An AJ Conti Novel

RUMOR OF DEATH

James A. Bacca

Luminare Press
www.luminarepress.com

Rumor of Death

Printed in the United States of America

Cover Design: Melissa K. Thomas

Luminare Press
438 Charnelton St., Suite 101
Eugene, OR 97401
www.luminarepress.com

LCCN: 2018968498
ISBN: 978-1-64388-049-5

*In memory of my sister Becky,
who believed in me long before I could see my own potential as a writer. This book is dedicated to her for providing the gentle nudge to start me writing.*

Not only would she be proud this novel is finished, she would be thrilled it takes place in Italy, where our grandfather was born and raised.

Thank you, Becky. You'll never be forgotten.

CHAPTER ONE

In the shadow of the majestic Alps, a bitter young man picked up his pen and opened his journal letting his words flow onto the paper before him.

Amidst the beautiful scenery, simmering anger coursed through his soul. He could feel the transformation throughout his body. His decision to look at himself and accept who he was made him realize *enough was enough*. His father's abrasiveness, coldness, and bullying no longer meant anything to him.

He taught me not to love, not to care. He taught me to kill. He will soon find out he taught me well.

Outside, I'll let the darkness envelop me. Even if seen, no one will be the wiser. My mind will be locked on my mission, the large door now protecting him providing little resistance.

I don't need the light, I know the room like the back of my hand. The familiar weapon calls to me from its resting place. Its weight only registers as the power I wield. I'll keep the weapon close to my leg so it won't be seen by any neighbor who may be on their porch.

The surge of adrenaline will come as I near the front door. I'll lock it behind me; then stop to pause at the opening to the living room.

He felt a tingling throughout his body as the pen paused an inch above the paper. He longed for this, to exterminate the very cause of the evil existing inside him resulting from his father's actions. He wanted his father to suffer for his wretchedness, to see his own death rapidly approaching, and the happiness the young man would enjoy.

His pen touched the paper again documenting the actions coursing through his mind.

There, in front of me, his large mass fills the recliner. I hear the shallow inhale, the turbulent exhale, repeating themselves in rhythm.

My soft soles glide over the tile surface without detection. Ten feet away I can feel the weapon start to raise.

I am so close I can see every twitch, every blink. No guttural clearing of his throat or movement of his head can stop me.

Who I will become thrusts aside who I once used to be.

My arm at its apex, I swing the wrench with all I have.

His larynx is no match for the heavy metal hitting him at full force. He fights for air that will never arrive. His eyes gaping, his hands to his throat—reality is setting in.

Once is not enough so I swing again. The blow to his sternum splinters bone, causing him to soil himself.

I gradually move to the couch and sit, my eyes fixed on him. Watching…waiting.

Setting aside the pen and pad, the still angry young man leaned against the headboard. He took a deep breath, contemplating what would surely come in the near future.

As his death slowly arrives, my birth will be complete, he thought. *The new me will emerge, ready for fresh prey.*

CHAPTER TWO

Being a detective in California is tough...so finding a corner market where you feel welcomed is a gift, any day of the week. AJ Conti felt relieved to have found such a spot.

Inside the Save Mart Supermarket nearby, I saw Francisco at the only open checkout. As always he waved and smiled when he saw me. He'd been there well before I moved in ten years ago. I liked shopping in the early morning when there were fewer customers. Francisco and I often chatted about his family and his kids.

Looking for a few essentials, I grabbed a handbasket. Lately, I ate out if I ate at all.

Looking ahead, I saw her...short dark hair to the base of ear lobes, a basket over her arm walking briskly like always. I hurried to the aisle where she turned.

I swore it had to be her. But...how? I asked myself.

Rounding the corner she stood ten feet away. Straightening up, she turned my way and I saw Bethany's brown eyes looking deeply into mine. She smiled, her cheeks rising, dimples at both corners.

Slowly, the delusion drifted away...the fateful day from four months ago taking its place.

I RELIVE THOSE PAINFUL MEMORIES DAILY. DAVID KIDnapped my fiancé, Bethany, hours before. He was angry at her for being the social worker years ago who destined him to a life of hell in foster care.

David had been my suspect in several other murders, and I realized Bethany was one of his targets. My partner and I cornered him in the house. He shot at us before he got away…with Bethany captive in the trunk of his car.

He called me on the phone, concerned my partner may have gotten glass in her eye when he shot in her direction. I was able to rationalize with him about having some good inside based on his caring about my partner. I begged David to care about mine and Bethany's future and let her live.

"Detective, I have been thinking about this for many years. I can't stop now."

I tried to reason with him about his sense of right versus wrong.

"I'll call you back." *Beep, beep, beep.*

From deep in my darkness I heard her voice, soft yet resolute when he let her call me.

"I'll always love you. You'll be okay, I'm—" *Beep, beep, beep.*

The phone went dead.

The dispatcher gave me the address of the call and I punched the accelerator, barreling down the road to her house.

The car door stood open, the front door ajar, blood drops on the tile leading down the hallway. Clues meant for me, to draw me in.

The bloody hand print on the open door to the master bedroom was like a seductive mistress, inviting me to come inside.

I knew I should not go in alone—I needed to get to Bethany.

David's lifeless body on the bed was what I saw first. Then my eyes dropped to the floor where Bethany laid. I rushed to her side, dropped to my knees, taking her outstretched hand. I cradled her lifeless body in my lap, rocking back and forth, tears rolling down my cheeks.

"Nooooo." I heard my own voice. My eyes starting to focus while I'm on my knees on the store's tile floor, covered in sweat, fighting back nausea.

People standing around me stare; eyes wide, mouths covered, not knowing how to help. A scared little girl hid behind her mother's leg.

"AJ, it's me, Francisco," his eyes full of compassion looking down at me, his hand on my shoulder…the only familiar face.

"Francisco, I'm so sorry." I stood and walked past him, but I heard his lowered voice speak to the crowd of shoppers.

"His girlfriend was murdered, and he found her body."

I headed for the doors, feeling every eye locked on me.

How do I get past this?

CHAPTER THREE

Some of the best skiing and magnificent scenery is located in Rumo, Italy, along with long and cold winters. Though the wind was still biting and the snow covered the ground, the anticipation of spring filled the air.

A YOUNG FEMALE BODY, FROZEN FOR NEARLY SIX MONTHS, now laid on her left side with her chest against the cement slope directly under the western edge of the bridge on a flat rock shelf. Less than ten feet above her head a single-lane dirt path crossed the Torrente Lavazzè River in Rumo. Throughout October her body remained in the shadows, direct sun unable to reach her during the short days of fall.

She froze solid by November…along with the river. The decomposition of her beauty halted when the winter temperatures continued to plummet. Solid as a block of ice, and lightly covered by blowing snow, her stiff corpse awaited under the bridge.

Each day the rising temperatures and longer days of spring allowed more sunlight to reach her. Her rigidity decreased, keeping pace with the release of melting snow from the mountains into the rivers.

The winter had been harsh, and the rising river ultimately took control of her destiny. Strong flowing waters moved her body from the flat rock shelf under the bridge.

Her body reached the lip of the waterfall, tumbling head-first over the moderate two meter cascade, plunging into the natural pool below...her journey had begun. The current gripped her legs the instant they submerged, pulling her downstream as her head and upper body bobbed to the surface. Pushed by the current, her legs swung toward the rocky edge where large rocks beneath the surface hid many traps.

The young woman's trek down river ended abruptly when her right foot lodged in a rock crevice. Her body swung around, twisting her already broken leg, lodging her foot even deeper. The flow of water forced her against the western edge of the river. Although her body tried to resist, the current would not be overpowered. Her back pressed up against a large slanted boulder, keeping her head at the water surface.

Her brief journey was complete. With unseeing eyes, Domenica Latia, two years out of high school, stared eastward at the *Centro Raccolta Materiali*, where the recycling for northern Italy's Rumo area took place.

CHAPTER FOUR

I sat in the corner of the Modesto eatery, large windows on either side of me, waiting for the police psychologist. Sipping my coffee I saw him walk inside. Dr. Papadopoulus, affectionately known as *Dr. P.* to all the cops in the county, grinned as he strolled over.

"Why'd you choose out here at the Fruit Yard for lunch?" Dr. P. asked.

"They treat me well and it's peaceful…less likely to run into people."

Dr. P. shook his head.

"AJ, people have forgotten all about you. There have been lots of headlines to take your place over the last four months. It's you who hasn't moved on."

I remained silent knowing not everything needs a response. Especially, since he might be right.

"I'm thinking of going to Italy. My grandfather's from a rural community at the base of the Alps called Rumo. My sister's been there several times, says it's like taking a step back in time…peaceful, nobody in a hurry."

"Unlike Turlock, Ceres, and Modesto in California."

I nodded. "Yeah, they used to be peaceful once, before the fast pace caught up to them like all the other towns up and down Highway 99."

"Not a bad idea AJ, as long as it's for the right reasons."

"Meaning…exactly?"

"How long have we been friends?"

"I don't know. We've been doing weekly lunch for at least ten years."

"Lord knows you've pissed my wife off enough times coming in my office right at 5 p.m. about some presumed dirtbag killer's psyche you're wanting to hook and book."

Frustrated, I snapped, "Where you going with this?"

"AJ, can you relax for two seconds? You have no problem trusting me for other things. Trust me now. In psychology-speak you're doing what we call *avoidance*."

"You're on crack, Doc. What the hell am I avoiding?"

"David, of course, and you know it. The piece of shit's dead and he still has control over you." He paused, staring stony-faced straight into my eyes. "Avoidance has never been you, regardless of how grueling things are. Use the same grit and courage which made you become a great cop to tackle this issue."

"You know this is different," I snapped. Lowering my voice I said, "I often wonder what went through Bethany's mind as the blade of David's knife fileted her throat wide open, blood spewing everywhere, and then him dipping his fingers in it, using it to write on the walls." I turned away, hoping I made my point clear.

Dammit, turning away played right into his hand, I thought.

"No, AJ, it's not different. Quit avoiding the issue. Trust me, please. Look, I realize you hate being sidelined. Still, you know as well as I do, not dealing with this is putting off the inevitable; it will screw with you later if you don't. Plus, I cannot in good conscience clear you to return to duty when you hardly sleep, you've lost a lot of weight, the nightmares and flashbacks haven't diminished, and you can't get past Bethany."

His stare softened, unlike his bluntness.

Part of the problem with a true friendship is they can know you better than you know yourself. I nodded…my way of raising the white flag.

"While you're in Italy it would be the perfect time for you to find purpose. Get involved. Find some ways to help other people. It will help you to finally get some rest and get past the nightmares. Then you can decide on your own terms what you want to do with your life."

"*Fine*, I promise to try. I can't promise anything else."

"That's all I'm asking. Man, you can be a hard-headed asshole." Dr. P. smiled from ear to ear.

All I could do was laugh.

He chuckled as he stood. "Get out of here. Go enjoy your homeland. I have to get back to the office and talk with clients who really want my help. And, AJ, keep in touch."

CHAPTER FIVE

In Rumo, Carabinieri Officer Bruno Caviglia noticed Corporal Amici leaving in a taxi. Captain Condello told him Amici's mother had become ill.

"I hope it's nothing serious," Bruno said.

"Hmm. I didn't think you cared about Amici."

Bruno explained he didn't care for some of the things Amici did, like his poor work habits, and being disrespectful to the citizens.

"Still, I have empathy for him and his family. I wish he would relax, maybe try to talk with people in a civil way."

"Good to hear. So, we've never had the chance to sit and talk since you transferred here from Verona. I've read what your personnel file says about you. Since it's only the two of us right now, plus we have some time, I thought we could have a cup of coffee, and maybe you could tell me a little something about yourself."

Bruno spoke of his desire to always become a police officer and felt his choices were limited growing up in Tivoli. Being on the wrong side of the law, like the Mafia, did not appeal to him.

"And, I wasn't about to become a priest."

"Me either." Condello smiled, his head swiveling. "A large number of the Carabinieri officers are exactly like us, as most are from the same four southern regions as the

Mafia. Tell me about America," Condello said, changing to a more interesting topic.

Bruno flashed a smile. "As a kid I read the paper and watched the news every chance I got, especially when the American police were mentioned." He recounted how he convinced his parents he would learn English along with getting a degree if they let him go to America. He described Eastern Nazarene College, in Quincy, Massachusetts, where he graduated with a degree in Crime, Law, and Justice.

"Many young people are leaving Italy. I would've thought you would stay in America."

"I had every intention to," Bruno said. "One of my professors, a retired Washington D.C. police officer, was great. He got me opportunities to ride with many different agencies. I maintained a 4.0 GPA, plus my English became pretty fluent. Everything seemed to be lining up."

"So, what happened?"

"My father had a heart attack. He passed away suddenly in November of my senior year. When I got home I barely had time to say I was sorry for not being there when dad passed before mom touched my cheek. '*To papà l'aria volest che te finisi l'università*,' she said in her heavy Trentino dialect. She made it clear, my dad wanted me to finish college. And, by the way she looked at me, I could feel her pleading not to argue about it. So, I went back to Quincy."

Bruno looked out the window…a moment of silent reflection.

"I never told my dad I majored in Crime, Law, and Justice," Bruno continued. "He thought I was getting a Business degree. It's what he wanted for me.

"He'd said several times many officers in Italy were corrupt due to the huge influence of the Mafia. I'd heard him talk with other people about the lack of respect the Carabinieri practiced. So, my own fear kept me from ever telling him of my dream.

"I did minor in Business though, so I didn't totally lie to him. Still, when he passed, I knew I must return home to be closer to Mom."

"Hmmm, I'm sorry to hear about your father. You have my condolences."

"Thank you."

Captain Condello knew the American agencies would have wanted someone like Bruno, a strong bilingual student with worldly experience. "You know any more languages?"

"Yes—German. My mother's from northern Italy, so she spoke some German. It made her happy when I learned to speak it."

The captain appreciated how much Bruno cared about his mother.

Bruno turned the conversation around to what his Lieutenant Colonel in Verona told him about Captain Condello.

"This could be interesting. What'd he tell you?"

"Years ago when you were a *Maresciallo*...a Warrant Officer, you were a *Ribelle* like me."

"Yeah, I once sported the rebel label, just like you." Condello dropped his half smile to ask, "What's that look on your face?"

"Nothing, sir, it's just the thought of you being gung ho...a rebel?

"*No way*. You're too calm."

Elbows on the desk, hands together covering his mouth, Captain Condello contemplated for several seconds before sitting back.

"The Lieutenant Colonel happened to be my captain at the time. A lot like us. He felt too many officers were, well, let's say not doing all they could. Still, over time he convinced me Italy is full of tradition and I should embrace it. He said I could accomplish more with a quiet demeanor than I could by rebelling. Rumo still has many people doing what their parents did decades ago. And the Carabinieri, it's bigger than either of us."

"The Colonel told me to pay close attention to what you say and do if I wanted to grow."

"Well, I'm not so sure about that. Although, I do believe your transfer will turn out to be in your best interest. This assignment can definitely help you grow—if you let it."

"I'm beginning to understand."

"I'm glad. If we can get you to have some patience with Corporal Amici, we'll have made progress." Captain Condello gave him a supportive smile.

Leaving the office Bruno became acutely aware of his growing admiration for his mentor.

CHAPTER SIX

Driving alone in his patrol car, Bruno enjoyed the peaceful Saturday morning. Taking in the area, he thought back to when he first arrived.

He transferred to Rumo in September; its eight hundred people inhabiting seven villages nestled at the base of the northern Alps. Why there were only three Carabinieri assigned to Rumo now made sense.

Capitano Condello was the territorial commander. He lived away from the Carabinieri office, which contained barracks on the top two floors for the lower ranked officers. At thirty-two years old, *Appuntato* Amici, the Corporal spent seven of his ten years as a Carabinieri in Rumo. It had not taken Bruno long to see Amici never seemed to be in a hurry to do much of anything—a typical dead-ender.

Still, did I really give him a chance? Bruno thought. *Or, did I prejudge him solely based on my troubles with the loafers in Verona?*

Driving on the main road in the village of Marcena, Bruno decided on Bar Lanterna for lunch. He loved the open atmosphere compared to other local bars. He admired the exterior, especially the beautiful flowers lining the windows.

Walking up to Lanterna's outdoor patio Bruno saw one of the regulars, *Radio Scarpa*, taking out the trash for the owner, Donatella. A few days before Bruno heard Radio Scarpa's real name, Rigo. Scarpa got his nickname, *Radio Shoes*, as he walked from bar to bar repeating stories he heard at the bar he just left. Bruno heard Scarpa's stories were always inaccurate due to his mental impairment. To Bruno, Scarpa seemed like a happy, harmless, older man who enjoyed people. He knew Scarpa loved helping anyone, especially Donatella, with menial tasks.

Bruno sat at his favorite spot, a large green picnic table, when the bar's owner appeared.

"*Giorno* Donatella."

"*Giorno* Bruno. Where's your partner today?" she asked as she set Bruno's usual order on the table.

Bruno explained why Amici went home, yet Donatella sensed Bruno had more on his mind. "You seem restless today, like something's bothering you," Donatella said.

"What do you mean?" Bruno said. "Nothing's bothering me."

"Something certainly is," Donatella stated matter of factly. "If you don't want to tell me? Fine!" Donatella pivoted to leave.

"Wow," Bruno sighed, watching Donatella through his squinting eyes. She stopped to look back, letting Bruno know he better complete his thought.

"Impressive. I mean your ability to read people like you do."

"Work in a bar as long as I have, you get pretty good at it. So?"

Somewhat embarrassed, Bruno began explaining about his having been judgmental in his opinion of Amici being unsociable and disrespectful to citizens.

"Now you realize you were being a little like him, maybe?"

By his reaction Donatella knew she nailed it. Before Bruno said anything further, Donatella described several reasons why Amici may have seemed so antisocial. "Especially the stress from his mother's illness," she concluded.

"You're probably right. Captain Condello's been on me to be more patient with him."

"Your captain's right. Everyone deserves respect. Seeing Amici in this new light might help you to realize it." Donatella walked away, leaving Bruno to contemplate what she said.

Twenty minutes later Bruno finished lunch when Donatella returned to clean tables. Tactfully avoiding their previous conversation she asked Bruno about his thoughts on Rumo.

"It's so different than my home down in Tivoli," Bruno said. "The entire region and your roads are so well taken care of. The benefit of being one of only five autonomous regions in Italy that don't pay taxes to Roma, I guess. When I get my own car I plan on exploring the region."

"You don't have one?" Donatella asked.

"No, making sure my mother has what she needs comes first, plus I need to pay off my American university loans."

Donatella nodded with an approving grin. "Are you able to visit her much?"

"As much as I can, I take the train to Roma at least once a month."

Donatella gave Bruno a "good for you" pat on the shoulder before going back inside.

CHAPTER SEVEN

The angry young man got up at four, thirty minutes earlier than usual. Excited, he hardly slept. He arranged to come in late at the Pomarella Apple plant, knowing his supervisor would not say no. His uncle happened to be the president of the board, something he regularly used as ammunition.

He wanted to check on her body at the river by the first hint of morning light, while avoiding being seen by any early morning trekkers. In November his motivation centered on his fear of her being discovered. This time became more personal; the excitement of seeing her body and re-living the kill inspired him.

He avoided parking close to the area and the walk took less than five minutes. What used to be tall grass next to the river barely reached his knees, packed down by the heavy winter snow. Stepping onto the grass he expected to see the portion of her head in plain sight and not hidden by large rocks under the bridge—she no longer perched in the nest where he laid her.

Somehow stuck with her head at water level, Domenica's dead eyes stared directly at him across the river. Seeing her exposed after nearly six months, made his head spin, a complex mix of exhilaration and bewilderment battling in his brain. Stay, or leave…desire versus pragmatic. Backing out of the grass he knew the time for her discovery would arrive soon.

The rest of his Monday he moved about on autopilot, working right through the morning break at the Pomarella plant. He could not stop thinking about her. At lunch time, sitting on the ground propped up against his forklift, his mind drifted to one of their last conversations.

"Listen, I can't stop you from leaving. Can you at least leave your parents a note for Christ's sake? Tell them you've gone to find yourself or something, so they don't worry themselves sick. I'm willing to help by taking you to the train station in Mezzocorona."

"All right, all right, I'll do it," Domenica said. She kicked a rock and dropped down on the wall near the bus stop. "I really need to leave before the heavy snows come. It's already October and I need to get to Germany, get settled with a job and find a place to live before it's too cold." She checked her phone calendar.

"I think I'll leave in two days. My parents will be gone to dinner at their friend's house and they don't plan to be home until late." She felt certain they would not check her room until the next day.

He replied, "Should work. Let's meet at the bridge across from the '*Centralina Comunale*' at about seven."

"Why can't you pick me up at the house?" she asked, resentment in her tone.

He explained if anyone saw him helping her it could make his life miserable. The rumors would race through town like wild fire. He suggested *Centralina Comunale* since she walked *Path Ten* there all the time…if anyone saw her they would not think anything about it. "In less than two minutes we hit the main road and we're gone."

She paused…then sighed. "You're right. Thank you."

He could see her bitterness remained. Nevertheless, she needed help getting to the train station—something he counted on.

"You're welcome." Smiling, he softly touched her shoulder, then manipulated her by suggesting she pack light so she did not have to drag suitcases around.

"Good idea. I have the perfect backpack. I can stuff it full."

CHAPTER EIGHT

While packing my suitcase and rethinking Dr. P's guidance about getting out of town, the doorbell rang. Looking out the window I saw Detective Seth Vantz's car. His timing could not have been more perfect. Before I could get to the door he rang the bell again.

"Patience," I yelled.

"Hurry it up, or I'll leave and take your hamburger with me," he yelled.

With too much on my mind, I had not eaten since lunch yesterday, so he had the upper hand on this one. I picked up the pace, not wanting to lose my double cheeseburger. Seth could be obstinate…enough to actually leave.

"What took you so long?" he asked pushing past me.

"I'm trying to get a head start on packing. It's been so long since I went anywhere…not sure what to take."

"Geez, it's not that hard," Seth said. "It's the base of the Alps, not the top. Long sleeves, jeans. Can't you ever keep things simple?" He started toward the kitchen.

"Grab the drinks. Let's eat."

We got along from the instant Seth first got assigned to the Detective Bureau three years before. Although he sometimes lacked couth, I admired his work ethic and honesty. Being one of the smartest people I knew was a bonus for him.

Over lunch we discussed his latest homicide.

"A drive-by killed a sixteen-year-old *wanna be banger*. Another round grazed the arm of a little girl." Seth said.

"Gang-versus-gang, then?"

"Yeah, one of the Sureño gangs from Fresno came up for retaliation, started shooting into the crowd."

"The older Mexican gang bangers hate drive-bys. They always wanted to go face-to-face, *mano-y-mano*. When I started, drive-by shootings didn't exist. There were a lot more stabbings, but no innocent victims."

"Sounds like the East Indian gangs with bats," Seth said.

"True. Using a bat usually means they target one person; whoever pissed them off, no innocent victims there either."

"Harder on us though, since a bat's easy to wipe down."

"Gotta take the good with the bad, my friend. I kinda prefer one straight forward crime scene with one victim. I'd bet you've got at least a good two hundred feet of crime scene with your drive-by."

"Oh yeah! They started shooting before they reached the house, then kept shooting even as they were driving away. Bullet holes in cars, houses, casings up and down the street. It took forever for the techs to photo, log, and diagram it all."

"Dumb question, any witnesses?"

"Not officially. Our Street Crime guys got some info from one of their CI's. One of our homeboys went to Fresno Thursday night and a Fresno banger came across our Norteño homeboy."

"They got Video?"

"None, can you believe it?"

"Is anyone dead in Fresno?"

"Yeah, the Fresno banger…not a scratch on our homeboy, so I hear." With palms open, Seth rolled his shoulders.

"Our dead guy didn't do the shooting down in Fresno?"

"Nah," Seth growled, pronounced disgust on his face. "Unfortunately, he paid the price for the stupid homeboy who was thinking with the wrong head. The dude goes to Fresno to see a girl with ties to the Sureños. He's still flashing red Norteño gang colors while in Sureño territory. The kid doesn't have any brains, although he must have nine lives."

"Did the Street Crime guys say how the Fresno bangers ID'd him?"

"Yeah. The chic in Fresno got beat down pretty bad for flirting with a Norteño. Word is she tried not to say anything, knowing they'd kill him. Supposedly she ended up in the ER with a broken arm and a messed up face. She finally gave him up."

"Man, the jerk's caused misery in two cities, and he's still walking around. You gotta like the old guys for their sense of justice."

"Not really, I don't have to. Kind of makes sense, though."

"Now I get why you look like hell."

Seth nodded. "Yeah, long weekend already. This week's shaping up to be even longer. Two prelims scheduled, plus a frickin rush follow-up on a rape I worked a couple months ago because the DA's investigators are too lazy to do their jobs. Sergeant Boykin asked me, so I said yes."

"Guess he wants it done right."

"Ah, the burden of competency…" Seth grinned.

I shook my head. "Be careful. This thing is ripe to explode into multiple shootings—all because they hit the little girl."

"Yeah, our gang guys are working with the Fresno Gang Unit, while our Street Crime people are trying to work with the *jefe* of our gang…trying to talk some sense into him.

He has to know his guy is toast for going into a clear-cut Sureño area for a chick."

"My advice is let Fresno PD take the lead. Their 187 happened first, they have more resources, and the next shooting is gonna be on their turf due to the little girl. They got Dics who solely investigate gang 187's, so let them roll with it, especially with your schedule this week. Stay on top of this."

Seth nodded and sighed. I could see the weight of finally being a lead detective hit him like a ton of bricks. For him, the intensity ratcheted up a notch.

"So, how long you gonna be in Italy?"

"Not sure. Ten days, maybe two weeks. I got an open ended ticket."

"You're coming back, right? To the PD I mean." Seth displayed resounding angst across his face.

Caught off guard, I pondered for a quick moment. *I've never even thought otherwise. Or did I*?

"Yeah, maybe, I don't know. I really need to get past all this first."

"BS," Seth growled.

"What are you talking about?"

"Doc gave you ways to get past PTSD. Stuff that's worked for soldiers. You're not even trying any of it, are you?"

"Ah, I get it. The two of you conspiring to try and control me."

"Who the hell cares?" The vein on Seth's temple kept rising in tune with his anger. "He's right; avoidance is your new best friend. You won't even answer my question."

My fist slammed on the table. I went to the sliding glass door and stared out. Silent.

Seth took a deep breath, softening his tone and said,

"Look, the bottom line is you're my friend. I care about you getting better." Seth made his way next to me, putting his hand on my shoulder.

"I'd love for you to come back to the PD; I don't want you to retire. Although if you do, it needs to be because you're really ready to hang it up. As long as you get better, nothing else matters. Dr. P. really cares about you, too. Can't you see that?"

I felt like I received a scolding from my mother.

"Yes, I can. Thank you. By the way, nice use of bad cop good cop, all in the same tongue lashing." I flashed a surrender smile.

Snickering, Seth said, "Thanks, I learned from the best. I ain't hugging you though." Sitting back at the table, "AJ, I want to know why you're really going to Italy," he said, genuine concern in his voice.

"I think it might do me good to get away from here. A place I can go to clear my head. We have distant cousins in Italy I've never met, but I'm not even telling them I'm coming. I need to relax. Truthfully, I'm exhausted, physically and mentally."

"I get it."

"Losing Bethany has screwed me up. If somehow I start feeling better like Doc thinks I will, I might try to connect with family there. I don't have a clue what to expect, but I pray this trip helps me deal with it all."

Seth nodded, a solemn look on his face. A few seconds later he grinned. "Look what you made me do simply to help you to get out of your own way."

"Don't you have to go dictate a report somewhere?" I asked, shaking my head and smiling.

CHAPTER NINE

The sun bouncing off the snowy Alps made the start of the workweek almost bearable.

In uniform, Bruno headed down the stairs ready for the new week having already enjoyed his morning walk and Cappuccino. Entering the office he saw Captain Condello pouring a cup of coffee.

"Morning, Sir."

Captain Condello looked over his shoulder. "Good morning Bruno. You've been out already this morning?"

"Yes, to Bar Podetti. I had a Cappuccino—real Italian coffee. Not whatever it is you're drinking," Bruno said, as he shook his head.

Bruno usually went to Bar Lanterna in *Mione*, or Bar Podetti in *Corte Inferiore*, when he had time. Otherwise he went to Bar Bivio directly across from the Carabinieri office. All three were coffee shops—and bars.

Captain Condello didn't flinch. He'd been teased by many an Italian after discovering the coffee he preferred from America fifteen years earlier.

"A little chilly out there still," he said, intentionally not acknowledging Bruno's comment.

"A little?" said Bruno.

"It's invigorating to breathe in the cool morning air while taking in this scenery."

"How's it been going…you meeting people in the area?"

"It's going well. I've started offering to help various people with their projects on my days off. No one's accepted yet, but I think they realize I want to be part of the community."

Before heading for his office Captain Condello told Bruno he heard positive comments about him, encouraging him to keep trying. Seconds later Bruno heard Corporal Amici coming down the stairs.

"Welcome back. I hope your mom's doing okay," Bruno said.

Amici stopped. He tilted his head as he pondered Bruno's comment, accepting Bruno actually appeared concerned about his mother's health.

"Thank you. She seems to be doing all right. I tried to convince her to go to the doctor," his voice trailing off.

Bruno saw the worry on Amici's face. "Don't you think you should still be there? I mean, I'm not prying, but you look a little worried. I'm sure Captain Condello would be okay with you taking some more time."

"I don't have any vacation time left," Amici said sorrowfully. "I can't ask him to let me go with no vacation time on the books."

Bruno could see the anguish on Amici's face. Bruno banked extensive vacation time, offering to donate some time to Amici, like other officers do in Verona. "I can ask Captain Condello to do the paperwork for me to give you some more time."

Corporal Amici looked at Bruno, in awe of his kindness, not a clue what to say. After some time he told Bruno he would consider it.

Fifteen feet away, Bruno saw Captain Condello near the door of his office. Condello shrugged and nodded. Which, was his way of telling Bruno he would do the paperwork.

FINALLY, TIME TO START BOARDING THE PLANE. I HOPED the flight to Italy would be as smooth as the first leg from San Francisco to Atlanta.

Throughout the flight I found sanctuary in the rear flight attendant area. I stretched my legs, got away from the surround sound of snoring, and avoided a possible nightmare by not sleeping. I had conversations with the three flight attendants and I enjoyed talking with Abri the most since we were relatively close in age. Feeling comfortable talking with another woman again almost made me feel as if I betrayed Bethany. Consciously, I knew I had done nothing wrong, although knowledge does not always outweigh emotions.

Toward the end of the flight I took my eyes off the blur of the movie in time to see Abri walking down the aisle between the seats. I smiled as she lifted her chin and eyebrows to motion me to come to the flight attendant area. Despite the captain's recent order to remain seated, I got up and followed.

"Alessandro, we have something for you." Abri said, with her coworkers by her side.

I loved the way she said my Italian name—nobody used it after I started school. My teachers began calling me *AJ* because too many people could not pronounce Alessandro.

Walking over to one of the countertops Abri grabbed a cup of coffee.

"We made this fresh for you, so we could all toast one another, as you Americans would say." Together we toasted to a great flight and my first day in Italy.

"Alessandro, we are going to be busy from now until we

land, so we wanted to say goodbye while we could. God bless you. Enjoy our beautiful country."

CHAPTER TEN

Sitting alone in the living room the angry young man's mind wandered. He pictured her beautiful face and her lovely petite frame—attractive. He could hear her taunting voice replaying in his brain and relived the scene.

"I'm leaving for Germany. I don't need you," she said.

His body shifted waiting for her to say she wanted him to go…but the words never came.

He remembered their last meeting. She moved toward him with authority, her backpack over her left shoulder, the sound of the river in the background as she crossed the bridge to him. Her anger at him for wanting her to stay showed in her every step.

He can see himself carrying her lifeless body to the flat rock surface beneath the small bridge over the river, laying her down facing the cement wall. He wanted to leave the area, but for some reason can't and tries to understand what is keeping him there…when he sees himself standing on the bridge. She is in the water, stuck in the rocks, her eyes are open, looking across the water. He stands on the bridge telling himself she had moved when he sees her head turn. It is his mother's face looking right at him. "You're still alone, you loser." And he imagined she laughed.

Lurching forward from the back of the couch, the sweat rolls down his face while his eyes take in the familiarity of the room.

Maybe I shouldn't have gone to see her, he thought.

He went into the bathroom to put cold water on his face and began clinching his fists as his jaw tightened. His first experience with those feelings occurred at thirteen, a time when his mother yelled at his father daily. One particular day she did something worse than yelling…she stormed out, never to return. She didn't pause to look at him, much less say she loved him or tell him she wanted him to go with her. He could not recall his mother's love or affection.

Staring in the bathroom mirror he realized she had given him something else, something more important.

This is your destiny you fool. Embrace it. Enjoy it, like you enjoyed killing Domenica, he thought.

His hands relaxed, calmness returning throughout his body. He recalled the intoxication from crushing her knee with the log, the pure excitement of watching her body twitch as he cut off her air. Thinking of killing again, it started to grow. He looked down and smiled.

CHAPTER ELEVEN

I looked forward to getting to Rumo, hoping it was everything my sister described. I grabbed my suitcase off the carousel and walked towards the same door as the young couple in front of me. They said something in Italian, bringing a smile to the guard's face as they kept walking. My suitcase previously cleared Customs in Rome, so the guard stopping me to check my passport surprised me.

After comparing the photo to my face for some time, he finally let me pass. Probably like all the cops back home who recognize a dirt bag when they see one, he could spot the tourists...Profiling 101. Unlike most people, I knew cops aren't the only ones who do it. All humans do it, even if they do not want to admit it.

I found the rental car company, intimidation setting in as I walked up to the counter. Fortunately for me, the young man who helped me spoke English. In less than fifteen minutes I held the keys to a small, grey four-door Audi.

The way my sister described Giorgio, the man I rented from, he sounded like a wonderful person. She guaranteed I could count on him and I decided to call him from the desk phone at the car rental company.

"*Pronto*," Giorgio said.

"Giorgio, its AJ Conti."

"Ah, yes. AJ. Where are you? Are you okay?"

"I'm fine Giorgio. I made it to Italy. I'm at the car rental site at the airport, getting ready to leave."

"*Perfetto*. You should be here in one hour and a half," Giorgio said.

Laughing, I said, "I don't know, Giorgio. This area is all new to me. I need to stop at the TIMI store in Cles to buy a SIM card for my phone, too."

"True, true. Okay. We will see you in two hours then."

We settled on me calling him prior to leaving the TIMI store.

Other than the signs being in kilometers, the first part of the drive seemed pretty easy. As I left the main highway the roads got narrower. I found the number of smaller cars zipping in and out of traffic to be a little menacing. Ultimately, I located the TIMI store my sister told me about where a young woman behind the counter greeted me with a smile.

I glanced at her name tag before asking, "*Parli inglese* Kara?"

"Yes. I speak English," Kara said.

"Great. I was afraid I wouldn't be able to get across I needed a SIM card for my phone."

With a straight face she said, "Maybe I should make you ask me in Italian." She stared at me for two long seconds before she laughed and patted my hand.

"You're good, you had me scared there," I said, shaking my head in relief.

We shared a relaxing conversation as Kara proceeded to guide me through the process.

"I got your phone ready, but you will not be able to use it for twenty minutes. It takes time to activate here in Italy."

"Oh, I had no clue. Hmm, can I use your phone there by the cash register to call someone who is supposed to meet me?"

"*Sì, sì*. It will be two euros."

When I reached for my money in my pocket she laughed. Realizing she got me again, I could not help laughing with her.

Walking around the counter I noticed a man standing at the back of the store with his arms crossed, staring at me. I stopped, then looked at Kara.

"Are you sure this is okay?" I asked, nodding my head slightly to the left.

Kara looked past me, smiled, put her hand in mine, and pulled me around the counter. "It's fine. Don't worry about him. He doesn't like the idea he cannot control his twenty-year-old daughter anymore."

The man barked something in Italian causing Kara to get angry as she responded in like kind.

Kara saw I had stopped. My eyes were wide and I slightly leaned my head her way, hoping she recognized my desire for an explanation of their conversation.

"He said I need to be more careful. Recently someone kidnapped a model in Italy and nearly sold her into sex slavery. He said I should not be so friendly with you; I don't know you."

"He's right, you know. I'm a detective in California, you really should be careful."

"I get it. I only want him to trust me a little more. I wish he would quit hovering over me."

I'd said enough. When I picked up the phone to call Giorgio I could feel Kara leaning into me.

Giorgio said he would meet me at the gas station he previously told me about in his directions. In typical Giorgio fashion, he did not wait long enough for me to respond before hanging up.

"Thank you for letting me use the phone."

Kara placed her right arm inside my left elbow and kissed me on my scarred cheek. She glared over my shoulder, then smiled as she looked back at me. "Let me walk you out, AJ."

Without trying I'd gotten myself in the middle of a family dispute. Walking toward the front door, it seemed like I could not get out of there fast enough.

When I got to the car Kara yelled from the doorway, her voice at me, her eyes looking into the store, "If you need anything, AJ, you have my number."

I heard the word *polizia* and the argument begin before the door had a chance to close. I had a pretty good idea what they were saying, even though I could not understand another word…time to leave.

CHAPTER TWELVE

Beauty enveloped me on the drive to Rumo. Seeing the large lumberyard on my right with the raging river right behind it, I knew I had made it. Coming out of the one hundred and eighty degree turn on the other side of the river I spotted the welcome sign, "*Benvenuto a Rumo*." Up the hill and around the next corner sat the gas station.

I recognized Giorgio next to his blue Subaru, although he barely looked fifty, not sixty like my sister told me. Otherwise, her description of him was spot on. Giorgio's huge smile made me feel like we met before—like I returned home.

"AJ," Giorgio said. No sooner had my feet touched the ground before Giorgio grasped my hand, followed quickly by a kiss on both cheeks.

"Giorgio, I presume."

"*Sì, sì*, your sister has told me all about you."

"Your English is good."

"Yes. I understand my English is much better than your Italian," he said, then laughed.

"So true. Unfortunately, I hardly speak Italian."

"No problem AJ, or do you prefer Alessandro?"

Not quite as elegant as when the flight attendant said it.

"AJ's fine, thank you."

"We have time to work on your Italian," he said, patting

me on the shoulder. "For now, let's get you to your house. I am sure you are exhausted from the long flight."

Before I could start my car Giorgio pulled away. I could not catch him, so I decided to keep him in sight. Giorgio had not gone more than a half-mile when he crossed the opposite lane and pulled onto a private road for two sets of double townhouses. They paralleled the main road, separated by a small stone wall.

The first set displayed a white exterior with beautiful wood accents on the balconies and an almost German or Swedish decor. Stepping out of the car, the panoramic view of green mountain tops nearly took my breath away.

I feel more relaxed right now than I have in months.

"I own this building," Giorgio said, pointing at the set on the left. "You will be in the house on the left. Nobody is in the one on the right. I still have work to do there. Your sister told me you wanted some privacy so I thought this would work the best. I hope you like it."

"I'm sure this will be perfect. Thank you."

Giorgio grabbed my luggage, and I followed him up the nineteen beautiful travertine steps to the first level of the house. The all white interior with large tile throughout gave it an almost elegant decor. I had no doubt I would be quite comfortable here.

Giorgio handed me the keys, informing me his wife wanted me to come over for dinner in a day or two.

"Dinner in a few nights would be wonderful. Do you want some money now?" I asked.

"No, no, later…for now you rest."

"*Grazie*," I said, extending my hand. Giorgio reciprocated, adding a kiss to each cheek before he left.

RUMOR OF DEATH

ALL DAY AT WORK THE ANGRY YOUNG MAN THOUGHT about her, seeing her in the river. Her discovery would cause a stir throughout the area. The rumors of her death would flow throughout Rumo.

My work's going to be the primary topic of conversation, he thought.

His plan to make it look like she left on her own worked beautifully. Only the mentally challenged old man saw him. He scared the old man enough over the past several months to ensure he would never tell anyone. Not perfect, although better than his first kill—the cat. His first human had been satisfying, to say the least.

His thoughts shifted for a moment to his father beating him regularly after his mother left. The beatings not only increased as each month passed, he almost felt his father searched for ways to hurt him beyond the normal occurrences. His resemblance to his father briefly passed through his mind.

He tried to convince himself for months not to kill anymore. He strained to persuade himself *he was normal*, similar to all the other young men in Rumo. He often got lost in thought about how he could kill again…the struggle in the back of his mind seething daily.

The cat proved to be a bloody mess. Suffocation would work for a while but he envisioned working his way into torture before the kill, and even numbering them to keep track. Domenica was now *Number One*. Ultimately, he wanted to experience ways to create pain, seeing their fear of dying, taking them to the brink of death before starting over.

He wanted to kill again, almost immediately after the first one. He even decided who would be *Number Two* after she snubbed him several times. His desire to make her pay grew so strong he never noticed she looked eerily similar to his mother.

Seeing *Number One* stuck in the river, staring straight ahead, settled the battle raging in his mind. The more he thought about it, the more his desire began to rise.

I plan to follow my fate. I will kill again.

CHAPTER THIRTEEN

I'd been up for over twenty-four hours. The clock said 2 p.m. but I wanted to stay awake, acclimate to Italy time, and get exhausted enough to actually have a good night's sleep.

Tantalized by the stunning view of the mountains and valley, I walked onto the balcony, soaking in the fresh air and the beautiful array of colors. The lake near Cles spanned a large portion of the valley. Despite being quite a distance away, it appeared majestic.

Hunger called, followed closely by the need to get my legs moving. I decided to worry about unpacking later… I locked up the townhouse, headed down the travertine steps and crossed both roads to the only sidewalk. *Uphill to the left, downhill to the right…is there any place level around here?*

Walking uphill I admired the varying portions of the town all around me. My sister informed me the town of Rumo has multiple villages, some above others because of the terrain. Right away I passed the road leading up to the village of Corte Inferiore, directly above the new village I crossed into, Mione. It reminded me of the Bay Area, crossing from one city to another on the same road without realizing it—minus all the congestion.

I came to a bus stop shelter with a small asphalt parking

area next to it. Across the one-lane road in front of me was a grassy area contained by a white wooden fence.

A short distance beyond the parking area a tall thin man worked in the yard of a lone three-story house. "*Buongiorno signore*," I greeted him when he looked at me.

"*Salve*," he said, smiling as if we had long been friends.

"*Bar Lanterna*?" I asked, pointing at the building with the five flags.

"*Sì, sì, Bar Lanterna*."

"*Grazie, signore*."

"*Prego*."

Approaching the bar I noticed drying laundry on the second floor balcony like several businesses in the region with families living on the floors above.

A woman walked onto the patio moving quickly, wiping down tables as if on a mission. She looked to be about five foot one, with dark curly hair pulled back and clipped on both sides, and she wore a white and blue short-sleeve silk shirt, and blue jeans.

She had to be Donatella by the description my sister shared with me, right down to her multi-colored scarf around her neck. I am not sure what I expected, but I surely did not imagine I would be so allured as to stare. Something about her; I could not take my eyes off of her.

When she spotted me ogling she glared at me, before breaking into a big smile. "AJ, Glenda's brother…*Sì*?"

"Sì," I said, unable to speak any other words.

She walked up to me and gave me a kiss on both cheeks. "She tells me on *WhatsApp* you were coming."

I became clumsy and retreated to my comfort zone, almost conducting an interview of Donatella about the beautiful décor of her bar.

"This woodstove, do you use it or is it only for decoration?"

Donatella canted her head. She looked at me similarly to how I felt—a fool for asking the question. She informed me they used it for heat, and punctuated my foolishness by pointing out how there were more trees around than they could ever use.

Donatella's cheeks rose slightly and her eyes widened when it registered to her why I might be acting like I had.

"Well, you've done a great job with this place," I said, trying to break the awkward silence.

"Grazie, now for you…what can I get you to drink?"

"I've been told, in Italy only Americans drink Cappuccino after noon," I said, striving to make my best *pretty please* face.

"Ahh, you *are* related to Glenda," Donatella said laughing. "I will do a Cappuccino for you. What to eat?"

"Maybe a salad if you don't mind, thank you."

Donatella darted inside and prepared my salad as I sipped on Cappuccino and stepped onto the patio. The view had me falling in love with the place even more.

Donatella brought an astonishing amount of food. Her meal showcased a wonderful mixture of simple, yet varying, tastes: a large bowl of salad, a platter with fresh bread, salami and cheese, and a bowl of freshly cut fruit.

"Wow, this looks wonderful."

Donatella placed it on the table, smiled, and walked away.

"Is it usually busier than this?" I asked, when she returned.

"Not at this time. But, in an hour or maybe a little more it gets busy most of the night. Some for gelato, later most come for the bar."

"How long have you been doing this?"

She paused and I instantly knew I may have overstepped my bounds. Donatella answered before I could retract the question.

"I was fourteen when my father died. I took his place. I run the bar for family. I have done it ever since. What do you do, as a police man?"

She turned that around on me quite nicely.

"I'm a detective. I investigate crimes against persons." I could see the obvious confusion on her face. "I look into people hurting or killing other people."

"Ahh, a lot of pressure *sì?*"

"Sì."

She patted the back of my hand and smiled softly.

"You can relax here. Enjoy your beautiful homeland."

Thirty minutes later, with a satisfied palate, I went inside to pay.

"I truly enjoyed this, Donatella. I apologize if I asked too many questions. I love your place, and I look forward to seeing you again. *Grazie*."

"*Prego*," Donatella said.

Our eyes met for what seemed like five seconds, my fingers fondling the change. She looked away, and then looked back at me. She turned and started wiping the Cappuccino machine.

Back outside I too felt uneasy. Strangely, I felt disloyal to Bethany, looking at Donatella like I did. Still, something about her piqued my interest—I relished the thought of talking with her again.

Coming out of my fog I saw the Corte Inferiore sign, so I turned and began the steep ascent. The slight chill from the dropping temperatures of the late afternoon disappeared as I reached the first semi-level area. Almost directly above Bar Lanterna, I found a series of beautiful multi-story houses, a school, and another bar—Bar Podetti. So many people were outside or walking, each of them greeting me kindly. The differences between Turlock and Rumo were palpable.

CHAPTER FOURTEEN

Lia Vender started the second Tuesday of May feeling it would be a pretty good day. By 4 p.m. she changed her mind as she headed to take her recycling to the *Centro Raccolta Materiali*. She had numerous things on her mind, none more pressing than getting ready for the family festa planned for the weekend.

Driving on the single lane road past the pizzeria, Lia's ten-year-old son, Marcello, excitedly pointed out the farm with live animals and the huge vegetable garden.

Pulling into the recycling area to her right past the farm, Marcello released his seat belt. The instant the car stopped he flung open his door.

"*Vado al fiume*," Marcello said. He bolted off as Lia opened the trunk. She smiled, knowing he loved to run over to the river to throw small rocks.

"Listen for me."

"*Va bene, mamma*."

Lia always whistled for him to return. Periodically, she had to whistle a second time. Marcello knew not to make her whistle three times.

Marcello sprinted through the parking lot, crossed the road and stopped at the edge of the grass across from the *Centralina Comunale*, a power station building where electricity is produced.

Marcello never broke his mamma's rules when he went to the *Torrente Lavazzè*, the best river in the area in his opinion.

Stepping into the grass with the largest strides he could muster, he made sure not to go over his age, ten. Picking up several rocks to throw at the target, he put the first one in his right hand, ready to count the number of hits. Looking at the flat cement wall under the bridge, he reared back when something caught his attention.

Marcello had no idea where his rock landed; his eyes were fixated on her. He gasped and jumped back, his heart pounding as the girl stared at him. For nearly a minute Marcello was frozen by fear, his mind trying to process everything, his knuckles white from squeezing the rocks. Marcello dropped his rocks as he shuffled backward, still unable to look away. Feeling the road beneath his feet he turned to run.

Something made Marcello stop. Looking at her again, the voices in his head competed, one telling him to leave, one telling him to stay. Still trembling, he cautiously headed for the bridge.

Marcello dared not go past the bridge—his mother's final rule. Afraid to get too close, he secretly appreciated the rule. From the bridge he saw she was stuck in the rocks, still staring at the grass where he stood.

Hearing his mother's whistle Marcello took off running.

Marcello racing through the parking lot so quickly after her first whistle surprised Lia. She thought she heard Marcello saying he saw a girl floating in the water.

"*Ho visto il corpo di una ragazza galleggiare nell' acqua*," Marcello blurted out.

"Marcello, you know how I feel about lying."

"Mamma, you have to believe me. I saw her." He grasped her hand and pulled.

"You have to stop making things up."

"Please, come look…I'm not making it up," he asked with pleading eyes.

Lia could see the seriousness on Marcello's face. *I think he's telling the truth,* she thought. But Ciro, the recycling worker who helped Lia, shook his head, *no, it couldn't be.* Marcello saw him, stopped talking and released Lia's hand. He got in the car, slammed the door and drew his legs up in front of him with his arms wrapped around them. Marcello stared at the back of the driver's seat; his mind could still see the woman's eyes staring at him.

Lia and Ciro discussed Marcello's imagination, with Ciro trying to make Lia believe Marcello was simply testing her limits.

Lia got in the car, looking at Marcello in the rearview mirror as she backed out. She saw him staring down, lost in his own world, his legs drawn up and slowly rocking in his seat. Though Lia tried asking him questions later, Marcello never spoke the rest of the evening.

Ciro started to walk toward the river shortly after they left. Something in the way Marcello reacted bothered Ciro.

What if it were true?

Before he could get to the road another car pulled into the parking lot requiring his attention. Ciro hesitated, looking from the river to the car, back to the river, then back to the car.

If I don't help them, boss is gonna be pissed. I can't afford to be in trouble again, he thought.

He looked at the river one last time. Despite the feeling of being coaxed by the river's mystery, he returned to work.

CHAPTER FIFTEEN

Having thoroughly enjoyed my walk through Corte Inferiore, I got back to my townhouse at sunset, feeling at peace as I watched it from the top step before going inside.

With everything unpacked and put away I brought out Doc's paperwork. The reading actually turned out to be more interesting than expected. I could relate to the fact nearly half of PTSD patients suffer flashbacks as well as experiencing nightmares, often exact replications of the traumatic event—referred to as *replicative nightmares*. I wanted to take back control of myself, willing to work through the traumatic portion.

Giorgio made sure the townhouse had Wi-Fi, so I researched Rumo's location in relation to other major cities Seth might recognize. I decided to send emails before getting some sleep.

Doc,

You wouldn't believe this place. The elevation is 3,300 feet, with the Alps literally in Rumo's backyard. There are more colors of green than I knew existed. The entire area is so unlike Turlock. The air is clear, it's quiet, and everything is so rich and vibrant in color. I would presume the closest example to Rumo near you would be the mountains near Yosemite. Tenaya Lake up at Yosemite reminds me of the lake near Rumo, except this one is a much more beautiful blue color.

Although I'm exhausted, I can easily say this is the most relaxed I have felt for months. So far I believe this might have been a great idea. I'll stay in touch.

AJ

I STARTED WONDERING HOW SETH'S GANG HOMICIDE investigation had progressed. I hated not being there to mentor him and hoped my absence benefitted him in its own way. For him to get the deserved recognition by the department, he needed to be lead investigator on major cases.

I wondered if Italy had any street gangs like we did throughout California. Our gangs shared many similarities to the Mafia, like the rank structure. Still, the Italian Mafia is one of a kind.

Fresno had one dead gang banger; Turlock one dead wanna be. Both died due to the color of the bandanas they wore. I hoped Seth and Fresno PD were able to do something before an innocent person died at the hands of a gun-toting juvenile. The days of gangs going *mano-y-mano* were long gone. Drive-by shootings were the new norm, even if innocent little girls got hit.

Seth,

I hope your week from hell is getting a little better.

Although I would love an update from you on your drive-by 187, I clearly do not expect one.

I made it to Italy. Rumo, for all intents and purposes, is a rural farming community. It's probably similar to many of the smaller farming based communities in the Central Valley not on the I-5 or Highway 99 corridors.

It is quite amazing being at the base of the Alps. The town of Rumo, Italy is located only two hours south of Innsbruck, Austria; and it is less than four hours south of Munich, Germany. When I saw Rumo was only about four hours southeast of Liechtenstein, I thought of you. It made me think of the movie we saw when we went to the Robbery-Home Invasion training in San Jose a few years ago, A KNIGHTS TALE, and Sir Ulrich Von Liechtenstein. You did a pretty good imitation of Sir Ulrich as I recall. Good times my friend!

I'll try to update you in a few days.

Best of luck on your busy week,

AJ

Exhausted, I went upstairs to complete my nightly ritual of sit-ups and push-ups. Despite it being eight o'clock, Italy time, when I finished, I decided I'd been up long enough and hoped I'd be able to sleep uninterrupted for the first time in several weeks.

I lay in bed replaying the last twenty-four hours. Shortly before nine o'clock I opened the windows to let in the cool night air and stood at the open window amazed at the quietness. Being so used to hearing sirens, trains, and speeding cars, the quietness stood out. I fell asleep in less than ten minutes.

CHAPTER SIXTEEN

Lying on his bed, staring into darkness, the angry young man thought about how it all started. Within a couple of months of his mother leaving, along with the regular abuse he received at the hands of his father, he found himself wanting to hurt something…something with a beating heart.

Seeing the neighbor's cat, his first plot started to form. The cat seemed small in size, with mostly white fur except for black and tan on its two back paws and around its face.

It's funny how I'd seen that cat for years, never really noticing it, he thought.

It took him a couple of weeks of using treats to befriend the cat before it would follow him.

On a summer afternoon, with no one watching, he called the cat across the grassy yard to the wooden doors of his basement-garage with its daily treat. Each day he had given the cat food closer to his garage, making sure to pet it before and after the treats so it would gain trust in him.

When the cat entered the doorway he dropped the food on the ground as usual. His dad's large pipe wrench had been strategically placed on the work bench right inside the door. The cat never saw it coming.

He could not recall how many times he struck the cats head, he only remembered nearly blacking out from the thrill invading his body. Coming out of the adrenaline rush his hands were shaking, almost uncontrollably. The euphoric feeling did not last long before panic set in. He hadn't thought about how to hide the cat, or get it to the woods. The blood everywhere punctuated his panic, causing instant cold sweats, especially with his father due home shortly.

A cat. Who would have thought a cat would have taught me so much, he thought.

His mind shifted. The past brought about an exhilaration. His trophies in the garage, the bell from the cat's collar, or the gold bracelet *Number One*'s mom gave her that she never took off, created a sense of bliss.

The thought of future kills evoked anticipation. The thrill of the hunt, and the risk of being caught carried him to a natural high.

His thoughts shifted to *Number Two*. He started tracking her after he tried three times to talk with her in the breakroom at work. She ignored him on every occasion. Each time she got up shortly after he sat near her, his efforts of a conversation quashed. She said she needed to go back to work…he knew better. For the past two months, he watched her daily routines as she left work.

Number Two had a petite frame, with short, dark brown hair. Her hazel green eyes and glasses nearly made him turn away from her at first. *Number One* had dark brown eyes and no glasses. The more he saw her at the Pomarella Apple processing plant, the more he found himself drawn to the small mole on her right cheek. The mole brought attention to her smile, a smile which seemed familiar.

He looked at the numerous pictures he took of her with his phone camera and could see her in his mind's eye. Her time had arrived. His excitement began to rise.

CHAPTER SEVENTEEN

My exhaustion worked to my benefit to allow me nearly four uninterrupted hours before the dream arrived. The sweating and the nausea made it difficult to get back to sleep and amounted to a few hours of light rest.

I sat on the edge of the bed and convinced myself I slept for nearly six hours. I realized Doc had it right, I subconsciously evaded longer periods of sleep to avoid the nightmares…I needed to start being in control again… time for a change.

I figured Doc might appreciate a little update, in addition to a little groveling on my part, however slight. I emailed him, apologizing for taking so long to listen to him.

It seemed a little too early to go for my morning run in an unfamiliar place. The time difference made it early evening in California, so I decided to send a quick email to my sister. I informed her I arrived in Italy and I loved the townhouse. I decided not to tell her I frustrated Donatella a couple times already, aware of her hard work toward building relationships in Rumo.

I hoped my future contacts with Donatella would not be disappointing. When I finished checking on the news I read the irritatingly tiny numbers in the corner of my computer, 6 a.m. and light enough to run. I headed out the door.

Unfamiliar with the back roads, I decided to stay on the main road heading north, the way I came in to town. I worked my way down the hill and through the majority of the town before I came to the one hundred and eighty degree curve where the lumberyard sat next to the river.

I barely finished crossing the bridge when a large German shepherd came running toward the edge of the lumberyard. He seemed excited as he barked at me, as if he were greeting me instead of protecting the property. I slowed down to take in the beautiful animal. When I looked directly into his eyes he quit barking and began wagging his tail, so I went to the fence to greet him.

I thought about my own canine, Bino, who worked with me in my early years with the department. Bino had been an eighty pound ball of fire who possessed all of the Alpha Male qualities, while at the same time being the perfect friendly dog everyone loved, except for criminals. Similar to a black belt in karate, he possessed confidence in himself without having to advertise or threaten in any way before taking care of business if needed.

Bino protected me on numerous occasions, often sensing what the person I detained was about to do before they did it. Thanks to Bino, I learned to understand German shepherds' abilities to use their noses well beyond what most people realize. Apart from having a phenomenal protective instinct of people they care for, Bino showed me shepherds can also recall people they do not care for. Retiring him proved tough, although being able to keep him at home before he passed had been special for me, much like him.

I wanted to take more time with this German shepherd, but decided it would have to be another time. He barked with a tone of disappointment as I ran away rather than the bark of wanting to catch the fleeing prey.

I ran approximately two miles before turning around to start my return. Passing the lumberyard again the shepherd was nowhere to be seen, only several employees moving about. I made my way back into Rumo, passing the gas station where I met Giorgio, the municipality buildings, and the Carabinieri office. I decided to pass my house and go up to Bar Lanterna. I could cool down there before having a much needed morning Cappuccino.

Running at this elevation shocked my system. My normal five mile run made my lungs feel as though I traveled three times farther, leaving no doubt about not wanting to check my time. The run confirmed no level road existed anywhere in this area.

CHAPTER EIGHTEEN

Walking to Bar Lanterna I saw a young man sitting at the picnic table. He looked to be about five foot nine, one hundred and eighty pounds, and in good shape. His short haircut, cleanly shaven face, and tucked in t-shirt told me cop or military.

"*Buongiorno, signore*," the man said, as I stepped onto the patio deck.

"*Buongiorno*," I replied.

"*Di dove sei*?" He paused. "*Hai fatto una buona corsa*?"

"*Americano. No capisco Italiano*." I said.

As Donatella approached she told the young man in Italian, "*Le nou a Rumo. Le n'afit dal Giorgio*."

Donatella spoke slowly, helping me figure out she mentioned me renting from Giorgio. I thought she said something about me being a visitor, but even when she spoke slowly she spoke too fast for me. Donatella turned and asked, "Water and Cappuccino?"

"Sì, *per favore*. Oh no, wait. What am I thinking? I don't have any money. I'll have some water please."

Donatella walked away while I chose to sit at a tall table with my back against the wall, mostly out of habit. All police officers I know do it to protect themselves. I also wanted to look out over the valley. Within minutes Donatella arrived with my water, surprising me with a Cappuccino.

Setting them on the table she quietly said, "You can pay me later. Don't worry about Bruno. He is local police officer. He's okay." She winked as she turned and walked away.

Donatella made my good morning even better. I lifted the Cappuccino, taking in a deep breath through my nose of the rich strong coffee odor. I sighed.

"I asked you before Donatella came out where you are from, and then if you had a good run," Bruno said.

"Ahh. I did have a good run, except for the difficulty breathing this thinner air."

"You'll get used to it. What part of America are you from?"

It felt a little awkward not to be the one asking questions. "California, a city in the middle of the state," I said. "You speak English well. Where'd you pick it up?"

"*Grazie*. I went to college in Quincy, Massachusetts. My choices were either learn English well or fail out."

"*Molto bene*. It sounds to me like you were successful. Donatella says you are a police officer?"

"*Sì*, I am a Carabinieri officer. It's easiest to describe as military police. The closest for you would be the state police. It is much more like a military system than you are used to."

"Where'd you go to the police academy?"

"We call it Cadet Training. There are five academies, as you would say. I attended the one in Torino."

When I asked how he did in training Bruno happily explained how he excelled in the mental aspects and the exams.

Ever the trainer, I wanted to be cognizant of his weakness. "So, what part of it didn't you excel at?"

"Let's say I did not immediately possess much skill at things like hand-to-hand combat, obstacle courses, and firearm training." Apparently one of his cadre told him he should be excelling with his natural abilities.

I raised my eyebrows, waiting to find out what happened. On cue, he replaced the silence.

"I made myself work on those, and finished tied for first in my class," Bruno said, a small proud smile on his face.

Something drove him to be at the top—I'd been there.

"Well, congratulations," I said. "Quite an honor…tied for first in your class, impressive."

"Thank you."

My concern, as a trainer and a visitor, was why a young officer who finished first in his academy class was assigned to remote Northern Italy and not a more populated area to take advantage of his skills. There had to be a reason. I decided not to go there—at least not now.

"So, you're renting from Giorgio?" Bruno asked.

"Yeah, right down the main road here."

Bruno seemed more at ease after learning about my accommodations. He explained Giorgio was known to thoroughly check out his renters before opening up one of his properties to them. "He must feel good about you."

"He gave me the impression he knows everyone," I said.

Bruno laughed. He described Giorgio as a good man who's well recognized as a result of working for the municipality of Rumo for decades.

"Thinking of moving here?" Bruno asked.

"Probably not…I'm not sure." I'd never given it a thought.

"You look too young to retire. Most people in Italy have to be over sixty."

I briefly studied Bruno. Pretty direct, yet I understood his thinking. The location in the world does not change how an officer would passively "interrogate" someone. All things being equal, I did not feel quite ready to reveal much.

"Trying to decide if I need a change in my life, is all."

"Ahh, *va bene*. Well, welcome to Rumo. Work calls. *Ciao signore*." Bruno stood, turned toward the door of the Bar, and yelled, "*Ciao* Donatella."

From somewhere in the darkness inside came her reply.

The look on Bruno's face told me he really wanted to stay and talk. I got the impression he liked having a conversation with an American so he could use his English. As for me, I simply wanted to enjoy the beautiful scenery, quite happy the questioning ceased.

There's something about him though, I thought. *Maybe the instant connection we felt because we both finished first in our academy class; or maybe something else. Regardless, I do like the kid.*

Donatella came out to check on my drinks. We looked at each other for a brief second, pausing like we had a common link. I could sense Donatella understood my desire for privacy, similar to hers. She gave me a faint smile, her lips barely turning upward, then quietly put a couple more napkins on the table. She left without speaking a word.

CHAPTER NINETEEN

Ciro tried several times the night before to get over to the river. The recycling plant stayed quite busy and Ciro helped customers until well after dark. And being so late he knew the chances of seeing something in the river were slim.

Throughout the evening, Ciro had been unable to get comfortable. He couldn't shake the thoughts running through his mind. He could see little Marcello's face as if he were standing right there. *What if* kept running through his mind. He hardly slept, an impending feeling in his stomach the boy might be telling the truth.

The next morning Ciro got up earlier than normal, not having slept well. Over an hour too early to go to work, he decided to go to Bar Podetti. He ordered a Cappuccino and tried to relax by reading the newspaper. Although the Cappuccino tasted good, he needed something stronger to kick start his day. He decided to have an Espresso as well. Despite the small cup, Ciro knew the Espresso would provide a good punch. If ever he needed a cup full of zest, it was today.

When Ciro finished the Espresso he felt ready. He reasoned if there were no dead girl, then he would need the extra *pick me up* to make it through a long day. If there were a dead girl, he would need the help getting through the stress of it all.

He headed to work. Nearing the last slanted overhang covering the large bins at *Centro Raccolta Materiali,* Ciro glanced toward the river and parked.

God, I hate to say this, but I hope Marcello lied, he thought.

Other employees were surprised to see Ciro there before 8 a.m., prompting their teasing about his wife kicking him to the dog house last night.

After joking back, Ciro excused himself and started walking toward the river. His heart rate and dread began building with each step.

During the night he realized they never asked Marcello where he saw the body. Since the boy could go on the bridge, Ciro figured it would be the best place to start.

Please Lord, let nothing be in the river. Not an overly religious man, Ciro felt a prayer could not hurt.

He crossed the open area in front of the building heading toward the bridge…the weight of his legs made each step more difficult. His worrying throughout the night gradually became fear with each stride closer to the grassy corner. The butterflies in his stomach turned into nausea, soon followed by light headedness as he passed the large wooden guy-wire pole on the corner. He reached for the rusty metal pipe rail on the bridge for support, afraid to look into the river.

Ciro stopped in the middle of the bridge, his head down, eyes closed as he started one last prayer. *Please Lord…*he did not know what else to say. Ciro slowly lifted his head, his eyes taking even longer to shift to the river.

"No," he screamed, as he ran to the far side of the bridge. *Why…Why didn't I come over last night*? After staring at her bobbing in the powerful rush of water, Ciro put his head in his hands.

"*Stava dicendo la verità*," he was telling the truth, Ciro said.

Ciro's coworkers, surprised he had not returned, were looking for him when they heard him scream somewhere by the river. They sprinted around the corner of the building, in time to see him holding his head and saying, "he was telling the truth." They rushed over fearing something terrible happened and from the bridge the reason he screamed became clear.

"Who? Who told the truth?" one of them asked.

"Yesterday afternoon, when Marcello ran back, he told his mamma and me. We didn't believe him. He told the truth!"

While his coworkers called the Carabinieri, Ciro sent out two texts. He knew Lia Vender, but not her phone number. One of them texted Lia's number to him.

"*Pronto*," Lia said. Silence. "*Pronto*," she repeated.

"Marcello told the truth."

Lia dropped the phone—she knew the caller.

CHAPTER TWENTY

The phone rang at the Carabinieri office in Cles.

"Carabinieri."

"There's a dead girl floating in the river by the recycling area in Rumo," said the male voice.

The young officer rationalized a body in the river in such mountainous country had to be a missing trekker, so he decided to first drink his Cappuccino. When he finished, he called Captain Condello directly.

"Captain, we received a call about a young woman floating in the river near your recycling area...probably a missing trekker."

"Who called, one of the employees there?" Captain Condello asked.

"Umm, not sure?"

"Is he waiting there for us?"

"He never said," the officer said.

Condello shook his head, realizing the young officer never took the time to ask any follow-up questions. Squeezing the phone, Condello punched the red button, and then dialed the office.

"Captain, good timing, I barely walked in the door." Bruno said.

"I got a call from the office in Cles," Condello said, seriousness in his voice. "They received a call about a dead girl in the river by the recycling area. Are you familiar with the area?"

"Yes. I've been on several walks by there."

"Get Corporal Amici and meet me there," Condello showed authority in his voice. "Be there in ten minutes."

Bruno hung up grinning. *There is another side to him*, he thought.

Corporal Amici had not made it to the office yet, so Bruno bolted up the stairs. He took a deep breath and then knocked on Amici's door.

Bruno repeated what Captain Condello told him. "You want me to get the car?" Bruno asked.

The door slung open. "No. I'm driving," Amici said before slamming it shut.

Bruno quickly dressed into his uniform and raced downstairs to the office—where he waited. Minutes later Amici ran down.

"Let's go," Amici said, bolting out the back door. They made it to the car before Amici dashed back in to grab the keys. Bruno kept a solemn face, trying to stay positive toward Amici.

By the time they arrived the news had been traveling fast. There were already twenty or so people gathered in the area, their cars parked along the side of the road. Amici parked next to the *Centralina Comunale* building.

Amici sprang out of the car, barking at the crowd to get back and stay off the grass. Bruno contained his excitement about finally investigating a serious case. He waited for Amici to finish yelling before he got out hoping the crowd would see they were different.

"What took you so long?" Condello asked. "I told you to be here in ten minutes. You're nearly ten minutes late."

Corporal Amici gave Bruno the evil eye. Rather than smile to irritate Amici like he used to, Bruno looked back with a pensive expression and shrugged his shoulders. From the bridge both men could see the young girl floating next to the river's edge.

"I'll grab the camera," Amici said.

"No. Bruno seems proficient with the camera, I want him to take the pictures. I need you to gather some of the men standing over there and start looking in the area for anything looking like it might be out of place," Condello said to Amici, pointing to the crowd. "Make sure you instruct them not to touch anything. I want them to show you what they found."

Bruno strode toward the crowd roughly ten meters in front of Amici. He knew many people did not care for Amici since he had not taken the time to interact with them like Bruno had.

When he noticed most of the crowd looking at him, Bruno quietly said, "What's happened in our community is an awful thing. Corporal Amici's going to need some help. Let's all pull together to find out some answers."

Bruno kept walking, smiled, and then grabbed the spare set of car keys from his pocket. Once inside the trunk he retrieved the digital camera out of its lockbox. Despite not being fancy, Captain Condello had let Bruno get comfortable with it on some of his walks so he would be proficient when the time came. He inserted a new sixty-four megabyte memory card, closed the trunk, and headed to the river.

CHAPTER TWENTY-ONE

I hoped I'd be able to have another conversation with Donatella similar to the day before. The number of people in the bar so early in the morning surprised me. Clearly, I'd been mistaken. After my second Cappuccino I walked inside.

"I'll go home and get you some money," I said.

"No, no. Pay next time you come in." Donatella pointed to her note pad with "*Debiti*" in bold letters at the top. I saw my name along with several others, every one of us owing her money.

I nearly said something when the phone in the bar rang. Donatella held up her index finger before answering and her expression indicated something had happened.

Several of the patrons began getting calls on their cell phones at the same time, including Donatella. Even before Donatella hung up many patrons were leaving the bar, talking excitedly into their phones. Despite not understanding what they were saying, their actions alone said something bad occurred.

"What's wrong?" I asked as Donatella hung up.

"A dead girl is in the river by the recycling area."

Where's the recycling area? How do I get there? The detective in me instinctively asked the questions before I realized it.

I lost sight of the bar as I pictured Bethany not moving, lying dead in her own river of blood.

"*AJ*. Are you okay?"

Donatella's voice brought me back.

"Yes, yes. I'm fine. Sorry. So, how would I get there, to the recycling area?"

"It's across from the lumberyard...next to the river. *Cognes pasarge per nir a Rum*."

Focusing on English for my sake had not been Donatella's priority. Still, I knew exactly where she meant...where I met the German shepherd.

Donatella became engrossed in conversation with the few patrons left as I slipped out. Walking away from the bar my internal conflict seethed. My resolution to get away and relax clashed with the detective inside wanting answers to the five W's; who, what, when, where, why, and the misfit, how.

How am I supposed to entirely shut off my inner detective? Besides, I'm not here investigating, I'm here looking like everybody else. Right, I'll keep my distance. With some semblance of compromise my relaxing would have to wait.

I jogged to the house where I grabbed a pair of sweats and my black Army hoodie. Figuring there would be quite a few cars, I decided a jog to the lumberyard would work best. I would walk in from there, hoping not to draw attention.

I passed the Pizzeria and could hear the powerful sound of the rushing water to my left, despite not being able to see the river from the road. Two patrol cars were parked near the municipal building on the right, and a crowd of at least thirty people gathered in the roadway looking toward the river.

Bad news travels fast in this small community.

Reaching the crowd I could see three officers talking on the bridge and recognized Bruno holding the camera. The oldest officer gave Bruno directions about what pictures he wanted, or so I presumed. He then turned and said something to the crowd. He waived like he was calling someone over to him, prompting ten men from the crowd to walk up on the bridge. Taking advantage of those men moving, I followed behind them, except I stopped a few feet past the guy-wire pole, short of the rusty pipe rail on the bridge.

Without thinking I started assessing their actions. I immediately had concerns about their tactics, like not freezing the scene, and using bystanders to search for evidence. I paused, taking in a deep breath, and told myself I did not work in a remote mountainous area like they did, and to quit judging. Still, it did not ease my preoccupation with going through my mental checklist of what needed to be done.

From my new vantage point I could watch what Bruno did while keeping an eye on the searchers. I also saw the dead woman for the first time, although seeing any details proved difficult.

I wondered how long she'd been there, considering most people lack being observant.

CHAPTER TWENTY-TWO

After giving directions to his officers, Condello stood on the bridge staring down at the young woman in the water. It had been a while since he investigated the death of a young person and planned to do all he could to determine her cause of death. He started with the person who found the body.

"Ciro, tell me what happened," Captain Condello said.

"I work at the facility here," he said, nodding toward the recycling compound. "Yesterday afternoon one of our regular customers, Lia Vender, and her son, Marcello, were here. Whenever they come, Lia lets the boy throw rocks in the river. He came running back with a story about a girl in the river. We didn't believe him. Then Marcello quietly got in the car and stared at us. Something about the way he acted, it made me wonder. I tried to get over to look after they left. I never could, we were busy until after dark."

"How old is the boy?"

"Ten or eleven, I think. He seemed pretty angry at us for not listening."

"Go on."

"It ate at me all night. I got to work early this morning to go look in the river. I saw her right away. It made me sick to my stomach. The poor girl…and me not believing the boy."

"What did you do then?"

"I texted a few people to get Lia Vender's cell phone number and called her. When I told her, I think she dropped the phone. I heard a loud noise, then—nothing."

Condello dialed Lia's phone number after getting it from Ciro. "*Pronto*," Lia answered.

"This is Captain Condello with the Carabinieri. We're down at the river by the recycling area. I'm told your son, Marcello, may have been the first one to spot a dead woman in the river here."

Lia could not bring herself to say anything, even when the captain asked her to get Marcello and bring him to the scene.

Expecting the call, Lia called in to work to tell them she would not be there. Arriving at the school ten minutes later, Lia nervously followed the staff.

Focusing on a book, Marcello heard loud whispering all around him. Feeling the excitement in the air he looked over the top of the book and saw his mother in the doorway, her lips clinched and pushing out, her head leaning left with her eyes on him for one second before she looked down and away—she knew.

Marcello stood, making sure to look at each classmate who teased him about telling a story of a dead woman.

Staring into each of their eyes, they all lowered their heads—vindication. Approaching his mother he saw her mouth the words, "I'm so sorry." Marcello pulled his shoulders back, showing no emotion as he walked past her. Marcello always believed someone would want to know what he saw, so he thought about what he would say, rehearsing it to himself several times.

Lia had to park quite a distance away. Walking up the road she put her left arm around Marcello, and together they passed through the crowd. Boys of Marcello's age normally did not want their mother's arm around them. Even though he tried his best to walk proudly with his chest out, his mother's arm provided a sense of security.

Nearing the bridge Lia recognized Captain Condello. She could not be sure, but she felt the captain displayed a condescending look.

He's right, I should have listened to Marcello, she thought.

"Marcello, am I correct?" Captain Condello asked.

"Yes sir."

"Can you tell me what you saw yesterday?"

"My mom lets me come to the river and throw rocks whenever we come here. I ran over there in the tall grass where I always go," Marcello said, pointing to the grass by the crowd. "I started to throw a rock at the wall under the bridge, then I saw her. Her eyes were staring at me, and I got a little scared. I started to run away. When I looked back, she was like, frozen there." Marcello's recall had taken over for the rehearsed statement. He looked up at his mother for reassurance, and she softly stroked his hair.

"It's okay, take your time. You're doing great," Captain Condello said.

"I kind of ended up on the bridge," Marcello said, his pace slowed considerably. "She looked real, like my grandma before we buried her." Looking down at his feet Marcello mumbled, "I thought she must be dead, too."

"Can you tell me what clothes you saw her wearing?"

Marcello shuffled backward, almost hiding behind his mother's leg.

"It's okay. You don't have to look down there again," Captain Condello said. "Can you remember anything she wore?"

"All I can remember is a gray sweater, and maybe jeans, I'm really not for sure."

Marcello gradually slid closer to his mother until he rested up against her. Seeing a bit of fear in the boy's face, Captain Condello ended the questioning. Condello explained to Lia he may have more questions for Marcello, although for now he could return to school. Condello put his hand on Marcello's shoulder.

"Thank you for all of your help. You're a brave boy."

Watching Lia and Marcello walk toward the crowd Condello spotted a man standing between the pole and the bridge railing who looked out of place. As Bruno approached the bridge Captain Condello got his attention.

"I want you to go with me to talk to him," Condello said, pointing toward the bridge railing. "I don't recognize him. He's much closer than anyone else.

"He's a new visitor to Rumo. I met him this morning at Bar Lanterna."

"Really. Well, I still want to talk to him. There's something about him," Captain Condello said.

CHAPTER TWENTY-THREE

Bruno appeared to be doing a good job taking photos from different perspectives. It seemed the other officer had finished instructions for the helpers from the community who were breaking into pairs to start combing the other side of the river.

When I scanned the crowd I noticed the men, especially the older ones, congregated in the grass about fifteen feet from the river. They were deep in conversation, often looking over their shoulders at the girl in the water. The women huddled together closer to the road, definitely involved in their own conversation. It seemed much the same at Bar Lanterna.

I watched the officer in charge interview a younger man who looked to be a local worker. Based on his clothes and gestures I reasoned he probably worked at the recycling area. Then the officer in charge spoke with a mother and young boy. I got the feeling the boy found the dead girl. *Smart move*, I thought, when he put his hand on the boy's shoulder; I could see the boy stand up straighter. With minimal personnel, and under these circumstances, I understood why they asked the mother to bring the boy to the scene. I noticed the men in the crowd continued talking amongst themselves, while the women seemed to be paying close attention to the mother and her son.

This is definitely different than any of my crime scenes.

Considering the lack of resources, I felt the officer in charge had been doing pretty well. I could not help wondering when he would get some support—like maybe a crime scene technician.

I saw Bruno and the officer in charge walking my direction. By the way Bruno looked at me, I knew they wanted to talk to me. For a second I thought of turning and walking away, ultimately deciding against it. I would consider it suspicious, so I expected they would also. "*Buongiorno* Bruno," I said.

"*Buongiorno signore*," Bruno replied. Bruno introduced each of us and proceeded to interpret throughout for Captain Condello.

"What are you doing here?" Condello asked, a stern look on his face.

"Watching, like everybody else."

"You're much closer than anybody else. You seem to be scrutinizing everything we do. There's something about you, you're not like the others."

I thought about playing it off as no big deal, then decided they did not have time to waste talking with me.

"You're right, I apologize. My people are from Rumo, this is my first visit though. I'm a homicide detective for a city in central California. Clearly, a lot of people were shocked about the young woman dead in the river, and I guess the detective in me couldn't stay away, so I decided to come take a look for myself. Again, I apologize."

"I appreciate your apology," Captain Condello said in a calmer voice. "We can talk again later, for now please do not come any closer, or others will think they can too." When Bruno finished translating, we all shook hands.

Time for me to leave; I'd seen enough. *Why am I here? I'm a fool for even coming,* I thought.

Turning to leave I could see both groups whispering and looking at me inquisitively. Passing them, I distinctly heard *poliziotto Americano.*

In less than twenty-four hours I managed to break my resolution for peace and quiet. Plus, I had not kept the deal I made with myself to stay back like everyone else. Now I was right in the middle of small town rumors. Disappointed, I made my way past the crowd.

Walking down the single lane road more people kept arriving and I noticed a young man on the opposite side staring at me. When I looked at him, his head jerked down and he rubbed his hands through his hair.

Odd smirk. He must be excited about seeing a dead body.

For a second I thought I recognized him, almost stopping to look again. Dismissing it, I headed back toward my house, trying to put the picture of the dead girl in the river out of my mind.

By 8:30 a.m. the word about the dead girl in the river in Rumo spread like wild fire throughout the break room at the Pomarella plant in Revò. He overheard other employees talking about getting texts from family members. He could feel his excitement growing, grinning ever so slightly, so no one else could see. He knew he had to go see the stir he caused. He told his supervisor he was ill and had to leave, fully aware he would not be challenged due to his uncle's position.

There were several cars along the single lane road leading to the recycling area. Walking along the parked cars on the west side, closest to the river, he saw a man he did not recognize in sweats and a black Army hoodie, walking toward him on the opposite side of the road. The man caught him staring, so he quickly looked down and rubbed his hands through his hair until the man passed.

Relax. You're too tense. Get control of yourself, he thought.

He knew the risk. The excitement of seeing the large crowd of bystanders made it worth it though. Seeing all the people who gathered gave him the chills, a sense of dominance as he had orchestrated such an event. The pleasure of success made him stand straighter, a proudness of his own accomplishment.

He tried to stay on the fringes, not wanting to get into conversations with anyone. He had his phone in his hand, using it as a decoy to make himself look busy. He had not been there long when something happened. All three Carabinieri went over to a young adult man, roughly his age, standing on the bridge. The mumbling from the crowd stopped, while people stared at the group on the bridge.

At one point he saw the young man hold up a tie-dyed shirt, then the crowd noise grew rapidly. Several people started saying her name…Domenica…and he knew he should leave but the rush from the excitement had him glued in place. He compromised with himself and moved down the road seven meters. He sat on a large boulder in the tall grass…facing the river, his side to the crowd, still pretending to be using his phone. He became light headed, the pure pleasure of it all setting in.

CHAPTER TWENTY-FOUR

Corporal Amici gave detailed instructions to the men assisting him not to touch anything. He also told them to gradually survey their area, afraid if they went too fast they might miss something. He separated the workers and sent them in pairs to look for clues.

Paolo and his friend were the youngest employees at the recycle plant, both part-timers. Since nobody would be bringing any recycled goods for a while, their boss suggested they help with the search. They were assigned to search the southwest side of the road, in a large grassy patch, ten meters beyond the bridge.

Paolo squatted down to inspect a log. "What do you think about this? There's nothing else like it in this open area."

"I agree. Let's tell Corporal Amici," his friend said.

Amici looked at the log, shaking his head. "Guys, we're looking for clues. Not things like logs, they're everywhere."

"We felt it was odd," Paolo said. "I mean, there aren't any other logs like it close to here. I don't know, maybe somebody used it on the girl."

"Look, we have a lot to cover. Don't waste time on foolish things like logs," Corporal Amici said, grumbling as he walked away.

They looked at each other, shaking their heads, offended how he spoke to them. Without saying anything, they turned and split up. Paolo went left, closer to the river, while his friend went right, closer to the slope of the mountain. Paolo spotted a blue backpack in the bushes next to the tall grass bordering the open area.

After pointing out the log and the result it brought, Paolo was not about to call Amici over to check it without looking inside first. He saw several pieces of clothing likely belonging to a woman. One of the pieces catching his attention had some writing on it. Pulling the white T-shirt out he could see it had tie-dyed sleeves as well as tie-dye on the sides. The shirt displayed writing from a hit song by the British rock band, Queen. Holding up the shirt he could see the writing on the front. The hair on the back of Paolo's neck stood up. *Oh crap*, he thought.

Paolo dropped the backpack and sprinted toward the bridge. He looked to his right at the woman's body trapped in the water. Aloud he said, *"Domenica, it really is you."*

Corporal Amici had seen Paolo racing toward the bridge and ran to catch up to him. "What'd you just say?"

Captain Condello had seen Amici rush to the bridge and hurried over, too.

Paolo turned to the corporal, astounded. "That's Domenica."

"Who's Domenica? How do you know it's her?"

Paolo pointed to the backpack saying he found it in the bushes. He then held up the t-shirt, telling Amici it came from the backpack.

Cutting him off, Amici nastily said, "What are you doing looking in the backpack. I specifically told you …"

Captain Condello put his hand on Amici's shoulder to interrupt his train of thought. Condello then looked at Paolo.

"Please, go on."

"Nobody else in Rumo has this," he said, holding up the shirt so they could see the writing on the front. "There're lots of people who've seen her wearing the shirt. Nobody's seen it around town for several months, which goes along with what Domenica said about going to Germany. She'd even posted it on her Facebook page back in October. Nobody ever saw any more posts after the date she planned to leave. It was common knowledge she wanted to get away from here. We all assumed she'd actually gone like she said, putting Rumo behind her."

Bruno walked over to the three men on the bridge. In an intense whisper, Amici caught Bruno up on the details.

"Corporal Amici." Captain Condello paused, staring at Amici long enough to get his displeasure across. "Calmly… get as much information as you can from Paolo, take control of the backpack and shirt after Bruno photographs them and the area where they were found. Then, go see if you can find her parents. Try to get as much information from them as you can before we bring them here to identify their daughter. They won't be of much help after they see her."

Uncomfortable, Corporal Amici directed Paolo with his open palm to the grassy area so he could attempt to get further information.

Bruno took the photographs and then returned to the bridge. "I think her leg is broken," he said to Captain Condello. "She also appears to have some bruising around her nose and lips."

"I know what you're thinking. Let's not get ahead of ourselves. If what Paolo told Corporal Amici about Domenica wanting to leave for Germany, and took her backpack with her, it is possible she sustained these injuries simply trying to leave the area."

Bruno asked, "Then what is her backpack doing in the tall grass on the far side of the river, nowhere near the water, yet she's in the river with a broken leg and bruising?"

Captain Condello put his hand on Bruno's shoulder. "Those are good questions. Until we have more information they remain unanswered. Patience." Looking toward the crowd Condello noticed the American had left. "Your American friend is gone."

"I'm not surprised. He probably gets too much of this back home."

CHAPTER TWENTY-FIVE

The hot water from the shower felt good. With my hands on the wall, I stood with my eyes closed letting it softly pelt my head. My mind drifted, caught between two worlds.

Lying somewhat on the surface in the river, her open eyes drew me in.

I moved closer and saw Bethany's face on the girl in the river, her eyes begging me to help her. Or was she begging me to help the girl?

Trying to focus on the Carabinieri and the men helping them worked for a short period. My eyes kept glancing back to the river, each time met by Bethany's staring back.

"Help her," I thought I heard Bethany say.

"I can't."

I could see Bethany's face. Her gentle look told me I needed to help.

I can't. I'm…I'm not ready."

I looked away in time to see the two Carabinieri walking towards me.

My mind flipped back to reality. My eyes opened

and I slapped the shower wall.

The juxtaposition of my not feeling ready, while hearing Bethany's voice telling me to help the girl, had me frustrated.

"There's nothing I can do," I said, trying to convince myself. "Not only am I not ready, I couldn't barge in and tell them I wanted to help."

I closed my eyes, again trying to focus on the warm water.

Bethany's eyes appeared. My eyes shot open and I jerked back. I shut the water off, put my hands on the wall and looked down.

What started as a relaxing shower ended with annoyance at myself for ever going to the river.

I decided to visit Donatella, and felt pleased to see no other patrons.

They must all still be at the river.

I spotted her washing dishes in the far corner.

"*Buongiorno,* Donatella."

"*Giorno,* AJ," she answered, tilting her head, confusion on her face. "Why are you here? I thought you would be at the river."

"What a mistake, I should have never gone. I started to get in the way, and it made me realize I needed to leave."

She offered to fix me something to eat, to which I accepted—of course.

"*Acqua naturale*?" she asked in Italian.

"*Sì, per favore,*" I said.

The corners of her lips raised slightly at my attempt to use Italian.

Since we were alone I decided to sit at the bar. Of the

two black vinyl square stools with rectangular shiny silver foot rests I chose the far one, closest to the east wall.

Donatella arrived with a large plate of salami, three different types of cheese, freshly baked bread, and apple slices. Looking at the food made me wonder how she could stay in business as low as her prices were and the amount of food she always provided. The smell and taste of fresh food made me forget about business issues.

While I ate, Donatella went back to washing dishes directly across from me. She broke the silence when she asked, "What did you mean, you started to get in the way?"

"The detective in me kind of took over. I started to get too close to her. I didn't realize how close until the captain and Bruno approached me."

"I'm sure you did not do anything wrong. Is being too close to the girl all that bothers you?"

I stopped from biting into a piece of cheese an inch from my lips, goosebumps forming on the back of my neck and looked at her.

She said, "I'm sorry, I should not be asking those questions. You do not need to tell me anything. It is a private matter."

"It's fine, don't worry about it," I said, a faint chuckle in my voice. I smiled hoping she would not see my angst. "My sister told me you Italians are private people. She said you're all nice and easy to talk to, as long as I don't ask about private matters."

Donatella grinned and nodded. "She is right, we are private."

"I understand. *Capisco, sì*?"

Her eyes sparkled. "Sì, *capisco*, means I understand."

"Well…I came here to get away from those kinds of

things at the river. I shouldn't have been drawn back so easily," I said, unable to hold back my frustration.

The caring look in Donatella's stare nearly made me forget about being so upset with myself.

Several seconds passed before Donatella spoke.

"Why are you, I am not sure how to ask it. What real reason did you come to Rumo?"

My hesitation…not based on not wanting to talk about it…but more due to being moved by her insight and ability to read people.

"We are a lot alike. We're both private people. Plus, we've both made a career out of reading people and trying to understand them. I normally do not share much about myself with anyone. But, I really enjoy talking with you."

I thought I saw her blush before she turned away. Donatella dried her hands before coming over to the bar across from me. Something told me she felt the same way.

"I came here because I needed to get away," I continued. "My last investigation four months ago, the killer murdered someone close to me…he killed my girlfriend, Bethany."

Donatella's eyes burst open wide, her right hand covering her open mouth. Gently, she placed her other hand on top of mine.

"I can hardly sleep, I'm exhausted, and, I haven't worked since it happened. I came here with the idea to get away, relax, and try to move on, I guess."

"AJ, I am sorry. I cannot imagine how difficult it is for you." Seeing her hand on top of mine she awkwardly pulled it away. Her eyes shifted to mine, then darted down to her hands, now cupped in front of her.

"Thank you. It's okay. I don't mind sharing it with you. I feel comfortable talking with you." I kept my eyes on hers until I saw the corners of her lips gently creep up. I told her about Doc, and how he encouraged me to talk about what happened.

I paused, trying to find the right words.

"I'd always believed as a detective I needed to have compassion, yet not so much it could take me away from thinking clearly, or staying on task. For years I've investigated people being killed, but not until Bethany's murder did I ever really know the sickening feeling of what loved ones were going through. I keep seeing her over and over, and as hard as I try, I can't save her."

Donatella crossed her arms, as if she were protecting herself. I could see her searching for what to say in the silence enveloping us.

"For me…it took a long time to get over my husband's death. He died in an accident, terribly hard for me. Worse for you…she, Bethany, someone killed her."

I could not believe Donatella shared something so private with me. I felt immense compassion for her and her sons. "Tragedy is tragedy. The people living through it are devastated. One is no worse than the other. All I know is, it's difficult to get past."

We looked into one another's eyes, sadly familiar with how each other felt.

Change direction. Say something positive.

"Actually, this may sound a little strange…I'm already feeling better."

"I am glad." Silence filled the room as she reflected. "What makes you feel this way?"

"Well, for the first time in four months an investigation interested me today. Plus, I've been able to sleep a little longer before the nightmare returns, so I'm getting more rest." I paused, unsure if I should say anymore. "And…you." I hesitated, seeing a faint sheepish smile.

Donatella lowered her head before uncrossing her arms, and putting her hands together on top of the counter.

She didn't walk away. Okay, good.

"I really enjoy talking with you," I said. "At first I felt badly, like it was wrong to enjoy talking with you, wrong on account of Bethany. I don't know. I think…I think somehow it's okay."

I could hear them before I could see them…several voices from entering patrons. Donatella softly put her hand back on mine, canted her head to the side, and faintly smiled her little smile before returning to drying the dishes.

I finished eating while listening to the buzz in the conversations, some of which had to do with me, having seen me at the river. Donatella looked at me when she heard someone say *poliziotto Americano.* I shrugged, deciding not to look at them as I ate my lunch. Although, I did find myself wishing I understood what they were saying.

I felt privileged Donatella let her wall down a little before people returned.

I wonder if it'll ever happen again. Time will tell.

CHAPTER TWENTY-SIX

Corporal Amici located Domenica's mother, Penina, at her house.

"Can you tell me when Domenica left?"

"October 19. She left us a note, said she wanted to see other places." Penina stepped out of the room, returning with the note, she handed it to Amici.

Mom and Dad,

Please don't be angry. You know I really want to go out on my own and I knew you would not approve. I am really excited about seeing other places and the experiences awaiting me. I will be in touch after I get settled. Mom, don't worry, I have been saving money for this for a while. I will have enough to be fine until I get a job.

I love you both,
Domenica

"Do you have any ideas where she planned to go?" Amici asked.

"I'd tried to call and texted her every day. She never responded," Penina said, her voice trailing off. "Obviously, we got worried when we hadn't heard from her. Her friends told us she posted on Facebook on October 19 her excitement about going to Germany."

Amici kept the note as evidence, carefully putting it in his pocket.

"Why are you asking about Domenica after all this time?" she asked.

Amici looked down, taking a few seconds to gather some courage before he looked into Penina's eyes. "Maybe you should come with me, over by the community building," he said softly.

Tears began forming in the corners of Penina's eyes.

Volunteer firefighters had made their way into the river to begin the process of extricating Domenica out of the water. Several firefighters held a metal framed basket, similar to those used to airlift injured skiers off mountains, while two others were dislodging her foot from the rocks. They submerged the basket under Domenica and slowly raised it, trying to prevent tearing her skin as they loaded her.

Firefighters on the flat ledge underneath the bridge used pulley ropes to guide the basket due to strong currents. Once safely on the flat ledge they got Domenica onto the grass next to the river where, ironically, she had originally been carried into the water months before.

One of the firefighters pointed out some blood on the rock wall which separated the two levels of grass. They notified Captain Condello as they set the basket on the ambulance gurney, covering Domenica with a crime scene blanket. When Bruno finished taking pictures of the blood on the wall ledge, he also collected some of the blood as evidence.

A few minutes later Corporal Amici arrived with Penina. All eyes were on the patrol car as a sense of stillness overtook the crowd. Amici stood outside of the car waiting for Penina. The creak of the car door broke the silence. It seemed to take a long time before she exited the car. She turned, looked over to the bridge and her heart sank when she saw what looked like a body covered with a yellow blanket.

Unable to move, Penina wept. When two ladies from the crowd came to her side, Corporal Amici breathed a sigh of relief. The women put their arms under Penina's, guiding her to the bridge.

Unknown to the onlookers and the police they were being scrutinized. The young man recognized Penina immediately. With a cruel and satisfied smile, he pivoted on the boulder, putting his back to the crowd, hoping not to be seen by her. He did not want to make any sudden moves or draw attention. The hush over the crowd made it easy for him to hear the weeping of a mother for her daughter.

He believed Penina recognized he was a sound influence on her daughter. While he often cursed his mother for not caring and for leaving him, Domenica had a mother who loved her. He cursed Domenica for only thinking of herself and her desires, and for making him do this to her mother.

Glancing over his shoulder he saw two women walking slowly, holding onto Penina. With each step getting them closer to the bridge, he took one toward the road, keeping his back to the crowd. Her scream shattered the serenity of the flowing water, causing his head to jerk around.

Walk slowly, don't draw attention, he thought.

He could hear his own rhythmic throbbing in his ears. When he got some distance down the road his mind stopped racing. The certainty of being out of sight allowed him to begin to relax.

The uncertainty of being seen, coupled with the stir he caused, invigorated him. He had not been able to imagine how stimulating it would be. It confirmed to him he would never again be normal—he had to kill again.

CHAPTER TWENTY-SEVEN

Captain Condello tried his best to position and cover Domenica to help minimize trauma to her mother. Lividity and waxy looking skin made it a difficult proposition and he wished he could have done more.

"I know this is difficult, I'm very sorry," he said, taking Penina's hand between his. "We need to determine if you recognize this girl."

Penina nodded her head, her eyes fixed on the yellow blanket.

Slowly he uncovered Domenica's face.

Instantly Penina let out an agonizing, shrieking scream of "*No, la me popa*," her knees giving out as she sobbed. The question had been answered.

Captain Condello knew one of the women helping Penina, so he whispered to her, "Can someone stay with her? She will need the support of her friends."

"Sì, *s*ì! We will take her home and stay with her," she said.

The women lifted Penina, steadily helping her remain on her feet, and consoling her as they departed.

Captain Condello looked at Domenica's face, overcome with a sense of sorrow as he replaced the blanket.

He used some of the volunteer firemen to hold up the blanket so officers could inspect Domenica's body for evidence.

"I've seen her before, on some of my walks," Bruno said. "She always seemed, pleasant."

How sad; she's so young, Bruno thought.

"The lividity on the left side of her nose and mouth jumps out at you. I can't see any signs of strangulation," Captain Condello said.

"She obviously laid on her left side after dying," Corporal Amici said. "I can't really see any other bruising. There's no way to determine what broke her leg without an autopsy."

The captain hesitated, looking at Domenica's face one more time. He bent down to get a closer look. "Look here. When the light hits her face from this angle …"

"I see it. On her cheek," Bruno said. "Those look like fingers. Am I crazy, or don't they look like they go from her mouth out to her cheek?"

"Thank you. Go ahead and cover her up," Captain Condello said to the firefighters. Condello's nod got his men to follow him to the grassy area where Paolo found the backpack. He felt they needed to discuss what they had before calling the Command Staff in Cles to ask for help.

"To start with, she planned to leave…I mean she even left a note. I have it in the car," Corporal Amici said. "It seems like she could have easily set her backpack down and somehow fell in the river."

"I have a bad feeling about this Captain," Bruno said, hesitation in his voice.

"Go on, speak freely," Captain Condello said.

"Something's wrong," Bruno continued. "Her backpack ends up in this tall bush, while she's down in the water? I don't like the bruising on her face; it's like someone's hand pushed down hard over her mouth and nose. I would swear those are finger marks on her cheek. Then there's the broken leg. It looks way worse than what I would expect from a fall on rocks from that short of a distance. It's pretty severe."

"Maybe some kids saw the backpack and moved it," Amici said. "Maybe they never saw her. If she slipped and fell she could have broken her leg and landed on her face, which might explain some of the bruising."

Following Captain Condello's advice from several days ago, Bruno paused and took a deep breath. "Even though your points are valid, I respectfully disagree," Bruno said, looking directly at Amici.

"Like Bruno, I have my suspicions," Condello said. "Although, Corporal Amici has brought up some good points, ones the Command Staff in Cles may seize upon, putting an end to this investigation, *regardless* of how we feel."

While the other two walked away Bruno remained, taking it all in. If Amici were playing the part of devil's advocate, Bruno could easily accept it being a valid role in an investigation. Still, he could not ignore his own concerns.

Does Amici really believe what he said, or is he simply taking the path of least resistance so we can close this case?

CHAPTER TWENTY-EIGHT

"Corporal Amici, contact the mortuary," Captain Condello ordered. "Bruno, gather the backpack as evidence."

Condello took a deep breath, and called the Carabinieri office in Cles. He identified himself to the young officer who answered and asked to speak with *Maggiore* Leone, the officer in charge in the Cles division.

"*Pronto*," Major Leone answered.

"Good morning Major. This is Captain Condello in Rumo."

"Captain Condello, Officer Biagi notified me of your situation. I've been waiting for your call."

"A few minutes ago we pulled the young woman out of the river. After looking closer, I feel uncomfortable about the circumstances of her death," Condello began.

"Go on."

"It appears she's been in the river for approximately six months. The winter temperatures preserved her body fairly well."

"Makes sense."

"There are no signs of strangulation, knife wounds, or gunshot wounds. However, she clearly has a broken leg, and we found her backpack on dry land up in some bushes almost twenty meters from where she got stuck in the rocks. Two of us believe we can see finger marks on her cheek by her nose and mouth on one side of her face. The other side is covered with lividity. Her foot on the broken leg was turned almost the opposite direction. Her foot had gotten stuck in the submerged rocks preventing her from going down the river."

Condello paused, trying to gather his thoughts about what else to say.

Major Leone asked about the girl's family, and wanted more information about the backpack.

Condello described the backpack stuffed with clothing and personal items, along with the shirt they used to identify Domenica.

"We interviewed her mother, who said her daughter left a note in October verifying her plans to leave the area. The note said she would contact them when she got settled. Some posts the girl made on Facebook matched what she said in the note. Her parents tried regularly to get in touch with her, but never heard from her again."

Major Leone paused.

"Are there any other signs of being beaten, restrained, or bludgeoned? Anything at all?"

Captain Condello shook his head and responded, "No, other than the finger marks on her face, nothing we can see at this point."

"Captain, you have an outstanding reputation, and I respect your feeling uncomfortable with this young woman's death."

"*Grazie Maggiore.*" *Here comes the denial.*

"You understand, for me to convince my superiors to send out the *Raggruppamento Carabinieri Investigazioni Scientifiche* (RaCIS) I have to have probable cause this was a murder and not some girl who accidentally met her death in the river. The closest of those four scientific investigation departments would be in Parma, so it would take some time to get them there."

The major went on about clear signs of foul play, repeating his difficulty in convincing his superiors to send the RaCIS such a distance on a questionable case.

Condello could hear the major's voice, although his thoughts were on Domenica. He could not help from feeling he'd let her down.

"Additionally, as I'm sure you are aware, a non-judicial autopsy is doubtful given your remoteness and the lack of trained physicians throughout Italy," Major Leone added. "Unfortunately, I do not believe I can do anything to help you at this point." He ended by providing the obligatory comment about calling him should any more information be discovered.

Captain Condello thanked the major, doing his best to sound appreciative in his closing remarks before hanging up.

No surprise, he thought.

Captain Condello's desire to do all he could to help determine Domenica's demise came to a screeching halt.

Meanwhile, Bruno placed the backpack in a large brown paper bag. While sealing the bag by the trunk of the car, he looked over at Captain Condello pacing, his shoulders slumped, the phone call over.

Man, it's like I thought. They aren't going to provide any assistance.

Captain Condello remained quiet until they were back at the office.

"I spoke with the major in Cles," Condello said, frustration in his voice. "He feels we don't have enough probable cause to validate a murder, or enough evidence for him to call out the RaCIS from Parma. Finish logging the evidence and photos, then do your reports so we can close this case."

Condello turned to walk away, then stopped. He looked back, and with a softer tone, said, "Corporal Amici, please return the backpack and its contents to Domenica's parents after the contents are photographed."

Captain Condello shuffled back to his office. Understanding Major Leone's perspective did nothing to quell his intuition something tragic happened to Domenica, not of her own doing. Sitting at his desk, he shook his head in annoyance as he buried his face in his hands.

CHAPTER TWENTY-NINE

Leaving the river he thought about going back to work, but decided he would not be able to focus. When he got home he went straight to the work bench in the basement and retrieved the bag he hid behind the wooden brace pieces attaching the bench to the wall. He pulled the cat's bell and Domenica's bracelet out of the bag and rolling them around in his hand, he envisioned adding to the collection.

The commotion he caused with Domenica elated him, especially when conversations among bystanders became almost heated about whether or not she'd been murdered. *Number Two* would add to the fear throughout Rumo after she went missing. He figured by the time they found her, if the animals did not get her first, nobody would be able to tell what happened to her.

He went upstairs to relax, took a seat in his dad's recliner, and gradually began to reflect on the past.

In his early years his mother seemed happy and smiled a lot. He recalled how she loved to have him sit on her lap so she could read him books.

His mother's happiness gradually drifted away as his father's discontent led to beating her. He could not remem-

ber the last time he saw her smile before she left. He always wondered if his father's unhappiness stemmed from not reaching the same level of success his brother had at the Pomarella Plant.

He thought it peculiar his father never tried to find his mother. He even had some thoughts his father seriously hurt her, or worse. Not only had he not seen her pack, she never said anything about leaving—she simply disappeared.

For several years he blamed his mother for leaving him, especially when the maltreatment got worse for him. It began with slapping, and progressed to punching when he got older. Those did not equal the severity of being held down and tortured, like the burns on his back.

At nine-years-old he discovered his father could kill after he got angry at their pet dog, Blackie. His father made him watch while he tied the dog to a tree, beat it with a shovel, and then forced him to dig the hole where they buried the dog. He learned his beatings could possibly be much worse. From that point on, he began to watch his father closely for signs of anger so he could leave to avoid suffering.

His own research into why he killed confused him. The more he tried to answer the question, the more confusing it became.

"It's time to stop. I can't change the past. Who knows why? Who cares? It's time I embrace who I am," he said aloud.

Done with logging the photos into the computer, Bruno turned his attention to Domenica's Facebook posts.

Before the young worker, Paolo, left the crime scene Bruno approached him. Paolo agreed to allow Bruno access to his Facebook accounts so Bruno could research Domenica's other friends and recent posts.

In the days leading up to October 19, Domenica posted regularly about it being time to leave Rumo. She clearly intended to go to Germany. Paolo told Bruno about Domenica having posted something on the night she left home, and then she went dark. Bruno found the post from Domenica, 6:38 pm on October 19. "Germany here I come! #Freedom #Superexcited."

Bruno discovered a more complex Domenica when he read her heartfelt post on Facebook from early in the day on October 19, regarding how much she loved her parents and how important both of them were to her. She mentioned not wanting to hurt them, hoping they would someday understand her desire to go see other places. Domenica's sincerity appeared genuine.

Domenica's last Facebook post caught Bruno off guard. She mentioned her "so-called boyfriend" smothering her, along with needing to get away from him. Then she posted, "Goodbye to Rumo!" All of the pictures Bruno had seen were of Domenica with groups of people, usually at parties, or a couple of her girlfriends; nothing even closely resembled a boyfriend or relationship type picture. He scrutinized each post back through September 1. No mention of a boyfriend—until the final post.

Bruno knew Major Leone would not consider his findings enough *probable cause* to investigate further.

Still, there's something about her final post that bothers me, he thought.

CHAPTER THIRTY

I wanted to see the area where my grandfather's family resided. My sister told me many homes in Rumo are referred to by the last name of the original owner. I longed to search for the home in Corte Superiore still known as the "Conti" home, and possibly meet a distant cousin or two like my sister had.

The beauty of the area compelled me to walk instead of drive. I went north along the main road and then turned east, hugging the ten foot brick wall in front of the Carabinieri building until I reached the sidewalk a couple feet beyond it. I looked around when I heard my name being called. I spotted him standing near the wrought iron fence on top of the wall.

"Bruno, *come stai*?" I asked.

"*Bene, grazie*. Using Italian, very good. Wait one minute, I'll be down."

"*No problema*." My asking Bruno, how he was in Italian, seemed minuscule compared to his ability to speak English.

"Where you headed?" Bruno asked, coming from the underground parking next to the building.

"Corte Superiore…to see my grandfather's family home."

"*Bene, bene*. Mind if I walk with you?"

"Not at all…busy couple days."

"Yes," Bruno said. "Sad, yet exciting, too."

"Those types of investigations are challenging. To good investigators, the challenge is exciting."

We came upon a small park with several climbing structures made of wood with four children playing, and two young mothers watching and talking.

"You seem, intrigued," Bruno intimated.

"Looking at those play structures, they would have been made of plastic in America. Yet here, they're built out of wood. They look so sturdy."

As we continued walking I asked, "Where exactly are the Dolomites?"

"Ahh, the grandest of mountains. They are beyond the mountain ridges in front of us. These mountains are beautiful. The Dolomites, they are magnificent."

Bruno began asking questions about my experiences. The standard fascination all young cops have, hearing stories from the old salts who sailed the streets before them. I'd done the same thing when I first started.

"What about gangs, are they as violent as the media makes them out to be?" Bruno asked.

"They can be. Rumo's nothing like where I came from… the way I see it, that's a good thing."

Bruno's youth wanted the adrenaline rush from action. Even so, he could see the value for the citizens in Rumo not having to deal with daily violence.

"Gang bangers will shoot at one another for having the wrong color bandana, or stepping one foot into the other's territory," I said. "They don't have any respect for life."

Bruno seemed a little unnerved by the statement.

"A close detective friend of mine got a gang-versus-gang homicide right before I left. It all started over a guy talking with a chick in the wrong place."

"Really?"

"Yeah, it happened between the Norteños and Sureños: two major Mexican gangs. After the first shooting, a drive-by retaliation shooting followed, killing an innocent sixteen-year-old and wounding a little girl."

"That's so bizarre," he shook his head in disbelief.

I explained how the older Mexican gang bangers used to take care of business.

"Unfortunately, these younger guys prefer to open fire, no care or concern about who they kill."

"Wow. Even though the Mafia is dangerous, at least they seem to have a reason for who they kill," Bruno said.

"They're mostly in southern Italy, right?"

"Yes. Despite the several families there, three or four are the strongest and most active."

Not surprisingly several American gangs have taken on many of the Mafia customs, like structure, rules, and loyalty.

"Much of the Carabinieri resources go to fighting the Mafia," Bruno said. "They are not beyond killing judges, ranking officers in the Carabinieri, or pretty much anyone who openly makes a stand against them."

Thankfully our gangs generally did not target cops or political figures. I shared with Bruno about a training officer I had who taught me to work at understanding people. He made sure I always started off showing respect, even to gang members.

"Did it ever pay off for you?" Bruno asked.

"Yeah, several times; once early in my career, I happened to be in the home of a gang member who had some reasonable rank. He had warrants for his arrest and I told the guy I'd wait for him outside. He realized what I was doing and said goodbye to his wife and young son, then met me outside. He never forgot it."

"What do you mean he never forgot?" Bruno asked.

"Years later while I'm trying to arrest a guy, I'm surrounded. Backup's minutes away and I'm about to get my ass handed to me. The crowd suddenly parts and the guy from years before walks up. He orders them to leave me alone. He tells the guy I'm arresting not to cause any problems. He gives me a sharp upward tilt of his head, and walks away."

Bruno had been locked into the story. I could see his wheels turning.

CHAPTER THIRTY-ONE

I wanted to learn about Bruno and told him, "No more shop talk…did you enjoy college in America?"

"Yes, immensely. I learned a lot, and it really helped my English. Great experience overall."

"Were you able to make many friends?"

"I had a tough first year. I didn't have much confidence then, mostly due to my poor English, but I made several friends over the next three years."

"Any girl friends?"

"I dated some. One girl…she had a boyfriend, a total jerk. We talked about it, she couldn't bring herself to leave him. I quit seeing her, turning my attention to getting experience by riding with police officers and volunteering at police departments."

I moved on, not having any desire to press him further on such a sensitive subject.

"This morning you said you finished tied for the top spot in your Academy class. If you don't mind me asking, what's somebody like you doing in a remote town in the mountains of northern Italy?"

"Nothing gets past you does it?"

I shrugged. "Sorry. You don't have to answer."

"It's all right." Bruno paused, trying to decide exactly how much to share. "My first assignment in Verona, I discovered

I didn't like working with lazy officers. Superior officers' acceptance of it bothered me even more. My captain there gave me the label of '*Ribelle*,' or rebel, after I questioned tactics, decisions, and work ethic. I spent enough time with police departments in America, I knew things could be done differently."

Bruno realized questioning a strong military system like the Italian Carabinieri usually ended in being passed over for good assignments and promotion—or worse.

"Well, it's refreshing to hear you have high principles and integrity," I said.

Bruno's face revealed his surprise.

"Bad cops make it tough for good, honest, hardworking cops…everywhere," I said. "The Amanda Knox murder case gave you guys a serious black eye. Trust me, there's been several of those in California, too."

"Like O.J. Simpson?"

"Yeah, like O.J. The trickle down from sloppy work affects us all, especially nowadays with all the social media crap."

"I don't want to be like those cops, giving in to the sub-standard norm," Bruno said. "They can make it hard though."

"Look, right is always right. Every case merits the best you can give it. Victims, like the girl in the river, definitely deserve your integrity. Don't let them get to you."

Bruno nodded.

"So, where's your family from?"

"Tivoli near Rome…my father passed away and my mother still lives there in the house they raised me." Bruno went on to explain being the only child he often took the train to visit her.

"I'm sure your father would be proud of you."

"Thank you," said Bruno, a wistful look on his face.

"Have you made many friends here? Or a girlfriend?"

"Not really, and no. Since I'm from southern Italy and in the Carabinieri, the people are slow to accept me. I understand though."

Between his daily walks, trying to talk with residents, and trying to learn the Rumo dialect, Bruno seemed to be doing all he could to win the people over.

Bruno paused, like people do right before they share something personal. "There is a girl…I've seen several times on my walks. We greet each other and she always smiles. I still haven't gotten the courage to talk to her."

"Look, you gotta quit being a wimp. It's time you man up. Go over there, stop and talk with her. Trust me, life might pass you by, and then you find yourself alone, like me."

When we made it to Corte Superiore I spotted it.

"There's my cousin's home," I said, pointing to the plain two-story white house with dark brown trim and accents, plus a huge basement-garage area. "My father's family, they were all raised right here."

My cousin was not home, so we walked around the house taking it all in, leaving me mesmerized by the thought of where it all started. The age of the houses in the area, descendants of original family members still living in them, and the area being farmed as it had been a century ago gave me a new understanding of tradition.

"You are touched by this, I can tell," Bruno said.

"Yes…deeply. It's hard to believe my great-grandfather built this house, farmed the entire area around it, including where some of these other homes are now, and I still have cousins living here. The tradition here…it's amazing."

After several more minutes of looking around and taking it all in, we began to walk back. Approaching the main road I had a view directly up a valley between two mountains. I counted seven other mountain tops beyond those in front of me. The valley gradually rose up, giving me the feeling as though I could walk up into the clouds if I were to follow it.

"What's this place, with the two large rollup doors?"

"Ahh, the *macelleria*...it's the butcher shop. The office doors are on the other side. This area is where they cut the meat. Of course, the family lives above the business...pretty normal in Italy."

This walk, filled with a variety of new experiences and views, brought about a relaxation I had not expected when I started.

"Is it just the three of you here, in Rumo?"

"Yes. You met the captain. The other one is Corporal Amici. Originally, he reminded me of those officers in Verona. Now, I'm really trying not to be so judgmental anymore."

"Outstanding." I tried to help Bruno understand all police officers learn the foundational things he came out of the academy with. The ones who excel take the time to learn how to read people and situations.

"Passing judgement means shutting down understanding, reasoning, and willingness to accept. When's the last time you asked him to go to morning coffee with you?"

"I...I've never asked him to go with me."

"Remember the gang member I told you about? Show Amici respect, it'll come back around to you. I promise."

Bruno hung on every word, he seemed to truly care. Even so, I felt I had become the real benefactor of our conversations. Focusing on learning about Bruno and mentoring him a little brought about a sense of calm, precisely like Doc suggested it would.

Damn, if he's not right again.

CHAPTER THIRTY-TWO

A couple minutes before 7 p.m.; I arrived at Giorgio and Wanda's looking forward to a homemade meal.

"*Buonasera*, AJ," Giorgio greeted me.

I took one step into their home and Giorgio called out to Wanda and a beautiful smile rounded the corner.

"This is my wife, Wanda," Giorgio showed his pride and his love.

"*Buonasera*, AJ. *Benvenuto in casa mia*," Wanda welcomed me to her home. Before I could respond, she gave me a kiss on each cheek.

Dinner already on the table, Giorgio handed me a glass of red wine. Wanda prepared a wonderful spaghetti dinner, accented with a fresh garden salad, fresh bread, and of course, more wine. After two helpings I had to move my plate when I saw Wanda ready to fill it again. Despite not speaking English, Wanda remained involved in our conversations, with Giorgio proving to be a sound interpreter.

"AJ, we hear you were at the river the other day and saw Domenica in the water," Giorgio said, translating for Wanda.

"You do?"

"Sì, *sì*. Rumo is not big. News travels fast here."

"I'm sure it does," I said. "A decent-sized crowd had gathered by the time I left."

"*All of Rumo* now knows you are an American police man,"

Giorgio said. Turning his head slightly, he stared at me out of the corner of his eye as if waiting for my explanation.

"Yeah, I could hear them telling each other as I left. What do you hear about the girl's death—Domenica, I think you said?"

"We were trekking with our good friends at *Val d'Ultimo* that day. The people I have spoken to say there is no way Domenica had an accident."

"Oh really," I said, intrigue in my tone. "What kind of reasons, or explanations do they give?"

"Ahh, reasons. Wanda says everyone hears Domenica left a note for her parents about leaving. Domenica told her friends she was going to Germany. Plus, I hear the young man helping the Carabinieri found a backpack full of clothes. An important thing, AJ, there is no *spiegazioni*… or reason she would fall in the river."

"What do you mean…why not?"

"There are two walking paths and they come together on the bridge over the river. Path Eight is the longest, it comes to the bridge on the opposite side of the river from the *Centralina Comunale*, our power station building."

"Yes, I saw it."

"Okay, so the one closest to the *Centralina Comunale* is Path Ten. Both of them come close together in the village of Mocenigo where we are. Path Ten is the best path for her to take."

"Why?"

"Path Ten starts in the village of Lanza above us, next to Domenica's house. The shortest path to the main road is by the lumberyard. So, it makes sense for her to stay on Path Ten. No reason to stop at the river, or be on the bridge. The road to *chiedere un passaggio*, um, um, to grab a ride is a short distance past the *pizzeria*."

I tried taking it all in without seeming to be overly wrapped up in it. I could not be sure if Giorgio told me all of this simply spreading the local gossip, or because I happened to be a detective.

"AJ, the whole thing makes no sense," Giorgio said, shaking his head. "Path Ten from her house brings her to Mocenigo. Then to a bus stop. Left is to Path Ten. Right is to Path Eight. Much confusion, why not take the bus? Her friends say Domenica talked of taking a train from Mezzocorona, well beyond Cles. She needs a ride to the train. It is too far to walk. If not taking the bus, who does she *aspettare* to give her a ride?"

Giorgio brought up some interesting points, ones I suggested the Carabinieri would follow up on.

"No," Giorgio protested. "They told Captain Condello the case is done, no more."

"Who told him?" I asked.

"Officers above him from Cles. Some of the things I say are people's beliefs. This is fact. The Carabinieri are done, no more for Domenica."

"How do you know?"

"AJ, many people were there to hear the captain on the phone. His own frustration made him forget how close the people were. When he hung up, the way he stood, they knew."

"Man, too bad." What Bruno described to me earlier seemed dead on.

"Captain Condello would keep going; I am sure. He is not happy about the order from his bosses," Giorgio said.

I listened intently. His comment about the bus stop made perfect sense. Domenica definitely needed a ride to the train, or take the bus. I had to admit, their reasoning seemed pretty solid.

"Enough of this, it is time for Grappa," Giorgio said.

"Grappa? What the heck is that?"

"Grappa is an Italian liquor." Giorgio exclaimed, a proud smile crossing his face, his shoulders pulled back. "You will like it. It tastes like a strong Brandy. Some Americans call it *firewater*." Giorgio rolled his eyes causing me to chuckle.

"We drink Grappa after a meal. It is good for you. It is illegal to make your own Grappa, but who cares. Homemadc is *superiore*. My good friend made this; it is excellent… you will taste and see."

One sip of the clear Grappa made me instantly understand why someone might use the word *firewater* to describe it. I could feel every inch of its descent. Giorgio and Wanda laughed, most likely at my contorted face. Quite an evening, punctuated with potent Italian Grappa.

When I left I followed Giorgio's directions to the bus stop and got out of my car to look around. Right away I could tell why people were saying the bus stop proved an obvious choice of where to pick up Domenica. The road is wider there, it has easy access, and it is close to her house. Although, I wondered if she may have been afraid of being seen since the area is well lit.

Thinking of Domenica brought about the vision of my seeing her in the river. Without notice I then saw Bethany lying beside her bed. I felt my heart pounding, beads of sweat forming on my forehead as I envisioned the puddle of blood around her. My knees nearly buckled, so I sat on the bus bench.

After several minutes I stood as the cool night air on the moisture covering my face made me shiver. *Twas Time for me to go.*

Sitting in my car I wiped my brow, my hand no longer shaking and deliberated about the entire day. Despite having wine and Grappa, a sense of intense desire to investigate once again surged throughout my body.

Feeling pretty relaxed I slowly made my way up the many steps outside my townhouse thinking about Giorgio and Wanda, telling myself what great people they are. My sister suggesting I come here proved to be a good idea, at least thus far.

Entering the townhouse I continued thinking about this trip and felt like I might be making progress. Going to the crime scene the other day left me unsure about what I was doing. Now, after listening to Giorgio, and seeing the bus stop, I had a different impression. The thought of investigating again no longer seemed like some far off improbable wish or something I would never be able to manage. Regardless of not being one hundred percent ready right then, for the first time in four months I had hope.

Having such a positive overall feeling made doing my exercises seem painless. I opened the balcony door to let the fresh air in, stepped outside, and looked in the direction of the lake. The half-moon provided enough light to be able to see the outline of the mountains in the distance.

I would've never expected this trip to be so worthwhile.

CHAPTER THIRTY-THREE

"Bruno, come in, please," Captain Condello said.

"Thank you, Captain, for agreeing to see me at your home."

"It must be important. I could hear it in your voice. Please, have a seat."

"Thank you, sir." Bruno hesitated, a little unsure if he was about to make a big mistake. "I know you said to close Domenica's case. I realize my being sent here to your station is a result of being labeled a rebel. It's important you are aware that's not my intent."

"Then, what exactly is your intent?"

"I came to ask for your permission to continue looking into this case. I don't want to cause you any problems. There's something inside of me, though, telling me there's more to her death than it being a freak accident."

Condello stroked his chin before he stood. "Wine?"

"*Wine*? No. No thank you, sir."

"White or red?" Captain Condello asked as he was leaving the room.

Bruno shook his head. *What's he doing?* "Uh, red. Please."

Minutes later Condello returned, handing Bruno his wine. Condello sat back down, not saying anything for what seemed like minutes to Bruno.

"We've been given orders," Condello began. "We must

abide by them. I understand exactly how you feel, I have the same feeling. However, I'm nearing the end of my career. I would like to help you—I cannot jeopardize my retirement."

Bruno recognized the risk to his captain and did not want to put him in a bad position. "I didn't want to sneak around and keep investigating on my own without your permission."

"Are you saying you're going to keep investigating, regardless of what I say?"

"No sir," Bruno exclaimed. "If I were going to do that I would not have come here. You said we need to follow orders, and I will. I simply felt I needed to try once more."

"Hypothetically speaking, if I gave you permission, what were your plans?"

"I'm a little ashamed to admit it, I really haven't thought about any," Bruno said. "I wanted to have your blessing first." Bruno talked about possibly seeing if AJ could help him, or at least give him some direction.

Condello swirled his wine in his glass, staring at the moving liquid.

"You stay active when out of uniform and free from the restraints of direct orders. I always like hearing about what you've done or found in your...*spare time*." He looked up at Bruno inquisitively, waiting to see.

It took several seconds before Bruno broke into a grin. "I fully understand, the case is closed, sir."

"Now, my wife has dinner ready," Condello said as he stood. "She told me to tell you, you're eating with us. I would suggest you think twice before saying no. You don't want to upset her."

Bruno stood, smiling as he followed the captain into the dining room.

Bruno enjoyed his dinner at the captain's house, even though his mind had been at the office on his computer the majority of the time. With Captain Condello's tacit approval to keep investigating, his first move would be to research AJ to verify his experience.

Back at the office Bruno started his research on Google at 9 p.m. After confirming AJ Conti's status as a detective for Turlock Police Department, he discovered a disturbing newspaper article about AJ written back in January.

> *Detective AJ Conti, the lead investigator in the homicide investigation, discovered his main suspect had killed Conti's girlfriend, Bethany Walker, before taking his own life. Bethany had been kidnapped, and according to an unidentified source, had been allowed to call Detective Conti minutes before being murdered.*

The writer of the article said she had two unnamed informants who verified Bethany had been the original social worker of the killer. He had been orphaned at ten-years-old after his family had been killed in a drunk driving accident. The writer clearly implied Bethany got herself killed by placing the boy in bad foster care.

Bruno found news stations in northern California with YouTube clips from their websites covering the killing. The information appeared identical to what he already read, the difference being they did show a distraught AJ being driven away by a fellow detective. The coverage ended by saying AJ had been put on paid administrative leave.

Bruno found the phone number to the sergeant in charge of the Detective Bureau. At 1 p.m. in California, 10 p.m. in Rumo, Bruno placed the call. Sergeant Boykin confirmed AJ's tenure with the department, along with his abilities as an investigator. Boykin directed Bruno to call Dr. Papadopoulus, who could better determine whether or not AJ could help in the investigation.

Bruno dialed it figuring he would not get any information out of the doctor. He told the receptionist who he was, where he was from, and what it was about. In less than a minute the doctor was on the phone.

Bruno explained his situation, along with his concern for AJ's well-being. Dr. Papadopoulus thanked Bruno for being sensitive to AJ's situation. "Look, I personally think it might be good therapy for him to help you out a little. It's not up to me; he has to make that decision. It's not something he can be forced to do." He stopped to check his watch. "I have clients waiting. I hate to do this, but I need to go. Best of luck!"

CHAPTER THIRTY-FOUR

The clock read 4:53 a.m. As usual, the same images arrived, this time shortly after five hours of sleep.

I could see David's visionless eyes as I entered the room. Blood everywhere, including the writing in blood on the wall. I woke up the instant I could see Bethany's feet on the floor by the bed. This time the nausea and vomiting never arrived.

Nightmares and flashbacks had been regular occurrences for the past several months. Not having the physical sickness which usually followed meant I was making headway.

Alcohol, I thought, suddenly recalling the two glasses of wine and Grappa the night before. I had no way of knowing if alcohol played a role or not. Truthfully, at that point I didn't care…this progress captivated me.

At one time Doc compared the healing process to a sculpture. He said I would have to learn to be okay with slowly peeling away a layer at a time until my complete return.

Feeling good, I walked to the balcony to check the temperature. With the early morning light I knew I would be safe from cars on my run, so checking emails would have to wait. I grabbed some euros, and headed out the door.

My mind seemed less on running than it did yesterday. Today I could see the culture throughout the area, making the run feel good.

What a great run. De-stressing, I thought. I enjoyed the special feeling I got inside after a good run when I started walking to cool down.

My body had been craving a good night's sleep…I had almost forgotten what it felt like. I felt more energized than I had in a long time and could smell the Cappuccino calling to me.

"*Buongiorno* Bruno."

"*Giorno* AJ" He smiled as we shook hands. "I trust you had a good run."

"Actually, I did. It didn't seem as hard on my lungs this morning." I could not resist adding a comment about a good night's sleep.

Bruno tacitly acknowledged my feeling well, but I could see on his face he had something else on his mind. He had a nervous look, the kind when someone wants to ask you something, blocked only by their own fear to do so.

"*Giorno*, AJ," Donatella said with a big smile. "Anything to drink?"

"*Buongiorno,* Donatella. I brought my euros today, so I would love a Cappuccino," I said jokingly.

Donatella grinned, shook her head and rolled her eyes, before leaving.

"Am I interrupting something?" Bruno asked.

Am I so obvious, or is he really that observant?

I had no desire to discuss my interaction with Donatella, or staring at her as she went back inside. At least not yet.

"So, what is it you want to talk about?" I asked.

Bruno started to say something but stopped, his mouth open with his face stuck in a *how'd he know* look. "Before I go any further, I want you to be aware of the fact I contacted Sergeant Boykin and Doctor Papa…Papa something, last night."

"What? Why'd you call them?"

"I called to verify you really had investigated homicides," Bruno said. "I had no reason to disbelieve you. You know as well as I do, it would have been wrong for me to share information with you about a case without checking you out first."

I nodded, waiting for more.

"The sergeant told me you're an exceptional investigator."

A nervous cop is no different than a nervous criminal. His inability to look me directly in the eye, his hands fidgeting with his cup, and his foot hooked around the leg of his chair spoke of his obvious uncomfortableness, along with telling me there was more.

He's got to learn to have more of a poker face, or every bad guy in the world will read him like an open book—like I am.

I put both elbows on the table, cupped my hands together in front of me, leaned forward, and slowly squinted my eyes to stare at him. I actually did not have a problem with him doing his research on me. Hell, I would have done research on me too.

Donatella arrived with my Cappuccino.

"Look, we can have a conversation, provided you're up front with me," I said. "You're hiding something though. I can see it in your body language. Now, come clean about what else you looked into, or we're done talking."

I looked at Donatella, whose eyes were wide open. She knew she walked in on something.

Bruno looked down, shifting in his chair. I had done dozens of interviews of serious criminals. This poor kid was no match. I understood he needed time to process it all. He had to come clean, he had nowhere else to go. So I waited, staring.

"I also researched news articles and news videos," Bruno said. He briefly looked me in the eyes before he looked back down.

"I found out about your girlfriend being murdered by the killer in your last investigation. I asked the doctor if he thought you were able to assist me."

Hearing his words I pictured Bethany lying dead on the floor. I felt sadness for her, for us, for our future.

I readjusted in my chair, unsure how long I'd been away thinking of Bethany. I looked at Bruno, raising one eyebrow and slightly tilting my head. I waited.

"The doctor said he thought it would be good for you to help me. Then he made it clear, the decision is yours."

Donatella stood in the doorway, shocked Bruno knew. Slowly she turned to me, mouthing the words, "I'm sorry!"

I nodded ever so slightly to thank Donatella, then looked back at Bruno.

"I apologize," Bruno said. "I got so caught up in what I wanted, I didn't even stop to think maybe you didn't even want it brought up," Bruno said.

I sat back for a short time before I let out a long sigh.

"Don't worry about it. Look, it caught me off guard, but you showed good investigative skills verifying I'm really a detective. I'd've done the same thing. Do me a favor though, be a straight shooter. Beating around the bush is usually a waste of time. Tell me what is it you really want?"

Bruno breathed his own sigh of relief before telling me he felt the girl in the river had been murdered. Of the three officers, Corporal Amici was alone in believing it could have been an accident.

"Captain Condello called the Cles office for assistance. They told him we didn't have enough evidence to warrant them sending out the RaCIS. They are our criminal investigation team."

I waited for more, sipping on my Cappuccino.

"I went to Captain Condello privately. I told him I would like to keep investigating the case, even though he told us to close it. He told me in his own way he won't stop me. I have to investigate on my own time, but Corporal Amici cannot find out."

Bruno painted a pretty good picture of what might happen to Condello's retirement if anyone in the Carabinieri found out. When Bruno mentioned being in over his head and asked for my help I could feel my chest start to tighten up.

I'm not ready, I thought. *Even though I'm headed in the right direction, I really don't think I'm ready. I feel bad for the kid.*

"Bruno, I respect your position, I really do. I hope you can respect mine. I came to Italy…to get away, to try to heal. Despite the fact I've recently started to do better, I don't think I'm ready. If it's any consolation, something tells me it's a murder. I'm proud of you for following your instincts."

"I'm sorry to hear that, AJ," Bruno said, a forlorn look on his face. "Truthfully though, I'm not surprised. I can't imagine how much this has affected you since it happened. I mean, reliving it over and over. So many things probably trigger flashbacks. I'm sure it's been difficult." Bruno stood. "Look, I need to go. Thank you for talking with me." He began to leave. He stopped, turning to look at me. "I'm really sorry, AJ."

"Thank you. Thank you for understanding."

Bruno nodded and walked away.

I sipped on my Cappuccino, running the conversation through my head, staring at nothing while I thought about it. Donatella moving the chair to sit down startled me.

"What are you doing?" I asked, quickly looking all around the patio. "What about your other customers?"

"AJ, there are no customers," she said. "You have been lost in your world for several minutes."

"Wow, I…I had no idea."

"This may be wrong, but I do not understand why you will not help Bruno. He tries to do the right thing. Captain Condello cannot…*compromettere*…his job."

"I know, I know. He can't jeopardize his career." I hesitated for a second. "I'm not confident I can help without going into a tailspin."

"What this is, a tailspin?" Donatella asked, a crease between her brows, confusion in her eyes.

"I'm sorry. It's like a dive straight into the ground. Like an airplane spinning out of control," I said, using gestures to show the plane spinning.

"*Bene, capisco*. You told Bruno you came to Italy to *migliorare*, mmm, to get better. Yes?"

"To heal. Yes, to get better."

"Maybe for you to get better you should help others, not only AJ." She softly put her hand to my cheek. "You are a good person AJ. You will do the right thing."

Donatella did not wait for a response. She quickly went inside.

What am I supposed to say to that?

CHAPTER THIRTY-FIVE

Incapable of getting earlier discussions with Donatella out of my head, I needed something to clear my mind. I thought of the one place I had taken pleasure in from a distance. I recalled seeing the signs to the lake when leaving Cles and decided to go there.

I walked around the north side of *Lago di Santa Giustina*, stopping in the shops close by. I admired how it looked sparkling blue from the water's edge. Despite trying to relax and take in the beautiful Italian scenery, I could not stop thinking about what Donatella said.

"*You will do the right thing.*"

I had an undeniable urge to go to the river after hearing of the discovery of a dead body. Still, I left the river due to my own hesitation to investigate again.

What if Donatella's right?

With an exceptional ability to get past the outer layers of a person, Donatella knew what to say to touch their innermost truth. I watched her interact with her variety of customers. I did not need to speak Italian to see they all trusted her. Many of them shared personal things with her. Her understanding on how to subtly guide someone intrigued me.

"*When things aren't going so well for you, go help others in need. You'll help solve your own problems*," I could hear my mother telling me—the same as Donatella.

At nine o'clock in the morning, Corporal Amici called Domenica's parents. After a short conversation, he hung up, and grabbed the backpack.

"Bruno, I'm headed to return this to Domenica's family."

"I think I'll stay here, try to finish reports and log photos," Bruno said.

Corporal Amici nodded as he headed for the back door.

Disappointed AJ would not help him, Bruno knew he still had try to figure out what happened to Domenica.

With Corporal Amici gone, Bruno got on the computer to see what he could find. He still had access to Facebook through Paolo's account. Back on Domenica's page, he decided to research friends common to both Paolo and Domenica. He found three. He began perusing their posts, paying close attention to the timeline.

One conversation in October caught his attention. It referred to Domenica having a boy toy.

"*That's why I never posted him as my boyfriend*," Domenica replied to one of their posts.

Posts on Facebook increased with each passing week about why Domenica had not contacted Paolo or the others. The posts reflected concern for her safety by early December after she never posted a word. There were even some posts demonstrating anxiety for her vulnerability to have been kidnapped, part of the human trafficking problem in Germany.

Bruno clicked off Facebook when he heard Amici walk through the door.

"How about we go have some lunch? I'll pay," Bruno said.

Bruno surprised himself, so Amici's look of disbelief did not shock him.

"Umm, sure. We should invite Captain Condello," Corporal Amici said.

"No thanks," Captain Condello said walking through his door toward the coffee pot. "I promised my wife I would come home today."

"Got it. Let's go," Bruno said to Amici.

When Amici headed for the door Bruno looked over at Captain Condello who nodded his approval.

Walking outside Bruno saw Amici getting into the passenger seat for the first time since Bruno arrived.

Maybe AJ's on to something, Bruno thought.

Driving away, Bruno stopped at the stop sign next to Bar Bivio, the bar across from their office. Radio Scarpa began crossing the road.

"*Buongiorno,* Rigo," Bruno said,

"*Giorno,*" Radio Scarpa said.

"Headed to Bar Bivio?" Bruno asked.

"*Sì, sì.*"

"What news do you have to share today?"

"I know what happened to the girl in the river. I saw the man who did it," Radio Scarpa said, excitement in his eyes.

Bruno looked at Corporal Amici. Both chuckled, behind hands covering their mouths.

"Okay, Rigo. Have a good day," Bruno said.

"*Ciao,*" Scarpa said, crossing in front of the car before walking into the patio area of Bar Bivio.

"Poor Scarpa. I think he means well," Bruno said.

"I guess. I wouldn't know. I have to admit, I've never spoken to him," Corporal Amici said.

"He's not bad. I think the stories he tells is his way of trying to fit in. So, I'm sure Domenica's parents are struggling."

"Yes. When I gave them her backpack with all of her belongings they both started crying."

"This has to be tough for them."

"Her mother, Penina, told me they were scared Domenica had been forced into the sex slave industry," Amici said. "They even hired a private investigator to try to find her. Obviously, he got nowhere."

"Poor kid. She really wanted to go see other places. She never even made it out of Rumo. Sad."

CHAPTER THIRTY-SIX

The fact I spent a large portion of my adult life helping others, especially those who no longer had a voice like Domenica, ultimately eclipsed any trepidation I still had.

No customers were inside Bar Lanterna when I walked in. The two gray-haired ladies sitting outside deeply engaged in conversation, some of it about me, of course, were all who remained from the lunch crowd. I sat on the stool at the bar near the cash register.

Donatella came out of the back kitchen area, a surprised look on her face when she saw me. The glint in her eyes told me she was pleased I had returned.

"AJ, good to see you. Can I get you something?"

"I'll take a Cappuccino if you don't mind."

"Americans," Donatella said. She shook her head, grinning as she walked over to the Cappuccino machine. Without looking at me she asked, "Did you tell him yet?"

"Tell who what?"

She looked over her shoulder, her head cocked, flashing me a look like I had made an imbecile of myself.

Turning back to the machine she said, "I'm pleased you came to the decision to help Bruno."

"You don't know that."

"Sì, *lo so*. Yes, I do," she stated, with the utmost confidence as she stared right at me.

"How?"

"I just do." She turned back to the Cappuccino machine.

Show off, I thought.

Donatella turned her ear toward me, like she knew she had me and wanted to hear me say it. I would have sworn I could see a smile by the corner of her mouth as it slightly moved upward. "I went to Lake Santa Giustina, walked around, and thought a lot about what you said. Your words were similar to what my mother used to say about helping others. I'm still not sure it will help me to get past my problems. What I am certain of is, my life has been negative too long. I'm looking forward to doing something positive."

"Your mother, a wise woman, like all women," Donatella said, followed by a huge grin, her head bobbing side-to-side as she set my Cappuccino on the counter.

"Trust me, AJ, it will help you too."

I felt reassurance from her confidence. For a brief second I actually believed her. I wanted to trust her, never having experienced anything like what I was going through. Strangely, I could almost feel her conviction.

"Before I forget, your cousin, stopped by," Donatella said. "He would like you to go with him to dinner to meet his brother and sisters. He will be here at 6 p.m. to pick up you and my sister."

"How did he even know…how did he plan dinner before we even met?"

The smirk on her face told me she knew the answer.

"What?"

"Your sister set it all up, she knew you would not. I told you, women are wise." Donatella laughed while walking away.

I barely finished my Cappuccino when Bruno sat next to me.

"AJ, I can't tell you how much I appreciate you changing your mind."

Donatella leaned her head around the door frame from the kitchen area. She stared right at me, a look of fulfillment on her face.

Not taking my eyes off of her I said, "It appears everyone else knows what's best for me, so I guess it's time I get out of my own way." I turned toward Bruno and said, "Let's go over to one of the tables. You can start telling me what you have."

Looking back over my shoulder at Donatella still in the doorway I said, "Oh, Bruno, by the way, apparently I'm being picked up around 6 p.m. to go meet my cousins for dinner, so we'll have to stop before then."

Donatella chuckled as she went outside to get the dishes left by the elderly ladies.

For the previous three months, the angry young man paid close attention to the employees at the Pomarella plant. He knew, in general, most people were not observant. He wanted to make sure who the meddlers were so he could avoid them. Relying on people's fear of reprisal based on his uncle being the President of the Board over his plant, he unofficially had access throughout.

In the last two weeks his focus had been narrowed to the office area where they kept the video camera equipment. He'd gone on three previous occasions to scout it out. The office staff always went on breaks together, which allowed for easy access without being seen. His goal the first time, locate all of the camera and recording equipment in the unoccupied office area. The entire set up seemed less detailed than he expected, so he disabled the recording device by unplugging it. He left the cameras alone so they still looked like they were working.

Early in the scouting process he overheard some of the plant electricians discussing the plant video equipment. Making sure he got close enough to hear their entire conversation, he discovered none of the office staff had been designated to be in charge of keeping track or maintaining the devices. He confirmed on his third time checking the equipment the electricians were right, after finding the recording devices still unplugged.

The picture on the screen displayed the many views throughout the plant, including the parking lots, despite the fact the red recording light remained unlit.

He smiled as he exited the office. Tomorrow would be his final check before he proceeded with his plans for *Number Two.*

CHAPTER THIRTY-SEVEN

I told Bruno he should prepare to be grilled for bringing me in to help, considering some attorney would probably question my mental stability.

"I hadn't even thought that far ahead," Bruno said. "I guess my answer would be I'll worry about it when the time comes. My gut says someone killed Domenica, so I guess I'm going to have to trust it. If I'm right, she deserves all the effort I can give her."

Bruno's integrity made my decision to help much easier.

He told me nobody originally reported Domenica missing since she left her parents a note. She had been home when her parents left for dinner at 6:30 p.m. and left before they returned, never contacting them like she said she would.

"Did she say in the note where she might be headed?" I asked.

"On Facebook ..."

I put up my hand to stop him. "Did she say in the *note* where?"

Bruno looked confused. "No, not in the note. Why does it matter?"

"Providing her parents specific information gives us places to start, and usually helps determine foul play much faster."

Unfortunately, I always found the more general the information the more difficult it is to determine foul play.

Bruno contemplated what I said. "Well, the note's pretty vague. She left in October, nobody ever heard from her again."

"How'd you identify her?"

"At first by Paolo, one of the volunteers helping Corporal Amici. He found her backpack in the bushes, looked through it, and saw a unique shirt she often wore. The shirt bore words from a song by a British band. Queen, I believe."

"Queen. Dang. She had good taste in music."

Bruno raised his eyebrows as if I were a little crazy, before saying Paolo identified Domenica from the bridge, finalized by her mom.

"You started to mention Facebook."

"Paolo told me everyone their age around town knew Domenica wanted to go to Germany," Bruno said. "He told us she even posted it on her Facebook account. Paolo is friends with her on it, so I asked him if I could use his account to do some background research. He agreed. Said he could easily change his password when I finished."

"Good use of a resource," I said. My first thought would have been a warrant, although his way seemed pretty smart.

"Thanks. Like Paolo said, it looked like she said goodbye to Rumo. On her last Facebook post on October 19 she posted she was going to Germany."

I wondered aloud if she mentioned someone picking her up.

"Not really," Bruno said. "She did mention going by train, which would be normal. It's common around here."

"Yeah, I heard her friends are gossiping about the fact she planned to take the train from Mezzocorona."

With his left eyebrow raised and his mouth left slightly open I could see Bruno wondered where I would have gotten such information. Even so, he didn't ask.

"There are quite a few walking trails around here," I said. "Do you happen to know if where you guys found her was a common way for her to walk?"

"Penina told us Domenica often walked Path Ten to meet her friends or catch a ride by the main road," Bruno said.

"There are paths on both sides of the river there, right?"

Bruno nodded. He verified Domenica's backpack and body were on the far side of the bridge from where I had stood.

"Imagine you were her. What's the most likely path she took from her house to the bridge?"

Bruno thought about it for several seconds before weighing in. "Well, I would probably take Path Ten, it's shorter and quicker. Plus, it goes right to her house."

"I agree," I said. In spite of it being pure speculation, I found I could usually pick one choice over another with basic reasoning. "The other thing is, she'd been itching to go somewhere. She's young, adventurous, and doesn't want to stay in Rumo. Wouldn't she want to take the fastest route out of here?"

Bruno smiled, realizing I had spent some time thinking about this.

"Path Ten puts her on the side of the river I stood on, not where Paolo found her backpack," I said.

Bruno began nodding his head as the picture came together. He realized he now had some basic reasoning to support his hunch about Domenica being lured to the other side of the bridge.

"Tell me, what makes you feel Domenica met with foul play?" I asked.

Like all young cops having to justify their beliefs to a veteran, Bruno's wide eyed, timid face did not surprise me.

"Well, her leg seemed shattered, I mean, way beyond normal for falling on rocks in the river," Bruno began. Still seeming a little unsure, I nodded approvingly to relax him.

"Plus, the blue covering half of her face, whereas on the opposite side it appeared like finger marks on her cheek and near her mouth."

"The blue is where her blood pooled, it's called lividity," I explained. "You're doing well. Keep going."

Slightly more confident Bruno explained his uncomfortableness with Domenica's backpack being found twenty meters from her body, and at the top of three meter high bushes. He finished by describing some blood found on a small rock wall near where they took Domenica out of the water, although they could not find any scrapes on her body.

"Those are the reasons so far. Circumstantial, I know."

After confirming Bruno collected blood samples from the wall, I moved on to anyone else possibly knowing Domenica's plans to leave October 19, or at what particular hour.

"Yes and no. On Facebook she spoke of leaving, going to Germany, and what day. Never the time."

"How about a boyfriend?"

"That one's confusing," Bruno said. He fumbled through an explanation about Domenica denying some guy being her boyfriend, although she tacitly admitted she used the guy for sex. "No name is ever mentioned."

"Only good for sex, huh? I wonder if he knew that. Maybe he looked at her that way, too, a good piece of ass. Or maybe *he* thought of her as his girlfriend."

I took pleasure in seeing Bruno write a note to follow-up with Penina regarding a boyfriend.

"While your reasons are circumstantial, they're decent enough for us to work off of." I educated Bruno about people going in the suspect pool until weeded out, along with all evidence, no matter how remote, following the same rule. Cognizant a lab would take care of the blood on the wall, I focused on Bruno's remaining reasons.

"Of your other three reasons, which one jumps out at you most?"

"Probably the backpack, it seems too far away from her," Bruno said. "I mean, it could be explained away by some kids finding it and throwing it there. Still, it's pretty clear she didn't drop it up in those bushes."

"I like the fact you have your belief, while at the same time also recognizing a plausible reason why it could be there."

Turning my head I noticed Donatella watching us. When she saw me look she flashed one of her slight smiles. It felt good making her happy.

I decided to finish up with Bruno since Elio would be arriving soon. We agreed to meet the next day after Bruno got off work, exchanging phone numbers so he could text me. Bruno left and Donatella introduced me to her sister Luisa, explaining Luisa and Elio were engaged. Luisa spoke limited English, leaving me a bit concerned how the rest of the night would go.

Minutes later my cousin Elio arrived. As a taxi driver and school bus driver his beautiful van doubled as his personal vehicle and his work vehicle.

"You and Elio look much alike," Donatella said.

Donatella was right, we did look strikingly similar. "There's no denying we're related," I said with a smile. I hesitated, nervous about asking Donatella to go with us. I finally took a deep breath and blurted it out.

"*Grazie*, I am not able," Donatella said. "I have to stay here at the bar." She softly placed her hand on my arm. With a look of appreciation she said, "*Mi dispiace*, I'm sorry, *grazie*."

We left to meet the rest of Elio's family in Cles. During the drive Elio and I gave our best efforts to use each other's language. Although Google translate helped, their regional dialect made communicating somewhat more difficult than I had anticipated.

At the restaurant we met Elio's brother Giovanni, and his sisters Anita and Franca, along with their spouses and children. One of Franca's daughters, twenty-eight-year-old Nadia, spoke excellent English. *Young people speaking English, a consistent theme it seems.*

The dinner began with food I usually got at Donatella's. The main course centered on *Torta di Patate*, a unique fried potato cake that has become a regular dish in northern Italy. Of course, wine and grappa were a must.

Four hours flew by and I would have never expected I'd have so much fun. I had not laughed this much in months. Giovanni was a gregarious storyteller even though his niece had to translate. I could not help but laugh, relax, and enjoy being in the presence of some of my new family. I recognized the twinge as the start of my enjoying life again, even if it was in small increments.

Another step in the healing process?

CHAPTER THIRTY-EIGHT

He wanted to relive killing Domenica before moving on to *Number Two*. Tonight, he wanted to enjoy *Number One* for one final time. Tomorrow, *Number Two* would get his entire focus.

He parked his car in Mocenigo, wanting to walk on Path Ten as she had. He calculated the odds were low someone would see him after eleven o'clock on Sunday night.

While walking he thought about having been attracted to her, captivated as much as he could be. He could not say he loved her, although he had been content.

"Look, you were good in bed," Domenica once said. "You made me grow, made me want more. Why the hell aren't you like that out of bed? All you want is this dead-end life, job security at the Pomarella plant. You have no ambition. You're comfortable…I'm not."

They had been out of high school for two years. Even though she had always talked about leaving, she never had. He believed she never really would, nonetheless, he had planned for the alternative.

Arriving on Path Ten in front of *Centralina Comunale* he recalled Domenica having been angry with him being across the bridge when she first arrived.

Crossing the single dirt lane bridge he saw the water flowing heavily, nearly twice what it had been when he had waited for her in October; the natural ebb and flow of the river.

On the other side he stood in the open area next to the final curve of Path Eight before it reached the bridge. He closed his eyes to see the night once again.

She called his name and waived him over several times. He stayed by the bushes, never moving.

"You wouldn't pick me up at my house, or at the bus stop," Domenica began, her anger rising. "Now you want me to come across the damn bridge."

He offered to wait for her, no matter how long it took.

She started across the bridge.

"Don't you get it? You wanted me to be like your mother. I even cut my damn hair for you, so it would look like hers. You're so stuck on her I could get you to do anything I wanted by threatening to leave. You wanted me to be like her. Well, you got it. I'm leaving. Exactly like she did."

"It's okay, go. When you come back I'll be here," he said. "I can see our future together. I'll be here waiting for you."

"Are you fucking deaf?" Domenica yelled. "I'm not coming back. We don't have a future together. I never loved you."

He could picture his Toyota Yaris, right where he now stood. When she reached the back of his car he raised his hand and she stopped.

"Is there any chance I can convince you to stay?"

"No! Absolutely not. You know what I want."

He slowly lowered his hand and turned away from her, certain it would draw her closer. The darkness nearly hid him. Extremely frustrated, she started to walk around the trunk of the car toward the passenger side. "Are we going or …"

The thud of the log he brought with him took her breath away. The bones inside her right knee gave way to the force. She instantly dropped to the ground as her backpack left the grip of her hand. He pounced on her, pinning both arms down with his knees and grabbing hair in both hands. He raised her head as she began to scream. With one swift and powerful surge he slammed her head into the ground. It stopped the scream and took the fight out of her. He positioned his hands over her nose and mouth, closing off her airways while pushing her head into the ground as hard as he could so she could not move.

"You think everything is about you," he said as he stared into her large panic filled eyes.

"Who's in control now? You stupid bitch."

Unable to mount much of a resistance, Domenica's life came to an end. You will never leave anyone again, he thought.

RELIVING THE PLEASURE OF THAT NIGHT LEFT HIS HANDS shaking. He could feel the tingling throughout his body once again. The cat had been a mess. The suffocation though, what a thrill. The rush lasted so much longer. The excitement from watching death arrive felt like one of his orgasms.

What a dumb bitch, he thought. *She got so angry, she couldn't see she became the lamb being led to the slaughter.*

He thought of the irony. She was in control—until she wasn't. Their destinies could have been so different.

His planning to put her in the river directly beneath the cement bridge worked perfectly once he got past almost being seen by the two girls. He discovered nearly getting caught brought about its own arousal.

Even the village idiot seeing me couldn't ruin the high I had, he thought. *He'll never say anything, not with my threats to kill his mother. Besides, nobody would ever believe him, not with all of his fucked up stories.*

Not until the Carabinieri were talking with the man on the bridge holding Domenica's t-shirt did he realize he had left the backpack.

Big mistake, he thought. *Panic is not an option in the future.*

Overall, he felt satisfied when walking back to his car on Path Ten. Despite a couple of glitches, *Number One* had turned out well. He had a good feeling about *Number Two* being smoother and cleaner—*Number Two* would be better. The time had come to focus on her.

CHAPTER THIRTY-NINE

Waking after another night of nearly five hours sleep validated my efforts.

Giorgio had called me the night before, telling me to be ready at eight the next morning; he wanted to take me to the *Santuario di San Romedio*. Exactly at eight I heard the honking outside, Giorgio's urging me to hurry.

I probably don't even need to lock the doors here, nobody else does, I thought as my key turned the deadbolt.

"I'm surprised there's not more accidents here in town the way people take these corners."

"There are some, those are not the good drivers like me." Giorgio smiled, and I could not help but chuckle.

The distance on the main road leading out of Rumo seemed to be around ten miles. That portion of the State Road had long been known for being exceptionally dangerous, with several blind curves; some nearly one hundred and eighty degrees.

"Now, *these* turns are dangerous. Many accidents here," Giorgio said, honking the horn as he slowed for the blind curves.

Once we cleared the dangerous curves Giorgio provided historical information, beginning with the vast amount of apples growing on the steep mountainsides, and how they saved a struggling economy. *Val di Non* means Valley of

Apples, an accurate term since they covered the entire valley.

Giorgio pointed out the Pomarella Apple Plant in Revò, a town with several villages similar to Rumo, twenty minutes away. He explained there are many Pomarella plants all over the valley, each with their own Board of Directors.

A little over forty-five minutes after leaving my townhouse we pulled into the public parking lot in Sanzeno. The path to *San Romedio* went through a variety of surroundings. The beginning of the walk went through a relatively flat area, followed by an uphill climb through the forest on a well preserved path. We exited at a large canyon with steep rocky sides. Amazingly a path had been cut through the rocky wall and a wooden rail erected to prevent falling to the road below.

Ten minutes later we came out of the rocks. The protective railing stopped as we reentered forest, despite the steep drop off on the side of the path. Our trek continued mostly downhill until we reached the point where the path and the road we had seen below us came together.

After an informative viewing of the churches we returned to Giorgio's car where he continued spewing historical Italian information at me. Giorgio obviously enjoyed his role as my guide, as well as being proud of his homeland.

Passing through Revò, Giorgio stayed on the road to the left instead of turning right toward Rumo. Within a short distance he pulled into the parking lot of the *Hotel Viridis* in Cagnò.

"What's this? Why are we stopping here?" I asked.

Giorgio smiled as we exited the car. "This is some of the best gelato in all of northern Italy. Plus, the view is perfect while you eat."

We were led to the corner table outside on a deck facing south. Looking out over the massive lake, I had a totally different perspective of *Lago di Santa Giustina*. The view of the lake, mountains, and blue sky was impressive.

"Wow, beautiful. I can't believe it's not busier," I said, continuing to stare out at the lake.

"It is still early afternoon. There will be many people in two hours."

"I drove by the bus stop you mentioned the other night," I said, taking another bite of gelato. "The spot seems perfect for Domenica to have been picked up if someone were going to give her a ride, or catch the bus like you suggested."

"Ahh. You are curious, yes?"

I chuckled. "Yes, it's in my nature as a detective."

"Good, good. The talk now is some people saw our local *donnaiolo*…I cannot think of a word for you. He talks with many women, tries to get them into bed with him."

"Oh, okay. A womanizer," I said.

"*Sì, sì*. A womanizer." Giorgio described some people seeing the man talking with Domenica, all of them positive it happened the night she supposedly left. "They saw him trying to *dare un passaggio*, umm, a pass on her at the bus stop, he put his hand on her *sedere*, right here," Giorgio said, his hand on his butt cheek. "She got angry at him. They saw her slap him and then go off mad onto Path Ten."

"Really. How are they so sure about it being the same night?"

"AJ," Giorgio said, drawing out my name.

"Rumo is not large like where you come from. It is small, so news we all hear about. We knew the next day. Domenica had left a note for her parents. Penina told friends, they told friends, you understand."

Nobody said anything to Penina or the Carabinieri after hearing of Domenica's note. In their minds she left town.

"Makes sense. Does this *donnaiolo* have a name?"

"Sì, his name is Carlo. Carlo Camioni," Giorgio said. "He lives in Rumo, in the village of Mocenigo near my home."

I wondered aloud if Carlo happened to be the type of guy who could hurt a young woman like Domenica. Giorgio seemed certain Carlo could hurt Domenica, although he could not believe Carlo would kill her. He said Carlo's wife left him over ten years ago to go live with her sister. She had apparently told some women Carlo would hit her.

"Why hasn't anyone told the Carabinieri about Carlo since they found Domenica in the river?"

Giorgio shook his head. He said when people heard the Carabinieri officially called it an accident, nobody wanted to go against the decision. "Maybe you can tell the Carabinieri?"

"Why me?"

Giorgio told me I had been seen talking with Bruno about Domenica's case, giving many people the hope I would help the Carabinieri.

Although Giorgio had made a statement, I could hear the question in his tone. I hesitated, not sure how to respond. Giorgio's expression said he hoped to take good news back to his friends. I did not want to mislead anyone.

"Giorgio, I'm simply helping Bruno, you know, to learn more about those types of investigations."

Patting me on the shoulder, a big smile on his face, Giorgio said, "*Eccellente*! I am glad to hear it."

My explanation obviously lacked clarity. I already knew Giorgio well enough to realize I would be wasting my time to try to get him to change his mind.

Two gelatos later, Giorgio drove us back to Rumo in less than thirty minutes. Pulling into the village of Mione I asked Giorgio to drop me off at Bar Lanterna. I tried to offer Giorgio some money but he refused. I no sooner started to close my door when he accelerated, whipping back onto the road.

I had barely begun walking toward the bar when I noticed the passenger door of the car in the driveway standing open, the side door to the bar ajar. That combination of open doors instantly brought about a thought of Bethany with no prior warning. I could see her lying in her own pool of blood, her throat fileted open, dead due to my inability to stop David in time. And here I was, about to enjoy myself talking with another woman. My guilty conscience halted me in my tracks.

Is this wrong?

I walked down the driveway and crossed the road, the hair on my neck telling me someone's eyes were on me. Glancing over my right shoulder Donatella stood on the second floor balcony looking at me. The expression on her face conveyed her confusion. I smiled, waved, and kept walking. I needed time to think.

What's happening here?

My initial confusion started to fade. I did not want to be a martyr to Bethany's death, exactly what David would have wanted.

A new juncture in life awaited me, a time where I could reinvent myself, or so I had read. Thanks to Bethany I had learned I no longer wanted to always be alone. I felt certain Bethany would not want me to be a recluse.

Needing or seeking a relationship per se had not entered my mind. Still, I had discovered I wanted to remain open to the idea. Somehow I needed to absolve myself of guilt.

Another apology seemed to be in order. First Doc, now Donatella. Two shots to my ego in the same week—all in the name of progression.

CHAPTER FORTY

Many people walked throughout Rumo, none more regularly than Anna Bertolli. She began walking all over Rumo as a little girl. And as an adult Anna preferred to walk any time she could.

She often walked to the *Pizzeria* at the north end of Rumo in the village of *Molini Località* where her best friend Marina worked at the restaurant. Best known for its pizza in the evening, the restaurant had a full menu of potential meals for lunch, too. Most afternoons when Anna got home from work she enjoyed walking, often meeting Marina so they could plan their evening. The walks were relaxing after the stress from work, the beautiful green scenery never getting old.

The driveway to the restaurant started at the beginning of a sharp one hundred and eighty degree curve which crossed the Torrente Lavazzè, the beautiful river running through the area. A large lumberyard had buildings and timber on both sides of the river and it sat across from the driveway leading to the pizzeria.

Anna had befriended the German shepherd guard dog at the lumberyard. She loved all animals, none more than the love she had for him. Something about his beautiful mixture of black fur along his back with the tan fur on his underbelly and legs caught her attention. She admired the shine in his dark eyes the most.

For three years Anna interacted with the dog, almost on a daily basis. She often fed him treats, staying to talk to him and pet his nose through the fence. He would jump with excitement and turn circles when he saw her, but he never barked at her. The frustrated owners tolerated the dog's behavior since it only happened when Anna was around.

Unlike many of the young people in the area who wanted to get away, Anna loved Rumo. To her it possessed a warm, inviting community atmosphere, set in what she felt were mountains of pure beauty with spectacular views. She could not see herself ever leaving.

Anna lived in a typical multi-story house in Corte Inferiore, a small village within Rumo. Her family owned the building for generations and it contained three floors, with the entire family living there.

Anna's favorite sister, Paola, had not married, but had been raising her two nieces since their other sister, Sofia, and her husband were both killed in an auto accident in Verona six years before.

Anna's parents, Eletta and Nicolò, had dealt with Sofia's death by throwing themselves into helping Paola raise their two granddaughters.

CHAPTER FORTY-ONE

When he heard *Number One*'s body had been found, he knew the time had come to make a move on his powerful desire to feel another life slowly drift away in his hands. It had been several days since her body surfaced and the Carabinieri had not shown up to question him yet. He felt comfortable no one would be able to prove he had killed her. He figured the Carabinieri would be so busy with *Number One*, no one would be looking for his next victim.

Earlier in the day when the staff was on break he walked into the office to check the video camera equipment one last time. He checked the recording machine; no light, the cord still hidden where he had put it when he unplugged it weeks before.

Number Two usually left fifteen minutes later on Monday's, which meant there should be no one else behind her. Waiting near the gate, he started walking away from the plant in the direction he knew she would take once he spotted her walking toward her car.

His palms started sweating as his plan began taking effect. He would know in a few minutes if it would be a success or not.

Anna Bertolli finished her shift at Pomarella Apple, the single biggest employer in the Val di Non province. She worked the six a.m. until two p.m. shift, except for Monday's when she had to do the previous weeks totals for her shift.

Whoa. Why'd I leave my sunglasses in the car? she thought as the bright sunlight made her flinch.

She spotted her late model Volkswagen Jetta amongst the four cars left in the parking lot area where the morning shift usually parked. She barely had enough time to get home, shower, and change into her clothes before she was to meet Marina.

Anna placed the man walking on the side of the road as someone she worked with at Pomarella. She recognized him as the nephew of the Board President of their plant, the one many did not like for always using it to his advantage. Anna had also overheard several people describe him as strange.

He had tried to talk with her a few times when he sat across from her in the breakroom. She felt badly about not being able to stay long so she could talk with him. Their lunchtimes were not the same, so she always had to get back to work.

What should I do? she thought. *I don't want to be late to meet Marina. Maybe if I drive by fast and act like I'm looking at my phone.*

Accelerating, Anna took her phone out of her back pocket. She faked reading a message while driving past him, a rush of excitement engulfing her.

Within seconds her guilt arrived when she recalled less than a month ago she needed a ride. Subconsciously her foot slid off of the accelerator.

I already feel bad for not staying to talk with him in the breakroom. I'm sure he thinks I dissed him.

The car slowed, her mind occupied with what to do.

What if he needs to go somewhere out of the way? Then I'd be really late. Still, I would hope somebody would stop to help me. Maybe if he needs to go too far out of the way I can tell him I'm sorry, I have to be somewhere.

Anna made a U-turn and drove back by him.

Dang it. He never even saw me, he's looking at the ground for God's sakes. I should turn around and go…I can't. I'll text Marina when I get to my house to tell her I'll be late.

Anna made another U-turn, driving up behind him. When he turned to look at her she motioned him to the passenger side with her index finger.

Walking toward the passenger door he smiled, as much for himself as for her.

I thought she would keep going, he thought. *This might be my lucky day.*

He opened the door and stuck his head in. "Are you sure you don't mind giving me a ride?"

"No, I don't mind," she said. "I'm not sure where you're going. I'm headed to Rumo. I live in Corte Inferiore, so I can at least get you to there."

"Perfect," he said, trying hard to look grateful. "I live in Livo," he lied, "so anywhere in Rumo would be fine, I can easily walk from there. I really appreciate this."

Pulling back onto the road she headed toward Rumo.

"How long you worked at the Pomarella plant?" he asked.

"A little over three years," she said. "You?"

"I started working there part-time while in high school," he said. "I didn't want to go to college, so when I had the chance to go full-time I did."

An uncomfortable pause hung in the air before she

finally said, "I've seen you at the plant in the breakroom a few times, although I'm not sure what you do. The times you came in I had to get back to work, so we didn't have the chance to really talk like this."

"Yeah, I thought you looked familiar, too."

You don't know what I do because you ignored me, he thought.

"I mostly drive a forklift," he said. "Every once in a while during the slow times I have to do other odd jobs."

I'm glad I stopped. He seems nice. I did the right thing, she thought.

"I understand," she said, nodding. "My boss does the same thing to me. It's like, the lazy ones do nothing. Since we work hard we get asked to do extra."

"Exactly," he replied.

He had driven the route at least a couple dozen times, clocking both time and distance to the first picnic area.

This small talk is working perfectly into my plan, he thought. *She hasn't suspected a thing.*

"And you, what do you do there?" he asked.

"Well, mostly I work on the line counting apples, checking for damaged ones," she said. "My supervisor has been giving me some extra duties, saying she likes the way I work. That's why I'm late getting off today. I guess it worked out for you," she said with a feigned smile.

"I guess so," he said, unimpressed by her smile. He let a few kilometers go by before asking, "Didn't you say you live in Rumo?"

"Yes. Why?" she asked, a quizzical look on her face.

"One of the guys at the plant told me a young woman had been found dead in the river in Rumo several days ago. I, you know, wondered if you had heard anything about what happened or if you knew the girl."

"Yeah—I knew *of* her. I haven't heard much other than I think she said something about going to Germany. I'm really not sure. I feel so bad for her parents, she's their only daughter."

"Sad. I wonder how she ended up…Did you hear that?"

"No. Hear what?"

"I think you might've ran over something, and it got stuck in your wheel well," he said. "There's a picnic area right around the next turn or two. Pull over there, I'll check it for you."

Anna thanked him as thoughts of being even later began running through her head. She spotted the picnic area so she quickly downshifted. She pulled into the beginning of the parking area paralleling the road.

Out of the several times he checked the picnic area the same time on a Monday only once had someone been there. Seeing no cars or people, he breathed a sigh of relief.

My calculations were correct. This really is my lucky day.

CHAPTER FORTY-TWO

Bruno was busy texting as I walked into my townhouse. He wanted to meet at Bar Lanterna at 4:15 p.m. I decided to use the time to check emails.

Surprised to see Sergeant Boykin had sent me an email the day before, I opened it first.

AJ,

Wanted you to know I spoke with Officer Caviglia from the Rumo area Carabinieri. He wanted to confirm you worked here.

I told him I had never heard of you!

Okay, I verified you were a detective. I had to be honest though, and tell him about your history. I told him you couldn't find your way out of a paper bag, the union is the reason I put up with you.

Seriously though, I wanted you to be aware he called. I told him to call Doc to find out if he thought it would be okay. Be careful. Hope to see you back at work soon. If you need anything, let me know.

Sgt. B

I laughed…at the same time I had a twinge of misgiving for not being there helping him instead of being in Italy helping Bruno. The feeling surprised me since I had not thought about the PD much lately.

With quite a bit of time to kill before meeting Bruno, I headed to Bar Lanterna. I needed to talk with Donatella, although I had no idea what I would say when I got there. I figured it would be best for me to go directly to being up front with her.

I felt more apprehension than if I were chasing a killer. Donatella slid a chair under the table below the TV as I walked inside. I heard someone say in Italian something about the "poliziotto Americano." I looked over my shoulder at the four older gentlemen sitting around a large table. Hearing the same comment I saw Donatella look over at me.

"*Ciao,* Donatella."

"*Ciao,* AJ," she said. "Are you sitting inside or out?"

"I thought about sitting at the bar until Bruno gets here, if you're okay with it," I said.

"*Molto bene*. I will get you a Cappuccino." She gave me her professional smile as she walked around the counter.

I sat at the counter on the stool closest to the wall to get as much distance from the table where the men were undoubtedly talking about me.

"Donatella, can I talk to you before Bruno gets here?"

When she looked at me I could easily see her skepticism of whether she should or not. Slowly, quietly, she shuffled over to me, nervously wiping the counter, waiting for me to say something.

"I know you saw me in your driveway earlier. I'm sorry if I hurt your feelings by not coming inside to talk with you. I…I had a thought about my girlfriend right before you saw me, I started wondering what I'm doing. I miss her…but then it all became clear. I now understand it's all right for me to move on, too."

"AJ, you do not need to tell me this."

"Yes, I do. I like being around you, and I want to be honest with you. I still think about Bethany sometimes."

"*Capisco*," she said. She stopped wiping the counter and put her hand on mine. "I understand. I still think about my husband, it has been *qualche anno*…a few years."

"I appreciate you being so understanding." I could see the empathy in her eyes.

Donatella's eyes shifted left, then back to me. "They talk about us now."

"Who?" My eyes scanned the room, seeing all eyes at the large table trained on us. I look back at her. "I'm so sorry. I should not have put you in the middle of the town gossip."

Donatella held my hand as I started to sit back.

"It is okay. Two of them have tried to get me to go eat with them. I said no. They probably have hurt feelings seeing the American in here, my hands on his. They need something to talk about."

Donatella kissed the back of my hand, then she put her hand on my cheek as she looked at the men and winked.

She looked back at me with an earnest face. "Thank you, AJ."

Donatella went back to the Cappuccino machine. She had barely begun making mine when I heard Bruno's voice greeting the men at the table. I stood, heading for Bruno's favorite table outside so we could have some privacy.

"The men in there are talking about the two of you," Bruno said as he took a seat.

"Yeah, we heard. She grabbed my hand, kissed it, then looked back at them and gave them a wink. It's almost like she's egging them on."

"Probably. One of the first things I learned when I got here, Donatella is quite capable of taking care of herself. Heck, she's probably had more stories told about her than she's heard from her customers. She can handle those guys, can you?"

CHAPTER FORTY-THREE

Anna stopped the car and started to text Marina after he got out.

Heading straight to the right front tire he bent down, feigning as though he reached up inside the fender. Seconds later he straightened up, waving her over.

Anna looked at her phone, then at him. *I'll finish this in a second*, she thought as she pushed the button to blank the screen. Anna turned off the car before getting out, putting her keys and phone in her pockets while she walked around the front of the car.

"There's something stuck up there, kind of behind the tire. Take a look," he said, pointing above the tire.

Anna squatted down, got on her knees, her right hand resting on the fender, her left hand on the ground. When she bent over to look into the wheel well he quietly moved behind her.

"I can't see …"

Grabbing handfuls of hair, he never heard her scream or felt her hands grabbing and scratching at his. His vision had narrowed, an all-white background surrounding her head, the front quarter panel directly behind it.

He slammed her head into the fender with such force, *one time…two times…three times…*it caved in. He felt her full weight as she went unconscious before letting her fall to the ground.

Slowly his senses returned to normal. He squatted beside her to catch his breath, trying to listen for cars. Convinced they were alone he rolled her onto her back. Pinching her nose while placing his other hand over her mouth, he waited for death to come. His excitement began to grow, its girth swelling.

Her twitching body brought an orgasmic sense of finality.

When all movement stopped he saw the large welt and discoloration on her forehead, realizing he hit her head too hard.

He heard a car coming from the direction of Revò so he pushed her body up against the tire hoping she would not be seen. Grabbing her glasses, he went to the passenger area to sit down, his back to the road. After the car raced by he relaxed, putting the glasses in the glovebox.

Taking a deep breath, he felt pressured, he needed to get Anna inside the car. He reminded himself not to forget anything like he had with the backpack.

With his hands under Anna's armpits he dragged her around the door. He tried to lift her to a seated position in the passenger seat…her dead weight made it more difficult than he anticipated.

Sweating profusely, the pressure mounted. Letting go of Anna for a second, he wiped the sweat from his face with his shirt. Changing his plan he grabbed her again, dragging her to the back door on the passenger side. He opened the door, propping Anna up in a seated position with her back against the door well. He hurried around the trunk, opened the back door, and got in the backseat, closing the door behind him.

With his hands under Anna's arms, he pulled as hard as he could. Anna's back scraped against the door well.

On the third attempt he got her up on the seat. With no cars coming, he stepped out and reaching inside he grabbed her by the shoulders, pulling her the rest of the way onto the seat. He closed the door and went to the passenger side.

He heard a car approaching and acted as if he was working on the tire. After the car sped past, he shut both passenger doors, then checked the area for anything that could be seen as evidence left behind. He went to the driver's door, his diaphragm pushed into the steering wheel when he sat, nearly knocking the wind out of him. Pawing the underside of the seat several times, he found the lever allowing him to slide the seat all the way back.

Catching his breath he reached for the keys, realizing he never got them. His mind raced, feeling they had been there too long. Two long minutes transpired before he got the car started after finding the keys in Anna's pocket. Despite mild temperature, beads of sweat rolled down his face…the neckline of his shirt drenched.

Making a U-turn he drove toward Revò, trying to take stock of his plan. He needed to get back to the Pomarella plant before anyone on the second shift went on break. He counted on the office staff to be like the first shift, oblivious to all of the video recording equipment.

Getting close to the Pomarella plant he slowed down to survey the parking lot one last time. He initially prepared to drive past if need be, but pulled in after seeing nobody there. Four cars remained where the first shift parked, his Toyota Yaris being one of them. He stopped Anna's car at the back of his, her back door even with his hatchback rear door. Leaving her car running, he surveyed the lot one last time.

Nothing moved so he pushed the button, hearing the familiar chirp. He got out and opened doors to both cars dragging Anna out of her car before using all of the strength he had to sling her into his car. Anna's upper body fell onto the gray carpeted hatchback, her head bouncing once on the carpet. He took another long deep breath, then grabbed Anna by the legs, throwing her the rest of the way in. Before closing the door he covered Anna with the blanket he brought from home.

He closed Anna's rear car door, then parked her car in the space he thought she had been in before. He turned her car off, put her keys in his right front pocket, and used his handkerchief to wipe down all of the areas inside the front of her car he thought he had touched. Spotting Anna's boss walking across the parking lot he tried to lay down out of sight. Typing something into her cell phone distracted her and she got in a small grey car two spaces on the other side of his. He peered over the door frame with one eye to watch until she drove away.

People in their own worlds. Amen.

He knew the odds of being seen were mounting with every tick on his watch. He scanned one last time, making sure he had not missed someone in the area. He got out of her car, swiping the bottom and top of each door handle once with his handkerchief. He scolded himself for having to spend critical time wiping the back door handles, the back seat not being part of the original plan.

Back in his car he took several deep breaths to calm himself before driving away. He did not want anyone he knew to see him that late on his normal route from work, so he went left. The comfort of not being rushed made the longer route worth it.

CHAPTER FORTY-FOUR

"All right, how about we take a look at those pictures," I said. *Impressive*, I thought after seeing Bruno had categorized the photos, along with setting up folders for each category.

"What you have there is generally the best picture of each one," Bruno said. He described taking four to five pictures of each item or area, often underexposing and overexposing on either end. He believed they were prepared for court if needed.

"These are good," I said, shaking my head in approval.

The next forty-five minutes I slowly made my way through the photos while Bruno provided his input.

"Even though I'm not a pathologist, I have to agree with you, those look like finger marks on her cheek. An autopsy would have been able to tell us more about any damage underneath the skin around her lips and nose. However, without an autopsy, we can't presume damage exists. What it does look like we have in our favor is the petechiae in the whites of her eyes."

"What is pateek…?"

"Petechiae. Those red dots you see in the whites of her eyes. It often indicates the likelihood of asphyxiation. Of course, a defense attorney will argue the petechiae could have come from the trauma of striking her head during the fall." I hesitated, wanting to make sure Bruno understood before I went on.

"As for her leg, my theory is for it to be twisted around in the rocks the way it had been would indicate a severe and complete separation of the bones. An autopsy would've helped here, too."

"I don't think anybody is going to believe she fell from the bridge," Bruno said. "I mean, supposedly she's leaving Rumo, right?"

"Unfortunately, a defense attorney would probably argue one fall from the bridge could be the culprit for the broken leg and the petechiae. Plus, they don't have to show why she slipped and fell—only the possibility it could have happened."

I paused to let it sink in. "The blood on the rock wall looks relatively old, it has no sheen, and its color all support the timeline. Truthfully, it's no help to us right now."

"Makes sense," Bruno said.

"I have to agree with you, this looks like a homicide. Proving it will be an entirely different matter."

"Do you always talk about what a defense attorney might say?"

I never looked at defense attorneys as scumbags like most cops. In an adversarial system I looked at them as my opponents. I told Bruno I had received good advice once from an old crusty defense attorney. "He said if I could think like a defense attorney while investigating, I would actually take away most, if not all, of their arguments." I hoped someday Bruno could see the value in it.

Bruno paused, shaking his head from side-to-side, a look of suspicion on his face. "I guess I can see in theory how it might work. I can't imagine it's easy to do."

"You already did it to some extent without realizing it. You didn't take one picture of each potential piece of evidence, you took four or five, each at different exposures and different angles. Not only does it help you as an investigator, it also takes away the opportunity for the defense to attack your photography."

Before I could say anything else Bruno's phone rang.

"This is a first," he said, his mouth puckered, his eyes wide with surprise.

"It's Corporal Amici. He's never called me."

My eyebrows raised as Bruno answered the call, wondering if Amici might already be responding to Bruno's attempts at respect.

I had difficulty understanding much, the conversation being in Italian. I could tell something had happened due to the grave expression on Bruno's face as he stared at nothing after hanging up.

"What is it?"

"Corporal Amici's mother has gotten worse, she's in the hospital with pneumonia. Since he has no vacation time left, I had offered him mine earlier in the week. He seemed confused and uneasy when I first offered it, so he turned me down. He called to ask if I might still be willing to give him some of my time. I said yes. I'm sorry AJ, I have to go. I want to make sure he's okay and help him get to the train station if he needs it."

Reaching into my pocket, I grabbed my keys.

"Here, take my car," I said, tossing the keys on the table toward Bruno. "He could use a friend right now. The train ride, wherever he is going, will be lonely enough. Take my car. Go."

Bruno looked at me with gratitude. He grabbed the keys and left without another word.

While Bruno walked away I contemplated his willingness to give up his vacation time to help a co-worker in a time of need. *He's growing on me*, I thought.

"Where is he going so fast?" Donatella asked, as she walked through the door to the patio area.

I looked at her, no longer surprised by nothing getting past her.

"He's going to help Corporal Amici, his mother is in the hospital. Amici has no vacation time so Bruno is going to give him some of his time. He went to take him to the train station. I'm proud of him."

"He needs to hear those words, from you. You are good for him." She hesitated briefly, looking at me caringly, her eyes touching my emotions. Before I could say anything we heard a man at the bar calling for Donatella. Without hesitation she went inside.

Sitting alone, reflecting, I began to accept the difficulty in setting my ego aside. I had many years of relying solely on myself. Bethany changed that. She helped me to trust someone else, to put someone else before me. Thankfully, she made me a better person. I could see her smiling at my helping Bruno. Goosebumps and tingling seemed to engulf me; I could almost feel her.

DUE TO THE LATE AFTERNOON HOUR, CAPTAIN CONdello expected to leave a message for Major Leone when he called the Cles office. Being connected to the major caught him off guard.

"Captain Condello. It's late. Is everything okay?"

"Major Leone, thank you for taking my call. I'm sorry

to bother you at this late hour. My apologies. I wanted to inform you about Corporal Amici's mother being in the hospital…quite sick. I have instructed him to go be with her since her husband has passed and he is her only living child. I know how strongly you feel about family, so I approved his leave. I hope you are all right with it?"

"Yes, that's fine. I would have done the same thing."

While Condello had the major on the phone he explained Amici not having any vacation time left, along with Bruno's willingness to donate his leave time under the circumstances.

"I appreciate the heads up, Captain Condello. There should not be any problem, especially in a family emergency like this. I may even provide Corporal Amici some free time given the situation once I receive your paperwork. Things must be changing up there."

"Sir?"

"Well, Corporal Amici has been known to have a chip on his shoulder for some time. And your newest officer has been there less than a year, yet he's donating time to Amici. You must be doing something to make those kinds of changes."

"For some reason Officer Caviglia seems to be getting through to Corporal Amici, so you're right, there are some changes happening. All positive, Sir. All positive."

"Impressive, Captain. I'll look into sending you a temporary replacement if it looks like Corporal Amici will be out for a while. Thanks again for the heads up. *Ciao*."

CHAPTER FORTY-FIVE

At five o'clock Nicolò Bertolli walked in the door. His daughter Paola had called him asking him to come home early, telling him Eletta had been acting strangely. He could see Eletta sitting on the couch crying, clutching a pillow to her chest, her fingers interlocked, rocking back and forth.

"I heard her scream about an hour ago, calling out Anna's name," Paola said, her voice cracking.

"Then she said, 'She's gone, I know she's gone.' She's been on the couch ever since, rocking and praying, exactly like that. She hasn't said another word."

"Oh my God. Have you tried to get in touch with Anna?" he asked, the color in his face going pale.

"Dad…she never came home," Paola said, tears in her eyes. "I've called, I don't know, at least twenty times if not more. She hasn't answered. I know the mountains block cell service between here and the plant sometimes. Still, she should've gotten service somewhere in there by now."

"Keep trying, call anyone you can think of who might have a clue where she would be." Nicolò had no words to comfort Eletta. He softly kissed her forehead, before turning for the door. "I'm going to drive around, see if I can find anything." Halfway out the door something told him to take Anna's spare keys.

Please Lord, not again. Not Anna, Paola silently prayed.

Word traveled fast throughout Rumo. Anna missing had people concerned; Eletta's comments had them scared. Nicolò knew people all over Rumo would be searching for Anna, so he decided to drive to the Pomarella plant where she worked. Pulling into the parking lot he saw her car. He knew Anna would have called if she had to work late. He stopped behind her car, unable to hold back his tears any longer.

After several minutes Nicolò forced himself to park his car. He wiped his eyes before going inside to speak with management and his heart sank when he learned Anna had clocked out hours ago.

Exiting the building Nicolò called his friend, Lorenzo, explaining he would need two drivers. Nicolò plodded over to Anna's car to find the doors locked. Waiting for Lorenzo, Nicolò took Anna's extra keys and unlocked the driver's door to look inside. He had to do something while he waited, although he had no clue what he should be looking for.

Nicolò sat in the driver's seat, attempting to gather his thoughts. Without any consideration he swung his feet in, put his hands up on the steering wheel, and tried to think of where Anna could be. Sitting there, he became certain something felt wrong. He looked around, trying to figure it out. Then it hit him, the seat position—he had no trouble getting his legs in. Anna could not have been the last person to drive her car; she needed the seat close to the steering wheel. Someone much taller than Anna had to be the last one to sit there.

Nicolò noticed dirt and grass on the back seat, definitely out of place for Anna who kept her car spotless. Opening the glove box Nicolò saw Anna's new pair of glasses, the right lens cracked. Stunned, Nicolò slowly got out of the car.

He walked around the car, his mind racing, trying to process it all. He scanned to his left down the passenger side once. His head jerked right, his eyes zooming in on *the* spot—the large dent over the right front wheel well. Tears formed in his eyes again, the reality setting in, his poor Eletta was probably right. The tightness in his chest and the difficulty breathing had returned from several years of lying low to accompany him through another family tragedy.

Nicolò sat back down in the driver seat of Anna's car, waiting for his friend, praying for his daughter. The twenty-five minutes it took Lorenzo and his son to arrive seemed like an eternity. Nicolò could not bring himself to get out of Anna's car. He handed Lorenzo his keys, and they followed him as he drove her car home. In a strange way Nicolò felt Anna comforting him along the way.

It had been two hours since Nicolò had left. Paola still had not found anyone who knew Anna's whereabouts. Eletta had not left the couch; she had drawn her legs up close, turned sideways, and laid her head on the back of the couch.

When Eletta heard Anna's car she raced to the door with hope. Nicolò's eyes met hers, his tears telling of his sorrow. Eletta slowly turned, shuffling to her bedroom where she laid on the bed in the fetal position, sobbing.

CHAPTER FORTY-SIX

I wanted to see where Domenica lived, as well as the path she took to the river to retrace the feel of her last walk. Giorgio agreed to pick me up and take me since Bruno had my car.

Giorgio drove me up through the villages of Scassio and Mocenigo before getting to Lanza, the highest village of Rumo.

"Where do you want me to drop you off?" Giorgio asked.

"Near Domenica's house. I don't want to talk with her parents, but I want to see her house."

"Then what?"

"Then I'll walk to the bus stop taking the same path she took to the bridge by the *Centralina Comunale*."

"I can go with you if you would like," Giorgio said.

"No, thank you. I need to do this alone. I hope I'm not offending you."

"No, no. *Capisco*. I heard some more news about Carlo."

"Really? Tell me."

"I heard Carlo talked at Bar Podetti about getting slapped by Domenica. Some men were teasing him. He laughed, said it was her *perdita*. I'm not sure the word."

It took me a second to realize Carlo had been bragging.

"Her loss?"

"Sì, sì. Her loss."

"When did it happen? Recently, or right after she went missing?"

"Carlo talking of getting slapped happened the same day they found Domenica in the river. Later, the same night. Several men, all heard him say this."

"Have they told the Carabinieri what they heard?"

"AJ, they tell me, I tell you. Nobody here wants problems."

"What do you mean?"

"The Carabinieri in Italy, they are sometimes not honest, not hard workers. Some can be *vendicativo*. I do not think ours are so much like that. Many people have their fears, from bad experiences, or from hearing what others experienced."

"Okay. So they're afraid to approach the Carabinieri, I get it. Did Carlo say anything else?"

"I hear he said to the men he had hoped for some young *figa*, umm, umm, a woman's part."

I laughed. "Tough to find the right words Giorgio?"

Giorgio grinned broadly. "Sì, *sì*. Tough. Carlo wanted some young *figa*. After Domenica slapped him, he says he went to a widow woman in Mocenigo."

Coming to a stop in a small parking lot which appeared to be for the graveyard off to our left, Giorgio pointed. "Her house is right up there. The white one."

"*Grazie*."

"AJ, the people of Rumo appreciate your help."

I started to respond about my not having done much, and then the reality of it all stopped me. They knew more about me than I did. I had been in denial about helping.

"You're welcome Giorgio. Please, tell them for me. It's the least I can do for the good people of Rumo. Oh, can you get me Carlo's address?" I asked as I got out.

"Sì. I will get it," Giorgio said, gratitude on his face.

He had made it home without seeing anyone he recognized. He parked his car in the front of the house mindful his father would want to park in the garage. He left Anna in the back covered with the blanket.

Sitting on his bed his mind vacillated between *Number Two* and the future.

H*ow long can I keep doing this here? People will get suspicious*, he thought.

Nobody should find her. The animals will finish her off. Even if she is found, the animals will have at least taken care of what happened to her. They'll presume she fell in a place she goes by every day.

I can't keep this up in Rumo. Maybe I should offer to go work at some other Pomarella plants when they need extra help. They have plants all over Val di Non. I'm sure my uncle will help me.

Once I get rid of my old man I can start over. New places. New prey.

He smiled as he lay back on the bed.

CHAPTER FORTY-SEVEN

Walking a short distance I came to Domenica's house. The house spoke of cleanliness and order. Yet Domenica wanted something more. Something told me she wanted freedom...she wanted to see other places. I wondered if maybe she felt smothered here, maybe from the cleanliness and order her parents expected from her.

I followed Path Ten by the two lone tall pine trees between me and the cemetery. The three light poles along the path, coupled with the ambient light, clearly lit the way. I noticed some activity in the backs of the homes to my left. Not surprisingly, none of the occupants even seemed aware of me. Walking being so common in the community, Domenica would not have drawn attention.

I passed a large vegetable garden with wooden slat fencing all around it, an old barn leaning to the right as if on its last leg, still protecting the firewood, even an old wooden stump carved to look somewhat like a horse, with a saddle on it for little kids.

Ahh, the simpler way of life. Maybe Domenica wanted excitement instead.

I went right, coming to the T intersection with the glass bus stop, the beautiful mountains behind it. With the street light, any person going by would have easily recognized Domenica, and the womanizer.

I continued walking along the sidewalk, picking up Path Ten, veering right down into the ravine. The Val di Rumo map in Donatella's bar showed Path Ten to be a much shorter, direct route to the *Centralina Comunale*, something Bruno and I both agreed Domenica would have been looking for.

In no time I heard the sound of the *Torrente Lavazzè*, and felt the drop in temperature as darkness quickly approached. Now I understood the long sleeved, V-neck, sweater. Soon I could see the light from the lone house on the path, the *Centralina Comunale* several yards beyond it.

Standing next to the river I recalled Bruno's pictures.

Something drew you to the opposite side of the river, what was it?

My years as a detective investigating these types of crimes told me Domenica would probably join the fifty-plus percent of all murder victims killed by someone they knew.

Someone didn't want you to go. We need to find your boy toy.

He had dinner waiting for his father when he arrived home shortly after seven o'clock, tired from a long week. As usual his father hardly spoke to him during dinner. A few minutes before nine o'clock he heard the familiar snoring, his father asleep in the recliner; the television on.

Logic told him *Number Two* had not moved, but his urge to see her and verify it overrode the common sense of not drawing attention. He went outside, surveyed the area, and opened the hatchback. His excitement started growing as he slowly pulled the blanket back.

Minutes later he walked along the side of the house to the backyard area. He opened one of the large, wooden, garage doors. Inside, he walked around his dad's car to the workbench where he retrieved the cat bell and the necklace. He took the keys off *Number Two's* beautifully crafted key ring, setting them on the workbench. Using a hacksaw he cut the first two letters away from the last letter, A. He threw the keys and the letters, P and S, in the trashcan by the bench. Holding the three items he treasured in his left hand, he closed his eyes while his right hand moved in rhythm.

CHAPTER FORTY-EIGHT

After receiving information from the Cles office about Anna having gone missing, Captain Condello called the Bertolli home. Nicolò told him Anna had always been consistent, regimented almost. She would call home if she were going to be late, in addition to laying out clothes she planned to wear if she were to meet her girlfriend after work. Anna did not call and the clothes were still on her bed.

"Did you contact the place where she works?"

"Yes," Nicolò said. "She works at the Pomarella plant in Revò. She normally gets off work at about 2:15 on Mondays. Today, she clocked out at 2:16. Nobody saw her afterward."

"And her car?"

"I found it in the parking lot. I could not find her keys anywhere in the car. I had to use our spare set to drive her car home." Before he could say any more Nicolò began to cry, handing the phone to Paola.

Captain Condello told Paola he needed a picture of Anna so he could fax it to other Carabinieri offices, as well as her physical description.

"Captain, Anna is my youngest sister. My other sister, Sofia, died six years ago in a car accident. My mother started crying at about four o'clock saying she knew Anna is dead. Please Captain, find her."

"I remember hearing about Sofia. I am so sorry. We will do our best. I'll be there soon."

"Thank you, Captain. I'll have those ready for you."

At ten o'clock the angry young man woke his father, suggesting he should go to bed. Without any resistance his father got up, made his way to the stairs, and headed to his room. The son let the television stay on for another forty minutes to be on the safe side. He peeked his head into his father's room at twenty minutes before eleven. Hearing snoring, he sensed he could leave without his father ever being aware he had gone.

"I'm at Captain Condello's house, getting ready to leave. I have some information you might find interesting," Bruno said.

"Good. I have some information of my own," I said.

"Really? *Molto bene.* Do you want me to bring your car to your house?"

"Nah. Meet me at Bar Lanterna. I'm heading out the door now."

"*Bene*, I'll be there soon."

I looked at my watch…ten forty-five. I ambled down the steps, a surge of excitement about hearing what Bruno had.

I walked across the small private road in front of my townhouse, continuing straight to cross the main road to the sidewalk on the far side. I no longer felt fatigued, my mind squarely on the rendezvous with Bruno. I never saw or heard the car coming from my left. The screeching of the tires shook me from my zoned-out state.

The hard braking lowered the front end of the car. Somehow my mind calculated options and I leapt, the sliding car narrowly missing me. Past critical situations trained me to think through the process, the ebb and flow of my heartbeat nearly unchanged. Unlike the driver coming to a stop millimeters from me, his wide, panic-filled eyes looked at me.

I fully expected him to be upset with me, yelling something in Italian. Instead, the young man's bulging eyes kept staring at me, his white knuckles gripping the steering wheel. He had a *deer in the headlight* look on his face, a panic from something other than nearly hitting me.

Stop, I thought, internally chastising myself for always scrutinizing like a detective, not giving the kid the benefit of the doubt.

No sooner had I finished scolding myself, he strangely diverted his head away from me so I could no longer see his face. He followed it with resting his arm on the top of the inside door panel, raising his shoulder even higher, much like a shield. His actions were awkward at best. The car jerked forward and began to roll away. He never said a word.

A blue Toyota Yaris, I told myself as I caught a glimpse of the plate. *CM 441*.

The significance of the driver's uneasiness had not been lost. I tried to provide the kid an alibi in my head but my gut told me otherwise. I decided to trust my instincts.

CHAPTER FORTY-NINE

His initial fear centered on being identified. *He's got to be a tourist, he's not from Rumo. Man, I'd swear I've seen him before though*, he thought.

His fear gradually diminished the more he rationalized the man would have been too scared to identify him after nearly getting hit by a car.

The cautious drive through Rumo provided him time to take several deep breaths. The large wooden sign saying "*Arrivederci da Rumo*" meant he needed to start looking for any signs of people or cars near the lumberyard.

The car coasted toward the one hundred and eighty degree curve while the stacks of lumber on the right became much clearer. A streetlight lit the beginning of the curve as well as a driveway to his left. The driveway descended down ten meters to an old wooden shop storing lumber, rising back up at an equivalent angle to the other side.

Not seeing another car or person in the area, he made a U-turn, parking at the mouth of the driveway farthest from the curve. The street light at the curve provided enough light for him to see without feeling too exposed. The area he chose had a small shoulder with no metal railing, which allowed him to pull his car up next to the slope running down to the river. He turned off the headlights, left the car running in case he had to leave, and popped the hatchback.

Without realizing it Anna chose the perfect spot to dump her body while he surveilled her, watching her walk by the steep, unprotected slope near this sidewalk to the pizzeria on at least a dozen occasions. People would naturally think she accidentally fell down the side of the hill.

He wanted to keep the blanket over her as he prepared to lift her, but it kept falling off. Frustrated, he hurled the blanket to the ground, slinging *Number Two* over his shoulder. He carried her a couple of steps to the steep hillside near where he parked.

He started to flop her onto the ground when he heard the dog barking from inside of the fenced-in area of the lumberyard across the river. He spotted the German shepherd, but not before the dog had him locked in by sight and smell. Laying her body down, he became apprehensive from the dogs incessant barking.

With both hands underneath her, he gave her body one thrust, propelling her down the embankment. Anna rolled, her swiftness dictated by the steep hill. Two seconds later her body slammed against a tree. He waited a couple seconds to make certain she had come to a complete halt before he stood, chucking the blanket in the back of the car.

With the lights off he drove three hundred meters toward town, pulling into a large grassy area on the shoulder near the "Community of Rumo Information" sign. An unofficial *parking* spot, his car would not draw undue attention there.

A sidewalk with metal railing and two streetlights separated the grassy parking area from the dumpsite. He pulled on work gloves before trudging back to the railing.

How stupid. A railing up here to keep someone from falling down the hill, yet nothing over by the driveway, he thought.

He found the end of the rope he had tied on to the railing the night before. After double-checking the sturdiness of the rope, he strolled down the sidewalk, taking stock of any onlookers. Confident of being alone, he moved to the edge where *Number Two* fell.

He slid down the hillside in a seated position, trying to stay in the path *Number Two* made. He dug his heels in at the last to prevent running into her. Turning her over, he aligned her forehead even with the tree she hit.

Her eyes will be the first thing eaten by the bugs or animals, so nobody will ever know I cut off her air.

Her body now perfectly situated, he stood to leave. The German shepherd's madness continued and he appreciated the fact a fence and river stood between them. So far the dog had been the sole witness; he wanted to keep it that way.

He trekked through the trees toward his car, hunting in the darkness for his exit. Finding the rope he used the previously tied knots, slowly pulling himself up the side of the embankment until he reached the sidewalk near the grassy parking lot. He untied the rope, drawing it up as fast as he could. He would worry about rolling it up neatly like his father had it another time. He felt he had already been there too long.

He started to take the gloves off when he heard the voices. The two young lovers were on the sidewalk by the curve, walking hand-in-hand toward Rumo. With silence and stealth he moved to the back of his car, ducking down behind the right rear tire. He worked his pocketknife out of his pocket, opening it as he heard them talking about their meal.

If they come toward the car I'll stab him first—aim for his throat. Then go after her.

Their voices fading, he closed the knife and put it back.

People are so unobservant, he thought as he popped the hatchback. He lifted the rear deck board, throwing the rope where the spare tire usually sat. He threw his gloves in, started the car and pulled toward the road with the lights off. He could no longer see the young couple, so he turned on the lights, pulling onto the road. Within seconds he passed the large wooden welcoming sign, *Benvenuto a Rumo.*

CHAPTER FIFTY

Surprised by the packed bar, I recalled what Donatella said about the increase in customers at night. *So much for privacy.* Bruno walked in carrying a manila folder and we sat at the only open table, the large one by the gelato freezer. Bruno told me he stayed with Amici until he got on the train and felt Amici genuinely appreciated it.

"I'm proud of you, for helping him."

"*Grazie*. And, thank you for your car," Bruno said.

I told Bruno about Domenica being hit on by an older guy while at the bus station in Mocenigo the night she went missing. "Giorgio called him a, '*donnaiolo*,'" I said. "Plus, the people who saw this, also saw Domenica slap the guy in the face before walking off on Path Ten. His name is Carlo Camioni."

"Interesting," Bruno said. "Maybe he got angry, then followed her. We need to find this Carlo guy and talk with him."

"I agree. So, what news do you have?"

Pulling out a picture from the folder, laying it face down on the table, Bruno said Captain Condello spoke with a family from Corte Inferiore, right above us. Their twenty-five year old daughter failed to return home.

"Okay. What makes it so interesting? She's a young woman who hasn't come home yet. In California nobody would even think twice about it. And, what's with the photo face down?"

"The picture is what makes it interesting," Bruno said, as he slowly turned the photo over while sliding it toward me.

"Wow. She looks a lot like Domenica. Except with glasses." I looked at the photo for another fifteen seconds, an uneasy feeling beginning to roll through me.

"This is not good. Please tell me she's like, irresponsible, maybe done this before."

Bruno shook his head, then described a responsible, family-oriented young woman who always told her family what her plans were. Bruno said she got off work on time, although she never contacted her family.

"This part though…I'm not sure if I believe or not. Supposedly, her mom felt at about 4 p.m. her daughter had died. I hear she's lying on the bed in a fetal position crying, repeatedly saying Anna is dead."

"You *should* believe it," I stressed with conviction. "There are some things probably not considered legitimate in a court of law, but they hold importance for you as an investigator. A mother's connection with her children is one of them."

"Are you saying you believe her?" Bruno asked.

"Absolutely. Especially with her behavior. Unfortunately, she's probably right, her daughter is likely dead somewhere."

"You think Domenica's death and Anna's missing are related?" Bruno asked.

"Uh, way too early to say. If Anna shows up dead, depending on the circumstances, then my gut feeling is it's pretty likely."

Until we knew more, we needed to stay focused on Domenica. We needed to locate Carlo, or at least confirm he spoke about talking with Domenica. Carlo and the boy toy were our only suspects for now, if you could call them that.

"Are you familiar with Bar Podetti?" I asked.

"Yeah. I go there for Cappuccino sometimes. Why?"

"Let's go," I said, sliding out of the booth. "If Carlo's there maybe we can chat with him. Kind of a cursory interview. If he isn't, maybe the bartender will verify some of it."

Bruno followed my lead. Donatella had started over our way, a confused look on her face.

"We'll be right back," I said. "Gotta go check something."

She flashed me one of her half smiles before heading off to help other customers.

We arrived at Bar Podetti in minutes. Before going in we discussed Miranda Rights. I explained how in America we did not need to read Carlo his Miranda Rights since this is informal along with the fact Carlo has the freedom to leave.

"Our laws are similar. So long as the person is not an *indagato*, a suspect, or an *imputato*, a defendant, we can talk with them with no reservation."

Neither of us believed Carlo reached the status of being a legitimate suspect, yet, so we went inside. Bruno walked in first, with me intentionally staying a step or two behind him. He went to the corner of the bar, keeping distance between him and the nearest customer.

Simone, the bartender, waived like he recognized Bruno. Finished with the customers at the other end of the bar, he made his way down to Bruno.

"Simone, I'm hoping you could help me."

"Sure, what can I do for you?" Simone asked.

"Is Carlo Camioni here?"

"No. Not right now."

Bruno looked at me, shook his head no, and then continued to speak with Simone.

"Yes, I heard him say it, I believe yesterday," Simone said. "He and his regular group were all here. The men were teasing him about her slapping him after he touched her butt. Sorry, I wish I could talk some more. I need to go, I'm working alone."

After they shook hands we left the bar. I told Bruno it seemed like he told the bartender what we heard…the bartender merely confirmed it.

"Yes, basically. Did I do something wrong?"

"No. Look, if you tell someone what you think before they can say anything to you, a defense attorney will accuse you of using coercion. So, when you interview people, say as little as possible, let the witness or suspect tell you what they saw. Never suggest it."

"I understand." Bruno then explained Simone heard Carlo talking with his friends yesterday when they teased him about Domenica slapping him after he touched her butt.

"Well, seems less like speculation now, more like probability since we have someone who heard him admit to being slapped by her. It's a start. What would a defense attorney argue?"

"I would say they would claim Carlo liked to gossip, maybe even elaborate a little to his friends," Bruno said. "There's no evidence, no actual witness yet."

"Ah, outstanding," I said, patting Bruno on the back. His smile told me he appreciated my positive feedback.

CHAPTER FIFTY-ONE

Not a soul out on the patio at Bar Lanterna seemed suspicious to us. Inside we saw a large crowd of people standing in the middle of the room with their backs to us. Other than the television, an eerie silence permeated the bar. I did not need to speak Italian to know there had been a bombing somewhere in Italy.

"We are used to hearing of bombings by the Mafia to take out someone they are after," Bruno said. "Terrorist bombings like this are not as common. Italy is not quite as bad as some other countries. Terrorist attacks throughout Europe are increasing, even in Italy."

"What are they saying?" I asked, pointing to the television.

Bruno shook his head, his eyes never leaving the screen. "About one hour ago a pipe bomb went off in the open grass area by the water fountain in front of the library at the University of Padua. At almost the same time, a car bomb went off in *Firenze*, sorry, in Florence. It exploded in the parking lot of the train station, *Campo di Marte*, two blocks from the University of Florence soccer stadium. There are at least two dead and a dozen injured in Padua, at least a half-dozen are dead in Firenze."

Donatella moved up beside me, her hands clenched together close to her chest. The people inside the bar were clearly shaken by the bombings, including Donatella. I put my arm around her to comfort her, as I had many people whose world turned upside down. She leaned her head on my shoulder, wiping away tears.

Oddly, some crimes made sense to me, like stealing when a person needs to eat. Killing innocent people by blowing them up made no sense on any level. "Not long ago Americans thought terrorist attacks were a European problem," I said.

"Now, with all of our recent terrorist activity, the reality it could happen at any time is approaching what you all have lived with for quite some time."

"True," Bruno said, sadness in his voice.

"I am sorry my friend; this is not the Italy we would hope you would see on your first visit here. I must go. There's a chance I could be called in."

Bruno paused long enough for us to shake hands. The look into each other's eyes spoke volumes. In spite of the danger of the job always being present, people like Bruno are willing to run toward it, not from it. I motioned for him to go when he tried to hand me my car keys. My car was the least of my concerns.

Donatella must have sensed the crowd about to break up. She sighed as she looked at me.

"They will either most leave to go home, or it will be a long night of drinking and talking." Wiping away tears, she scurried back behind the bar.

A small number of the people had returned to their tables, the majority had left. I took a seat inside at one of the small tables so I could see a little more about the bombings. I had not been there long when Donatella came up to the table. She stood there, peering at the television with me.

"Scary isn't it," I said.

"Sì, much for a mother whose sons are young adults who travel into areas like Padua and Firenze," she said, pointing to the screen.

"Here in Rumo, a terrorist bomb will not happen. Where it is a lot of people, especially young people, there is always a risk in Europe."

I nodded. No words would comfort her from such a reality.

Donatella fidgeted, still looking at the screen.

"AJ, I am sorry for crying on you," she said. "I should not have."

Before I could respond she left. I felt like we were two people trying to get to the same place, living life again after tragedy; it seemed like neither of us were really ready.

CHAPTER FIFTY-TWO

The cool night air felt good on my walk home. It had been a full day, one I savored, other than the bombings. I sensed more movement, ever so slightly, toward living again, not merely existing.

I walked into the townhouse at two minutes past midnight, consumed by absolute exhaustion. I had been exhausted for months from stress. This felt as though my welcomed friend had returned…the familiarity of fatigue from working long hours on an investigation. I stayed true to my routine, did my exercises, and looked at the clock at 12:43 a.m. Sleep called, I listened.

THE GERMAN SHEPHERD RAN ALONG THE FENCE FOR over an hour. Instinctively he ran to get a drink of water from his bowl, preparing for the next move. He ran back to the fence between him and the river, then slowly walked along it with his head down as if tracking something. He stopped close to the end of the fence near the roadway.

He had never left the fenced-in parking lot at night, although his drive to get to his friend consumed him. He began to dig at the one spot along the entire fence line where the asphalt did not meet up with the fence. Soon he worked his paw in between the two, little by little breaking off flakes of the asphalt. At first he could only use one paw. Intuitively, he alternated paws. After forty-five minutes, despite all of his toenails bleeding from being sanded down by the rough asphalt, he had worked enough asphalt away for him to get both paws in to dig. The softness of the dirt beneath the asphalt and fence made it easier for him to quickly create a sizable hole.

After fifteen more minutes of digging he raced back to his water bowl for a long drink. When he returned he began to work his way under the fence. He never stopped moving his body; minutes later he stood on the outside of the fence.

The Shepherd instantly ran to the river on a direct course for Anna. He stopped at the river's edge instinctively assessing the power of the flowing water. Shrewdly, he scampered up the side of the hill along the outside of the fence to the roadway.

Paying no attention to his bleeding paws he bolted along the roadway next to the guardrail along the bridge high above the river. On the far side of the bridge he turned to the one wooden work shed on the opposite side of the river. Following the asphalt drive downhill he raced past the shed, up the drive on the other side and at the top he cut right, angling down the grassy hillside toward Anna.

He made a path through the tall grass until he came upon her. He slowly walked along her entire body, using his nose to take in all of the odors. Getting to her head, he tried to wake her by licking her cheek. Despite the odor of death, he tried several more times to nudge her with his nose and lick her to get her to move. Unsuccessful, he turned three circles before softly lying down near the back of her head. His bloody front paws extended out beyond her shoulder blades while he gently rested his head in the crevice of the back of her neck.

CHAPTER FIFTY-THREE

I slept soundly for hours before my adversary returned in the early morning, taking its normal route.

I RACED TOWARD THE HOUSE WHERE I SAW DAVID ON THE bed, his eyes staring at me. This time I went further. I saw the writing on the wall, the red blood running in spots. His words meant for me, a clarification and it felt like a dagger to my emotions. I could see Bethany's legs and torso beside the bed, blood all over her clothes.

MY EYES OPENED...I SAT UP ON ONE ELBOW. SWEAT, panic, and vomiting no longer played a major role. Instantly, I knew I had progressed. I began to get real sleep; deep sound sleep. The clock said 6:17 a.m., yet I felt rested. I looked forward to another day.

The long hot shower revived the sore muscles in my legs. The lengthy trek, along with the number of stairs from San Romedio, helped remind me of muscles I seldom used in the flatlands of California.

I contemplated Carlo as I let the warm water pulse onto my legs. I had interviewed many suspects of varying cultures with court certified translators who understood to relay the questions exactly like I asked them to maintain continuity. Bruno's dialect from southern Italy, versus the unique Italian dialect in Rumo, had me concerned. Still, he had already surprised me with his ability to listen. He seemed to be a fast learner. It did not take long before I concluded I could trust Bruno to do the job well.

I mean, they're all Italian right?

A good night's sleep, a hot shower for my aching legs, the cool brisk morning air on my walk to the bar and soon a Cappuccino…life looked pretty good right then.

I walked into Bar Lanterna a couple minutes after seven, not expecting to find it empty. Donatella stood in the middle of the bar looking at the television, the bombings still the main story.

My God, she never rests, I thought.

"*Buongiorno,* Donatella."

"*Giorno,* AJ. You look *rinfrescato*, umm, relaxed."

"I am. Thank you." Pointing to the screen, I asked, "What is it they're saying now?"

"They say the daily market where people sell their crops inside the walls of the university in Padua, they are not allowed in today. They also say the restaurants inside the walls, they take the place of the market later in the afternoon or early evening, will not be allowed to open tonight. The bombings, they hurt many people in different ways."

I understood. All of us naturally mourned for those killed, yet the bombing reached far beyond the dead. "Those who died all have friends and family who are hurting right now."

Politely Donatella tried to smile. "Thank you for trying so hard to understand us, our culture. And me."

I took her hands in mine, looked deeply into her eyes, red from crying and lack of sleep.

"You're welcome. I can say the same thing about you, trying to understand what I'm going through." I drew her close and we quietly held each other.

"We have our troubles. We are like a *paio*," she said, as she backed away, crossing her middle and index fingers.

Realizing the meaning, I smiled. "A pair."

"Sì, a pair," she said with a little chuckle. Donatella headed for the bar when she heard someone approaching.

"*Buongiorno,* Bruno, *come va*?" I asked.

"*Sto bene, grazie*," Bruno replied. "Using Italian greetings, *Bene, bene*, it's a start."

"I figured I'd get the few Italian words I can say out of the way right off the bat," I said with a smile. "There's no way I could give you any help if I had to speak Italian all day."

Bruno laughed. "I'm glad. I wouldn't have the patience to listen to you butcher it all day."

We laughed. I appreciated the fact Bruno had loosened up, allowing us to joke with one another. We might need some laughter later on, the natural stress reliever for cops.

"*Giorno*, Bruno," Donatella said as she walked around the counter carrying a tray. She went to the large round table near the gelato cooler. "The cappuccinos are ready. Sit here, it is the best place for you not to be interrupted." Placing the cappuccinos on the table with a stack of napkins and two spoons, she looked at us with a curious expression, obviously wondering why we had not moved yet. "Sit, sit."

We had no sooner slid into the booth when she returned with plates and a tray full of pastries. Without a word Donatella used the tongs to put two pastries on each of the plates. She knew Bruno liked the fruit filled ones, while I preferred cream filled. She departed as quickly as she had arrived to go about the business of preparing for her day. We looked at each other and smiled, both admiring her energy.

"I'm a little surprised to see you here today."

"Me, too. Captain Condello said the major told him with Corporal Amici on emergency leave due to his mother's health, we were not going to leave our post, they would draw from other areas."

"Any news on the missing girl?"

"No, unfortunately, I had hoped we would have gotten a call from her parents, or even another Carabinieri office, saying she had been located. No such luck."

CHAPTER FIFTY-FOUR

Tommaso arrived at the family lumberyard a few minutes before seven. Zeus, their German shepherd, did not greet him when he unlocked the gate and pushed it open. Although not normal, he presumed Zeus would find him soon, so he went about his business.

Over the next fifteen minutes Tommaso made his way around the lumberyard unlocking doors and getting equipment turned on. While he headed to the office he realized Zeus had never shown up. Tommaso unlocked the office, then walked around the parking lot, buildings, and piles of lumber calling Zeus's name. Other employees joined the search. Looking up to the end of the property nearest the road Tommaso saw the dirt on the asphalt. He sprinted over, surprised by the hole Zeus dug. Tommaso called Zeus's name as loud as he could, again and again.

Zeus kept hearing his name. Excited, he tried nudging Anna. When she didn't move Zeus took off toward the path he came down. He had not made it far before he returned, licking Anna's cheek. Whimpering and barking, he could not get her to move. He left her side, going a little further the second time before returning once again. After nudging her several more times he laid down.

The last call from his owner had a higher pitch. Zeus' ears perked up. He began barking several times in a row before he raced up the path. Reaching the sidewalk by the bridge he barked three times. Not bringing about the desired response, he took off running again next to the railing toward the lumberyard. At the far side of the bridge Zeus stopped to bark at Tommaso.

Tommaso spotted Zeus running across the bridge. He ran to the corner of the property excitedly calling out, "Here boy, here!"

Zeus would not go down to the fence. Instead he kept turning and running toward the bridge, returning each time after looking back and Tommaso had not followed.

Realizing Zeus was trying to tell him something, Tommaso took off at a dead run for the gate. Zeus ran along the road toward the gate until he could see his owner coming. Barking and turning a circle, Zeus took off toward the bridge.

In spite of the fact Tommaso had no idea what may be wrong, something told him he needed to trust Zeus. Two other employees saw Tommaso sprinting, so they followed. Twice Zeus stopped, giving them time to catch up. Zeus ran down past the wooden building and up the other driveway where he waited for them. When they got near him, Zeus ran down the side of the hill where he stood by Anna, barking.

"Oh my god," Tommaso said, gasping for air. "It's a girl,"

They looked at each other, astonished by what Zeus had done to get their attention and direct them to her.

One employee, a volunteer firefighter for the town of Livo, took two steps toward the girl. Zeus growled.

"Be careful," Tommaso said. "The hair on the back of his neck is up."

The third man said, "We need to get help. He's not going to let anyone near her."

"He'll let me, watch. Come here boy," Tommaso called.

Zeus held his ground, looking down at Anna each time Tommaso called him. When Tommaso tried to move closer to the girl, Zeus met him with the same growl.

"Boss, we need to get help," the third man repeated.

Tommaso and Zeus stared at each other for several seconds before Tommaso nodded. They went back through the grass toward the driveway.

Zeus turned a couple of circles, resuming his position by her neck, whining ever so softly as he laid his head down across his legs.

"Captain Condello. I wish I could say good morning, but so far it hasn't been. What can I do for you?" Major Leone asked.

"It's about to get a little worse, Major. We have a report of another dead young woman. This one's not in the river, although she is on a pretty steep embankment by the river. She is less than a kilometer from where we found the other dead girl last week."

"Have you already started investigating it?"

"No sir, we just received the call, I wanted to notify you right away. I'm concerned there may be a connection and I suspect you might be having the same feeling. Due to the bombings, I assume we won't have any support."

"Most of the resources available have been sent to help the two bombing locations. I wouldn't expect to get any assistance from the RaCIS to help with evidence collection if I were you. The bombings were likely from the same group, the preliminary information suggests a terrorist group.

Unfortunately, your one dead body, now two, don't hold the same importance to the administration as the bombings."

"I understand, Major. Still, in case there may be any connection, and with Corporal Amici being gone, I would like to ask for your support. Well, a favor really."

"Go ahead, say it. I'm listening."

"We're fortunate to have an American detective here on vacation from California who has worked many homicide cases. He has family ties to Rumo with some cousins in the area. I would like to be able to use him as a consultant on this case, with your approval, of course. It's been many years since I worked these kinds of cases, and Officer Caviglia lacks experience."

Captain Condello fidgeted in his chair, mindful his odd request meant Major Leone would have to be willing to go out on a limb for him.

"Make an identification tag with our logo, it needs to state he is an American consultant. If he has a badge with him, ask him to use it with our ID. We will not supply him with a weapon. Under the circumstances I can approve this, at least until we can give you some help out there. Please make sure I get regular updates, especially if you find any connection."

"Thank you Major."

CHAPTER FIFTY-FIVE

Bruno and I had taken the last bites of our pastries when his cell phone rang.

"*Pronto Capitano*," Bruno said. "*Sì, sì. Sono al bar con* AJ." He paused. "*Può venire anche lui perche* Corporal Amici è *andatovia*?" He waited again. "*Va bene. Ciao Capitano*."

"Let's go." Bruno said. "Your suspicions were probably correct. We have another dead girl, down by the large lumberyard at the end of town across from the pizza restaurant. I told the captain we are together and I asked if you could come since Amici is gone. He said yes, we're meeting him at the office first."

I took one last drink of my Cappuccino, amused by Bruno's youthful exuberance.

I remember being like that when I first started. Someday he'll understand.

"We'll pay later," Bruno said, heading for the door.

Silently I slid out of the booth, ambling toward the cash register, reaching in my pocket for euros.

"We have to go *now*, AJ," Bruno snapped, obviously frustrated with me.

I laid down twenty euros on the counter. "*Ciao*, Donatella."

"*Ciao*, AJ...Bruno."

In a calm, steady voice I said, "You need to slow down. A dead body's not going anywhere, the one thing you have in those cases is time." Since I had his attention, I explained rushing to the scene almost always leads to rushing at the scene. In the meantime, cops often destroy their own evidence.

"Slowing yourself down before you get there, you take control of the pace of the investigation."

I took Bruno's slight nod as confirmation I got through, maybe.

"One more thing…if I'm going solely as a bystander, that's one thing. If your captain wants my help, we do it my way."

Bruno did not say a word as we walked to my car. Getting inside, Bruno said, "I'm trying to decide what to tell the captain. Maybe I'll tell him you agree with us about Domenica probably being killed…we need to be careful with this investigation in case the two have something in common." Bruno rambled on about how the captain is not like Amici, he will want to do it the right way. I listened as Bruno continued convincing himself what to say.

At the Carabinieri office I followed Bruno inside.

"*Capitano!*"

Putting his hand up to stop Bruno while looking at me, Captain Condello said in English, "Not now Bruno."

The captain speaking English stunned Bruno, who stared wide-eyed and mouth open.

"What? You don't know everything about me," Condello said to Bruno. "I spent some time in America, learned some English like you did. Now, I need to get AJ his official Consultant identification." Condello turned to me.

"I've already run this by Major Leone. He's in support of us using you as a consultant."

I nodded, and grinned at the captain, who totally caught Bruno off guard.

"Bruno, close your mouth and go get your uniform on," Condello said.

Bruno shook his head, still a little shocked, before bounding up the stairs to his room.

"We cannot provide you a weapon. I hope you understand."

"Not a problem, Sir," I said.

"Do you have a badge of some kind?"

"Yes. I have my flat badge with my American police ID," I said, reaching for my back pocket.

Condello held up his hand. "*Bene, bene*. I need to take your picture and laminate this ID for you before we go to the scene."

"Sounds good. I would like to say one thing though."

"AJ, relax. I would not ask for your expertise, and then try to control you." Condello explained it had been years since he investigated cases like these. He admitted to being a little overwhelmed by a second body showing up, in addition to still having limited resources.

"In return for not controlling you, all I ask is for you to make it look like I'm making the decisions when anyone other than the three of us are around. I cannot afford to have the people in this valley questioning my ability to make decisions."

Smiling, I said, "I bet. As fast as rumors fly around here that would not be good. I'll make sure nobody questions your being in charge. The last thing I want to do is cause any problems. Thank you for trusting me."

Condello nodded. "It's probably best for you to show up in your own car rather than '*the new American*' getting out of the Carabinieri car."

"Yeah, I agree."

Captain Condello finished my ID about the same time Bruno came downstairs. They drove off ahead of me while I waited in my car for several minutes, hoping my getting so deeply involved would not set me back.

CHAPTER FIFTY-SIX

I decided not to park too closely, so I turned into the driveway of the pizzeria taking a few deep breaths before walking back down the driveway.

I crossed the road, taking in the lumberyard on the other side of the river to my right. In front of me, well below roadway level, stood an old wooden work shed.

I noticed what looked like consistent blood spots on the sidewalk. Left, right, left, right…pretty evenly spaced. Blood spots continued down the driveway toward the work shed.

Looking over the railing at the shed below I remained on the sidewalk. The long driveway came up the opposite side to a widened asphalt area where the patrol cars were parked.

The streetlight by the railing gave me a bad feeling. It probably helped the killer see things clearly, while at the same time it meant we had no witness since he would have been easy to see. Dumping her right off the main road in a decently lit area…I wondered if he liked the risk of being seen.

The trail of blood spots came up the other side of the drive, drifting toward the grass bordering the asphalt parking area. No one had seen me yet, they were busy talking and looking down the side of the hill.

So much for any possible evidence where the killer might have parked.

I could see a path had been made through the tall grass going down the hillside at an angle. There they were—I could see them both and knelt down, not wanting to startle him.

The German shepherd was lying by the woman's shoulder with his head facing me. I realized I'd met the dog before when I jogged by the lumberyard. Having been a canine handler early in my career, I appreciated his being in the protection mode—I could not approach too quickly.

"Those blood spots belong to you, don't they buddy," I whispered, still squatting to minimize any threat to him.

They still don't have a clue I'm here.

"You're trying to make sure nobody else hurts her, aren't you? You're a *good boy* for protecting her," I said in a quiet, high-pitched tone. While I continued praising him, the dog slowly stood, lightly wagging his tail.

Poor guy, he's hurting inside.

He laid down by her feet, ears slightly back, continuing to stare at me. We were starting to make a connection.

Gradually I made my way back to the patrol car closest to the people and waited.

Bruno and Captain Condello finally saw me. Condello said something to Bruno who nodded, then walked toward me. The group by the hillside briefly stopped talking when they saw me.

"*Il poliziotto Americano*," one of the men said.

Giorgio nailed it, the whole town of Rumo knew.

Bruno thanked me again on behalf of Captain Condello. I had no difficulty showing him the respect his position deserved.

"Now, we have a problem," Bruno said. "There is …"

"The dog protecting the woman," I said, finishing Bruno's

statement. "Sorry, bad habit. I'm working on it. Go ahead. What were you saying?"

Bewildered, Bruno asked, "How'd you know?"

"Remember what I said earlier about approaching slowly?"

Bruno nodded, a foreboding look on his face like he knew the training had begun.

I described the dog's bloodied footprints on the sidewalk, along with the trail he left up to the path in the grass behind the cars. "I've been here, I'd guess, roughly five minutes, squatting down by the path, talking with the dog."

It baffled Bruno, who first looked at the drive, then at the path, then back to me. I reached out and grasped his right hand. Loud enough for the others to hear, "Absolutely. If I can provide any assistance for Captain Condello I'd be happy to help."

Finally, Bruno realized my intent. He walked me over to meet with Captain Condello, and we shook hands, too. We quietly agreed to speak English unless others were around, using Bruno to translate in those situations.

"He doesn't know what to think about your English," I said to Captain Condello, nodding in Bruno's direction.

With a hint of a smile Captain Condello said, "It's normal. Many people my age do not speak any English. He will see in due time, he and I are more alike than he realized."

"I'm right here. You don't have to talk about me like I don't exist," Bruno said, a bit of frustration in his voice.

I grinned slightly, the youngest officer being at the mercy of us more experienced, wiser men. I patted Bruno on his shoulder for reassurance.

Once I established Bruno had crime scene tape I directed him to get the bystanders back to the sidewalk, move the Carabinieri cars, and then get the tape up from the sidewalk railing by the shed to the railing near the "Welcome to Rumo" sign. Something told me to have him put tape up to block off the open grass area by the Welcome sign also.

Bruno did what I asked, so I had yet to see his rebel side.

I asked Captain Condello if he believed Domenica had been murdered, to which he said yes.

"Someday when I have time I will explain the Italian Carabinieri system. Bruno's frustrations are felt by many officers, myself included. As for now, simply accept it is far more military in structure than American police departments. I love being a member of the Carabinieri, but it's not the kind of system where one can be an individual since you are part of the larger organization."

I appreciated their frustrations. I loved being a detective, despite often struggling with administrators' decisions. We could definitely compare stories.

"I think you comprehend as well as I do, the chances of these two bodies showing up in this quiet, family-type community, and not being connected is pretty slim."

"Sadly, I do, AJ."

CHAPTER FIFTY-SEVEN

When I got to the edge of the hillside, I saw the dog lying by the woman's head again. Without standing he crept along the ground so he could turn to look up at me.

Although I never claimed to be a *Dog Whisperer,* I had long ago learned I needed to trust their intelligence and instincts. There are some people dogs connect with better than others and I considered myself fortunate to be one of the former.

"I don't run the show here, bud. You're going to have to work with me. They're gonna want to get to her soon." As far as I was concerned we could wait until he was ready to let us down there since he had bled for her.

Bruno walked up behind me saying he thought we might have to put the dog down to get to her. The dog bound to his feet, barking aggressively. I glanced at Bruno, nonverbally telling him to leave with a quick tilt of my head.

"Good boy," I said. "I'll be back in a minute." Once the dog laid down I stepped away.

I asked Bruno to find out what he could from the people on the sidewalk. He told me the woman and the young kid were merely bystanders. The oldest of the three men up front, Tommaso, happened to be the owner of the lumberyard and Zeus, the dog. The other two men were Tommaso's employees who followed him. Zeus had dug out through the asphalt and dirt to get underneath the fence. Apparently when he heard Tommaso calling for him, Zeus came back, got them, and took them to her.

"So, they made it all the way down to her?" I asked.

"No. That's the strange part," Bruno said. "Zeus wanted to show them the woman, only he would not let them get close to her."

Tommaso told Bruno they followed the same path as Zeus. He said they had gone about seven meters before Zeus started growling at them.

"Nice," I said, pleased with what Bruno learned. "So, then these marks I see in the grass right here are from somebody else. Wouldn't you agree?"

"Yes, they were all sure they went in from over there at an angle through the tall grass, not up here," Bruno said.

Captain Condello walked up joining in on the conversation.

"What are we going to do about the dog?"

"Zeus, his name is Zeus. I think I've built up a little bit of a rapport with him. If it's okay with you I would like to see if I could get him to let us in. I want to try to preserve the area as best as possible. If we have to drag him out of there, who knows what evidence will be destroyed."

Captain Condello thought about it as he walked over to the edge and looked down.

"I'll give you thirty minutes. If not by then we need to discuss other options."

"Fair enough," I said. I sent Bruno on a mission to get a leash for Zeus from Tommaso, along with directions of what I wanted him to do with it once he got it.

After Bruno headed for Tommaso I eased over to the edge of the hillside, squatting down. Seeing me, Zeus stood and slowly wagged his tail before lying back down.

"Good boy Zeus. I'm going to come see you," I said in my high-pitched tone.

Standing, I turned my attention to Captain Condello. "This might be a good time for you to call Bruno over, loud enough for others to hear, tell him to give me the directive to go see if I can get the dog before you have to take another course of action." I could see the appreciation on his face when he caught on.

Condello called Bruno over, doing as I had suggested. After Bruno translated I replied formally, "Yes sir," then walked over to where Zeus had run down.

My descent began a few feet below Zeus's original path. He stood, watching me closely. I took my time, constantly talking to Zeus, praising him often, working to build his trust.

I turned slightly left when adjacent with the girl, slowly making my way toward her. I paused beside each tree while I worked my way closer, keeping a close eye on Zeus' body posture. Two trees away from the girl I squatted down and leaned against one.

"You're a good boy," I said in a soft tone.

"She's your friend, you did everything you could to protect her, making sure nothing else happened to her. I want to help her be with her parents one more time. I know you saw who did this, the same way I'm certain you understand I'm here to help her."

Zeus made his way over to me, looking directly into my eyes with complete sadness. I stayed squatted and continued talking while I softly petted his head. After a short time Zeus turned, looked back at me as if to say, "Come with me," and we began our walk back to her together.

I HEARD THE LEASH LAND SOMEWHERE BEHIND ME about the time I got to the young woman. Zeus went up near her head, did one complete circle, lying down with his jaw up against the top of her head.

I crouched down by the girl, my eyes taking it all in, trying to determine what belonged, versus what might possibly be evidence. Scanning up the hillside toward the spot where I believed she had been dumped, I could see what appeared to be two shoe tracks with disturbed ground in between them.

This reminds me of being a young kid in New Mexico, sliding down a hillside in the snow.

I recalled how I tried to stay on my feet, often falling backward and sliding down on my bahooda, as my mom used to call it. The tracks I left in the snow were almost exactly the same as the tracks I could see down the hillside.

The shoe tracks were two to three feet apart, while the grass on both sides appeared disturbed at least another foot. When I looked at the bottoms of the young woman's tennis shoes, I could not find a correlation of mud and grass from the hillside.

Even though the girl's pants had mud and grass all around them, they lacked the heavy stains in the buttocks area of the jeans I expected to see.

The backs of the girls' shoes caught my attention. Both shoes had even dirt marks extending up from the heel about an inch on the back seam of the shoe. The dirt marks did not appear consistent with the muddy type soil on the hillside.

Drag marks. They dragged her somewhere else, then dumped her down this hill.

The girl's shirt on her back had crept up about an inch from the waistline of her pants. I saw what looked like possible scratch marks on her back knowing I would have to wait to confirm it until after pictures were taken. Then I noticed her forehead.

What are the odds her head would end up resting against the tree?

I realized a defense attorney would argue it would be possible for her head to strike the tree as she came to a stop, bounce back, then roll up against the tree as gravity would be drawing her downhill towards it.

She would've had to slide on her feet with her head upright, then go horizontal right before she struck the tree, in order to perfectly end up against it. The more I looked, the more convinced I became the possibility seemed remote at best.

Looking at the tracks one more time I could see they came within a foot of where the girl stopped. The killer wouldn't follow her down here except for one reason—*to stage her.*

Looking at her head one last time I spotted something in the back of her hair. Inspecting the area closer without touching her, I smiled. I understood how lucky we were. A lab would have to confirm it, although I felt certain she had carpet fibers in her hair. Tangible evidence—assuming we could get some assistance in the future.

I softly petted Zeus' head.

"We need to go now boy," I said, looking into his eyes.

Zeus stood, licking her cheek one last time and I turned to begin walking the path Zeus had taken, him walking next to my left leg. I stopped for a brief second to pick up his leash.

He doesn't need this, I thought.

Carrying the leash, we walked up to the asphalt driveway area together, side-by-side, stopping at the crime scene tape. Handing Tommaso the leash, I knelt beside Zeus, putting my arm around his neck.

"I'm proud of you," I whispered in his ear.

Zeus licked me on the face and then stepped toward Tommaso. His gait slow, his steps gentle on his raw front paws.

The crowd of people seemed stunned by Zeus being so subdued, not to mention letting *the American stranger*, a man none of them knew, grab him around the neck. Tommaso reached down and petted Zeus on the head. Without saying a word he turned on the sidewalk to head back to the lumberyard, Zeus by his side.

CHAPTER FIFTY-EIGHT

He called in sick to work, having hardly slept. When he did, seeing *Number Two* lying against the tree with her back to it instead of her head like he left her jolted him awake. Her eyes had been looking at him, staring directly into his. He awoke to being covered in sweat, the possibility *Number Two* had been moved running through his head.

At 8 a.m. he walked up the steep hill to the main road. Turning left, he arrived at *Famiglia Cooperativa* in less than a minute. His intention had been to get a few food items for his father. The two women's conversation derailed his plan.

"I heard they found Anna Bertolli's body," the clerk said, putting the purchased items in the bag the shopper brought with her.

"Nooo!" the shopper replied, shock in her voice. "Please tell me she ..."

"I wish I could...I heard she's dead. My brother-in-law who works at the lumberyard down by the bridge said he saw her. When they tried to get to her Tommaso's German shepherd protected her. He wouldn't let the men get close to Anna."

"Oh my God. I feel so bad for her parents. I can't find the words," the shopper said sorrowfully.

"Such a sweet girl," the clerk said.

"You don't think somebody killed her, do you?" the shopper asked.

"I'm not sure. My brother-in-law texted the American policeman people talk about is there, helping the Carabinieri."

The shopper started to cry.

The clerk went around the counter; the two women hugged and cried.

Temporarily paralyzed by the conversation, the women crying shook him from his stupor. Setting the small hand held basket down on the floor, he headed for the door.

Walking, his body subconsciously functioned to get him home while his mind focused on Number Two. The internal conversation bounded back and forth.

"How could she have been found?"

"Nobody saw me. The couple had no clue about me."

"Did you leave anything behind?"

"I looked over the area before I left. I made sure I got the rope from the metal rail."

"You can't go there. It's too risky."

"I have to see if what they said is true."

"It's foolish to go."

"It's exciting. Dangerous, but exciting."

Reaching his house he never went inside.

The drive from his village of Mione happened robotically. Rounding the corner near the edge of town by the wooden greeting sign, he could not believe his own eyes.

"My God. They were right," he said.

The fear and the sheer excitement were one. Faintly shaking, the hair on the back of his neck tingled. He stared—intoxicated.

The two Carabinieri cars parked along the sidewalk railing where he had tied his rope nearly brought him to a complete stop. His internal conflict continued to rage.

"*Turn around.*" Still, at the same time, "*Keep driving. Slowly.*"

The car crept forward, things coming into sharp focus. Noticing the crime scene tape from the back of the Carabinieri car to the sidewalk rail he felt his chest restricting. His breathing labored.

The car continued to edge forward. He functioned in a fog, no realization of his actions beyond his eyes scanning the area behind the crime scene tape.

Then he saw him—the American.

The man he nearly hit the night before stood next to the dog from the lumberyard. The car jerked to a stop.

The pressure in his chest became heavy, like an elephant sitting on him.

CHAPTER FIFTY-NINE

Tommaso began walking away with Zeus when I turned to my right. The car stopped almost directly across from me and the face flashed through my memory.

That's him, the same kid who almost hit me last night.

Our eyes met…his face read fear. Quickly turning his head away from me, he forced the gearshift into its slot.

"Stop! Stop! *Polizia*!" I grabbed the crime scene tape, lifting it to go under.

My eyes shot over in time to see Zeus looking in my direction when he caught it—the scent.

Clearing the crime scene tape I hesitated for a split second, instinctively reaching for my gun on my right hip that did not exist.

Unnerved for a split-second, my mind shifted gears and I began racing toward the car. I could see Zeus locked onto the driver's fearful body odor. I would not be alone.

Zeus instantly hit full speed, aiming for the open driver's door window. The man floored the accelerator as the two of us were converging for his door. Zeus leapt for the open window, his jaws open for the attack. The driver, seeing Zeus at the last second, instinctively leaned away, jerking the car to the right. Zeus's jaws snapped together, narrowly missing the driver's shoulder.

Zeus hit the door before dropping to the ground in front of me.

The gears engaged, the tires grabbed, and the car sprang to life, leaving the area at a high speed.

Tommaso and I reached Zeus at the same time. Before we had time to worry about injuries, Zeus sprang to his feet ready to chase the car. Tommaso grabbed Zeus' collar, snapping the clip of the leash onto the collar's dead ring.

I looked up and the car had gone too far for me to get any more of the license plate than I had from the night before.

A young woman stood by the stacks of lumber across the street, her hands together, slightly covering her mouth. A frightened bystander I presumed, the car having headed directly at her for a brief second. I could not believe my eyes. The woman had the appearance of a young version of Bethany, right down to her petite frame and her short dark hair. I had to force myself to turn and head for Captain Condello.

Marina and Anna had been friends for over ten years. She dreaded something bad had happened when Anna failed to show up the evening before at La Vecchia Segheria. Anna would have called her to tell her if her plans had change, but Marina had not received a call. She tried several times to call Anna during the night, never getting any response.

Shortly after eight in the morning Marina drove the main road through Rumo toward the pizzeria. She knew Anna walked the same route to meet her after work. As she rounded the last turn by the Rumo sign she saw the Carabinieri cars and several people near the bridge. Slowly driving by, Marina nearly got sick when she saw the crime scene tape. She stood by the stacks of lumber knowing she could not handle talking to anyone about her best friend.

Marina had been standing for a few minutes when she saw the man come up the hillside with the German shepherd next to him. She did not recognize the man, the dog on the other hand she had seen before at the lumberyard. Anna befriended Zeus, regularly talking to him and giving him treats.

Looking over the crowd Marina noticed one of the owners of the lumberyard, a frequent customer of the pizzeria.

A blue car entered her peripheral vision and stopped.

The man with Zeus yelled, "*Stop! Stop! Polizia!*"

Zeus jumped, and the driver leaned in her direction as Zeus tried to bite him. For a brief instant the car started towards her, the driver's face clear and panic in his eyes as he stared in her direction. She knew immediately she recognized him.

Though her mind raced at full speed, it felt like slow motion as she connected the dots. Believing the man and the dog somehow recognized the driver tipped the scale causing her to cover her mouth with her hands.

She stood motionless as the car sped off. Zeus went to his owner, but the man who yelled at the driver stared at her, almost as if he knew her. When he finally turned away Marina exhaled deeply.

Catching up to the dog's owner she asked, "*Scusi. Ci hai giat*à?" she asked, taking a chance they may have found Anna.

"*L'è la femma che me tegniva fieterà el ciain*," the man said.

Hearing him say the woman who always fed his dog, Marina turned and threw up. In the distance Marina heard him ask if they were friends as she took off running to her car.

Marina did not want to be the one to tell Anna's parents. She also knew she did not want them to hear it from a stranger who would not show them respect. Wiping away her tears, Marina knew she had to make sure it was Anna before she went to their house.

Marina drove her car to the same area she had been standing, backing up to one of the stacks of lumber.

Putting her head in her hands the crying returned.

CHAPTER SIXTY

Several things were running through my mind while I crossed under the crime scene tape. So much had happened in such a short period of time.

Wait a second, she looked like Bethany and I didn't have a flashback.

I spun around, but she had already left. Taking a few steps I spotted her, running in the general direction of where I had parked.

Not having a flashback, especially with her close resemblance to Bethany, pleased me. On the other hand, realizing our likely suspect drove away did not.

It's still progress right? I'll take it.

Walking back toward the hillside a sense of clarity overtook me. Trying to figure out the identity of the young man in the car would have to wait. Resources were limited to the three of us. We needed to preserve the crime scene and the woman's body first. As much as I wanted to go after him, I had to prioritize our responsibilities…we had a homicide on our hands.

"The young man who fled in the blue car is almost assuredly our suspect," I said to Bruno and Captain Condello.

I paused long enough for the statement to set in, not long enough for questions.

"He almost hit me on the road last night. I sensed by his

reaction he seemed worried about something…strangely, it didn't seem like it had anything to do with almost hitting me. The car is a Toyota Yaris. I have a partial plate, CM441, and I'm pretty sure two more letters are behind it. I'm not positive, though. Maybe you could get somebody in Cles to start trying to hunt down the missing letters. We also need a BOL out for the car."

"What makes you think he's our suspect?" Bruno asked.

"The panicked look on his face last night, being at the crime scene today, driving off quickly when being spotted, and Zeus recognizing him, as strange as it may sound."

"At Cadet training they told us people who start fires are often in the crowd. Is that true with killers?" Bruno asked.

"It can be. Some collect trophies from their victims, some return to the scene to relive the thrill, some do both. A defense attorney would say the guy has to leave town, and this is the main way to go. He got caught up in seeing the police cars and the crime scene tape and panicked when I yelled at him. I would argue the same thing. All we need to do is come up with the evidence to disprove the argument. Easier said than done, right?"

"Well, it seems like you're pretty convinced he is our suspect though," Captain Condello said.

"Yes, sir. I am. This is a small community and word sure seems to travel fast." *Sometimes accurately, sometimes not so much*, I thought.

"I think he probably heard we were here, and he had to come see for himself. The look on his face, I don't know, it felt like we surprised him. Like he couldn't believe she had been found so fast."

"All right, I'll contact the office in Cles to get them started on the BOL and the license plate," Condello said.

The crime scene already had the appearance of a homicide. Sadly, I felt pretty certain the victim would turn out to be the missing girl from last night. I began to feel a drive inside of me I had not had in a long time.

"I think this guy might've had her in his car last night when he almost hit me based on what I believe are carpet fibers in her hair."

Bruno commented it might have been a long time before anyone found the girl had it not been for Zeus. I had to agree...even though Zeus would not technically be considered a witness, I had no doubt in my mind he knew who killed the girl.

Captain Condello informed us not to expect assistance from the RaCIS for evidence collection due to last night's bombings. "They were likely from the same terrorist group; our investigation probably means nothing to the administration right now."

Strangely, there was comfort in being put on notice from the beginning so we did not keep looking over our shoulder for help. I had confidence Bruno and I could handle it.

"When I'm done with the call to Cles, I'll start getting names and any information they have," Condello said. "If you need help from the volunteer firemen to get her body up the hill tell me, I can start making phone calls."

Heading down the hillside Bruno and I stayed on the path Zeus had already made. We began placing markers near items to be photographed as evidence and collected.

While Bruno began photographing I squatted by the girl's head. I looked to my left where I saw a path through the tall grass leading away from the girl's head, parallel to the roadway.

"Bruno, come over here, tell me what you see."

I had him squat by her head, facing away from her and asked him to scan the whole area.

After a brief period Bruno cautiously said, "It sort of looks like some kind of a path to my right, in the tall grass."

"*Perfetto*," I announced, excited he saw it. "I think so, too. We need to photograph it and follow it. See where it takes us."

After a short distance the path abruptly stopped.

"How far do you think we went?" I asked.

"I'd say maybe three hundred meters," Bruno said. "Look, on the hillside going up toward the road."

We could see concentric disturbances in the grassy hillside, alternating from left to right, in a nearly equal distance from each other.

"It looks like they go all the way up the hillside to the metal guardrail by the sidewalk," I said.

Bruno began placing placards and photographing the path while I inspected the first few disturbances more closely.

"Any idea what they might be?" I asked.

"I hope this isn't too crazy," Bruno began, "it kind of looks like toe marks, like someone climbed up the hill there."

"Ain't nothing crazy about it. Hell, I think you nailed it. You're doing great, man. Keep trusting your instincts. This is too coincidental for the path to lead from her to here, turn ninety degrees, and go up the hill. There are no slip marks or areas where it looks like a hand might have been used for balance. So, if I had to guess, I would say they had a rappel rope waiting."

Bruno looked at the disturbances one last time, shaking his head. "How do you piece the puzzle together so quickly?"

I let his question slide by and asked him to get the captain over to the guardrail directly above us.

Two minutes later Captain Condello leaned over the guardrail.

"Can you look at the last two meters of the railing for me?" Condello being a seasoned-officer, he did not need for me to give him specifics, he knew to look for anything out of place. Besides, I wanted Bruno to see first-hand how to ask an open-ended question without leading the person. I had seen good statements and evidence tossed as "fruit of the poisonous tree" because some cop coerced someone by saying too much.

Condello inspected the railing closely, using his flashlight to highlight it. "At the top and bottom where the metal is sharpest it appears like there may be some kind of a rope fiber. The fibers on both look similar from what I can tell."

CHAPTER SIXTY-ONE

Racing through the countryside between Livo and Cles, his mind nearly kept pace with the car. Encountering traffic near Cles brought his concentration back to driving.

His whole body tingled, scared and excited at the same time. The challenge level had grown dramatically, meaning he would have to make some quick changes.

The man he almost hit the night before had to be the American policeman people spoke about.

The Carabinieri increased their skill level with the American. The test will be, can I elevate mine? His lip rising on one side broke the solemnness on his face, a nefarious smirk settling in.

Excited by the pressure, he began thinking of what he would say to the American when they were face-to-face. Would he tell him about his past as a child…what he had to endure? Maybe he would tell him *Number One* and *Number Two* both got what they deserved, one for trying to abandon him, the other for dissing him three times.

His speech to the American started taking shape.

Nearing the piazza toward the middle of town he saw the sign, *Parrucchiere*, for the hair salon. Suddenly he knew—make some changes to himself. First, he had to take care of the car.

Remaining on the main road he recalled some used car dealers. Nearing the area, he saw a dealership on his left, although they were all higher end cars. Seconds later he found it, a small dealership.

Finding the right car did not take long. An old, faded green, 2008 Fiat Panda hatchback would be the perfect change.

This will throw the American off, he thought.

Seeing the young kid approaching, he knew it would be a quick trade since the kid would focus on his commission. In under an hour he drove off the lot in the Fiat.

He drove the short distance to the Poli supermarket and decided to get the items for his father he should have gotten at the Cooperativa earlier. While shopping he thought about *Number Two*, and how they found her so quickly.

He had watched the wooden shed area for several minutes and no one had gotten out of a vehicle where he dumped the body. He felt certain it would not have been a lumberyard employee, they had no reason to look down the hillside.

Placing the bread in the basket, it hit him.

The damn dog! He must have had something to do with it.

Sergio realized the dog being outside of the lumberyard with the owner, not on a leash, could not have been coincidence. He definitely played some part. For his role, the dog needed to go—with poison.

After leaving the market he drove back to the piazza square. Many of the businesses could only be reached by walking, so he parked in the public parking area directly across from the large three-story Carabinieri office.

He parked close to the main road, watched for a few seconds and got out. Not seeing any police activity in the area he bound up the first set of stairs to a sidewalk where he quickly fit in with the crowd.

Within minutes he found a small curio-type shop catering mostly to tourists. He picked out a cheap pair of sunglasses with a thick black frame, silver earpieces and nearly oval eyeglass.

Continuing through the shop he spotted maroon baseball hats with a large Italia insignia on the front. The hats were adjustable with a Velcro strip in the back. He found a mirror on the wall nearby and tried on the hat, deciding he liked the look. After paying, it was time to find a salon.

He spotted a small jewelry store right down from the tourist shop. Until now he had never thought about earrings as part of the change. The ones in the front window area caught his attention and something told him to try it. He knew studs were allowed at the Pomarella plant so he chose a sterling silver pair. Fifteen minutes later he walked out of the store, a stud in each lobe.

Turning right he continued through the piazza where he found the *Parrucchiere*. A cute, young girl with tattoos up and down her arms greeted him.

"I want a different look, not over the top though," he said. "And I want it blonde."

With a smug smile, she grabbed his hand.

"Don't worry, we will start conservative this time. You'll be back." She winked and laid him back in her chair.

Over the next couple hours she bleached, washed, dried, and cut his hair. Sitting him up she gave him a chance to look at the final product. He smiled—she nailed it.

The sides and back were now stubble. She shortened the top by at least half of what it used to be and had slicked it back in the front. The more he stared at it the more he liked it. He gently kissed the back of her hand as he slid one hundred and fifty euros in it. Staring at each other, smiling, he stood and walked out, neither of them saying a word.

Leaving the salon he slid on his new sunglasses. His appearance had changed enough he would be hard to connect to the old Toyota. He walked with confidence, feeling empowered. Approaching the public parking area next to the Carabinieri office he passed by two officers. He greeted them, receiving head nods in return as they kept walking and talking to each other.

Try to keep up with me now, mister great American policeman.

Leaving Cles he chose a route taking him by the lake, through Cagnò, and by the Pomarella plant as if he were going home from work. He had been in Cles for several hours, so he could not imagine they would all still be at the lumberyard. Fighting his urge to drive by there one more time, he decided to play it safe—the back way home was best.

CHAPTER SIXTY-TWO

After collecting the rope fibers we needed to go back down and move the girl's body to see if there would be any evidence. Bruno grabbed his camera and evidence collection kit.

"We need to take our time as we examine her, along with the immediate area around her. I've always believed the body will talk to you if you listen," I said.

Bruno looked at me as though I were deranged. "What are you saying?"

"Obviously a dead body can't actually speak to you, so you can stop looking at me like I'm totally crazy," I said with a grin.

"It's kind of like the difference between hearing someone and actually listening to them…an investigator can do the same thing. You can hear the body speak to you, kind of like the obvious outward signs…or you can choose to listen to the little things it has to say. I've found it's usually the fine details a body shares with you that are most important."

I gave him examples of the way the body is laying, the direction of a mark or bruise, the placement of a hand, or the faintest fiber could all be speaking about what happened.

"You'll understand better as we go along."

Bruno shook his head, trying to take it all in. After pointing a few things out, I hoped he could start picking up on it without me directing him.

I slightly lifted the back of her shirt while Bruno photographed the abrasions. Something pressed all the way across her back, scraping downward from the middle of her back to the waist of her pants. The scrape marks were even and consistent. I already knew she had been dragged. These marks gave me the feeling she must have been pulled up against the edge of something to make such a consistent pattern.

"What is her back telling you?" I asked.

Bruno paused, followed by giving me the exact same assessment.

"The bruising seems slight, almost more of a scratch really. Plus, the dirt on the back of her tennis shoes is consistent with her being dragged."

"I agree," I said. "That bruising is so slight because she was probably already dead. No blood circulation."

When I laid her shirt back down I thought I could see frayed threads. Using Bruno's flashlight I saw the disturbed fibers were roughly the same overall dimensions. On my mental *to do list* I added having her shirt inspected by the lab and compared to the marks on her back, whenever we finally got access to some technicians.

We wanted to look at her face so I carefully rolled her, laying her on her back.

"Why so, gentle?" Bruno asked respectfully.

"She's already been dealt a bad hand, the least I can do is treat her with dignity."

Looking closely at her face, the obvious large bruise and welt on her forehead stood out. "Tell me what you think about this bruise," I said.

"Hmm, it appears to cross a large portion of her forehead. In some ways it's kind of like the scrapes on her back are, um, um, *simmetrico*. There's way more bruising than on her back so I would say it probably happened before she died. I'm not sure how to explain it, it's pretty obvious though, the bruise is not from that tree," Bruno said, as he pointed first to her forehead, then to the tree.

This kid's got some natural instincts for this, I thought.

"Excellent. Once again, we agree. There's nothing consistent with her hitting a tree at high speed coming down the hill. Separately, you're dead on about the difference in this bruise compared to marks on her back, and whether she had blood pumping or not." I held a ruler for him to show height and width as he snapped a couple photos of the bruise.

"She looks like the picture of Anna Bertolli," Bruno said.

"Yeah, pretty sure it's her, unfortunately."

When Bruno finished photographing Anna's forehead I told him to open her eyes, so we could see if we have anything.

"What do you mean? What are we expecting to find?"

"Quit making it more difficult than it is," I stated. "Open her eyes, tell me what you see. Remember, let the body speak to you, don't predetermine what you expect to find."

Bruno being new to this stood out like a sore thumb. Gradually getting past his uneasiness, he finally knelt closer once he had them open.

"The whites of her eyes are kind of bloodshot…different though, almost like red dots," Bruno said.

"Those dots are petechiae. Remember Domenica, I commented how they often show up when a person has been strangled or asphyxiated. Now Anna has them too. Even though we can't say it's the same killer, at least we can say there's a common link at this point. Keep them open for a second, I'll snap some photographs."

I wanted to check one more thing before we went to talk with Captain Condello.

"Let's look under her fingernails, see if she left us anything."

"I'm guessing you're expecting to find something there."

I shrugged my shoulders.

"It's not so much I'm expecting to find something, remember, don't predetermine. I've seen a lot of victims who were choked or asphyxiated scratch their killer while trying to claw the killer's hands away from their face or their throat. Occasionally you'll actually get some skin deposits under their fingernails. Since ninety percent of the population are right-handed, odds are that's where we'll find something—hopefully."

Looking under each fingernail on Anna's right hand Bruno said, "*Merda*! I think I see deposits on a couple of them." Grabbing his flashlight, he took another look.

"I'm pretty sure there's something under her middle finger and her thumb. You want me to try to get it out for evidence?" Bruno asked.

"No, not yet," I said. Certain kinds of evidence collection demanded better lighting. "We'll put some bags over her hands and tape them closed until we can get to a better location where we can clip her fingernails to preserve it all. Let's go up and talk to the captain."

"*Merda?* What the heck does it mean?" I asked with a chuckle.

"Shit," Bruno said, a little red faced.

"Oooooo. Better be careful, you might start using foul language hanging around me." Slapping him on the back, I laughed.

At the top we saw Condello pacing while on the phone. He spoke in Italian, quite rapidly actually, his frustration rather obvious. Neither of us were about to interrupt him.

Walking towards us shaking his head, Captain Condello said, "We will definitely not get any assistance. I had hoped with two dead girls in the same week, and this one likely being a homicide, Major Leone would consider getting us some help. He said he can't afford to redirect the RaCIS to help with evidence collection."

He took a couple deep breaths to calm down before finishing.

"The one piece of good news is an officer in Cles sent a list to my email of possible license plates with the same letters and numbers from the one you gave me earlier, AJ. I have not had time to look at it yet."

"Not a problem," I said, intentionally trying to stay positive. I sensed they would follow my lead.

"It's good we have the list, maybe we can get something off it. For now, we need to get Anna's hands bagged, get her up the hill, and then get her to wherever it is you all would send a dead body. We need to make sure nobody works on her wherever you take her until we get a chance to look at her one last time and to cut her fingernails."

"I will work with the volunteer firemen to get Anna up the hill," Captain Condello said. "I can coordinate them picking up her body and preserving her hands. The firemen and the people from the mortuary will do exactly as I ask."

"We need to re-interview Domenica's parents, see if she had a boyfriend," I said. "If she did, a picture of him would be helpful, and any information about where he lives and what he drives. I think it's probably gonna be a dead end, but we have to start searching for any connection between these two girls; my gut says one killer did both of these. We also need to meet with Anna's parents. I'm curious to hear what they have to say."

"Let's go talk with these families," Bruno said. "It will work better if we are together. They probably would not feel comfortable with *just the American policeman*," he finished, with a sarcastic tone and a half-grin.

CHAPTER SIXTY-THREE

Bruno and I drove to Domenica's house in his patrol car. On the way I asked if he heard from Amici.

"Yes. I asked him to text me when he arrived. He said they allowed him to visit his mother for a couple minutes, since he got there so late last night. He didn't say anything about how she looked, and I couldn't decide if I should ask or not."

I shook my head to show him support. "Well, I'm glad he's there with her."

We were silent until we arrived. "You can run with this since you have more information about what Domenica said on Facebook. Please, let me know exactly what you asked and what she answered?"

"Got it," Bruno said, knocking on the door.

Domenica's mother, Penina, opened the door, not uttering a word. Her eyes were bloodshot and swollen.

"Ma'am, I am Officer Caviglia. This is AJ Conti, an American police consultant," Bruno said in Italian.

Penina looked at me, her sad eyes not shifting back. I pulled out my consultant ID and my badge. She never looked at them—she remained focused on me. Stepping aside she nodded her head for us to come in and directed us to the living room. We sat on the couch, she sat in a chair off to my right.

"Ma'am."

"Penina. Call me Penina," she directed.

"Yes ma'am, sorry, Penina," Bruno stumbled. "If possible we'd like to ask you and your husband a couple questions."

Penina told us her husband chose to comfort himself with alcohol at the bars ever since the private investigator turned up nothing.

"Ask your questions."

"Domenica talked on Facebook about leaving. Neither of you knew anything about her going?" Bruno asked.

"Her father and I don't do Facebook," Penina said angrily, before pausing to regroup. "Sorry. No." Her tone had softened and she remained somber. "Domenica regularly talked about America and Germany, always in passing."

Bruno translated after she answered like we had discussed.

"Did Domenica have a boyfriend?" Bruno asked.

"Yes, at least I would say so."

"What do you mean? It almost sounds like you're unsure."

"I would say something about her boyfriend, if he wasn't here she would glare at me and tell me he's not her boyfriend, they're only friends," Penina said.

"They had been together for almost four years though, since high school."

"Do you know his name?"

"Yes. It's Sergio. Sergio Fezzi, I believe. He lives in Rumo, in the village of Mione, although I'm not sure exactly where."

Penina described Sergio as a nice, grounded young man. She felt Domenica needed someone like him. They liked the fact he was a hard worker, a forklift driver at the Pomarella plant. Taking care of his father after his mother up and left them one day pleased them, too. Domenica did not feel the same way though.

"So, did it seem like a good relationship to you?"

"I felt bad for him," Penina said. "He really cared for her. She...she basically used him. It made me sad."

Penina told us she had seen Sergio two or three weeks after Domenica left. He seemed nice and respectful to her, no different than before. When Domenica came up in the conversation, she said he almost got angry, going on about Domenica's selfishness. He said, "She only cared about herself."

When Bruno translated, I stopped him.

"Ask her again if Sergio said, 'Domenica only cares about herself,' or only 'cared about herself.'"

Bruno asked Penina the question for me.

Pausing, she said, "I am pretty sure he said she only cared about herself." She looked at me like she did not understand why I wanted to know, although she never asked.

"Cared, not cares. Past tense, right?" Bruno asked me.

"You got it," I said.

When Bruno asked Penina for a picture of Sergio she said she did not have one, but did recall he drove a blue Toyota hatchback though.

"Is there anything else you feel is important?" Bruno asked.

Penina turned, facing me directly. Moving to the front of her chair she gently placed her left hand on my forearm.

"I know my sweet daughter did not have an accident. Someone did this to her. People are saying you investigate these types of things in America. Please help us to find out the truth."

Putting my left hand on top of hers, staring straight into her sad eyes, I listened to Bruno's translation.

"Please tell her I am so sorry for her loss, we promise to do our best."

Bruno translated. Penina's lips moved up, not to a smile,

more to an appreciation. Patting my arm, she said, "*Grazie signore. Grazie.*"

Penina's crying began as she hurried out of the room. We saw ourselves out.

SITTING IN HER CAR NEAR THE STACKS OF LUMBER across the street from the crime scene, Marina replayed in her mind when she first met him. Domenica introduced him as her boyfriend, then winked and shrugged ever so slightly, like, "Whatever." She recalled it had been at least a year ago.

Marina remembered Domenica called him Sergio. It seemed to Marina he had clearly been infatuated with Domenica. She recalled thinking Domenica was anything but infatuated, she liked Sergio for the sex.

Like others in town, Marina had heard of Domenica's plans to leave Italy someday.

I wonder if Sergio still lives in the same place he told me about when we first met, she thought.

Normally Marina would not have remembered the location except she had an aunt who lived in a house catty-corner to his.

Marina decided she needed to leave when she saw the young officer and the other man heading for the patrol car. She did not want them to see her and drove away as they got in. Marina went through Rumo, and entered the village of Mione.

Slowing as she approached the curve by Bar Lanterna, Marina turned near the bus stop. Knowing her aunt had gone to Bolzano, Marina parked her car so she could watch

Sergio's house. After nearly an hour with no activity, Marina heard a car coming. A small, faded green, old Fiat passed in front of her with a young man driving.

The car parked next to a three-story, white home Marina believed was Sergio's. When the driver got out Marina could see Sergio had tried to drastically change his looks. Hours before when she saw him he had dark hair, exactly like when she first met him with Domenica. He changed the color to blonde, and cut it much shorter on the sides.

After Sergio grabbed grocery bags, and headed into the first floor of the house, Marina started her car and left before he came back outside.

CHAPTER SIXTY-FOUR

"Isn't Bar Podetti up by Anna's house?" I asked.

"Yes, near there. Why?" Bruno asked.

"If you don't mind, before we go to Anna's house, maybe we can swing over there to see if Carlo Camioni is in the bar. If he's there I want you to translate like you did with Penina."

Walking into the bar, the bartender nodded to the right. Carlo sat in a booth near the back corner, his arm around a girl thirty years his junior. At the table I flashed my badge and ID, Bruno standing by my side in his uniform.

"It might be time for you to leave now," I gently said to the girl when she looked at me. Sure enough, my experiment worked—she understood English. She scrambled out of the booth, heading straight to the bar to watch us.

Sitting next to Carlo, I pointed for Bruno to sit across from me.

"So, you realize why we're here," Bruno said.

"Yeah. I heard you were asking around for me."

"What can you tell me about Domenica, the dead girl in the river?"

"I got nothing to hide. I saw her at the bus stop, sometime in October, pretty close to the Eurochocolate Festival, give or take a few days. I had my window down, saw her on the phone. The road's wide there so I got pretty close, heard a little bit of her phone conversation. She looked angry, apparently someone wouldn't pick her up. I got out of my car, walked up to her, offered her a ride."

"So what happened next?" Bruno asked.

"She turned down my offer. I didn't want to give up so easily. I smiled and got closer to her. I suggested she could stay with me for a night at the hotel in Cles. I reached out and put my hand on her butt. The instant I touched her she slapped me."

Carlo chortled, until he saw neither of us smiling.

"When she took off walking I started laughing. I told her, 'You don't know what you're missing.' She flipped me off, kept walking. Last time I saw her she was in my rearview mirror."

"Are you positive you never saw her again?"

"Yeah, I'm positive. Ain't seen her again. You want to hear what's funny?"

"What?"

"The dumb bitch would still be alive if she would have let me have some pussy," Carlo said, chortling again.

No sooner had Bruno finished translating when my elbow struck Carlo in the ribs. He bent over toward me gasping for air when my elbow got him square in the nose.

I slid out of the booth and Bruno followed, a shocked look on his face.

Rolling my shoulders, I said, "Maybe the asshole will learn to show some respect."

By the smiles on all the faces in the bar, apparently a lot of people besides us considered Carlo an asshole.

FIDGETING NERVOUSLY, BRUNO ASKED, "BEFORE WE GET there…I'm hoping, maybe…can you do this?"

Bruno had never done a death notification, so I agreed to do it. I explained the keys were being direct, but compassionate.

"Truthfully, most of the time they already know."

Pulling up to Anna's house I noticed a Volkswagen Jetta closest to the house, with a newer Suzuki Vitara behind it. We already knew Anna's father brought her car home. I figured the Jetta to be Anna's, protected by the Suzuki.

I no sooner got out when another car pulled in behind us. When the thin, dark haired woman driver began to get out I would have sworn I saw Bethany getting out of her car in my driveway as I stood in the doorway of my house. I froze right where I stood.

Bruno flung his door open and stood, thankfully startling me back to reality.

The girl stopped next to Bruno's car.

"So, are you related to these people?" I asked in English.

She stared at me for nearly ten seconds, her head canted to her right. "*Scusi*," she said, stepping around Bruno.

Right before she reached the house, I said, "I saw you get a good look at him this morning."

Coming to an abrupt stop she turned, glaring at me through squinted eyes. Silent, she turned back around and went to the door, walking in without knocking.

"What's that about?" Bruno asked.

"It's my way of confirming she'd been across the street from me when the guy fled this morning."

"How'd you know she could speak English?"

"Didn't for sure. Ever since I arrived in Italy I've heard a number of young people who speak English, at least to some extent. Kind of like the girl with Carlo. I took the chance and it worked."

The thought of mentioning how much the girl looks like Bethany crossed my mind, fortunately no more than a split second. If Bruno did not see my frozen stare before getting out of the car, then why bother.

I knocked on the door and within a few seconds a young woman appeared. I would have sworn it was Anna who answered, only ten years older.

"*Parli inglese*?" I asked, hoping someone spoke English.

"Yes, I do," she said. "Can I help you?"

I identified myself and Bruno, then showed her my consultant ID. I learned she was Anna's sister, Paola, and she offered to translate for me.

After Paola let us in the family gathered together in their living room, with the exception of Anna's mother who refused to come out of her bedroom. I had always believed the best way to tell a family their loved one had died was to gently say it right away, followed with being sorry for their loss. Which is exactly what I did.

The instant I finished the death notification, I said, "I realize this is difficult for you all. I need to ask some questions as soon as you are able to talk with me."

Paola, Nicolò, and the young woman all hugged each other while crying. At the same time we could hear Anna's mother crying in the bedroom.

After several minutes Paola wiped her eyes and took a deep breath. Her voice crackling, Paola said, "I will interpret for my father."

"Thank you. Can you tell me when you first believed Anna might be missing?" I asked.

"I think around three o'clock yesterday when my mother started saying she knew something bad happened to Anna. By the time I called my dad, close to four, asking him to come home from work, my mom said she knew Anna was dead."

Through Paola, Nicolò told us he learned Anna had gotten off work at 2:16 p.m., normal for her on Mondays. He found her car in the lot, although he had to use spare keys to get in. He found the seat all the way back instead of close to the steering wheel, her purse still under the driver's seat, an out of the ordinary dirty back seat, her broken glasses in the glovebox, and a new dent in the fender.

"Can you ask your father if it would be okay with him if I look over Anna's car?"

Before Paola could ask the question Nicolò shook his head yes.

Nicolò said something to Paola in Italian.

Turning back to me, tears forming in her eyes, Paola said, "My father said to tell you, he's certain God brought you here to find the killer of his daughter. Please, find my sister's killer."

Looking directly at Nicolò, I said, "I will do my best, I promise."

I stole a look at Bruno having a hard time with his emotions, along with everyone else in the room, myself included. I could not remember the last time I cried with a family.

Gathering myself, I turned to Paola. "In case we happen to come across a set of keys somewhere, can you tell me if there might have been anything special about Anna's keys? Maybe the number of keys, if any are colored?"

"Wait here one minute," Paola said, quickly taking off for another room. In the awkward silence I slowly made my way over to Nicolò, gently putting my right hand on his shoulder in an effort to say how sorry I was. The instant we made eye contact Nicolò broke down in tears, covering his face with his hands. The young woman sat next to Nicolò, trying to console him through her own tears.

Paola returned with a set of keys in her hands.

"Our sister Sofia, who was killed in a car accident, had given Anna and me this special key ring at Christmas the year before she died. You can see the silver letters are the first letters of each of our names. Sofia had one made for herself, too, so we all had one."

Pulling out my cell phone I took a picture of Paola's key ring. "It's beautiful how the letters flow together," I said. "Unique."

Paola broke down, rushing over to her father's arms. I set the keys on the kitchen counter.

The time had come for us to step outside.

CHAPTER SIXTY-FIVE

"What does her purse still being under the driver's seat mean to you," I asked Bruno as we walked around Anna's Jetta.

"Hmm, probably this had nothing to do with robbery."

"Dang, they did teach you something at Cadet training," I said, both of us grinning.

"I think I found the dent Mr. Bertolli spoke of," Bruno said, pointing at the top of the right front wheel well.

It seemed obvious the car had not been in a wreck since we could not find any paint transfer or cracking.

"You think the killer did it?" Bruno asked.

"Without a doubt." The dent appeared consistent with Anna's forehead, about two inches thick, about five inches long, and similar to the size of her bruise. When I asked Bruno where the dent came from he made the connection to Anna, too.

Bruno retrieved his camera and began taking photographs of the dent. Standing back, I stared at the passenger side of the car, thinking …

We discussed the possibilities of where Anna might have been attacked and Bruno brought up the driver's seat being moved for a larger person. That corresponded with no robbery based on her purse, which begged the question, why even get in her car if attacking her in the lot?

"I'd say he attacked her somewhere else, then took her car back to the plant," Bruno said. I smiled at his progress.

The door handles on the passenger side appeared to be freshly wiped down. Opening the right rear passenger door I found white cotton fibers at the bottom of the metal doorframe in three places.

"Do you recall what type of shirt Anna had on?"

"A white cotton shirt, I think maybe a t-shirt, right?" Bruno asked.

"Exactly. Kind of like these white fibers on this doorframe. And, look here," I said, pointing to the back seat.

"Blades of grass and dirt smudges on the vinyl seat. Anna supposedly kept a clean car," Bruno said. It seemed pretty clear to both of us Anna had been dragged into her car.

Something caught my attention on the far side of the back seat. Leaning in for a better look without disturbing the other evidence, I could not believe our luck.

"A spot of blood," I said, pointing to the front edge of the seat. DNA analysis would confirm what I already suspected, the blood spot and the skin under Anna's fingernails were from the same person—her killer.

I could not help being surprised by his leaving such evidence behind, given Anna had almost assuredly not been his first victim.

He must've been rushed or he would've cleaned this up.

"Don't her glasses being in the glove box seem kind of strange to you?" Bruno asked.

"Very. I haven't quite figured it out. In any case, all of it together, including the glasses, points to him being rushed. Or maybe nervous, I guess."

"Well, I think it all supports Nicolò's beliefs, the suspect had to have driven her car," Bruno said.

We were putting the camera and evidence in Bruno's car when we heard the house door open. Looking up, Paola was walking toward us.

"The Pomarella plant called," she said angrily, holding up her cell phone. "My father asked them yesterday to check on the video of the parking lot after he saw several cameras. One of the board members called to tell us the video cameras were not operating."

"Inoperable," I said in disbelief. "Did he or she say why?"

"When I pressed him about it he finally said the system accidentally got unplugged so it did not record," Paola said.

Damn. That's no coincidence.

I nodded, trying not to show my disgust, making it worse for Paola.

"By the way, since you're here, the girl who walked in right before I knocked on the door, who is she?" I asked.

"Marina, Anna's best friend. She works at the Pizzeria when she's not in classes at the University of Padua. She worked yesterday and Anna made plans to meet her when she got off work. She's been here off and on since last night, trying to comfort my parents."

"Okay thank you," I said, politely asking Paola not to touch Anna's car. "Please have Marina step out here for a quick second? Again, I'm sorry for your loss."

Paola began to tear up when she tried to say "thank you," and headed back inside.

MARINA STEPPED OUTSIDE, CROSSING HER ARMS IN front of her as she slowly began to walk toward me.

"Marina, I believe it is." *Hold it together, she's not Bethany,*

"I know you understand English so I presume you speak some. I'm not sure why but you seem like you're avoiding me. I suspect for some reason you don't trust the police, or maybe it's me. Anyway, I could see you were trying to comfort the family and I really respect you for that. I've written my number on this paper, all I'm asking is for you to take it and think about calling me if you can think of anything that would be helpful." I extended my hand with the paper in it.

Looking first at the paper, then up at me, Marina slowly reached her hand out. She took it, crossed her arms again, turned and headed toward the house.

I did not move, waiting to see what she would do.

At the door Marina paused. She unfolded the paper, looked at it, refolded it and put it in her pants pocket. Reaching for the door she hesitantly looked over her shoulder. Seeing us still looking at her, she turned her head.

"Marina," I barked to get her to stop. Then, with a softer tone, "Since you don't want to talk to me, and I'm pretty sure you want us to leave, it might be helpful if you moved your car so we could back out."

Marina went in the house, returning with her keys in her hand. Passing by me she looked up making eye contact and I noticed the slightest grin in the corners of her mouth. She backed her car into the road, keeping the engine running while Bruno backed out.

I made sure to wave at her, hoping to help her relax so I could build on her one slight grin. Her left hand barely came off the steering wheel enough for it to open up before returning to the wheel.

She pulled back into the driveway and walked to the doorway without looking back.

"She's holding onto something, possibly the driver of the car this morning," I said.

"Why don't we press her then?" Bruno asked, stopping in the middle of the road.

"Not yet," I said, wiggling my index finger at the windshield to tell him to get going.

"We have our hands full as it is. Besides, I think she's coming around. In an interview of a suspect, if you press too hard or too fast they lawyer up. Give them a little space, take your time, let them come to the conclusion they need to talk. We can give her a little time to see if she wants to cooperate rather than be forced. Not much time, but a little."

CHAPTER SIXTY-SIX

I had Bruno go to Bar Lanterna so I could get a soda.

"I'll stay here. I need to call Captain Condello, see what he wants us to do," Bruno said.

The quiet caught my attention before I saw Donatella behind the bar with her back to me.

"Hey there."

Donatella looked over her shoulder and smiled. She turned as I approached the stools, placing her hands together on the lip of the bar.

"Any chance I can get a soda to go?"

"How are you doing?" she asked, pausing…my soda not her priority.

I could see the concern for my well-being in Donatella's eyes.

"We finished speaking with the families of the two girls. I never struggled with it before but today was difficult, and sad. Actually though, staying busy helps keep my mind occupied."

Gently laying my hand on hers I said, "Thanks for asking."

Donatella's eyes shifted, her hesitation brief before turning to get my drink. She returned with an eight-ounce bottle. Seeing my smug smile, she chuckled.

"*Capisco*, I know, you think all Italian drinks are *piccoli*," her thumb and index finger almost touching.

"You read my mind," I said. "*Va bene*, the prices are *piccoli*, too." I grinned.

Setting the bottle on the counter Donatella said, "You can pay later when you have more time."

"I wish I could stay and talk with you, especially since nobody else is here."

"That would be nice." She looked past me, and said, "Bruno is waiting for you."

I looked over my shoulder, then back at her.

"Right now, you need to go," Donatella said. "Helping find who did this to Domenica and Anna, is what is important." She patted the back of my left hand and retreated into the office area out of sight.

Grabbing the bottle I took a long first drink walking toward the car. I felt pretty certain Donatella might be attracted to me, although she could be a tough read at times. I wondered about her ability to move on beyond her husband. Given my confusion about Bethany I totally understood.

No sooner had I concluded she might be interested in me, my internal devil's advocate wondered if Donatella would be telling herself not to get involved with an American who is going to leave. My ego felt like it was attached to a yoyo.

The man in the community people called Radio Scarpa walked by the car on my side. We greeted each other prior to Bruno backing out.

"Amici and I talked with him the other day. Scarpa told us he knew who killed the girl in the river," Bruno said as he chuckled.

"Did you question him?"

"No, of course not. He's Radio Scarpa. Why would I?"

"*Stop*. Pull back into the driveway," I said.

"You can't compartmentalize anyone in an investigation. Once you put them in some convenient section in your mind it's hard to see them as anything else."

Reluctantly, Bruno spoke with Scarpa and translated for me.

Turning to me, Bruno said in English, "He still says he saw what happened at the river and who did it. Like the other day."

Scarpa appeared certain he saw the man at the river with the girl a couple of days before the Eurochocolate Festival in October. He had been walking up the path by the community building. Shortly after he passed the bridge he saw the man.

"He held the girl, like a doll across his arms. Her arms and legs, they dangled," Scarpa said, holding both of his arms straight out, palms up.

The man saw Scarpa and got angry. He threatened to kill Scarpa's mom if he told anyone, then yelled at Scarpa to leave. Scarpa ran. When he looked back, the man was carrying the girl under the bridge.

"Did you see anything else?" Bruno asked.

"He laid her down under the bridge," Scarpa said. He watched the man get out of the water, slip going up the wall, ultimately driving off toward the pizzeria.

Scarpa felt dizzy and sweaty, so he went to the bus stop in Mocenigo to sit and rest. He said he has gone by the river several times since then and the girl remained under the bridge.

"Did you say anything to anybody?" Bruno asked.

"Nooo. He said he would kill my mom," Scarpa said, wide-eyed. "I didn't want my mom dead."

Bruno paused and waited.

Perfect Bruno, let him fill in the silence. I wondered if Bruno understood the technique or if it were by accident.

"Sometimes when I'm here he's at the stop sign over there," Scarpa said, pointing across the street.

"He points his finger like a gun, he pretends to shoot me." Scarpa's right hand demonstrated the action.

Scarpa did not know the man, although he had seen him before in Mione. Even though he could not determine the man's age, he compared the man to being young like Donatella's boys, not old like him.

"Can you remember what kind of car he drives?" Bruno asked.

"Blue. It's a blue car," Scarpa said.

"Thank you. If you see him again while we're here, tell us or Donatella," Bruno said.

"Sì, *sì*. *Ciao*," Scarpa said, walking off matter-of-factly to grab the newspaper on the table.

"Scarpa seems, kind of literal, like he doesn't grasp the importance of any of this," Bruno said.

"Does he need to grasp the importance to accurately repeat what he saw or how he felt?" I asked.

Bruno's reddened face and hustling to the car convinced me I might have gone too far, something else I had a tendency to do according to Sergeant Boykin.

"Good interview. You never led him once. Now we have a good idea our suspect lives somewhere around here," I said, my feeble attempt at trying to be positive.

"*Grazie*," Bruno said while getting in the car. "The fact is I should not have dismissed Scarpa so easily, simply because of some *etichetta*…I'm sorry, I'm frustrated with myself… all based on some label people may have given him."

"Look, you did a great job talking with him, making him comfortable enough to share something frightening to him," I said. "Don't beat yourself up, you really did do a good interview."

Bruno nodded, the corners of his mouth moving up slightly, the redness not so prevalent anymore.

Driving away from Bar Lanterna I saw a small white car ahead of us turn in our direction.

"It looks like Marina's car," I said.

Passing, Marina and I looked at each other, neither waving nor smiling at the other. Bruno had taken his foot off of the accelerator so we were coasting at a snail's pace. I looked over my shoulder and Marina's brake lights came on at the bus stop catty-corner to Bar Lanterna.

"She's turning right, wait, she parked between the bus stop and the house there," Bruno said, keeping an eye on her in the rearview mirror.

"I knew I'd seen her spotless white VW Polo before," I said. "It had to have been when I visited the bar. I never paid attention to who it belonged to. Well, the good news is it'll be easy to find her if we need to talk with her again."

"True, especially since Bar Lanterna seems to be your second home," Bruno said as he shifted into first gear.

"Or has it become your first?" He shot me his best rendition of a parental face, the one stating, *I'm not going to say anything, but you are about to get yourself into trouble.*

"Well, dad, if you must know, I went to Bar Lanterna to get a soda, nothing else," I said with a smirk on my face. "And, I'm glad I did. Now, we know who lives across from the bar."

"Yeah right. Because we finally left Bar Lanterna so you weren't distracted anymore," Bruno said, with a deadpan stare.

I laughed, *this young buck's trying to bust my chops.* I was enjoying the hell out of it. He could dish it out, I wanted to see if he could take it.

"Lest we not forget my friend, because of me wanting a soda, we now have an eyewitness named Scarpa. Do you happen to know who he is?"

Bruno's head jerked my direction, the look on his face caught somewhere between shock and distress.

I busted up laughing, causing him to do the same.

In less than a minute we were in the Village of Marcena. Turning left across from the Carabinieri office Bruno went by the parking lot next to Town Hall.

"One quick question," Bruno said.

"Oh, now we're back to police work?" I asked flashing a smug smile.

Bruno's eyes narrowed, I could almost see the daggers.

He still can't figure out how to take me sometimes.

"Why didn't the suspect kill Scarpa?" Bruno asked.

Now, my turn to wait for *him* to fill in the silence.

"What? Aren't you going to answer me?" Bruno asked, his tone bordering on irritation. "Why you looking at me like that?"

Patience. Wait for it.

"Ahh crap," Bruno said. "He didn't need to kill Scarpa. Who around here would believe Scarpa's story? We didn't."

Ta da. I'm really liking this kid. Watching him grow brought a sense of satisfaction.

Donatella knew this would happen.

"Enough said—can't keep the captain waiting," I said.

CHAPTER SIXTY-SEVEN

"Visits before the burial are often done in the home here, usually right after the person has passed. Unless it's a situation like this," Bruno said. He told me the dead are often not embalmed, with the person usually being buried at the graveyard the next day.

Arriving at the graveyard, we entered a grey, almost obscure, structure there where embalming's or cremations took place.

Walking in the door we saw the captain talking with a middle-aged man who did burial preparations and he offered to stay and assist us. Anna lay on a shiny smooth metal table and in some surreal way she had a content look about her.

"This looks like a standard autopsy table I'm used to seeing in California. Does this mean we have a pathologist coming to do an autopsy on her?"

Captain Condello slightly leaned his head sideways, pursed his lips and shook his head once.

"It's not so easy in Italy, I'm sorry to say. The Italian justice system became an adversarial system like America's in 1989. We can get what is called a judicial autopsy ordered by the prosecutor or a judge. Unlike America, frequently, actually most of the time, a pathologist for the prosecutor is appointed, a pathologist at the family's request is present, and the suspect or defendant can have a pathologist present as well.

"It is rare for a judicial autopsy to be approved, especially with no suspect or defendant named. It is perceived as unbalanced or unfair. One of the major complaints by police and prosecutors in Italy about autopsies is the breakdown or loss of evidence, with too much time needed to get approval for one. It's a much slower process than what you are used to."

"So, without directly saying it, you basically told me we aren't getting a judicial autopsy anytime soon."

"*Corretto*," the captain said, nodding.

I needed a tape recorder to document evidence we saw. Bruno had one in his briefcase in the car he offered to get.

"I'm sorry to hear about your system erring so heavily on the side of caution," I said. "In cases like this, an autopsy is critical. Sometimes the best evidence is below the surface. More importantly, it's found by someone *other* than a cop."

"Unfortunately there is a lack of trust here. I wish I could fix it somehow," Condello said, shaking his head.

Condello put in a request for the major in Cles to speak with a prosecutor about an autopsy. Not expecting one, we agreed we needed to get what we could before too much body decomposition.

I pulled one of the overhead lights closer to Anna's head, trying to get a better look at the bruise on her forehead.

Turning on the tape recorder Bruno identified the four of us in the room, the date, time and location, as well as the victim, Anna Bertolli. He then laid the recorder next to Anna's head. I enjoyed seeing Bruno's comfortableness with talking into a tape recorder since most young officers I had worked with were not.

I explained to Bruno he had pictures in his camera of the dent on the fender of Anna's car showing the separation of the two-inch wide border around the tire compared with the remainder of the smooth fender. I then pointed out the corresponding rounded marks on Anna's forehead consistent with the rounded edge over the wheel. The darkness of the bruising caused by the rounded edge indicated a deeper trauma. An autopsy would have brought it all together for Bruno—and a jury, too.

Bruno noticed Condello nodding his head, his eyebrows raised.

After looking at the picture in the camera once more, Bruno went to work on capturing the marks and bruising I mentioned, while I retrieved some tools from our helper.

After I cut off the paper bags around Anna's hands, I wrote my initials, along with the date and time, by the cuts on the bags. I then carefully cut Anna's fingernails placing each one in its own container, marking which finger it came from.

After nearly two hours, combing over her body several times, the three of us agreed we had photographed, documented and recovered as much of the evidence as we could without an autopsy.

Checking one last time to make sure we properly bagged and identified all of the evidence, we locked it away before we sat in Captain Condello's office.

"What did you two find out when you went to Domenica's house?" Condello asked.

"Penina, Domenica's mother, was cooperative," Bruno said. "She told us Domenica had a boyfriend, sort of, by the name of Sergio Fezzi." Bruno described Penina's comments about Sergio, concluding with where he lived and car he drives.

"You run his driver's license yet?" Condello asked Bruno.

"Yes, sir. No surprise, they are short staffed in Cles due to the bombings, so it could be a while."

I wanted Bruno to understand the necessity of logically piecing things together, so I used Sergio as an example.

"Sergio gets abandoned by his mother, Domenica *selfishly* intended to leave according to him, and he goes from being a nice young man to angry young man pretty easily. Sergio's use of past tense likely indicates he knew Domenica had died, and his blue Toyota Hatchback he almost hit me with then showed up at the scene. It all spells out a connection. I'm not ready to say for sure this is our guy, but I will say the evidence is definitely mounting."

"You mentioned him working at a Pomarella plant," Condello said. "There are several in Val di Non. If he happens to work at the same one Anna did, it could be our link."

"Penina said Sergio worked at the Revò plant, same as Anna," I said.

"Man, we need that driver's license photo so I can see if he's the same kid."

CHAPTER SIXTY-EIGHT

I shared the information about Carlo Camioni with the captain, and then told him we stopped at Bar Podetti to talk with Carlo. "We found him in a booth with his arm around a girl decades younger than him. Bruno did good interviewing and Carlo admitted to seeing Domenica in October at the bus stop.

"In a nutshell, he offered to take her to a hotel in Cles, admitting he put his hand on Domenica's butt. She slapped him in the face, exactly like our unknown witness or witnesses saw. Carlo then made a comment Domenica would still be alive if she would have let him have some young pussy."

Captain Condello's eyebrows squeezed together to form a crease…I could tell he got incensed by Carlo's comment, too.

"I owe you an apology, sir," I said.

"I don't understand AJ. What for?"

Looking first at Bruno, who broke into a smug smile, I turned to the captain and said, "Well, sir, Carlo's last comment kinda pissed me off. I sort of…elbowed him in the ribs, then somehow my elbow found his nose."

"You should have seen it, the whole bar seemed pleased with AJ," Bruno said in my defense.

Condello chuckled. "I wish I could've seen you wipe the

smirk off his face. I'll get word out for him not to waste time trying to make a complaint. Man, I wish I could've seen it."

Seeing Condello's reaction, I knew he had my back.

"So, tell me about the Bertolli's," Condello said.

"I identified the people there, along with Anna's mother who never came out of the bedroom where we could hear her crying. I unofficially confirmed Marina was the girl across from the crime scene when the car sped off. Something tells me she knows the driver."

I explained nobody at the plant saw Anna leave, although she clocked out on time. I showed him the picture I had taken of Anna's key ring so he could see the uniqueness. Then, in detail I outlined the evidence surrounding Anna's car.

"I would be surprised if the drop of blood on the back seat is not the suspect's, given she had skin under a couple fingernails."

"Unfortunately, the Pomarella plant called the Bertolli's to tell them the security cameras were not functioning," Bruno said.

"They claim the recorder had been accidently unplugged. AJ and I think that's a crock, using his word."

Condello smiled. "It sounds like all of the interviews were productive. My gut says we're on the right track. I have to say, I have a bad feeling he may try to kill again."

Shamefaced, Bruno looked at Captain Condello. "There's one more interview we did."

"Really." Condello sat forward, putting his elbows on his desk, his hands to his chin, "And?"

I intentionally looked away from Bruno trying not to make it harder for him. He already seemed to be doing a good job of beating himself up.

Bruno verified the captain knew Radio Scarpa. He explained what Scarpa told him and Amici a couple days before.

"We chuckled and blew it off as Scarpa telling another one of his stories."

Silence filled the room. Bruno looked at me pleadingly and since he came to my defense earlier, I could not leave him hanging out to dry.

"Bruno did an excellent interview again," I said, winking at Condello without Bruno seeing it. Condello faintly nodded and I knew he understood I already spoke with Bruno about it.

"I actually think Scarpa saw the suspect holding Domenica in his arms seconds before placing her under the bridge—it's not just a story. With young kids and people like Scarpa, threatening to kill their mother is enough to shut them down, they don't tell anyone."

"Scarpa only saw the man one time?" Condello asked.

"No, he's seen the suspect in Mione across from Bar Lanterna a few times," I said.

"When the guy's been at the stop sign across from the bar he uses his fingers and acts like he's shooting Scarpa. Poor guy's scared, so he didn't tell anyone."

"What do you think?" Condello asked. "I mean, even though it would be easy to dismiss with it being Scarpa, it sounds somewhat convincing."

"Well, based on my training and experience—what the hell, I sound like I'm testifying in court—I think Scarpa really was afraid to say anything. That is, until he started hearing the rumors and people talking about Domenica."

"Do you think these cases are linked?" Condello asked. "The same suspect?"

"It definitely feels like it. If they are related, you can almost bet there'll be another one. If these were his first two, then the good news is it might take him a while to get to number three. The problem is we can't say for sure, and the time line almost always gets closer as they continue to kill more. If these two aren't his first, we could be in trouble."

"Why were both bodies close to where people could come across them?" Captain Condello asked, a quizzical look on his face and shaking his head. "I realize they still could have decayed or been taken by animals, even from there. It's the proximity to civilization which has me confused, when really there is no reason to be so close. Around here, in a short drive, they could have been dumped anywhere in the forest, probably never found."

"In my opinion he likes the idea of the danger in getting caught. It's kind of like a couple who likes to have sex in an elevator. The thrill of almost getting caught makes the act more exciting, at least in their minds."

"Hmm, I must say, I'm pretty concerned—I don't feel good about this," Captain Condello said.

"Whether the suspect is Sergio or not, it seems like the guy's organized, not over the top though. We need to hope he slips up so we can find him before he kills again."

"Well, it's been a long day. I suggest we get some rest, get back after it tomorrow," Condello said.

Within minutes we were all leaving the captain's office. "I'm exhausted. See you tomorrow," Bruno said.

"Hey—you did well today. Go get some rest," I said.

Bruno pursed his lips, a smile almost surfacing.

CHAPTER SIXTY-NINE

I stopped at my townhouse to turn on the lights and grabbed my computer figuring I could get some emails out. I stood on the balcony for a moment taking in the day and decided a walk in the cool night air would be good.

Nearing the bus stop I looked at the lone house to my right. Marina's family members, or so I presumed, had always waived and greeted me. Why did Marina respond to me the way she had? At first Marina's protective wall seemed to be due to her friendship with Anna. I pondered the possibility of some other reason—something I knew nothing about.

Lights were on in the top floor, the balcony door open. I hoped Marina might step outside but when she didn't, I crossed the street to the bar.

Bar Lanterna appeared hectic, to say the least. No tables were empty outside, and a large number of younger adults were moving around the tables engaging in conversations. Inside I spotted the last available table up against the wall, directly under the TV. I could feel the eyes on me, hearing the now familiar *poliziotto Americano*. I did my best to ignore them.

Donatella and her teenage sons were working hard. Not getting served in a hurry did not bother me—good sleep came in five-hour increments if I was lucky, so I had time to kill.

Looking around the room waiting for my computer to boot up I saw people were no longer turning away to talk about me. I decided to research the bombings in Padua and Florence and disheartened by the death toll having risen again, I clicked off the internet. I'd had enough death for one day.

No sooner had I placed the arrow on the email icon when I looked up and saw her approaching. Our eyes met, Marina giving a thin tight lipped smile—for one, brief, second.

"*Buona sera signore*," Marina said.

I grinned at her attempt to stay away from English, then responded, "*Buona sera signorina*."

Marina planted her right hand on her hip, canted her head to the right, and looked at me through squinted eyes, like she could not figure me out. Although she looked like a younger Bethany, a more strong-willed personality than Bethany had begun to emerge. I stared back with a look of conviction, determined not to be the first one to look away. Time dragged before Marina finally looked down, putting her hand on the top of the chair.

"Do you mind if I sit?"

"Ahh, the young lady does speak English. Please, sit," I said closing my computer. I watched Marina pull the chair out from under the table further than she needed to, sitting erect guarding herself with crossed arms and feet standing out.

Marina took a deep breath as her eyes focused on the table. She apologized, saying it had been difficult losing her best friend and she wanted to appear strong for the Bertollis who now faced the death of a second child…Anna being their youngest.

"You were respectful and compassionate toward the Bertollis. I appreciate the way you treated them. I hope you can forgive me." Her eyes drifted up to look at me as she finished.

"Thank you, I understand. I'm so sorry you lost your best friend."

Still tense, her guard remained up.

"That had to be hard for you to go be with the Bertollis, I have the utmost respect for you doing it. Your parents obviously raised you well." Although she did not uncross her arms I noticed her shoulders relaxed.

It's a start.

"How is it an American police man is helping the Carabinieri?"

"I'm here on vacation, I happened to speak with Bruno several times. I had told him about being a homicide investigator, so they asked if I would lend some advice."

"The talk around town is Anna had been beaten and… and …"

"Raped," I said, helping her finish.

"Oh my God. *No*?" Marina gasped.

"There's no evidence of it," I said, my palms facing her. "I can't talk much about the case. I will say, *that* rumor definitely needs to come to an end."

"There are so many things being said right now, I'm not sure who to believe," Marina said. "People are starting to get scared. Some are even locking their doors now, no one ever locks their doors."

I understood being afraid, although this killer is not the kind who bursts through the door to abduct someone.

I wanted to find out more about Marina, the person. This seemed like a great time to change the topic.

"So, you're a college student?"

"Yes, I go to University of Padua."

"Wasn't the university one of the locations of the recent bombings?"

"Yes. Late last night I didn't think my day could get any worse, and then my roommate sent me a twitter link…I couldn't believe it."

"I've been out of touch with social media," I said. "What's being said about the bombings?"

"Of course there is panic right now. Most of it refers to Europe being under siege."

Europeans definitely have more direct concerns than Americans solely based on the sheer number of terrorist attacks. People in America get hysterical when an attack happens, followed quickly by complacency it won't happen again, at least not in their neighborhood.

"I have been able to find out through tweets most of my friends were not on campus at the time," Marina said. "We have one friend who has not responded to anyone." With tears filling her eyes, she grabbed a napkin, covering her face.

Enough about death. "What are you majoring in?" I asked.

Marina wiped away the tears, taking a second to compose herself.

"I am studying social work, and taking classes in psychology, too. I hope to be able to help people who may be struggling, who want to change their lives."

Subconsciously my eyes went up and to the left as I stared at nothing beyond Marina.

"I am sorry if I said something wrong," she said, her eyes peering at me probingly.

Refocusing, I said, "You didn't…I recently lost someone

close to me, a social worker, it made me think of her. In fact, you look a little bit like her. Would you like something to drink?" I asked, as I stood. I had no desire to go into any more detail.

"Please. I would love some wine. Donatella knows what I prefer."

I returned with two glasses of wine. "One of Donatella's sons helped me, he said he knew what you liked."

Marina extended her glass, waiting for me to extend mine.

"*Cin, cin,*" she said as the glasses touched.

Seeing the look of bewilderment on my face, she smiled. "It's an Italian custom, a little more formal than *salute*. I have read in America you touch glasses like we do, usually for a toast. Ours is similar except we do it more often."

Grinning and nodding, I said, "All right, I'll try to remember for the next time we have drinks together."

Marina raised her glass again. "Here's to our two friends who have passed. We hope they are in a better place."

As we toasted, I looked deep into Marina's eyes. We were trying to read each other. Clearly by accident, she had touched on the one area in my life where I had vulnerability. Even so, Marina recognized she had leveled the playing field some as she relaxed her posture, no longer so guarded.

For twenty minutes we sipped wine, each sharing a little about our past. Something about Marina made me appreciate her. Yet, my gut said to be careful. The juxtaposition intrigued me.

"I must go," Marina said, sliding her chair back. "Thank you for the wine and conversation."

"I appreciate you stopping by. I've enjoyed getting to know you. Again, I'm sorry you lost your best friend."

Marina pushed her chair under the table, quietly looking at me. Turning to leave, she took three steps and stopped. Pausing for several seconds as if in a dilemma, she finally turned, and said, "I think the driver's name is Sergio. I met him one time—several years ago." Not waiting for a response she left, walking through the door into the darkness.

Bingo. I knew it. That's the same name Penina gave Bruno.

Smiling, I took a sip of wine. Not pressuring her paid off. The edges of the puzzle were starting to come together.

An angry young man sat within earshot watching their every move as he admired his newly bleached hair in the bar mirror. Neither of them noticed.

CHAPTER SEVENTY

Sergio got to the bar shortly after the American detective, watching him sit at the table under the television.

Staying out on the patio he requested a raspberry gelato from the young waiter. He could overhear untruthful rumors being spread about the dead girl found by the lumberyard. Gossip being what it is, some people were saying the girl got attacked on one of her walks, while others said they had heard the girl had been raped.

Being the cause of the disruption pleased him.

This is perfect, he thought. *People add to my story before passing it along.*

Sergio took a seat straddling the end of the bench by the patio entry where he could keep an eye on the American. No real reason existed to follow the American beyond his desire to learn about his adversary. Two could play the game. The changes he made to his appearance gave him confidence the American would not recognize him.

Sergio was finishing his gelato when he spotted her crossing the street. She walked into the bar from the door near the driveway, never looking at the people on the patio.

He watched her confidently stride over to the American's table, putting her hand on her hip, tilting her head to the side. It gave him pleasure to see the American detective did not intimidate her, remaining there for some time before she finally took a seat.

I have to get closer, he thought. *She's going to tell him about me. If she does, I'll have to eliminate her quickly.*

His ability to make quick assessments had gotten a little better, although he preferred time to think and plan. Inside the bar he stayed close to the gelato freezer while keeping an eye on the two of them. Her back faced him, while the American seemed fixated on her.

Go now! Get to the stool, my back will be to them, he told himself.

Moving with purpose, while trying not to draw attention, he kept his head turned toward the bar while he headed for the open stool next to the wall.

He felt excited to be so close to them, listening to their conversation. Despite his English not being excellent, he believed it would be good enough to understand most of what they were discussing.

In the mirror behind the liquor he saw the American stand. His muscles tightened as his knuckles became white clenching the beer bottle.

His eyes were locked onto the mirror, the distance diminishing rapidly. *Shit, he's coming here.*

His right elbow twitched from the contact.

"Sorry," the American said.

"*Nessun problema*," he replied, his right hand raising slightly as if to waive it off. He started to take a drink, hoping to look relaxed. He put the bottle down when he noticed his hand shaking.

Hearing the American ordering drinks helped his muscles back off slightly from being on the brink of fight or flight.

Swing the bottle, aim for his head, he thought, silently

hoping he did not have to. At least not there.

When the American turned to walk away he picked up the napkin under the bottle to wipe his forehead. He fully grasped his own bravado almost cost him.

He decided to prepay for his drink in case he had to leave quickly. He found himself straining to hear her, wanting to learn more about her as she spoke.

A social worker, helping others. Honorable, I guess.

Hearing of her friend at school not responding almost touched him—then he dismissed it.

He listened to them for over twenty minutes, yet she never mentioned his name or said anything about seeing him. When he heard her say she must go, he slid off the stool. Hearing her chair back up, he made his move for the door, blending with the crowd. He glanced over his shoulder, confident neither of them noticed him.

She bought herself some time, he thought. *I'm still going to have to kill her. At least now there's no rush. People would think something's wrong if I killed her too soon. It's okay. I'll get to her in due time.*

CHAPTER SEVENTY-ONE

As I reflected on my conversation with Marina I realized time had flown by. The quick jerk of the chair startled me as Donatella sat.

"Wow, you're sitting. You feel okay?"

She cocked her head left, giving me the universal *smart ass* look. Donatella wanted to hear what Marina wanted. Instead, I turned it around, getting her to tell me about Marina. No surprise, she described Marina as a beautiful girl who adored her parents. Then she surprised me.

"Marina can be pleasant, she also protects herself often," Donatella said.

"Guarded?"

"Sì, guarded."

"About what?"

"Many people feel they cannot get on her bad side. They feel she is, I don't know how to say it in English."

"Vengeful, or vindictive?" I asked.

"Yes, they think she would get revenge."

I told Donatella how Marina happened to be at the Bertolli home when we were there and she had been cold towards me.

"She came in here to apologize."

"Anna was so nice, to everyone," Donatella said, a pained look about her. She described how several people would not talk with Marina. Anna apparently did, and they soon became best friends.

"Marina is taking Anna's death hard. If she acted cold, then you saw the face people always talk about."

"Would she hurt the person responsible for Anna's death?"

Donatella carefully scanned the bar first.

"Yes, some think she could. I cannot give you a reason *specifica*, some they feel it is possible. I do not think so, I wish others did not feel this way. I have to be careful, they are my customers."

Pausing, I thought about what Donatella said and weighed the risk of sharing more with her. I didn't know enough about Rumo or the people, but I had to trust someone, and right now Donatella happened to be the one.

I told Donatella about Marina being at the crime scene and seeing the driver of the car before it sped off.

"She wouldn't talk to me at the Bertolli's. Right before she left here she told me she knew the driver's first name. Even though she didn't say anything else, I kind of sense she knows more."

"She does, *probabilmente*," Donatella said, a look of concern on her face. She nervously looked around the bar once again and stood, saying, "I need to help my sons, and then we can talk."

Within a few minutes Donatella returned, setting down a Cappuccino for me and cleared away the wine glasses.

I sipped my Cappuccino, intrigued by Donatella's comments and blatant nervousness. She had more to say, though not until we were alone. In her own way, Donatella had already confirmed my suspicion there was more to Marina.

I watched Donatella and her sons with great interest, admiring their closeness. Her teenage sons willing to help their mother instead of being out with friends impressed me. Not surprisingly, both sons gave Donatella kisses on her cheeks before leaving.

Did I make the right choice devoting my life to being a detective, not having a wife and family? I asked myself.

Pondering, I felt an emptiness inside.

Donatella made her way to the chair across from me, clasped her hands on the table, and stared down. I leaned forward, softly placing my hand on top of hers.

"Look, you don't have to tell me anything you don't want to. I get it, this is uncomfortable for you," I said, removing my hand and sat back and waited.

"It is just…this is something I have never told anyone. I love Marina, she grew up with my sons, I want to be wrong. Her parents are wonderful, I do not want to lose their friendship. Promise me you will not say a word to anyone I told you anything about Marina. Promise you will not use it unless there is no choice, *assolutamente*."

I sat erect, putting my hand up like I would in court. "I promise you I will not say anything. I will not use what you say unless I absolutely have to. I swear to God."

Before my hand returned to the table Donatella stood and walked away, making her way around the bar. She appeared seriously worked up and I wanted to put a stop to it.

"Donatella, I'm really impressed, your sons have been great tonight," trying to change the conversation.

She returned with a large glass of wine and sat. After taking several sips she looked directly into my eyes and then her stare shifted to the wine glass she held firmly between her hands.

"Many years ago, Marina was seven, a family with a

little boy one year younger *hanno vissuto in* the house next door," she said, pointing over my head without taking her eyes from the wine glass.

I noticed Donatella's English worsened as her look into the past became more focused.

"*Nome del ragazzino* Dante, Dante Zaccaro. One afternoon Dante, Marina, and my boys were playing." Donatella described the kids playing for thirty minutes before they ran up to the table to get the drinks she made for them.

"I walk outside to go clean a table. I saw Dante touch the bottom of Marina's glass, right when she drank. Something red, a juice of some kind I think. His touch on Marina's glass makes her to spill the juice on her blue dress. She wore the dress two times a week, always. Dante is laughing loud. My boys smiled. They saw me so they did not laugh. I try to teach them to laugh at a person hurts them."

Taking a large drink of wine, her eyes stared into the past. I waited.

"Marina is stiff, no fear, angry, so she stares at Dante. I hurry over to start wiping up the mess. Marina set the glass on the table, she walked away, no words. Marina never wore the dress again."

I had a terrible feeling where this might be heading.

Donatella twirled the wine in her glass, staring at its rotation. "Later…the same evening…Dante is missing."

Two days later Marina's father, Aldo, had been putting firewood under lean-tos in his backyard. "Past is *collina ripida*, very up and down," Donatella said.

"Steep? Like a steep hill?" I asked.

"Steep hill, *si*." Donatella said Aldo told the Carabinieri his wife Clara honked the car horn out front. He went to see what she needed and she said she was going to Cles after she dropped their son off at the soccer field. As Clara drove away Aldo looked down the embankment and spotted the neighbor boy, Dante, directly below the sidewalk railing.

The Carabinieri ruled it an accidental death. They dismissed the tracks from small feet below the lean-tos in Aldo's backyard as Dante trying to climb back up the hill. "The Carabinieri said it looked like Dante crawled toward the road where he went *incosciente,* and died."

Donatella finished her wine with two large gulps.

She said the day they found Dante everybody in the area cried.

"Then, Dante's parents blamed Marina. Many people say she is not upset enough, not enough tears."

Donatella waited over a week before saying anything to Marina. She made sure nobody else heard them. Donatella asked Marina if she knew anything about how Dante might have fallen down the hill.

"I do not forget, she looks at me scared, like confused if she could talk to me."

Marina never said a word to Donatella, and Dante's family moved shortly after the funeral.

"AJ, people here *la gente parla*."

She could not think of a word, so I used my Google Translate app, discovering it meant rumor, gossip or hearsay.

"Poor Marina lives most of her life as a *voce della morte*… a rumor of death."

"Ahh, when people talk about Marina, the rumor is always part of their conversation."

"Sì, *sì*. Always. Marina became quieter, almost afraid to

talk to people. They can be mean. Until Anna."

"How has Marina been around you after Dante?"

"It is funny thing. After, she comes over here all the time, even hugging me." Donatella said she and Marina had grown close and Marina never looked at her angrily.

"Many people mistake Marina's quiet as evil. My sons tell me many times over the years how people think Marina is angry, when my boys say she is not." She even said her sons told her when they were younger, after Dante died, kids would tease Marina about having what they called *sguardo della morte*, her death stare.

"She has always been sweet to me, she's never done anything else to make me to be suspicious."

"Tell me if I'm wrong, I sense you've always felt she had something to do with Dante's death. Even if it was an accident. Am I right?" I asked.

Donatella started to take a drink of wine, until she saw an empty glass. Hesitating before looking at me, she finally said, "Yes, I have always felt this way. I think it is an accident, not like many others think here. Dante goes missing the same day he ruins her dress, to them she does not show enough emotion. It does not mean she hurt him."

"Did her parents ever say anything? Do you even think they have seen the, whatever you called it, the death stare?"

"Clara, her mother—happy person. No. Aldo, he is nice, also. If there is any *disciplina*, Clara made him do it. Maybe he has seen her look unhappy. I do not think he saw *sguardo della morte*."

Donatella got up, taking her wine glass and returned with a half full glass of wine.

Donatella described how Aldo had twice come to the bar acting worried about people saying Marina had something to do with Dante's death. Once the Carabinieri ruled it an accident Aldo relaxed. He never said another word about it. Donatella even told her husband how Aldo acted strangely at first.

"Do you know if Aldo went down the hillside by the sidewalk once he saw Dante?" I asked.

She considered it for several seconds before saying, "No, I don't think he did. Why do you ask?"

I explained the natural response by a parent like Aldo whose daughter, Marina, is roughly the same age as Dante, he would immediately go check on the boy's welfare—unless Aldo already knew Dante was dead.

Donatella's eyes narrowed as she hung on my every word.

"Or, maybe Aldo no learn of Dante until after. Maybe he is scared for Marina."

"That's possible. Maybe Aldo warned her, told her not to talk to anyone about what happened. I mean, the whole town blamed her from the beginning, so anything she would say might make it worse. Marina does not strike me as a killer. She understands right from wrong, she has feelings and emotions about people, even though she had to build a wall to protect herself from nasty people. Something might have happened, I do not believe she killed Dante on purpose."

Donatella nodded. I could tell she seemed pleased my thoughts were similar to hers.

"What did Marina say about the man's name?" Donatella asked.

"She said his name is Sergio, she didn't know his last name," I said.

I took a sip of the last of my cold Cappuccino. I told Donatella about Bruno and me meeting Penina, and her telling us Domenica's boyfriend had been Sergio Fezzi.

"He works at the Pomarella plant in Revò. Anna Bertolli worked there, too. Right now he is the one link between the two dead girls we have."

"I know this Sergio Fezzi. He lives down below Marina's house. The road goes down by a church, there are several homes in there. I am not sure which one he lives in, it is down there by the church. He lives with his father, his mother left them years ago. I have never heard anyone say anything bad about him."

It sounded like the same person given the similarity with the mother leaving.

"My sister, the one you met, works in Revò at Pomarella. Next time I see her I will ask if she knows anything about Sergio," she said, standing, grabbing my cup and her wine glass.

"It is late, you need to go rest. I am sure Bruno will call you early." She had a dispirited look on her face when she turned to go to her office.

When I reached for the handle of the door Donatella came out of the office area to the bar.

"Please, do not say word to anyone?" Donatella asked, a pleading look on her face.

I acted like I zipped my lip, and winked. Donatella returned a fake smile.

Walking home I replayed what Donatella told me. Marina originally left me feeling uneasy, then I realized over time she would have naturally become protective about whom to trust. The fact she gave me the name, Sergio, told me I had made headway with her.

Walking in my door I realized I had never gotten to emails. Sitting in the recliner with my computer I touched base with my boss and a few family members over the next forty-five minutes. I fell asleep in the recliner sometime around three.

CHAPTER SEVENTY-TWO

Marina believed Domenica had once told her Sergio Fezzi worked at the Pomarella plant in Revò. She doubted if he still did.

It was common knowledge Pomarella employees typically work five days a week, except for the rush at the end of the apple season when they are required to work six or seven days a week. Marina's doubts about Sergio were based on seeing him the day before when he should have been at the plant if he still worked there. Following him would be the one way to find out for sure.

She set her alarm for four thirty in the morning hoping to be in place by five. From her house she went to Vender Lumberyard to wait and see if Sergio passed. From his house Sergio would have to go right past Vender Lumberyard if heading to Revò. Marina backed her car in so she could see the main road.

She had been there for twenty-five minutes when she spotted Sergio in the faded green Fiat Panda leaving Rumo. Marina tried to keep her distance far enough from the Fiat so Sergio would not become aware of being followed.

Within twenty minutes they made it to the town of Revò. Driving through town she somehow lost sight of the Fiat but drove to the Pomarella plant to see if she could find it. Approaching the plant she spotted Sergio walking across the parking lot with several other employees, and continued on, giving him time to get inside. Making a U-turn, she waited five minutes before driving through the parking lot to find where Sergio had parked.

Marina's next vigil centered on identifying a hiding spot where she could watch Sergio leave when he got off work. Once satisfied, she headed back to Rumo shortly before seven o'clock.

Marina believed her boss would give her the days off she requested after learning of the death of her best friend. She needed to meet with him before eleven, which would provide ample time for her return to Revò and be in place by 1 p.m., an hour before Sergio should get off work.

She needed to email her professor at the university to reschedule an exam she missed. Like her boss, she felt her professor would understand when told him about the murder of her best friend.

Though Anna's death had been upsetting to Marina, the real reason for the time off centered on her being consumed with feeling Sergio had killed two people she knew. Unsure of the Carabinieri's abilities to solve the murders, in spite of having an American detective helping them, her main goal had become discovering as much as she could about him.

Waking up in the recliner at seven thirty, I realized I'd gotten four hours of uninterrupted sleep. *Something's working,* I thought. *Not sure if it's the fact I'm helping with the investigation, or what. Whatever the reason, I like it.* A feeling of happiness flooded through me.

The shave and shower rejuvenated me even more. I checked emails and saw a new one from my sister who sent me a list of all the cousins in the area, complete with their names, addresses, and phone numbers.

Surprisingly, we had several cousins throughout the Val di Non region. Perusing it I noticed three asterisks, presumably to get my attention, fully aware I would most likely do exactly what I did.

You should at least meet your third cousin Aldo, his wife Clara, their daughter Marina, and their son Matteo.

The realization of what I read pushed me into the back of my chair. My heart began racing and I instantly felt a tightness in my chest about destroying any family ties my sister had worked so hard to procure and cultivate. Closing the computer, the uncertainty surrounding Marina raged in my head.

The detective in me says I can't trust her yet. On the other hand, her intelligence, her personality, and now our blood lines have me wanting to believe her.

The beautiful crisp morning and bright blue sky went unnoticed. Passing the bus stop I looked at Marina's house where I saw Aldo in the backyard stacking firewood. Almost as if he knew he were being stared at, Aldo turned to look at me.

No time like the present.

Approaching the backyard I spotted Marina looking out of the French doors from the second floor. Seeing her father walking toward me she swiftly turned from the window, the curtain flying in the wake of her movement.

"*Buongiorno signore. Aldo, sì?*" I asked, pointing at him.

"*Buongiorno. Sì, sono Aldo. No inglese signore.*"

Marina came bursting through the door and Aldo and

I paused, looking at her. Gathering herself, Marina tried to walk over slowly but we were already shaking our heads and grinning.

"Your timing is *perfetto*," I said looking at Marina. "You can interpret for us, if you don't mind." I asked her to tell Aldo about my relationship to Glenda. Marina froze, her mouth open.

"Are you okay? You look like you saw a ghost," I said with a smirk. "*Go on*, tell your father we're cousins."

Slowly Marina told Aldo what I had said. Instantly Aldo broke into a large smile. Grabbing me by my shoulders he kissed me on both cheeks. Aldo began calling for Clara, boisterously sharing the news with her when she came out. Clara's smile nearly outdid Aldo's, and she too proceeded to kiss me on both cheeks.

We exchanged pleasantries for several minutes with Marina as the interpreter. Before I had to go to meet Bruno, Aldo and Clara said they wanted me to come to dinner one night next weekend.

"I would love to," I said, smiling at Marina.

She glared at me before telling her parents. They beamed at my acceptance, hugging me before I left.

"Marina, thank you for your help," I said.

Marina turned without a word, briskly walking into the house. Smiling, I looked at Aldo and Clara, who both had their palms up and their shoulders raised. Even in a foreign country some gestures are universal.

CHAPTER SEVENTY-THREE

Sergio had gotten used to getting funny looks from fellow employees at the plant, usually resulting in a swirl of voices in his head and strange sensations to hurt someone. The double takes because he changed his appearance did not bother him, in fact several people had even nodded approvingly. By his morning break at nine, Sergio began feeling comfortable with his new look.

Sergio had long been a loner at work, including breaks and lunchtime. None of the employees were his friend outside of work. Generally he liked being alone, although he got upset if he thought people were laughing about him behind his back. The last two people who openly laughed at Sergio had been fired within twenty-four hours. Supervisors in the plant made sure to point him out to new employees, cautioning them about how they should act around him.

Sergio had used his uncle's status to his advantage so many times, most of the employees, if not all, kept their distance. His direct supervisors actually liked him as a forklift driver. He worked hard, never wasting time talking with other employees. Still, no supervisor would think of denying any of his requests for days off.

Getting close to the break room Sergio started taking off his leather work-gloves as the pain on the backs of his hands caused him to pause. He remembered the gouges she had left. Pulling his gloves back on he continued toward the break room.

Walking up to the open door of the break room Sergio heard his name. He stopped short of the doorway, listening closely. One woman appeared to be doing most of the talking.

"I'm telling you, he's a freak," the woman said. "Even if I liked the changes, a new hair color and earrings don't change the fact he's a freak. No matter what he does to try to fit in he's always going to be the misfit nobody wants to talk to."

Sergio heard other voices in the room comment about her statement, telling her she should be careful.

"Look, I'm from Rumo, there have been rumors about him and his dad for years. There's even one his mother left them years ago, she didn't want to be around them anymore when she realized they were both strange. Even on Facebook people have said his supposed girlfriend planned on leaving him before she *accidentally* fell in the river. He's strange I'm telling you. He's a freak."

Just as the woman finished her statement Sergio walked around the corner, stopping in the doorway. Unlike the others in the room who immediately looked down acting as though they were eating or drinking something, Rosa Tevini turned and stared at him. Lowering her chin in disgust, she confidently got up from the table, throwing the remnants of her snack in the trash container. Rosa stood tall, staring back at Sergio as she approached him.

"You don't scare me, you fucking weirdo," Rosa snarled, a deepness in her voice.

"Even now, you walk in here wearing your work gloves. What an ass. Everyone else leaves their gloves at their work area. You? No, you wear yours in here. You fucking think you can intimidate people with your powerful uncle. Well, you don't intimidate me. *Now*, get the hell out of my way, FREAK."

Rosa stepped toward the open doorway as if he were not even there.

Sergio could feel the anger boiling inside. His fists clenched, the inferno inside making him flush with hatred. The room began to spin, everything kaleidoscopic to him. Her hand on his shoulder pushing him out of the doorway brought him back to reality. He turned, allowing her to pass without saying a word.

Almost as quickly as the anger had risen inside of him, now rose the fear from what she had said about his mother. He could feel the color leaving his face as he again began to get lightheaded. The kaleidoscope returned…he felt outside of himself…seeing the people in the room staring at him. He told himself he had to get out of there quickly and he turned, almost stumbling through the doorway.

Out of the room he leaned up against the wall for support, his knees about to give out. His head would not stop spinning and he gradually began to hear the low whispers inside the break room slowly growing in volume. Sergio concluded he had to leave before somebody saw him and staggered back to his forklift without any recollection of how.

Leaning against the forklift tire, eating his lunch, his thoughts centered on punishing Rosa. The risks of doing something to her too soon were hardly processing through his grey matter. His mind drifted, seeing her in front of him, tied to a tree. The others were killed right away…not Rosa. He could hear her bones breaking, see the blood dripping from the cuts. He knew she would faint from pain, probably more than once and he planned to take his time. Before returning to work he had convinced himself, though risky, no woman would treat him the way she did and get away with it.

The angry pounding in his chest returned. He took his trash to the closest dumpster, intentionally taking slow, deep breaths as he returned to his forklift.

In the past he overheard Rosa say to others how she likes to go running or walking to stay in shape. He would follow her outside of work until the right opportunity presented itself. He planned to enjoy punishing her. Unlike the other two, he would make sure no one ever found her.

Unmarried, Rosa enjoyed spending time staying exceptionally fit. Her small frame, or being thirty-five, could not keep her from trying anything recreationally and physically of interest to her. Similarly, her strong self-confidence would not allow her to back down from saying what she thought.

Rosa tried her best to put what happened in the break room out of her mind. She could not help wondering how many days she had remaining before she would be dismissed for her comments. In the meantime, she needed to be cautious.

Trust your gut and watch your back, she thought.

CHAPTER SEVENTY-FOUR

I saw Bruno sitting at one of the square tables on the patio as Donatella came outside when I walked up.

"Ah, my favorite customer," Donatella said with a smile. "You must have gotten some sleep. Cappuccino? Pastry?"

"I slept for about four hours, never woke up once. I would love them both, *grazie*." Donatella gave me a quick flash of a smile before going inside.

"I've been ready to go since seven. Do you have any idea how difficult it was to sit here waiting for you?" Bruno asked, an almost disgusted look on his face.

I could not talk about last night, so I ignored the question. "Anything on the partial plate yet?"

"Yes, I've been working on it since I got here. You'll like this. The plate is CM441JP, registered to a blue Toyota Yaris belonging to none other than Sergio Fezzi," Bruno said with a smile. "I've already walked by his house, down there," he said, pointing to the road across the street next to Marina's house.

"There are several homes past the church, so it took me a little while to find Sergio's house. No cars are there, so I put out a BOL as you would call it."

I gave him what I liked to call a dual-purpose nod, partially to acknowledge his good police work, secondarily for being pleased with his overall progress.

Donatella arrived with my Cappuccino and pastry, setting them on the table. I excused myself to follow her back inside, instinctively looking around the bar. There was nobody else besides the two men in the corner, heavily involved in a discussion.

"Hey, guess what? Aldo and I are cousins." Excitedly I told her about the email, as well as my conversation with Aldo and Clara.

Donatella nodded before turning away from me. For a brief second I did not understand why, then it hit me.

"You knew this last night when you were telling me about Marina, didn't you?" I asked, almost in a whisper.

She turned to look at me, confusion on her face.

"Yes, I knew. I did not know what to do. I thought your sister told you all about your cousins here."

Donatella realized she had not said anything the instant I spoke of Marina, leaving me confused.

"Everything I told you last night is true," Donatella said, tears in her eyes. "I am sorry for not telling you." She turned, running to the office area, closing the door behind her.

I returned to the table and sat. Staring at Marina's house, I rationalized she had done nothing wrong as far as this investigation went. I could even go so far as to say she felt unsure of sharing information with the American police officer based on a lack of trust. After the way she had been treated most of her life, not surprisingly, trust did not come easy.

Still, what role did Marina play in Dante's death? And Aldo, did he know more than he shared?

Knee deep in family versus responsibility, I finally told myself the past had no bearing on the current investigation. I needed to let go, I needed to focus on helping Captain Condello and Bruno catch this killer.

"Hey, you okay?" Bruno asked. "It's like your mind's elsewhere."

"I'm great," I lied. "So, where do we go from here? Penina said Sergio worked at the plant in Revò, correct?"

"Yes. I happened to think about it this morning." Bruno described the work schedule at the Pomarella plant and said he doubted if Sergio still worked there.

"I mean, he drove by our crime scene yesterday morning."

I stood, putting enough euros on the table to pay for it all. "Why don't we walk down to Sergio's house so you can show me where it's at?"

Donatella stepped into the doorway, watching us cross the street. I needed a little time, maybe some distance, too.

Bruno commented about seeing me talking with Aldo and his family and paused, like he expected me to tell him about it.

"Yes, you did." I stared, messing with him.

"And?"

I laughed, continuing to stare. Bruno did not see the humor. Finally, I explained Aldo and I are cousins, so I thought I should stop to say hi.

The silence between us remained until we reached the bottom of the hill by the large water fountain close to the church.

"What's on your mind? Something's bothering you," I said.

Bruno stopped turning to face me.

"One of your family members is part of this investigation. Up to yesterday you described her as evasive, you weren't sure you could trust her. Now I'm wondering how Marina being a family member will affect your ability to investigate objectively."

"Wow, pretty direct."

"A couple days ago you wanted me to be a straight shooter, not to beat around the bush," Bruno said matter of factly.

"Fair enough." His comments actually impressed me, on many levels. I admitted how in America I would probably be removed from the case.

"I believe right now I can still be objective. It's your call, though. If you want me to walk away, I will."

Pausing to take in what I said, Bruno finally pointed to a road barely two feet wider than my car directly between the two houses across from the church. "We go through there, turn left, turn right and Sergio's house is right past the fountain.

Bruno remained quiet while we walked, processing what I said. Or at least I hoped he had.

The directions were perfect. A short distance beyond the fountain I saw the plain two-story, all-white home. I pointed to the house, not saying a word, and Bruno nodded.

I slowed my pace taking it all in. A road ran along the front of the house on the first level. It separated the field behind the fountain and Sergio's home. I walked along the west side of the home on a narrow road separating Sergio's house and his closest neighbor.

The back of Sergio's home opened up to a yard, flowing into a rolling hill full of trees. Walking in the backyard we saw two wooden garage doors with a lock in the hasp. The garage sat underneath the first floor of the home on the western end. A wooden lean-to shed with stacked wood sat on the eastern end of the backyard, along with a large vegetable garden. No other homes existed on the eastern side.

An elderly lady with a colorful cooking apron stepped onto the balcony of the third floor, grabbing the rail for support. "*Seo drè che zerciao che l'om che l'abita doi piani sora de mì*?" she asked.

"She asked if we were looking for one of the men who live on the floor below her," Bruno translated.

"Tell her we wanted to talk with the young man who lives here. See if she says his name's Sergio Fezzi?" I asked.

Bruno translated, her head nodding as she responded

"*Grazie signora*," Bruno said. Turning to walk away, he said, "He lives there, she says he usually gets home at three."

Approaching the church Bruno's phone rang. When he hung up he told me Sergio's Toyota had been located at a small used car dealership in Cles and the people there were waiting for us.

Driving to Cles, Bruno barely said a word. After passing Livo I broke the silence.

"Go ahead, ask me whatever it is you're thinking. You're nervous about something. Hell, you wear your emotions on your sleeve. You're making me nervous. What is it?"

Bruno took a deep breath. "I've never been in a critical incident, but I've read a lot about them." Bruno wondered if my lack of sleep and nightmares were what he could expect if he were ever involved in a shooting.

"You're all over the frickin map today," I said.

"What do you mean?"

"First you question whether I can investigate objectively, then you ask what it's like to be in a critical incident. You're covering a lot of ground, is all."

"Sorry, you don't have to answer it then," Bruno said, looking a little uneasy as his cheeks turned a light shade of red.

"No, don't be. I like the fact you're not afraid to ask difficult questions." All young officers wondered these same things, so it did not surprise me Bruno did, too.

"There really is no right or wrong way to act after a critical incident. People react differently." I explained the theory behind most departments in America removing an officer from duty, making sure they see a psychologist before returning to work.

"This is the worst I've ever experienced. Shrinks would tell you it's because I loved Bethany. I think...the real reason is...I couldn't get there in time to save her. I've had to shoot people before and that's not always easy to get past. Still, none of it compares to not getting there in time for someone you love."

Near the Poli market Bruno slowed to turn into the car dealership.

"I appreciate you sharing that with me," he said.

Getting out I asked Bruno to see if the Cles office could get us Sergio's driver's license photo. Then I said, "Actually, my shrink said it'd be helpful for me to talk about it, he was right. Talking with Donatella, and you, has been good for me. Now, let's get to work on this car so we can start tightening the noose on this case."

CHAPTER SEVENTY-FIVE

I counted fifteen cars on the lot, none were the Toyota Yaris. Since they said they were waiting for us I figured the car had to be here somewhere. I did not hold out much hope that nobody had started cleaning Sergio's car.

A nicely dressed older man came outside first, obviously the owner. I guessed him to be in his late forties or early fifties.

A kid who looked maybe twenty, a couple inches taller than the older man, and an easy hundred pounds less followed a good five paces behind. The young man had the *lectured to* walk, shoulders slumped over, eyes looking at the ground.

Bruno and the older man began talking in Italian.

"I'm the owner of the dealership," the older man said. "This is my son. He sold one of our cars to the man who brought in the Toyota Yaris, who used it as a trade in."

The owner, looking at his son still staring at the ground, bopped him on the back of the head with his open hand.

"He got caught up in seeing the Toyota had more value than the car he sold the man, he failed to remember what I taught him—normal people don't bring in a decent car to trade for a worse car unless something is very wrong.

He apologized to Bruno at least three different times.

Looking at me, Bruno said, "He told me the Toyota is in

the back, nothing's been done to it. It still has the plate. He said his son is lazy. He should've started cleaning it, instead he sat watching soccer all day after Sergio left. Fortunate for us, huh."

"Amen," I said, both of us chuckling.

The owner took us around the back of the building to the Toyota. He apologized one more time, grabbing his son's arm, pulling him as they turned and walked back to the front of the building.

"In America most detectives would get a search warrant. Some might search it while they waited for a tow truck calling it an inventory search. What about here?"

"The search laws are different here. Basically, it's easy to get permission to search, even after the fact. Captain Condello already took care of it for us."

Bruno took photos of the exterior of the car and the license plate, CM441JP. I opened up the hatchback door and smiled, nodding with approval.

"The carpet fiber looks like the same as ones in Anna's hair," Bruno said looking through the camera lens.

"I'm thinking the same thing. The blanket needs to go as evidence. Pretty unlikely he has a blanket in the back and doesn't use it to cover her up until he can dump her. We can check for her hairs and any other transfer evidence later."

After finishing with the hatchback photos we put the blanket in a large brown paper bag. I set the bag off to the side, my back turned to Bruno.

"You're not going to believe this," Bruno exclaimed, surprise in his voice.

I turned to see him holding up the rear deck board from over the spare tire.

"What is it?" I asked.

"That has to be the rope he used to climb up the hillside,

right?" Bruno asked, even though he already knew the answer. The rope took up almost the entire spare tire area.

"Either this kid has never seen a television show about forensics, or he totally panicked after we saw him at the crime scene. Get some pictures before we remove it," I said, holding the rear deck board.

After taking pictures Bruno lifted the rope out.

"It looks like the knots were tied roughly two to three feet apart, perfect for climbing up the hill," he said.

We were putting the evidence into the trunk of Bruno's car when another patrol car pulled up with one young looking officer.

"*Qui c'è l'immagine che avete chiesto*," he said, handing Bruno the picture he had requested.

"*Grazie*," Bruno said, taking the picture, looking at it, then handing it to me.

"It's him, no doubt about it," I said, staring at Sergio Fezzi's driver's license photo. "Let's show it to the kid, see if he says it's the guy he sold the car to."

Walking into the office Bruno went directly to the son, showing him the picture, asking if he recognized the guy.

"Yeah, it's the dude who drove the Toyota Yaris out back," he said.

Smack. "Show some respect," the owner growled.

"Yes sir. He's the same young man," the boy said, rubbing the back of his head.

"What car did you sell him?" Bruno asked.

The owner stood, handing Bruno a picture and the accompanying paperwork for a 2008 Fiat Panda, license plate AW249WL.

"We'll be towing the Toyota Yaris sometime in the next day or so," Bruno said. "I'm directing you not to touch it. Also, you need to leave the crime scene tape we have around it."

"I understand," the owner said, downcast at the thought of losing money.

Closing the door as we were leaving we heard the owner start yelling at his son, calling him "*stupido*." We looked at each other and started laughing—at the kid's expense.

Marina was pleased with the outcome of her visit with her boss and her call to her professor. Her boss told her to take all the time she needed, he seemed genuinely sad about her having to deal with the death of her best friend.

Notwithstanding her professor being respectful about Anna, he seemed more straightforward and businesslike regarding her taking his exam. He gave her ten days to make up the exam without any consequence.

Marina arrived home by eleven and decided to eat before she headed to Revò. As she placed the top piece of bread on the ham her brother walked into the kitchen. When Marina turned to get a napkin he pounced, grabbing the plate. He took a huge bite of the sandwich, smiling with full cheeks before he rapidly exited the kitchen.

She and her brother had been trying to steal each other's food since they were little. She decided if she hurried she still had time to make another one.

Marina finished her sandwich as her brother walked into the kitchen, grinning like a Cheshire cat.

"I really have to be somewhere soon. Since you stole my first sandwich, the least you could do is clean up the kitchen," Marina said, more like a mandate than a statement.

She did not wait for a response as she left to grab her car keys. She knew he would be able to tell she was serious.

Poking her head into the kitchen, she said, "Thank you baby brother."

Before she could say the last word he had already slung dish soap at her, hitting the wall next to her head. They both laughed as Marina turned, heading for her car.

Marina knew she had ample time to get set. Driving by the Pomarella parking lot she could see Sergio's car still parked. She went past Pomarella one last time as she headed for the parking lot at the *Parrocchia Di Revò*. When she got to the Parish parking lot she made sure she could see both ways on the road.

She had no idea what Sergio's plans were for after work, so she wanted to be able to go either direction once he got on the main road. Rolling down her front windows, reclining her seat enough to be able to relax, Marina found her favorite radio station playing American music.

CHAPTER SEVENTY-SIX

Driving back to Rumo we stopped at my place to pick up my car so we could separate. Bruno had not eaten all day and suggested we stop at Bar Lanterna for a quick lunch and agreed to meet by the bus stop.

Pulling into the lot I looked around, not seeing Marina's white VW Polo at her house, I thought *She's probably over at the Bertolli's consoling them. Good for her.*

Walking into Bar Lanterna I scanned the room for Donatella.

"Grab us a place to sit. I'll be there in a second," I told Bruno.

Heading for the back room, I theorized the need to speak with Donatella privately outweighed the possibility of someone getting upset with me for walking into the private office area.

Finding Donatella in the kitchen making someone's salad, I felt a terrible pang in my chest when I saw the pleading look on her face. I could not put her at ease fast enough.

"I'm sorry about leaving earlier and not saying goodbye," I said, my arms up, palms facing her.

"It was wrong, I apologize." I told her I knew it had been hard for her to tell me about Marina, and my own selfishness put my thoughts first.

"I want to make it clear, I've really enjoyed talking with you and getting to know you. You're a wonderful person."

Despite her watery eyes, I spotted a faint, bashful smile.

"*Grazie*, AJ. *Grazie*." She moved toward me, softly placing the tips of her hands on either side of my chin before giving me a kiss on each cheek. Turning around, Donatella grabbed the salad plate, blissfully heading out to the bar.

I followed, spotting Bruno outside on the deck at one of the smaller tables. Bruno stared inquisitevely and I presumed he wanted an explanation of why I went to the back, which is always off limits to customers.

"What? I really wanted to apologize to her for not saying goodbye and leaving so quickly this morning. She's been nice to me, so I wanted to tell her."

Bruno half smiled and half smirked.

"Rrright. Whatever," he said, nodding his head.

"How about we do some meat and cheese so we don't take up too much time?"

Happy to stay away from any uncomfortable conversation about Donatella, I said, "Great. I want to get to Pomarella today to get a feel for the area, see what I can find out."

"You okay going alone?" Bruno asked.

"Yeah. I've noticed quite a few younger people can speak some English, so someone at the plant has to be able to translate for me. That leaves you here in case he comes home."

Donatella arrived, and Bruno began speaking Italian to her. Thankfully he kept it short. Turning to leave her eyes met mine and she gave me a quick wink, out of Bruno's sight indicating *Apology accepted*.

Bruno asked, "Why do you think he left the blanket and the rope in the car? I mean, it seems so foolish"

Pausing, I pondered the question.

"There could be several reasons and if I had to guess, I'd say he's in over his head. If he's able to keep going he'll get better, making less mistakes. They all do. Right now, he probably hasn't thought much about contengencies."

I had never claimed to be an FBI profiler with their Behaviorial Analysis Unit. Regardless, I believed we were dealing with a young organized killer who had not yet reached his full stride. He had to have done some reasonable planning to lure Anna somehow. Obviously, he did not count on almost running into me the night he most likely dumped her body, or the next morning at the crime scene. He clearly knew Anna regularly walked by where he dumped her, probably figuring it would be weeks before she was found.

What he didn't count on was Zeus.

"The chances are he made a rash decision about dumping the car," I said. "Leaving those items in it, his mind had to be racing. With more experience he would have had contingencies and most likely would not have unraveled so quickly."

Donatella arrived with our meat, cheese, and bread, setting them on the table. A couple minutes later she returned with two glasses of fresh water.

She said, "I forgot to tell you earlier, I spoke with my sister about Sergio Fezzi. They both work the first shift, from six in the morning until two." Her sister agreed with her coworkers, Sergio is different. She told Donatella what bothers them most is the special treatment he gets simply due to his uncle being president of the board.

"What kind of special treatment?" Bruno asked.

"She said he always gets to leave when nobody else is allowed to take time off."

"Man, was I wrong. Now I'm sure he still works there," Bruno stated.

"Everything points that way," I said. "You used good logic, none of us had a clue about his uncle this morning." I deduced Sergio would not be at the plant if I went to do some follow up since it was past one thirty. The odds were more likely he could be coming home soon.

"Maybe you should stake out the house while I go to the Pomarella plant," I suggested.

Pulling out twenty euros I handed it to Donatella, and said, "The change can go towards my morning Cappuccino debt, we need to go." Nodding her head, she took the twenty and walked away. Bruno and I grabbed several pieces of meat and cheese to take with us.

"I'll go to the lumberyard a little ways past the little family grocery market, wait for you to call me. You need to go to the house, see if he's made it home yet. If not, find a place to hide so you can watch the house. If he's there I'll come to you. *Do not* confront him until I get there. If he's not there maybe I'll pass him along the way."

I drove the short distance and pulled into the Vender Lumber gravel lot, parking at the far end. The dash clock read 2 p.m. Now I had to work on having patience, despite really wanting to get to the Pomarella plant. Bruno's safety took precedence.

I parked my car and watched the house, Bruno's text read. *No activity yet so I'm going to go take a closer look. I will let you know.*

CHAPTER SEVENTY-SEVEN

Sergio could not recall the various faces in the break room except for Rosa's. Each time he visualized her face he could feel himself getting angry, so he tried to avoid thinking of her.

Sergio wanted to work hard, giving the impression he had not been affected by Rosa's outburst in the break room. He intentionally greeted other employees with a simple finger wave or a quick chin raise when he passed them on his forklift. He had acknowledged more people in one morning than he usually did in a week.

Sergio knew how the majority of the people at the plant felt about him. He respected Rosa for having the guts to say how she really felt. Although he would make sure she would pay for it, he admired it, nonetheless.

He left his forklift at lunchtime to grab his food, before returning to eat alone. Sergio's hard work for the day paid off when his supervisor told him there were no other jobs for him, letting him leave fifteen minutes early.

Deciding he would wait for Rosa in his car, Sergio watched the doors closely. At two o'clock employees from the first shift started coming out into the parking lot. Not knowing what Rosa drove, Sergio had to scan through the female employees. The metal door closest to the parking lot had the highest number of employees walking through, so he focused on it.

With three quarters of the cars gone Sergio started thinking he must have missed her. Blinded by anger for missing her, he began squeezing the steering wheel so hard his knuckles were white. He never saw the metal door open. Only the reflection off the door closing caught Sergio's attention.

Flinching, his eyes adjusted after three quick blinks and he saw her walking to his left. Relaxing his grip, he understood what took her so long. Rosa wore a light green, V-neck, short-sleeve shirt, tan cargo shorts and brown trekking shoes. Walking with purpose, Rosa headed to the blue Ford Focus.

MARINA SAW SERGIO WALK OUT INTO THE PARKING LOT at a quarter to two. She sat up straight as she got ready to start driving.

"All right you jerk. It's time to start following you so I can make sure you don't kill anyone else," Marina said.

Sergio not taking off immediately had her confused. After ten minutes she began feeling uncomfortable.

Picking up her cell phone she opened up her contacts and scrolled to "American Detective" and clicked. AJ's number from the Bertolli's showed on the screen. Starting to touch the number to call him she paused, not quite sure what to say. Clicking back to the main screen she set her phone down on the passenger seat. Minutes later dozens of employees began walking to their cars.

Maybe he's having car trouble, and he's waiting for help, or someone to pick him up, she thought.

"Good for you," Marina said with a benign smile. "You

traded for a lemon. You deserve it. Trading cars isn't enough to get past me anyway. Maybe the cops, not me."

Marina saw a woman walk out into the parking lot by herself. She had no clue Sergio happened to be watching the same woman.

Sergio's brake lights flashed red, staying on for less than ten seconds before the dullness returned. Marina sat up straighter, subconciously reaching for her keys. She slowly relaxed back into the seat when the brake lights went off. She saw a newer looking blue car drive slowly in front of Sergio toward the exit. Marina whipped her head left when Sergio's brake lights came on again and began creeping forward.

"Did she get in the blue car?," Marina said aloud, near-hysteria setting in. Her hands slapped onto her cheeks, the pressure pushing her lips into an oval. Her foot began bouncing, mirroring her heartbeat.

"Oh my God, I think she did. Not so quickly after Anna. Crap, I've got to tell AJ."

Reaching for her phone she saw the blue car turn out of the parking lot followed by his car quickly driving to the parking lot exit. Marina saw Sergio sit at the exit despite no oncoming traffic. She began counting by thousands, reaching six before Sergio finally turned right, following the blue car. Marina typed a message as rapidly as her thumbs would move.

It's Marina. He's up to something, following a woman. They just left the apple plant. I'm following him.

Send!

CHAPTER SEVENTY-EIGHT

Working on patience only lasted so long. Reaching for my phone to send Bruno a text it dinged. Perfect timing. I opened the message.

"Where the hell are you?" I shouted. One second, two seconds. "Come on, tell me where you are."

No matter how long I stared at my screen, I did not see another message. Touching the phone icon I went to recent calls to get to Bruno's last call to me. Pressing Bruno's number I heard the ringing. Bruno answered.

"I got a text from Marina, she says Sergio is up to something following a woman from the plant. The scary part is, Marina says she's following him."

"It makes sense, he's definitely not here. I'm almost at my car. I'll come to you," Bruno said.

I knew Bruno would turn right at the church taking the fastest route to where I was. Standing by my car at the far end of the gravel lot, I spotted the front of his car as it crested the hill.

Pulling up next to me I opened the car door before it came to a complete stop.

"Maybe we should take both cars," Bruno said before I got in.

"We're dealing with a killer who's stalking a woman. Unless we absolutely have to, we're safer together. Besides,

I could easily get lost."

"Get in," Bruno said.

"The problem is I don't know where we're supposed to go. I texted back, asking where they were going. She hasn't responded. Marina doesn't understand what she's dealing with. This guy's dangerous. He'll definitely kill her if he finds out she's following him," I said, concern on my face and trepidation in my thick voice.

"Did you try to call her?"

"No. I don't want to put her in danger. If she's walking behind him I don't want to startle him by having her phone ring."

Bruno mumbled aloud if Marina would not answer a text, she definitely would not answer a call. He paused, thinking of options.

"Here, use my phone to call Captain Condello. Give him Marina's phone number, see if he can get the process going to start pinging her phone. Up in these mountains it's a fifty-fifty shot at best. If we can get anything, at least we'll have an idea what direction to head." Bruno took off towards Revò, rationalizing maybe we could cover some ground before Marina texted again.

"I can't lose someone close to me again," I said, looking directly into Bruno's eyes, my voice almost cracking.

"You need to call Captain Condello. We're not going to lose anyone," Bruno said, a look of conviction in his eyes.

Damn it, this is exactly what I worried about, Bruno thought. *There's no way I could tell him to back off the investigation now*.

I quickly made my way through Bruno's phone finding Condello's number.

"Pronto," he answered on the second ring.

"Captain, it's AJ. We have an issue, we really need your help. The young woman at the crime scene who saw our suspect, Sergio, she's possibly following him right now. She sent a text saying he's following a woman…she's following him. I haven't heard back from her and it's been several minutes. We need to start pinging her phone through cell towers."

When Captain Condello was ready I read off Marina's number.

"If Sergio realizes he's being followed, he'll kill her," I said. "We're leaving Rumo right now to go to Revò."

"I'll get right on this," Captain Condello said. "Whatever you do, don't expect miracles up in these mountains."

I normally don't, especially in solving a case. This one is different, she is family. In all likelihood we needed a miracle, and I was not beyond accepting a little help.

MARINA SAW THE BLUE CAR HEAD WEST OUT OF REVÒ, Sergio following in his Fiat ten car lengths behind. Marina was waiting at the parish parking lot exit when Sergio went past her. She wanted to keep the same distance between her and Sergio that he kept behind the blue car. Her impatience got the best of her when her foot tapping the accelerator accidently went too far.

"Okay, she's not driving over the speed limit," Marina said, talking to herself. *Sergio is keeping his distance behind her. I've got to do better at not being so close.*

Marina's focus on tailing slacked off, she had so many things going through her head. Twice it caused her to get within four car lengths of Sergio.

"Damn, that's the second time. Keep your mind on Sergio."

In ten minutes they had covered the six and a half kilometers from Revò to Sanzeno.

Marina slowed way down as the blue car neared the T intersection in the town of Sanzeno. Sergio turned left after the blue car, keeping a good following distance. Marina punched it to get to the T intersection. Looking left she could still see the back of Sergio's car, so she slowly made her turn to follow.

Marina had driven a few hundred meters when she saw Sergio's brake lights. Ahead of Sergio's car the blue car turned right, but Sergio went straight, pulling over to the right shoulder ten meters later.

"All right jerk, what are you going to do now?"

Marina saw the woman had pulled into a public parking lot. Marina turned into the same lot and parked in the first available space. She could no longer see Sergio's car from where she had parked. In her rearview mirror, Marina saw the young woman getting out of her car, obviously dressed to go for a trek.

Okay, you're going to walk the trail to San Romedio. What the hell is he going to do? Follow you?

In a short distance the woman's walking gathered pace. She went out of sight on the beginning of the trail leading to the five churches of San Romedio.

As the woman went out of view, Marina caught Sergio's car in her rearview mirror coming back the other direction. She punched the accelerator, her tires slinging gravel as she backed up rapidly. Pulling onto the main road, Marina saw the back quarter panel of Sergio's car turning left onto the road leading to San Romedio.

"What are you doing now? Are you going to San Romedio to watch her as she comes out the other end of the walking trail? Is this what you did with Anna, watched her like this? You're not getting away with this."

Marina did better at keeping her distance on the eight minute drive to the parking lot of San Romedio. She saw Sergio pull into the lower parking lot and park in one of the last parking spaces on the left, Marina pulled into one of the first parking spaces on the same side. When he began walking her direction through the parking lot she laid across the front seats, hoping he would not see her.

"Damn. He's going onto the trail. I didn't expect all of this. Crap, what do I do? I can't call AJ. He'll tell me to back off. I can't, not now."

CHAPTER SEVENTY-NINE

Bruno drove northeast out of Rumo, keeping a safe, yet steady pace.

We had gone around two kilometers when Bruno approached one of the most dangerous blind corners on the route. We heard the honking horn and slowly rounding the corner we saw the motorcycle lying on its left side in the middle of the roadway. A small red car sat in the road directly behind the motorcycle.

Bruno stopped, turning on his emergency lights.

"Man, a car coming quickly around the blind curve behind us would never have time to stop," Bruno said.

"I'll take care of it, you take care of the accident," I said.

I ran back to the blind curve with flares, trying to slow down any approaching cars. Bruno found the driver of the motorcycle in the back seat of the red car with what looked like a broken left ankle.

"We didn't see the accident, I think we came upon it right after it happened," said the elderly driver of the car. His wife nodded in agreement.

Bruno wrote down the information of the two vehicles and the three people. The elderly gentleman offered to take the motorcyclist to the hospital in Cles since he already had the man in his car. When the motorcyclist agreed they took off. Bruno moved the damaged motorcycle onto the roadway shoulder, throwing its debris to the closest roadway edge.

"Wow, almost twenty minutes. Any texts from Marina?" Bruno asked, as we were getting back in the car.

"None. I've texted her a few more times. Still no response."

Approaching the end of the blind curves where it intersected with the road to Revò, Bruno's phone rang.

"It's Captain Condello," I said.

Bruno pulled over to the right shoulder.

"Hello, sir. It's AJ."

"We got some solid pings on her phone in the Sanzeno area," Condello said.

Looking at Bruno I said, "Sanzeno."

Bruno put it in first gear, made the right turn, and barreled toward Revò.

"It pinged in that area not long ago. I don't have any more information, I'll contact you as soon as I get anything else."

"Got it. We're heading there now." Hanging up I turned to Bruno. "Sanzeno, any ideas?"

"The two obvious things would be the museum, or, the five churches at San Romedio. It's late afternoon, she got off work a short time ago, so maybe she lives in the Sanzeno area." With the number of towns and villages around Sanzeno, Bruno's earlier comment, "it's a best guess kind of thing," seemed accurate.

We did not want to put ourselves too far away in the wrong direction to help if something happened. We agreed we needed a staging point, and Revò seemed like the best place.

Not knowing a definitive direction had my blood pressure starting to rise.

Rosa enjoyed most of her treks, although the trail to the base of the five churches at San Romedio topped her list. She stopped at one of her two favorite spots to look back through the valley toward Cles at the beautiful mountains in the background. Rosa wanted to make sure she could be back before dark after walking to San Romedio, so she enjoyed her stop for less than two minutes.

Within ten minutes she had reached her second favorite spot, the rock walled canyon where the trail had been carved out of the solid rock on the western wall of the canyon. She enjoyed leaning up against the wooden railing on the trail, watching the birds who made their home in the canyon walls. She especially loved to see the peregrine falcons gracefully soaring throughout the canyon, as they were right then. Rosa could watch for hours, but darkness was not far off. After five minutes she continued on, pleased to have seen them soaring through the air.

Rosa made her way through the trail in the rocks, staying close to the railing, seldom having to duck her head to avoid hitting rocks. She had greeted three different groups of people walking the opposite way, each time stopping underneath the rocks, allowing the taller people to stay close to the railing to prevent hitting their heads.

Close to the end of the canyon she admired the transition from the solid rock walls back to mountainous terrain. Passing the last railing Rosa noticed a man approaching from the opposite direction. She continued scanning the mountainside to her right for a few more steps. When she looked back to the trail the man had stopped less than five meters away. Rosa recognized his face—her eyes widened, she gasped, but she could not move, paralyzed by fear.

CHAPTER EIGHTY

Sergio turned right out of the parking lot, walking away from the five churches at San Romedio in the direction of the walking trail. Marina got out, trying to follow him. Sergio walked with purpose, not looking at any of the beautiful scenery around him and never once looked behind him in her direction.

Marina waited to get closer until Sergio got off of the roadway onto the dirt path. Losing sight of him as he left the roadway and headed up the dirt path, she ran along the road in an effort to catch up. Gasping for air, she feared she could not keep up with him. He was a man on a mission.

Sprinting twice more on the nearly level parts of the trail, Marina somewhat kept Sergio's pace. She had been on the trail several times with family and friends, including AJ's sister. The rapid pace, along with trying to keep her eye on Sergio, left Marina unsure exactly where they were.

Rounding a corner, she saw Sergio stopped on the trail and crept forward, trying to get closer without being seen. She had taken five or six steps when she saw the woman walking the opposite direction on the trail. Even from a distance Marina could tell she had been the driver of the blue car Sergio followed. For the first time in nearly fifteen years apprehension overtook her…the woman was in trouble.

Oh my God, she thought.

Sergio, seeing the total fear in Rosa's eyes provided more intensity to the fury and loathing he already possessed for her.

I'm going to beat the living pulp out of you before I strangle you, bitch, he thought. *You're going to suffer.*

Sergio pounced on her before she could move a step. The first sound of her screaming met with his right fist connecting with her jaw. Losing peripheral vision around him, Rosa looked to be under a microscope.

Seeing her head whip back, hearing the breaking of bones in her jaw, the beating he craved to give her had begun. Falling to the ground on the edge of the trail, Rosa's head and right shoulder were over the edge. Reaching down with his left hand to grab her shirt, Sergio planned to pull her back up for more.

Rosa kicked, a near miss from squarely hitting him in the groin. Catching enough, he doubled over groaning. Looking down the steep hillside she instinctively knew her best chance for survival was staying on the trail, hoping someone would come. Rolling away from the trail edge, Rosa began crawling away.

Still reeling from the kick Sergio reached out, grabbing her right ankle. Rosa rolled onto her right elbow, kicking wildly with her left foot. Sergio let go of her ankle, barely turning his head in time as her left foot shot by his face.

Free from his grasp Rosa rolled onto her back, kicking with both feet as hard as she could. Connecting with his left hand and chest, Sergio had to step back to catch his balance.

Sergio kicked as hard as he could, connecting with the back of Rosa's left leg causing her to scream from the excrutiating pain. Her legs stopped kicking long enough for Sergio to pounce, grabbing her around the neck with both hands. Choking her with a strength he never had before, he pulled her up into the air, her feet not touching the ground.

Rosa felt utter terror, her airway closed from his squeeze. Pure anger stared at her.

His eyes. Go for his eyes! she thought.

Instantly she reached for them, scratching and poking with all she had. Her middle finger hit the target, catching Sergio's left eye. Releasing her throat, his left hand instinctively reached for his own eye. Partially falling back, Rosa's right foot touched the ground, and she gasped for air.

Grabbing blindly with his left hand Sergio got hold of her shirt by the shoulder. Rosa scratched his left cheek one last time before he picked her up and slung her. Grazing the first tree closest to the trail, Rosa began tumbling down the mountainside. Her left leg glanced off the side of one tree, her right knee squarely hitting a large one causing bones to break. Coming to a stop face down, Rosa's left shoulder rested near the base of a tree.

Placing his hand over his left eye Sergio looked over the edge of the mountainside to see where Rosa had stopped. Staring at her for nearly a minute he could not see any movement, she did not appear to be breathing.

Sergio's senses were gradually returning to normal when he heard voices to his right. He could see two women walking on the last portion of the trail in the rock canyon. He looked down at Rosa one more time, fixated for ten seconds, not seeing any movement. Time for him to leave.

I'll come back in the darkness to finish you off if you're still alive. You aren't going anywhere, he thought. Still covering his eye, Sergio began walking on the trail back to his car.

CHAPTER EIGHTY-ONE

Marina watched in terror as he tried to kill the woman, but unable to move she hid in a fetal position behind the tree, praying for help to come. His pace appeared slower as he left, hurt from the woman fighting back, especially with the groin kick. After he rounded the curve out of sight Marina sprang down to the trail, racing to the spot where he threw the woman down the mountainside.

Marina could not see any movement. Looking to her right she saw the two women walking her direction. Afraid to yell for help in case Sergio remained in the area Marina began wildly waving her arms until the women spotted her. Both of them moved as quickly as they could through the last part of the rock canyon, running to Marina once they cleared it.

Seeing both of the women were easily in their fifties, Marina knew she had no choice except to go to the injured woman alone. The steepness of the mountainside meant Marina could easily slip, possibly plummetting to her own death.

I've got to get to her quickly, Marina thought. *I don't have time to slalom left to right. I've got no choice.*

Sitting down Marina slid on the soles of her shoes and the bottom of her pants. Digging in her heels Marina stopped five trees shy of the injured woman. Bracing herself with the trees, she made her way to the injured woman's side.

"Is he gone?" the woman asked softly through nearly pierced lips, trying to keep her jaw from moving.

"Oh my Lord, you're alive," Marina said, pure shock in her voice. "Yes, yes, he's gone. We need to get you help right away."

"Help me to the trail," the woman said, sparingly using as few words as possible.

"My God, can you do that?" Marina asked.

The woman nodded.

"What's your name?" Marina asked.

"Rosa."

Marina helped Rosa rollover and sit up. Wincing in pain, Rosa closed her eyes for a few seconds. Reaching with her left hand Rosa grasped Marina's, took a deep breath through her nose, then nodded her head indicating she was ready. Marina pulled, helping Rosa stand on her unbroken leg. Rosa shrieked in agonizing pain before pursing her lips until the agony subsided.

Marina could see something visibly wrong with Rosa's right leg, her knee twice the size of her left one. Placing Rosa's arm over her shoulder Marina asked, "Are you ready for this?"

Tears formed in the corners of Rosa's eyes.

"I don't want to die here," she whispered. She looked up the mountainside, taking as deep of a breath as she could and looked at Marina with conviction in her eyes, nodding once.

They slowly began moving left to right up the hillside, setting goals of what tree to reach before resting.

Dear God, this woman is so strong. You saved her from death. Please help us to get up this hillside, Marina prayed silently.

"Don't let him win. You can do this," Marina repeated at each turn. Rosa never spoke. Instead, drawing strength from Marina's words, she put every ounce of effort into the focus of not giving in.

The two bystanders were able to get over the edge far enough to help Marina lift Rosa the last three meters of hillside onto the path.

While the women laid Rosa on her back, Marina put both of her hands on her knees trying to catch her breath. The huge sense of accomplishment got overshadowed by the feeling she had to somehow gather the strength to go after Sergio.

"I'll go down the path…until my phone gets reception… I'll call for help," Marina said, gasping for air. "Can you both stay with her?"

Both women were saying yes when Rosa sat up on her left elbow, extending her right hand. Marina walked over taking Rosa's hand in both of hers.

"Thank you," Rosa said, in her muffled voice.

Patting her hand, Marina smiled, then turned and began running down the path.

CHAPTER EIGHTY-TWO

Sitting in Bruno's car in the parking lot of an autobody shop on the highway leading into Revò from both Rumo and Cagnò, we waited for the next piece of information. Antsy, both of us were pacing around the parking lot.

Ding. Ding. Opening up the text from Marina we read it at the same time.

Attacked woman on path to San Romedio. Past canyon. Helped her. 2 women with her. Needs ambulance. On path closest to the parking lot. Going after him.

"Damn! She's trying to get herself killed," I nearly yelled as we ran to the car.

"We're a good twelve to fifteen minutes from the parking lot there," Bruno said, starting the car. "Call Condello, let him know what we have. He'll get the ambulance rolling."

Before I could answer Bruno, my phone rang.

"Yes, Sir."

"We finally got another ping, she's in the area of San Romedio," Captain Condello said.

"Yeah, I got another text from her right before you called. He attacked a woman on the path to San Romedio, past the canyon close to the parking lot. The woman is alive, two women are with her, but she needs an ambulance. We are headed there now from Revò. The problem is our witness ended her text saying she's going after him. We have no idea where. We need to find him quick. He's starting to unravel."

"I'll get the ambulance started," Condello said, an anxiety to his voice I had never heard.

"Tell Bruno I'm headed his way. Keep me updated." Captain Condello hung up.

Turning on the lights and siren, Bruno punched the accelerator.

Placing her cell phone in her right rear pants pocket, Marina took off running on the path as fast as she could.

Figuring Sergio had at least a thirty-minute jump on her, Marina worried she might not find him again. Back on the main road leading to the parking lot Marina stopped running, not wanting to draw attention—and to catch her breath. Quickly glancing at the lot, she saw four cars. Late afternoon meant less people.

Looking down at the key remote as she got it out of her pocket she pressed the unlock button, hearing the click. Marina pulled the handle of her driver's door.

At the same time the door cracked open, Marina felt the tip of a knife under her rib cage on the right side, and the yanking of her hair at the nape of her neck.

"You scream, I'll fucking kill you right here," Sergio said in a quiet, stern voice directly in her ear.

"We're going to slowly turn and walk together to my car."

Nodding her head, Marina softly let go of the car door handle. Feeling him looking around to make sure they were alone, Marina pushed the keys against her pant leg. Hoping the plastic of the key fob and the rubber key caps on her two keys would mask the noise, she let go of them right as she said, "I'm not going to cause any problems, I promise." The key fob hit her shoe laces before sliding to the gravel lot.

At the back of her car they turned left to begin walking toward the far end of the parking lot. Several meters from her car Marina knew she had gotten away with it. Nearing the last two cars on the right, she realized what Sergio had done. He had moved his car from where he originally parked it to the opposite side where a larger, black, four-door Audi blocked it from view. Sergio had backed in so close to the Audi, his driver's door could not be opened wide enough for him to get in or out.

"Face the car," he said, when they were adjacent to the passenger door.

Letting go of Marina's hair Sergio grabbed her hands, pulling them behind her while pushing her into the side of the car.

What's he tying my hands with? It's thin, smooth, like maybe nylon.

Placing the palms of her hands together he wrapped the cord around her wrists several times.

After checking his work, Sergio grabbed the back of her shirt, pulling her to the left until he could reach the door handle. Opening the front passenger door, he took hold of the cord, setting the knife on the dashboard. Sergio sat, turned to face forward, and pulled her back up against the door frame.

"You have two choices. You can sit down on your own, or I'll drag your ass into this car," Sergio said.

"You don't have to pull me in," Marina said. "I'll get in. I promise." After Rosa, Marina knew she needed to cooperate.

"Then sit down on the edge of the fucking seat," he demanded, pulling her hands down towards him.

Sergio tugging on her hands caused her head to hit the door frame as she sat on the passenger seat.

Lifting his left leg over the gearshift knob, Sergio straddled the seats, letting go of her hands.

"Now turn, get in the seat."

Marina swung her legs inside the car, shifting her weight and hips until she got comfortable, if it were possible with her hands behind her back.

Sergio slid in the ignition key. When he lifted his right leg over the gearshift knob, Marina saw him wince.

Oh yeah. I hope Rosa got your nuts good.

Sergio pulled the car forward far enough to be able to open his door. Leaving the car running, he got out and ran around to her door. Reaching across her, he tried to latch her seatbelt, taking three attempts to get the right angle.

With the left side of Sergio's face right next to her, Marina could see the numerous scratches to his cheek, as well as around his red and watery left eye. Marina smiled inside, proud of Rosa for putting up a good fight.

After he closed her door he ran back around, getting in the driver's seat. Putting the car in first gear, he reached up onto the dashboard to grab his knife, setting it next to his right leg.

Marina recognized the Swiss Army knife. Her brother got the same sixty-five milimeter blade last year for Christmas.

In some weird way Marina appreciated the fact he did not have a large hunting knife. Even so, she knew she still had to be careful. After what she witnessed with Rosa, she had no doubt Sergio definitely had the capability of killing her with a Swiss Army knife all the same.

"I admire your work," Marina said, her eyes fixed on Sergio.

Driving through the lot at a normal speed so he would not draw attention, Sergio looked over at Marina twice.

The look on his face, his narrow eyes...he's confused. I need to keep playing that angle.

"I'm serious," Marina said. "I saw what you did to the girl on the path. When I saw you throw her over the edge, I kind of got a rush from it." Marina tried her best to put a smile of excitement on her face.

Sergio stopped the car and turned, staring at her for at least five seconds. Without a word he turned back to check for traffic before pulling out on the road toward the rock canyon. In less than a minute he looked at Marina one more time, seeing her still looking at him with a smile on her face.

"After you left I watched the two ladies. One looked much younger than the other and she started down to check on the girl. The one who stayed on the path asked her, 'Are you sure she's dead?' Seconds later the woman does the Catholic cross on her chest, then begins praying. I quietly snuck onto the path and took off. She never saw me."

Marina's head was bouncing like she was proud of herself.

Sergio did not respond immediately. Instead, he kept glancing over at Marina for short periods.

"You've been following me since this morning when I drove to work," Sergio said. "Then you're sitting in your car in the parish parking lot, following me again." He paused before saying, "You're either terrible at tailing someone, or you just didn't care if I knew."

"Exactly, that's what I'm trying to tell you," Marina said, trying to sound excited. "When I saw you stopped in the roadway down by the lumberyard, I started figuring it all out. I thought it was brilliant what you did with Domenica, putting her in the river under the bridge so she wouldn't be found right away. Then, the other girl. The whole town knows she walks everywhere, she's always talking to the stupid dog at the lumberyard. And this chick, I've never seen her. I figure you chose this place because she goes walking here. Smart."

She winked.

When Sergio looked at her again, Marina saw his face softening slightly.

I've got to keep going, or I'll be next, she thought.

Nearing the end of the rock wall canyon she heard the sirens.

"Do you hear it?" she asked. "Those are sirens, the ladies must have called for an ambulance."

Pausing, she could see his eyes getting wider and his knuckles turning white on the steering wheel as his car slowed down.

"Quick, quick, turn right into the gravel area by the barn, pull up on the far side of the tractor over there."

Without hesitation Sergio turned, pulling up alongside the tractor out of plain view. They had been stopped less than ten seconds when they saw the Carabinieri car with its emergency lights on turning right through the curve and accelerating as it went into the rock canyon area out of sight.

Feeling his eyes on her she slowly nodded her head, smiling as she looked over at him. Sergio raised his eyebrows, pulled around the tractor and got back on the roadway. In less than two minutes they were in Sanzeno turning left onto the road heading to Revò.

CHAPTER EIGHTY-THREE

I would bet Bruno drove through the rock canyon faster than he ever had before. He turned off the siren when we had less than a kilometer to go, dumping the emergency lights when we could see the first parking lot below San Romedio. He whipped a U-turn in the parking lot in case he needed to leave quickly.

Stepping out of the car, I saw the familiar white VW Polo to my right. "There's Marina's car," I said.

We looked at each other briefly, neither wanting to mention the white elephant in the room. *He might have her.*

We went over to check her car.

"The door's not shut, and the keys are on the ground. That can't be good," Bruno said.

Kneeling down I picked up the keys. Holding them in my palm I contemplated the possibilities.

"Unless…she intentionally did this to tell me something."

"What are you saying," Bruno asked, a curious look on his face.

"Chances are almost nil she left the door ajar and dropped her keys *before* following Sergio to the path. After he attacked the girl, it's possible Sergio could have waited for Marina. Maybe he knew she tailed him. I'm hoping the keys and the car door are her way of saying she made it back to this parking lot. I would almost guarantee he would have picked up the keys and closed the door if he had seen them. It's not great news, but at least there's still a chance she's alive somewhere with him in his car…*if* I'm right."

"I see what you're saying," Bruno said. "Look, I understand she's related to you—I have no choice." Both of us knew Bruno had an obligation to try to find the injured woman so she could receive medical attention.

"No, I get it. Go help her," I said, patting Bruno on the shoulder. "You know I have to try, right?"

Bruno nodded, the look in his eyes telling me he knew nothing he could say would stop me. Bruno's car needed to stay so the ambulance could see it, and he might need it.

"I'm going to take Marina's car. Go find the woman, I'll let you know if I find anything."

For a brief second Bruno put his hand on my shoulder, looking directly into my eyes. In his own way I knew he wished me luck in finding Marina alive. I nodded to thank him before he took off running to the walking path.

Not wanting to come off as fake, Marina decided not to say anything, letting Sergio take it all in.

Somehow I'm going to have to kick it up a notch, she thought

Remaining quiet after they left the barn, she could see Sergio nervously looking for more Carabinieri as they passed through Sanzeno and Revò. With his mind occupied she tried twice to reach her phone in her right rear pocket. She could not get it out without the risk of losing it on the side of her seat, or worse yet, Sergio seeing her. After passing through Revò, Sergio seemed to relax, getting to her phone would have to wait.

"When I realized what you had done, I knew I'd found someone I could talk to who would understand," Marina said, peering at Sergio.

"Understand what?"

Marina turned, staring out the passenger window at nothing.

I hope He can forgive me for the lies. Here goes.

"When I was seven years old I had a favorite dress. I wore it as many times a week as my mother would let me. One day the three neighbor boys and I were having some juice. One of the boys, Dante, intentionally made me spill red juice all over my dress. When my mother told me she could not get the stains out, I knew Dante had to pay."

Marina described how she went outside, convincing Dante to come over and play. They played inside for about fifteen minutes. Then she convinced Dante they should go outside into her backyard.

"I acted like I saw something over the edge of the hill behind our property. When Dante leaned over the edge to see, I pushed him. He hit several trees as he rolled down the hill."

Pausing for effect, she looked over. Sergio eyes were locked on her, like a vulture waiting for death.

Oh my God, it's working. Look at his eyes.

Marina then told Sergio she watched for awhile before she went down the hill at a gradual angle like her father had taught her. She squatted down, staring into Dante's eyes as he gasped for air, trying to ask for help more than once. When he quit breathing she climbed back up the way she went down.

"I had taken the last few steps from the hillside up to my backyard when my dad pulled up. I don't think he saw me on the hillside, but I'm not sure since we never talked about it. I never wore the dress again. I haven't been able to tell this to anybody until you. Nobody else thinks like we do."

Marina told a killer a story of evil, hoping for a kindred connection between them…in his mind. She imagined how someone like him, with such evil inside, would normally not share their story. She hoped him hearing a story from a person he believed to be of like mind would provoke a sense of relief in him. For her, deliverance would not come. She wished her own darkness of carrying a burden which did not exist, yet others had slung on her, would depart like the cold of winter.

She longed for a new spring, a chance to live life with excitement, helping others. Sergio had killed two women, maybe three. Marina knew she had to stop him, or more would die. Continuing to stare out the window, thankful for no conversation, Marina listened to the consistent hum of the road noise.

CHAPTER EIGHTY-FOUR

I drove as fast as I could under the circumstances. My two times to San Romedio did not exactly leave me feeling certain of all of the turns in the various towns, and Google Maps in an area where cell phone reception was shaky at best was of no help. When I finally made it to Revò I decided to call Captain Condello. Recognizing the auto body shop Bruno and I had been at earlier, I pulled into the parking lot. Locating the last call from him, I pushed the button to call him back.

"*Pronto*,"

"Captain, it's AJ. I realize you're headed to meet Bruno, but I could really use your help. I need you to see if your people can get me the information on Marina's phone one more time. I have an idea where she may be headed, but not an exact location."

"I will give it a try, AJ. I can't make any promises."

I thanked him for trying before he hung up.

Back on the road heading west I drove slowly until I found what I had been looking for…the road out of Revò toward Rumo. A much more comfortable road, I punched it, believing I had several minutes before the final turn onto the winding roads to get to Rumo.

Where would I take her if I were him, I kept asking myself.

I felt uneasy, quite conscious of the fact we had minimal

information on Sergio to really evaluate what made him tick.

Without warning it popped into my head what Marina had told me…*no one ever locked their doors.*

Sergio slowed down through all of the blind curves on the last road to Rumo, not wanting anything to happen with a woman tied up in his car. He had almost been caught two nights before when he nearly hit the American in the road while he had Anna in the back. He had no doubt it had messed with his focus, preventing him from thinking clearly when he tried getting rid of her body.

He could not afford to make any mistakes with the woman in his car now. He needed time to think about what he might do with her. She seemed different and he felt confused. Rounding the last sharp curve he momentarily glanced at her.

"What happened to the boy? Did they ever find him?"

Marina looked at him, smiling.

"I wondered if you were ever going to talk to me," she said, an aching in her chest. Pausing for a few seconds Marina looked back out the passenger window.

"Yes, a day or so later. The funny thing is, they found him down the same hillside, almost under the main road near our front yard, not the backyard where I pushed him."

"Maybe he crawled over there before he died. You said you were seven, so it would have been easy for you to think he died when he didn't."

Marina turned to look at Sergio. She pondered what he said, at least for his benefit, despite having always believed someone or something had moved Dante.

"I had never thought of that. You're probably right."

Watching him closely she could see by the nodding of his head and the slight grin on the corner of his mouth he liked a woman to admit he was right. She could never have imagined the information from her college psychology classes would help her to weave her way through the mind of a killer.

Slowing down, Sergio made the gradual curve to the left. Marina saw the large wooden sign greeting people entering the town of Rumo. Passing the lumber yard he veered slightly left into the housing area in the village of Mione.

"We're almost there," Sergio said softly.

It seemed obvious they were heading to Sergio's house. Marina did not want to upset him, so she chose to remain quiet, she knew Sergio was trying not to draw attention by driving slower than the average Italian on the streets between the houses.

What a dumbshit. By going this slow he's doing exactly what he didn't want to do. Good, maybe someone will see me.

When they reached the church he turned on the narrow road between the houses, arriving at his house seconds later. Marina noticed Sergio intently looking around to see if any residents were outside. He reached out and grabbed a handful of her hair, pulling her down to lay across the center console. He passed by the front of his house continuing down toward the backyard area.

For a brief second Marina thought Sergio might be going somewhere else as he passed by his backyard. She had no sooner finished her thought when he came to a stop, putting the car in reverse. He backed up into his yard, placing her car door a couple meters away from two large doors leading to a basement-garage. After nearly ten seconds Sergio told her to sit up. He turned the car off, took the keys, grabbed his knife, and got out.

Watching him, she saw him scanning the area as he made his way around the car over to the garage doors. Sergio unlocked the padlock on the doors and barely opened the left door wide enough to walk in, leaving the right door closed.

Walking over to Marina's door, he scanned the area one more time. Feeling comfortable they were alone, Sergio opened the door and bent in to unsnap Marina's seatbelt with his left hand. He looked directly into her eyes as he slowly backed away, making sure to pass the knife in his right hand directly in front of her face. Marina looked at him, nodding to confirm she understood his silent message.

Softly grabbing Marina's elbow, Sergio helped her to stand. He slightly released his grip but left his hand there to guide her. Sergio removed his hand, closed the door, then gently put his hand back near her elbow, guiding her through the open doorway into the basement-garage.

"Wait here," he said, grasping her arm in a manner to get her to stop while he reached back, closed the door, and flipped the light switch up. Leaving her standing near the doors, Sergio walked to his right, opening the long door to the storage cabinet.

"I'll get you something to sit on," he said, pulling out a white metal folding chair and opening it up. He took the chair to the center of the room, setting it to face the wooden doors. He returned to the cabinet and gently closed the door until it latched.

Placing his hand softly between her shoulder blades, he guided her to the white chair.

CHAPTER EIGHTY-FIVE

Looking at the clock on the dash of Marina's car I had driven a little over ten minutes. Seeing signs for the villages of Tregiovo and Lauregno told me I was getting close to the final turn. Despite wanting to drive faster, I knew I could not afford to miss my turn or get lost. Minutes later I spotted the turn to Rumo and as I turned my phone started ringing.

Pulling to a stop on the narrow shoulder, I did not recognize the number. I pushed the answer button, praying Marina might have gotten free.

"Hello."

"*Il Capitano Condello mi ha dato il suo numero signore. Il numero che ci ha chiesto di controllare dovrebbe trovarsi da qualche parte nei dintorni di Mione*," the man said, in a different Italian accent.

"Slower, please. *Più piano per favore*," I said, hoping I asked it correctly.

I knew the first part had to do with Captain Condello giving him my number. The man spoke so fast I did not catch anything else. Bruno had told me most of the Carabinieri are from southern Italy, so they have different accents and dialect than the people in northern Italy, especially in the Alto Adige region.

"*Più piano per favore*," I repeated.

"*Il Capitano Condello mi ha dato il suo numero signore. Il numero che ci ha chiesto di controllare dovrebbe trovarsi da qualche parte nei dintorni di Mione*," the man said much slower.

Using the Spanish I knew to help me, I surmised Marina's phone had to be somewhere in Mione.

"*Grazie, signore. Grazie*," I said.

Hanging up, I sent a text to Bruno telling him the pinging put Marina's phone in Mione, my best guess being at Sergio's house. I tossed the phone into the open area beneath the stereo, put the car in gear and took off for the sharp, blind curves.

BRUNO HAD BEEN WORKING HIS WAY UP THE TRAIL FOR several minutes, wondering if he was close. He stopped for a brief second, an overwhelming feeling he needed to check his phone for a message. No bars…even so, he could not shake the feeling.

He heard the scream for help. Sliding the phone in his pocket he took off, racing around the last two cutbacks on the path.

He saw the one woman standing, frantically waving her arms.

"She's not breathing, she's not breathing," the woman screamed. The second woman was kneeling beside the head of an unconscious young woman, undeniably the one Sergio attacked.

The woman on her knees kept rocking back and forth, prayer hands together at her chin, her head tilted to the sky. She kept mumbling, most certainly asking for a miracle,

Bruno presumed. She had not even reacted to his being there, instantly giving him the feeling she would not be of any help.

Bruno turned to the woman standing as he dropped to his knees on the opposite side of the injured woman.

"What happened?" he asked, feeling for a pulse on the woman's neck.

"Rosa said her tongue piercings were loose," the woman said rapidly.

"My friend knelt beside her, talking with her, so she told Rosa to open her mouth. Rosa had a lot of blood on her tongue. When she reached for the studs Rosa started choking. *Please* do something?" She pleaded, her eyes locked on Bruno.

For a split second Bruno's mind slowed to a near halt. He could feel a pulse, but Rosa's lips were turning blue. He talked with himself in his mind, telling himself to do the Heimlich.

Reality returned as he heard the woman pleading with him to do something. Bruno slid into position straddling Rosa's legs, placing one hand on her abdomen slightly above her navel. Placing the other hand on top of the first one he rationalized her not breathing took precedence over abdominal problems he may cause.

"Please Lord," he asked, pressing into Rosa's abdomen with quick upward thrusts. He hopped around beside her head and started to roll her on her side, then stopped. Unsure of any neck injuries, he chose to leave her on her back, doing a finger sweep instead. Nothing came out. When he tried to do rescue breathing, Rosa's chest did not rise. Moving down to face her he placed his hands in position once more.

Bruno had a flash in his mind of AJ telling him doing

something to another human being was not easy at first, almost as if you are afraid to hurt them.

I need to push harder, Lord. Please, be with us?

Bruno thrust with a pressure he had not reached the first time. He quickly positioned himself beside Rosa's head doing another finger sweep. He felt something touch his finger and he guided the object slowly to the surface. One bloody silver stud.

"There's another one, there's another one. She had two," the woman screamed as her hand grasped Bruno's shoulder.

Bruno handed the woman the stud, preparing to do another finger sweep. He glanced across and the woman continued her rhythmic rocking, praying fervently.

Keep praying, he thought. *I was wrong. I can't do this alone.*

His finger began the sweep. Suddenly he felt a tingling. Bruno's cheeks raised slightly as he felt a strange sense of peace. Slowly he moved his finger from Rosa's cheek closest to him across her tongue. Midway he felt the roundness. He knew he could lodge the stud deeper in her throat if he missed. The peace he felt guided him to keep going.

Flick, his fingernail slid off. *Flick,* it came off again, the difference being this time he felt some movement.

Closing his eyes Bruno pictured the stud in his mind. He put his fingernail against it one more time. The movement of the stud caused him to open his eyes and pause.

"Is it there?" she asked, slapping his shoulder half-a-dozen times in rapid succession before his head whipped around, his stare telling her to stop.

He slid his finger the rest of the way, guiding the second stud to the surface. With delicate precision he grabbed the stud in his fingertips, handing it to the woman.

"Oh my God, you got it," she yelled, taking it in her hand.

Bruno could not see any exchange of air and Rosa's pulse started getting weaker. The prayer woman's unwavering rocking persisted, providing Bruno confidence about the outcome. He gave Rosa one breath, seeing the rise and fall of her chest. He paused, hoping she would breath on her own. Something told him he needed to deliver a second breath, so he did. Waiting, he met with the same results. Thoughts began racing through his mind, questioning all of the possible mistakes.

The woman slapped his shoulder, getting him to refocus.

"Again, again," she said, rolling her hand in quick circles.

Bruno provided Rosa with a third long breath before sitting back on his knees, feeling for a pulse.

Several short sputtering coughs began to flow from Rosa, followed by a larger gasp for air and her eyes opening. Lack of recognition overtook her eyes as they darted side to side.

"It's okay, you were attacked by a man. He's gone now, we're here with you," Bruno said, gently laying his hand on her shoulder, softly looking into her eyes.

The woman did the Catholic cross on her chest and stopped rocking, tears flowing down her cheeks past her wide smile. The other woman dropped to her knees and they hugged.

The woman who talked him through it softly touched his cheek and said, "You saved her."

Bruno smiled as he stood. He slowly turned, looked skyward, silently saying, "I was but the tool."

HEADING FOR THE LAST CURVE BEFORE I WOULD SEE THE "Welcome to Rumo" sign I punched it, my adrenaline kicking into a new gear. The tires hugged the road as I accelerated through the turn, crossing over into the oncoming lane to clip the inside corner like a racecar driver.

When I came out of the turn I saw him frantically waving his arms. The look of sheer terror covered his face. We had the same thought, could I get this car stopped in time before I ran into the back of his logging truck which had overturned and blocked both lanes entirely?

I had no choice. Straight on would kill me. Going left meant rolling down an embankment. Right became the selection by default. I jammed the gearshift knob into second, released the clutch, turned nearly twenty degrees to the right to follow the angle of the truck, and hoped the ABS would work before I slammed into the solid rock wall a few feet beyond the shoulder.

The man in the road jumped out of the way, watching as I slid past. There are times in life where regardless of skill, a person needs luck. Mine arrived in the nick-of-time. I crossed my arms in front of my face, turning my head to the right a split second before impact.

CHAPTER EIGHTY-SIX

Sitting Marina down on the chair, Sergio began pacing behind her. His eyes caught glimpses of things passing by as his mind slowly started to spin, the tingling inside reaching out into the fine hairs on his neck. The voice in the background told him to kill her, while at the same time a strong desire to keep her alive kept the voice in the distance.

I'd like to get to know more about her, he thought.

Sergio had never shared what he had done with anyone like she had shared with him about the little boy. His fear centered around how difficult it would be to kill her if he began to really like her, especially since she knew of the others. Turning around to go back the other direction, his eyes naturally gravitated to his first instrumentality of death…the wrench.

One blow to her neck is all it would take. No blood. I don't have to see her face or look in her eyes. She won't have a clue what hit her.

MARINA PAID CLOSE ATTENTION TO SERGIO'S STEADY pacing back and forth. Although she could not see him directly behind her, she could feel his pause as he turned. His pace slowed. She turned her head to look over her shoulder, seeing him slowly come to a stop at the large wooden work bench, placing his hands on it. As he paused, staring at the work bench, Marina realized she needed to do something quickly. Somehow she knew he could not kill her with the knife. He needed to be physical, like he had been with Rosa.

"Can I ask you for a favor?"

Sergio slowly turned his head to look at her, his hands still on the work bench and he silently turned back toward the bench.

Seeing him look away Marina acted quickly.

"*Please,* you have to believe I'm no threat to you, right? There's no way I could say anything to the Carabinieri about you, or you could tell them what I did to Dante. Please, my arms are really hurting, all I'm asking is for you to maybe tie my hands in front of me. Please?"

Although not tied to the chair, Marina deduced it best not to startle Sergio so she remained seated while waiting to see what he planned to do.

The battle within him of what to do had him nearly disoriented. He tried to contemplate what she had said.

She did expose herself to a life in prison, similar to me. Without her, the Carabinieri and their American don't have enough evidence to prove I killed any of them. Damn, what do I do?

Seconds later he relaxed his hand, laying the knife on the work bench.

Maybe it's worth not killing her right away. Hell, she has as much to lose as I do, he thought, trying to convince himself.

The air bag exploded onto my crossed forearms and left side of my face. I had managed to slow the car enough to keep the impact from being overwhelming. Nothing felt broken and the burns to my arms did not even register as I scrambled to undue my seatbelt and get the bag off me.

The door jammed from the impact, although my shoulder provided enough force to send it flying backward. I jumped out of the car, immediately seeing the gap between the truck bed full of logs and the wall I had hit. I heard the man coming up from behind me saying something in Italian. All I could think of to say was "*polizia*," and took off.

Once I made it through the gap I hit a dead sprint. I had run the hill before, but never at all out speed. Nearing exhaustion as I reached the peak directly across from the lumberyard office, I crested the hill, starting down the residential street between the multi-story houses. The rhythmic slapping of my shoes while running downhill slowly increased as my breathing almost got under control.

I rounded the last corner, seeing Sergio's house. No car! Incomprehension and near terror gripped me.

Ahh shit. Where? Where would he have taken her if not here?

Sergio turned, walking towards her.

"Go ahead, stand up." He gently placed his hand on her elbow.

Marina cocked her head to the left, doing her best to have a look of compassion.

"Thank you sooo much, my arms are really hurting."

Marina stood, slightly turning right to make it easier for Sergio to get to her hands. Sergio untied the knot and began unwrapping the cord from around her hands.

"Man, I appreciate this a lot. They've been cramping since we turned on Rumo road, all those dang hairy curves."

With her hands free he reached to grab her wrist. His instinct to hold onto her somehow diminished as his fingers began to wrap around it. Gradually he pulled his hand away, staring down at her with softer eyes.

"Turn around, put your hands together in front of you."

Her cheeks dimpling, and the corners of her eyes wrinkling, Marina turned and intentionally looked him straight in his eyes as she slowly leaned her head to the side.

"Ohhh, this is so much better. I appreciate you doing this for me, thank you," she said, with softness in her voice.

He stared into her eyes, sensing she understood him and appreciated him. Still, his internal struggle raged…she had to go, but how could he? The scale in his head balancing her destiny favored life. He briefly looked at her dimpled smile before he intentionally looked down at her hands as he began to get nervous and sweaty. Slowly, gently, he started wrapping the cord around her wrists, tying a knot at the end.

Wanting to appear submissive, Marina immediately sat back down on the chair when Sergio finished tying her hands.

The distinct change in lighting when they first walked in prevented her from noticing the white garage utility sink next to the freezer on the wall opposite the work bench. After her eyes adjusted, she saw it while he had been pacing. A white Cappuccino cup with the Italian flag sitting on the top ledge of the sink next to a small Styrofoam cup caught her attention.

"This feels so much better," she said, lifting her hands to show him.

"Good. I'm sorry about how I've treated you. I had no idea why you were following me," Sergio said, looking at her eyes.

"It's all my fault," Marina said. "I should have done something, anything, instead of following you. I wanted to talk to you, because I admire you. Honestly though, I didn't know how to tell you. Instead, like a fool, I made you think I was a threat."

Marina lowered her head, looking at the ground, hoping he bought her feigned embarrassment. Feeling the soft touch of his hand on her left shoulder, she slightly turned her head away from him, smiling to herself.

"I'm not sure how I would have reacted if you would have approached me. To be honest with you, I'm not sure why I didn't attack you and kill you on the walking path like I did her. You surprised me the other night when you were in the bar with the American and didn't tell him anything about me. And, something about how long you've been following me intrigued me, so I guess, now you can see why I didn't kill you right away."

Replacing the smile with shame, Marina slowly turned her head to look up at him.

"I'm really glad you didn't," she said. The corners of her lips turning upward, she stared at his eyes until he sheepishly lowered his head.

"Could you do me one more favor? Please?"

When Sergio looked up she said, "I could really use a drink of water if you don't mind?" Looking over at the sink, hoping he would follow her eyes, she looked back at him with a pleading look on her face.

Sergio gave her a tight lipped smile, nodding before he slowly headed for the sink.

While he walked toward the sink Marina interlocked her fingers, placing them on the chair between her legs. She pushed down with her arms enough to help her lift her hips and slide them to the front of the chair while keeping her feet in the same position.

When Sergio looked over his shoulder Marina tensed, certain he heard her. She smiled, afraid the fakeness of it stood out. When he turned back to the sink Marina knew she was in the clear.

CHAPTER EIGHTY-SEVEN

The flash hit me…Bruno and me talking with the old lady up on the back balcony behind Sergio's house. In my mind, I pictured the wooden doors and the locked padlock in the hasp. I bolted for the backyard.

There they were…closed, but unlocked. The front of Sergio's car faced me, the passenger door no more than ten feet away from the wooden doors. My gut said they were in there. The question remained, was Marina still alive?

I moved up to the doors and closed my eyes. I would need at least one good eye going from the bright sunlight to the darkness of the garage. I felt close to being physically spent, the altitude having stolen my oxygen. I took several deep breaths to try to regain some control after the run. I had no idea what to expect, beyond the obvious; he was a decade younger and possibly stronger than me. Lacking oxygen would make it worse. I took the deep breaths, listening at the door.

I strained to hear something, anything besides my own heartbeat. Silence.

I prayed to hear her voice. I heard what sounded like running water, but no talking. The combination of those two could not be good, not good at all.

Please Lord, don't let me be too late again, I silently prayed.

MARINA COULD SEE HIM GRIN AS HE TURNED BACK TO the sink.

It's now or never, she stood while Sergio focused on the cup and water.

When he turned on the water she moved. Walking on the balls of her feet, she crept as quickly and quietly as she could to the work bench. Keeping an eye on him, Marina could see Sergio had his right hand on the knob, the paper cup in his left hand, his left index finger under the water testing for coldness.

She turned and began to cross what seemed like the width of a soccer field toward him.

If he looks over I'm done for. Run for the door. Stab him if he gets close.

Sergio turned the knob with his right hand to shut off the water. He began to turn to his right when the movement in his peripheral vision caused him to stop. Instinctively his head canted to the left.

Marina had the Swiss Army knife above her head cupped in both hands.

The movement of his head exposed the unclothed spot between his collar and jaw. Marina swung both hands at the spot as hard as she could.

The blade of the knife parted the skin, sinking into his neck. Water sloshed, splashing the wall above the faucet as his left hip pushed against the front of the sink.

Marina let go of the knife, slowly backing away.

Sergio dropped the cup, reaching up with his left hand to yank the knife out of his neck. Bright red blood spurted from the nicked artery, hitting Marina in the face, chest and arms.

Her eyes round, pupils pinpoint, and her mouth stuck open, Marina was transfixed.

Sergio looked at the knife, then at her.

"You bitch," he said, with pure ire.

His right fist struck her squarely in the jaw, Marina's feet leaving the ground. She flew through the air, landing at an angle, the majority of her weight on her right shoulder. The right front side of her head slapped the concrete, bounced up, then struck it one more time as her limp body slid across the cement floor.

"You fucking bitch," Sergio said, putting the knife in his right hand. He advanced toward Marina's near lifeless body…a new resolve to kill again.

Sergio angrily kicked the chair as hard as he could sending it flying into the large metal vise on the work bench before crashing into the cement floor. The noise from the metal chair drowned out the squeak of the large wooden door.

CHAPTER EIGHTY-EIGHT

I opened my left eye when the silence was shattered. From inside the garage a male voice yelled. I pictured Sergio abusing Marina inside, so I yanked open the large wooden door. Sergio kicked a metal chair at the same time I crossed the threshold, masking the creaking of the door. I sprang to my right to prevent being silhouetted.

Opening my right eye I had instant focus in the dimly lit garage. The chair bouncing near a workbench to my right drew my attention first. Then, on the opposite side, I saw Marina fifteen feet away, face down on the cement floor, not moving.

Sergio stared at me. I knew the look, a dirtbag cycling through his options, fight or flight. Our eyes met for a split second. The knife in his right hand, Sergio made his choice. He stepped toward his prey. Instinctively I reached for my Glock on my right hip, grasping air instead. Marina still had not moved. When Sergio took another step toward her I bolted after him, months of built up anger and rage taking control.

"You killed her you motherfucker," I screamed.

Sergio spun, raising the knife above his head before he swung downward across his body. I pulled up to my right, raising my left arm. My skin parted, no match for the knife. The strength of Sergio's thrust buried the blade in my bone.

My mind registered the blow, but the pain kept its distance. Strangely, I knew Sergio was not an accomplished knife fighter, or he would have slashed, thrusting from below.

Coming out of a red fog she opened her eyes at the loud noise of metal hitting something. She wanted to stand but the throbbing in her forehead and jaw were too much. With no strength to move, she stayed face down, the cement biting into her cheek, blood leaking from her mouth.

Think, think, think, she told herself. The pounding in her head made it nearly impossible. *What do I do? I can't stand or run. I can't do anything. Oh my God. All I can do is play dead but I may have one chance. Kick him, aim for his groin. Then run, run for the door.*

She heard him yell. The recognition of his voice brought a respite of hope. Then the fighting began.

AJ, be careful, she thought, before dizziness returned, nearly passing out from the pain.

I grabbed Sergio's knife hand to keep him from stabbing me again. The knife handle snapped off, leaving the blade trapped in my ulna. Arterial blood sprayed from Sergio's neck covering everything in its path, making his hands and arms hard to grasp.

He's ten years younger...stronger...jacked up on adrenaline. Hold on...just hold on.

Grunting, Sergio's furious eyes widened. His free hand grabbed my shirt and shoved me—hard. Despite the blood loss his strength seemed juiced on adrenaline.

He drove me backwards, my kidneys slamming into the edge of the workbench.

Pinned, hot pain shooting through my body, I saw his hand reach for the pipe wrench. If I did not do something quickly we would all end up on the cold cement.

I rolled my fingers, swiftly drew my arm back like a bow, and followed with a quick strike.

The shot to his trachea stopped his reach for the wrench. He instantly grasped for his neck, leaving a narrow window of opportunity for me to thrust both hands to his chest, hoping for even a slight bit of distance between him and the wrench. Despite bleeding out and having difficulty breathing, Sergio's eyes remained locked on the metal device.

Close enough to smell the rancid odor of the blood and sweat soaking his clothes, I began to see it…the first sign of weakness.

Now. Do it now.

I lunged for the wrench, doing a backswing straight off the workbench. He saw it coming in time to raise his right arm, an instinctive effort to block the heavy tool and I felt his forearm shatter from the blow.

"You're going to pay for killing her," I shouted, swinging again.

His eyes saw it coming, too late for him to move. The working end of the wrench caught him square in the sternum. He gasped hard, knocked back, half bent over. I thrust one last time, hearing his clavicle snap.

He let out a gutteral sound as his legs gave way, dropping first to his knees, then on his back, the fight in him ebbing away before my eyes.

Sergio lay there—pale, not moving, his eyes focused on me. He raised his head, anger still in his eyes.

"*Non ti fuoi fidare di nessuno di loro.*" Sergio said. "*Ti deluderanno tutti, proprio come mia madre. Hai vinto signore poliziotto Americano, hai vinto.*"

The raspy voice from my shot to his throat, coupled with the fact he spoke in regional Italian, left me wondering if I would ever know what he hoped to tell me with his dying words.

Gradually the blood stopped spurting from Sergio's neck. As the last pulses of blood seeped from his wound, he slowly laid his head back on the cement. Not long after his eyes no longer focused.

Throwing the wrench on the workbench and stepping over Sergio, I bolted over to Marina.

I KNEEL DOWN BESIDE HER, LOOK INTO HER FACE. BETHany, I can see Bethany's face. I slowly reach out my right hand to feel for a pulse in her neck.

She's alive. She's still alive.

Opening her eyes, she looks at me.

"Is he dead? Say he's dead."

"Yes, he's dead."

"Thank you for saving me."

Softly she closes her eyes, the pulsation in my fingertips ever so strong.

I softly brush her hair from her face, whispering in her ear. "Shhh, you are going to be okay. I'm going to get you some help."

I gently slide my arms underneath her, pick her up and carry her outside.

I look down at her as I step into the afternoon sun. She is alive.

The sunlight on her face, Marina opened her eyes, adorned by a faint smile. For the first time in months a sense of complete tranquility overcame me.

CHAPTER EIGHTY-NINE

The cool night air made me feel alive as we walked up the sidewalk, looking out over the community. I moved my hand toward her, touching the back of hers. She looked up smiling, putting her hand in mine.

We walked for a while, silent, enjoying each other's company. Donatella directed us across the road and up the path to Corte Inferiore. Half way up we stopped, turning toward the lake.

"It's beautiful," I said, looking first at the silhouette of the mountains and then at her. I softly put my hands on her cheeks, looking deeply in her eyes, and then leaned forward. I felt the warm tingling in the hairs on my neck as our lips came together. When I finally pulled away I leaned my forehead against hers.

"Thank you," I whispered. "You have been such an inspiration for me." She brought her lips to mine, gently pressing into my chest.

When we returned to Bar Lanterna we sat at the table looking out toward the moonlit lake. I took a sip of my soft drink, set the glass down and looked at her. "I've barely been here a couple weeks. I've been busier than if I'd stayed home and gone to work."

"Ahh, you would not have had as much fun," Donatella said. "You go see Marina at the hospital tomorrow? *Sì*?"

"Yes, I'm going in early." Fortunately, Marina didn't have any major head injury, although they did have to do surgery on her jaw. She had been kept pretty heavily sedated, so I wanted to be there in the morning, hoping she would be more alert.

"What are people saying about Marina?" I asked, afraid they would say her going after Sergio was based on evil.

"Most say she is brave for helping the Carabinieri, and to help Rosa like she did," Donatella said.

I felt a sense of happiness, hoping she may not be judged so harshly by the community in the future.

"You are what people talk about. How you got there in time to save Marina, how you were able to keep an angry, strong young man from killing her. The whole town thinks you are a hero for saving her."

The softness on Donatella's face had my eyes locked on her as she placed her hand on top of mine.

"Thanks to you, I feel I am ready to deeply care for another person, so you have saved me too."

Donatella smiled, kissed fingers on her other hand and gently placed them on my lips. I looked at her meaningfully, a tight lipped smile crossing my face. Donatella slowly stood, turning to go inside the bar. With each bar light that went out I relaxed deeper into the chair, staring out at the mountain tops touching the night sky in the horizon.

I slept for almost seven hours, feeling better than I had in a long time. I had no idea if the pain pills helped keep the nightmares at bay, or if it was solely for another reason. Either way, I didn't care. With clarity of mind I looked forward to seeing Marina.

I walked into Marina's hospital room in Cles a little before ten. Her parents got up from their chairs at the foot of Marina's bed. Clara started crying as she hugged me.

She moved back, holding my hands in hers as she said in broken English, "You save my *bambina. Grazie*." Clara gave me a long *thank you* hug before turning to look at Marina, thankful she had not been killed.

Aldo's watery eyes stared at me as he moved toward me. He grabbed me by the shoulders, gave me a bear hug, and then grabbed me by the shoulders again.

"*Uomo buono,* AJ. You good man. *Grazie, grazie*." Aldo walked over beside Clara, said something softly, and they left the room, Aldo's arm wrapped around Clara's shoulder.

I quietly slid over to the side of the bed, gently placing my hand on Marina's. She opened her eyes and tried to smile. The pain prevented her from moving too much.

Smiling tenderly, I said, "I'm so glad to see you're going to be all right." I gently wiped her forehead. "You're a hero. You saved Rosa's life. They say she'll fully recover over time. I am so proud of you."

The middle-aged nurse walked into the room and started to get upset when she saw a stranger. Then she noticed the bandages on my arms and relaxed.

"You American, stab, kill man do this *mia* Marina. *Molto bene*," she said.

When Marina looked at me I shrugged my shoulders and winked. She barely nodded her head, the corners of her lips faintly turning up. The nurse checked Marina's IV bag and site before heading back to the nurse's station.

I told Marina, Sergio said something at the end in a raspy voice after I had punched him in the throat. I told her I thought he said something about his mother, but I had a hard time understanding him.

"He pretty much had bled out when he said it, and then he simply laid back and died."

With her index finger Marina motioned for me to come closer. I moved within a couple inches of her face.

"He said, you cannot trust any of them. They all disappoint you, just like my mother," she said softly, looking directly in my eyes.

"Really," I said.

"He also said, you win mister American policeman, you win."

"No surprise, it's actually fitting. Killers like him often look at the police as the foe they have to beat. Lucky for me, I had you on the police side," I said, with a wink.

Marina gave me a slight smile, followed by a tear in the corners of each eye.

"I did not kill Dante," Marina whispered. "I went inside, when I came back out I could not find him, so I thought he went home. After we heard he never did, my dad and I saw him. He was already dead."

"And your dad?"

"Scared for me, he feared people would blame me. He waited to call the Carabinieri is all. People blamed me anyway." Tears began flowing down her cheeks.

I softly kissed her on the forehead, then whispered in her ear, "I don't blame you. I'm so glad you are going to be okay. You rest now, get better. Your whole life is waiting for you."

I softly dabbed the tears with a tissue, brushing the hair from her face before quietly leaving the hospital room.

I felt pretty certain Marina being family had not clouded my judgement. My instincts told me she did not kill Dante, and she had told the truth. I had worked enough investigations in my career to realize parents often do foolish things to protect their children, so Aldo's actions, whatever they were, did not reach the level of egregiousness I had seen many times before. Who am I, a non-parent, to judge Aldo for wanting to keep his young daughter from a life of ridicule and rumor?

I hope the people in Rumo can finally see in Marina what I see, I thought, strolling through the hallways.

Before he left, AJ made sure Marina knew he felt she had such promise, plus a chance for a great career. Hearing AJ leave the room Marina's mind drifted back to the garage.

Leaving the garage the sunlight on her face told Marina she would live

"Your life would not be the same if people knew what you did," AJ said. "I've had to kill several people in the line of duty. So, it was me that stabbed him in the neck. Nobody will question that. Trust me."

Marina looked at AJ, tears forming in her eyes as she nodded in agreement. His willingness to be "the one who killed Sergio" would forever change her life.

Opening her eyes, laying in her hospital bed, Marina lightly smiled.

AJ believes in me. In his own way, he freed me from the rumor of death which has followed me since childhood.

Hearing the familiar click from her mothers shoes on the tile in the hallway Marina softly closed her eyes. She needed her rest—thanks to AJ, she had her whole life waiting for her.

CHAPTER NINETY

I walked into the Carabinieri office and Bruno smiled when he saw me.

"I'm sorry, I should have been there with you," Bruno said.

"Don't be sorry. You saved a young woman's life. I'm proud of you." Bruno pursed his lips, an embarrassed smile hidden underneath as his eyes darted down to the ground.

"And, Donatella tells me your actions have already started more positive comments about the Carabinieri, at least in this part of Italy. So, you see, in more ways than one you were meant to be there for Rosa."

Bruno nodded, his shoulders going back as his chest pushed out and his head tilted back. Not quite complete victory body language, but close enough. He deserved to be proud of himself.

Reaching into my pants pocket I pulled out a beautiful silver key ring with the letter A on it. Separately, I had the individual letters, P and S, which matched the A.

"After they took Marina off in the ambulance I found this hidden on Sergio's work bench while I waited for you, the P and S were in the trash can next to the bench. Can you do me a favor, return those to the Bertollis? It's not much, but they deserve to have it back instead of it sitting in an evidence bin." My eyes began filling slightly with fluid.

Bruno put out his hand, staring at the key ring after I gave it to him. Looking at me, Bruno said, "That poor family has suffered enough. Yes. It's the right thing to do. I'll do it later today."

I thanked him by patting him on the shoulder.

"How's the arm?" Bruno asked, trying to change the subject.

"It's fine. They x-rayed it before they took out the blade, stitched me up, gave me some antibiotics and a painkiller, then kicked my ass out the door," I said, a sly smile on my face. "They had two seriously injured women, so my little arm injury and airbag burns didn't amount to much."

Bruno laughed. "I'm almost done with the reports," he said. "I'm finishing up on your statement. Man, you were pretty fortunate to be able to fight with him as long as you did. He seemed pretty violent. You were lucky you got the knife away from him long enough to stick him in the neck before he stuck you in the arm, otherwise we would be doing your death certificate."

I forced a smile. "Yep, pretty lucky."

I had no idea exactly what Bruno believed happened, but I felt uncomfortable not being up front with him. I believed he would understand if I told him, yet did not want to put him in a compromising position. Sometimes the less we know, the better.

"So, do you mind if I look at the photos?"

Bruno tossed me the thumb drive.

"You can use Amici's computer."

I sensed again the sly look on Bruno' face having a deeper meaning, but I could not decide if I wanted to go there. Instead, I scanned through the pictures, quickly finding the ones of Sergio's garage. After going through them all twice, I decided the photos I had been looking for were not there.

"Where are the pictures of Marina? They on another thumb drive?"

"No." Bruno paused. He slowly turned from working on his report to look at me.

I squeezed the edges of the mouse as I tried to look him in the eye and fake being relaxed.

"There are none," he said.

"What do you mean there are none?"

"By the time we got to the hospital, they had already cleaned Marina up to prepare for surgery. With a dead suspect, I convinced the captain we probably did not need Marina's clothes. I figured the medical report would be sufficient."

Marina still had Sergio's blood on her clothes when Bruno arrived at the hospital. In his own way Bruno told me he figured it out, and he understood why. Looking him in the eye, I slowly nodded, closed out the computer, and tossed the thumb drive back to him. Not talking about it provided him plausible deniability, although I did not believe he would ever need it. The people of Rumo were happy the killer was dead. In their minds, Bruno and Marina were heroes.

We stood and shook hands.

"Look, I want you to know, I think you have a gift for this stuff," I said. "You did an excellent job. Also, you asking for my help, I can't tell you how much it helped me work through some things. I owe you, in more ways than one. Thank you."

"I appreciate you teaching me, I learned so much from you. You're much more patient than I am. With your help, I now believe I'm heading in the right direction. You are going to stay in touch, yes?"

"Absolutely, I want to hear how it goes with you and the girl you're afraid to ask out."

We laughed before I turned, heading for the door.

"Only once, right?" Bruno asked.

I turned around, pausing as I looked at him. Now I had no doubt—Bruno gave Marina one free pass for me. I gave him one nod of acknowledgement, turned and went through the door.

I knew I liked him. He recognizes Marina has had to live under the rumor of death cloud most of her life, the truth would seal her fate as the evil person she wasn't. Yet, he has enough moxy to put me on notice it won't happen again. He's gonna do well.

CHAPTER NINETY-ONE

I sat in Doc's lobby not having read a word of the magazine in my hands. My mind remained in Italy…I'd been there a few weeks, yet it felt much longer.

"AJ, good to see you. How the heck are you?" Dr. P. asked while walking toward me.

I stood as he extended his right hand. While we shook hands I quickly thought of how we would have kissed each other on the cheek in Italy. I smiled inside.

"Come on in. I want to hear all about it."

"It's good to see you Doc. I hope you enjoyed the updates from Italy."

"AJ, those were a breath of fresh air…hearing you were trying to help others. Then to hear you were getting better. Well, to someone like me, that's always exciting."

"I'm sorry about being so resistant before I went to Italy. I learned a lot about myself while there."

"Look, I'm glad you were finally able to reach some peace. Nothing else matters. So, tell me about the nightmares. I've been dying to hear this."

"This may sound a little strange to you, but this is how it really happened."

"AJ, nothing's strange. We're all individuals. Each of us heal in our own way."

"I had watched our suspect die, which is a story in

itself for another time. I went over to the young girl on the ground, who happened to be my third cousin's daughter. Her name is Marina. I knelt down…beside her." I could feel the lump in my throat.

"AJ, it's okay. I'm not going to think it's strange, or you're crazy. Relax, when you're ready, tell me."

Even though my good friend, the police psychologist, told me he would not think I'm crazy, it did not automatically relieve my sense of insecurity.

He's your friend. Trust him.

"I knelt down beside Marina, then I saw Bethany's face. I felt for a pulse and she had one. She opened her eyes, asked if he was dead. I said yes. She…she thanked me for saving her."

The tears I had held back for months were now coming, a feeling of relief consuming my body. My friend, compassion and understanding on his face, slid the tissues closer, then sat back and waited. Patiently, quietly, he waited.

"She closed her eyes. For an instant I got scared, until I felt her strong pulse. I brushed her hair from her face. I told her she's going to be okay, I would get her help. I picked her up and started to carry her out. This is…the really strange part."

I looked at Doc for understanding. He was like a rock, not a hint of disbelief.

"When I looked at her face, I saw Bethany's face, until we stepped out of the garage. When the sunlight hit her face, Marina opened her eyes, then smiled. Exactly at that moment I felt at peace. Something in me told me the nightmares were done. I felt Bethany with me, telling me it would be okay for me to move on."

Looking at my friend through my tear-filled eyes, I saw

happiness on his face…happiness for me. Doc exhibited the epitome of understanding.

We sat quietly for some time. He had the ability to read me like I read suspects. Doc sat forward, a kid's interest on his face. He put both arms on his desk, and interlocked his fingers.

"Now, tell me all about the Italy investigation."

Smiling, I thought, *It's good to be back.*

CHAPTER NINETY-TWO

It had been a few days since I saw Doc. I had been cleared to meet with one of the Rangemasters to qualify before I went back to work. I felt good about putting a couple hundred rounds through my Glock again. I walked through the gate, heading for my car when Seth pulled up.

"Lunch?" Seth asked.

"I'm great. Thanks for asking."

He broke up laughing, and I was not far behind.

"Get in. I'll bring you back," Seth directed, like usual.

Seth showed a Cheshire grin staring at me.

"What the hell are you grinning at?"

"I'm so happy to have you coming back, I'm breaking tradition. I'm going to let you be King of the Car."

"Oooooo. Aren't I the lucky one? I feel special."

"You should. Only on the way to lunch, though. I don't want you to get a big head."

"Asshole," I said and smiled.

"You're welcome." The Cheshire grin still present.

Seth had a way of making sure I did not get the last word in. Apparently a bad habit of mine that he felt compelled to help me fix.

"How'd your week from hell go?" I asked.

"Better than expected. The cases in court were continued, again. No surprise. The follow up the DA Investigators should have done went smoothly. Sergeant Boykin's happy."

"What about the homicide?" I asked.

"An interesting one, to say the least. Not sure how the Fresno Dic's did it. Their Gang Unit guys must have their stuff together."

"Really? What happened?"

"The Fresno lead detective called, asked us to back off for twenty-four hours to let their Gang Unit do their mojo. Sure as shit, they did something. The shooter of our drive-by fell on his sword and gave a statement. Couldn't have cared less about anyone being shot…except for the little girl. Young guy, turned eighteen a few days after they arrested him. Knowing our system, he'll be back on the streets before he's twenty-five with some clout for having done prison time."

"Damn. Some nice work by their Gang Unit," I said.

"Yeah. Still not sure how they pulled it off, all I know is it worked. We're hearing through our Street Crime guys the shithead who started this whole thing is probably going to Mexico. I guess they've already seen graffiti with the dude's moniker followed by 187."

"He's as good as dead then," I nodded. "He needs to unass the AO and run. Sounds like this whole thing kinda ended pretty well for you then."

"Yeah, can't complain."

"So, how do you like being lead detective?" I asked.

"I didn't feel ready, even though you had been saying I could handle it," Seth said.

"Now, truthfully, it feels good. The downside, if your team doesn't have your same drive it's tough not to get pissed off."

Seth now realized we always had each other to lean on, both of us willing to give whatever we had to solve a case. Now, separate teams meant we were both going to be alone.

"I worked with Bruno, a young Carabinieri officer there. He was good for me because I had a chance to do a lot of teaching. He's like us, ready to do whatever needed to be done. He hates lazy officers and his speaking out got him sent to Rumo. Ended up working out for him, and for me, too. It goes to show, the cop profession everywhere has its fair share of lazy ass slobs."

"I think most of our bureau is pretty good, don't you?" Seth asked.

"Oh yeah. Most will do what you ask. They may not initiate stuff, they'll work for you, though."

"You happy to be coming back?"

"I think so. A lot happened on the trip, made me start really assessing things. I'm feeling pretty good physically and mentally for the first time in months. I'm excited to get back to work, maybe a little unsure of where my heart is, though. I think I need to do it, if for no other reason than to close out a bad chapter, so to speak. For the first time in my career I really am confused about how long I want to keep doing it."

"Told you before, all I care about is you. It's great to hear you're no longer reacting to all the crap. You look like you have your life back again."

I did not have an ounce of doubt about my friend's sincerity.

"Thanks. Now, as King of the Car, I say let's go inside, it's time to eat. You're paying, my liege."

We laughed together, something I had been missing.

CHAPTER NINETY-THREE

It had been a good day. Qualifying on the range, hearing Seth talk about his family, and sitting down with Sergeant Boykin to hash out the details of getting back to work had left me feeling content.

The sun had almost set when I pulled up to Bethany's still unsold house. I briefly looked in the living room window before walking around back. I hesitated prior to looking in the master bedroom window.

While I scanned the room with all of its fresh paint and carpet, my thoughts revolved around what transpired six months before.

My gut said we were close to the end. I had figured it all out, but not before David kidnapped Bethany.

My cell phone rang and Bethany's name popped up. *Yes, she's okay*, I thought as I answered it.

"Bethany, sweetheart, where are you? I need to come get you, David's after you."

"AJ…my dear AJ," Bethany said, the fear in her tone palpable. With a soft, quivering voice she said, "I love you…I'll always love you. You'll be okay, I'm …" WHOOSH, a faint sound of air. Flop. The phone was still on, but muffled.

"Bethany! Are you there? Bethany?"

Beep, beep, beep. The phone went dead.

Time seemed to stand still. Finally our most senior dispatcher spoke to me. Never tension in her voice, this time it quivered, eerily similar to Bethany's, as she gave me the location of the phone.

I punched the accelerator, barreling down the road. I already knew how to get there. He had taken her back to her house.

I could see the car in the driveway as I rounded the corner. The driver's door and trunk had been left open. Something told me not by accident. In the background I heard our dispatcher say something about the closest backup being a minute out. I could not wait. I drew my Glock, praying for the opportunity to use it as I raced toward the front door. The door had been left ajar, so I paused as I pushed it open. The silence took my breath away. The throbbing in my chest rose with my foreboding.

I entered needing something...movement, noise, screaming, gunfire...anything. The pounding of my heart was all I discerned.

Nothing appeared out of place in the front of the house. I moved to the hallway with its blood trail, a fatal funnel in its own right. I took my chances, moving quickly. The spare rooms were clear, leaving the open doorway at the end of the hall calling me.

David summoned me with a large bloody handprint on the open master bedroom door. The familiar smell of blood met me. *Maybe she fought back. Please be alive*?

My back hugged the wall, my senses heightened knowing David had to be in there with the rest of the house clear. I did a quick peek around the door frame. Instantly my knees buckled. My peripheral vision departed, overtaken by a whiteness surrounding the writing in blood on the wall above the headboard…his message for me.

I'm sorry, Detective.
She chose my path.
My purgatory, thanks to foster care.
She took my opportunity of a good life from me.
I have now returned the favor.

Stalker

Somehow I stood, I had to find her.

His lifeless body took up the bed. The butcher knife in his hand, the hole in his chest, was his way out. His dead eyes stared at me in the doorway, he knew it would be my entry point.

When I scanned to my right I spotted her foot on the floor on the opposite side of the bed. I rushed to her, stopped by the shock of what I saw. I could not believe my eyes. I told myself to move, but my legs were like weights.

Bethany's blood was everywhere. Her eyes were closed as I felt for a pulse I knew would not exist. Against all of my crime scene training, later to be judged harshly, I dropped to my knees and gently lifted her head, cradling her in my lap as I cried.

Bethany coming to me through Marina had left me able to face real life again. I felt a sense of peace and finality. A sense I had moved on…I would no longer continue to be haunted.

When I got home I went to the kitchen to make coffee. The detective in me rationalized when the phone went dead David, aka Stalker would have had to hurry, not knowing how far away from her house I would have been. I had learned the unfortunate art of how to think like killers, so the closer I got, the more I could picture what he had done.

The severity of the slash to her throat spoke of his pure anger toward Bethany, along with his adrenaline rush as the climax neared. Bethany would have gone unconscious almost instantly, or so I often hoped. Bleeding out would have been fairly quick. He needed her dead to have time to write the message on the wall for me to see. I believed he knew I already understood his motive, but he had to make sure, so he wrote, using what the lab later determined to be Bethany's blood.

As I sipped my coffee I contemplated the methods killers use to reach their motives, how so often their motives are logical in their minds, even though society struggles to understand. I read once from a famous FBI Profiler: serial killers are motivated by many complex factors.

Bethany could have never known what would happen to David by helping to initially place him in the home she did decades before.

David's life before foster care, the accident which killed his family forcing him into the system, and the horrors he experienced created his complex factors, leading to his basic motive of having to blame it all on someone. For him, that someone was Bethany.

CHAPTER NINETY-FOUR

I had been home a month, back at work for two weeks. Sitting at my desk working on my latest homicide case, my desk phone rang. The familiar voice made me smile.

"*Ciao amico mio*," Bruno said.

"Brunooo," I said, a bolt of energy hitting me as I sat up straight. "It's good to hear your voice."

"You told me to start trusting my gut. Well, my gut told me you would be at work at 11 p.m. Why are you still there, AJ?"

"I caught a homicide about twenty hours ago. Two drug dealers had a shootout. Just sitting here trying to piece it together. It's what, eight in the morning there, right?"

"Yes, exactly. Try not to kill yourself working all the time, my friend. I may need your help again someday."

I appreciated Bruno calling me his friend. "Don't worry, I'll be ready when you need the help."

"Do I hear an underlying meaning, like you're giving it up?"

"Not yet, but maybe for the right reason…maybe consulting on a homicide in Italy and having the honor of working with my friend, Officer Bruno Caviglia of the Italian Carabinieri."

"*Molto bene*. I will remember this AJ."

Hearing the news about Corporal Amici was bitter

sweet. He had returned to work, but his mother passed away from pneumonia. I asked Bruno to pass on my condolences.

"How are you two getting along?"

"Actually, we're doing well. We've even gone on a couple of treks together." Apparently, Amici could not stop thanking Bruno for donating his vacation time.

"That's awesome man, proud of you and the way you handled the whole thing."

"Thank you. By the way, have you spoken with Donatella?"

I chuckled. "You can't BS a BS'er. You already know the answer." Hearing his laughter confirmed it.

"Yes, we've Skyped a couple of times already. It's been nice."

"Good. I'm happy for you. So, would you like an update on our case, if I'm not interrupting anything?"

The kid skipped right over him and the girl there he likes. Frickin smooth. I felt the sly smile in my cheeks.

Bruno's timing was perfect, I definitely needed the break.

"I have my coffee, my feet are now on the desk, go for it."

"Yesterday, around 10 a.m., Captain Condello got a call—from Serafino Fezzi, Sergio's father. He said someone had been shot at his house, nothing else. So, of course, the three of us go rushing over there."

Bruno took a seat at his desk and started to put his feet up until he saw Captain Condello looking at him.

"Remember the little old lady you and I spoke to, she told us there had been a single gunshot from Sergio's house. The front door was already open and we could see Serafino slumped over, so we went in. He had a self-inflicted gunshot wound to his temple."

Probably despondent over Sergio, I thought.

Bruno described Serafino's detailed suicide note. He also said Serafino had been cleaning out Sergio's room when he found a notebook under the mattress.

"The writing on the front of the notebook says, *Kill Book*," Bruno said. "Serafino left it opened next to his note, on a *specific page*," he said.

"Okay. Now you've really got my interest."

"I thought it might," Bruno said, a hint of pleasure in his voice. He explained the *Kill Book* had details of Sergio's plans to kill Domenica and Anna, plus details of how each kill went.

"He even had details of how he would get a transfer to another Pomarella plant so he could find 'fresh prey' as he called it."

"Hmm. Interesting. What the heck derailed him?"

Bruno told me they took a more detailed statement from Rosa, who said she pissed Sergio off when she confronted him in the breakroom at work the day he attacked her. "We couldn't find her anywhere in his *Kill Book*."

"Ahh, makes sense. With all of his errors I always felt he wasn't quite the organized killer he would've become if we hadn't stopped him."

"The page his father had the *Kill Book* opened to described him killing Serafino. One page, very dramatic… in a nutshell he hits his dad in the throat with a wrench. He describes in detail how his dad is fighting for air. Sergio then describes hitting his father in the sternum, sitting on the couch while waiting for his dad to die."

Neither of us spoke for several seconds.

"You thinking what I'm thinking?" I asked.

"Yeah, it plays out pretty much what you did to Sergio… with his wrench, too."

"Damn." I could not bring myself to say anything else.

"Eerie, right?" Bruno exclaimed.

We agreed Sergio probably planned on killing his father before he transferred Pomarella plants.

"Serafino states in his suicide note how he had not been a good person."

Nothing shocking there, other than he admitted it.

"He put in details about killing the dog, and exactly how he killed his wife. He told Sergio she abandoned them. We found his wife and the dog buried by a large tree below his property, right where he said they were."

Serafino described himself as a monster for what he did to make Sergio turn out like he did—a monster who deserved to die.

"Then he signed it, dated it, he even put the time on it… the exact same time he called Captain Condello."

I could not help thinking Sergio's mother might have been the sane one in their family.

"I appreciate the update. It kind of answers final questions we all had."

"Yeah…I thought you might want to hear how it ended. I'll let you go. Oh, by the way, Captain Condello put me in for a promotion. I won't hear anything for a couple of months."

"I got a feeling you'll get it. You deserve it." I hoped the kid realized how lucky he was to have someone like Condello mentoring him.

"Thanks for the call. Stay in touch."

"I will. *Ciao amico mio*."

Hanging up I sat there, feet on the desk, still sipping coffee. My thoughts went to the caring people in my life, who helped me during the dark times after Bethany's murder. I owed a debt of thanks to family and friends, including those from Italy, who stood by me while I found my way back from darkness.

I pondered all the information about Sergio's mother, wondering if her love would have made a difference.

The stack of homicide binders on my desk caught my eye. The longer I stared at them, the more I thought about Italy.

What am I doing, here?

THE END

ACKNOWLEDGEMENTS

To my wife, Kristina, who patiently assisted me through this process by reading, editing, and supporting me in every way possible. Special thanks to Britne and Kortne for being unofficial editors, right alongside their mom.

Many thanks to my sister JoAnn for reading my work from front to back, providing her encouraging words of support. A special thanks to my sister Glenda for discovering Rumo, Italy, and all of the wonderful people there we have gotten to know and love.

Made in the USA
Middletown, DE
08 February 2019